I0761677

GOD'S JUNK DRAWER

BOOKS BY PETER CLINES

STANDALONE BOOKS

God's Junk Drawer

The Broken Room

Paradox Bound

Dead Men Can't Complain and Other Stories

The Eerie Adventures of the Lycanthrope Robinson Crusoe

The Junkie Quatrain

THE THRESHOLD UNIVERSE

14

The Fold

Dead Moon

Terminus

THE EX-HEROES SERIES

Ex-Heroes

Ex-Patriots

Ex-Communication

Ex-Purgatory

Ex-Isle

GOD'S JUNK DRAWER

PETER CLINES

Published in 2025 by Blackstone Publishing
Cover and book design by Bookfly

Printed in the United States of America

First edition: 2025
ISBN 979-8-8748-3087-8
Fiction / Science Fiction / Time Travel

Version 1

Blackstone Publishing
31 Mistletoe Rd.
Ashland, OR 97520

www.BlackstonePublishing.com

AP WIRE
September 26, 1984
THIS STORY HAS BEEN UPDATED

Authorities continue their search for a family of three that went missing during a camping trip this past weekend. James Gather and his two children, Beau and William, had been white water rafting Saturday afternoon on Dead River and did not arrive at their campground to meet friends as scheduled. Law enforcement was contacted when the family did not appear after several hours. Search parties were formed and have spent the past four days searching for any sign of the family.

Gather's wife, Cynthia, had died one year previous, and the rafting trip was intended as an anniversary event. The family had taken many such trips and vacations in the past, and Gather had told friends he hoped this one "could be a celebration of her life and not just remembering her death."

On Tuesday morning, a section of the Gather family's raft and pieces of camping equipment were discovered by search party members approximately four miles downriver from their last known location. Working off the remains, Fontana Township Sheriff Gerald David believes the family's raft came apart high on the rapids and plunged them down . . .

THE BOSTON GLOBE
October 13, 1984

After three weeks, authorities have called off the search for the Gather family. James Gather and his two children, fifteen-year-old daughter Beau and nine-year-old son William, went missing in September while on a white water rafting excursion that was part of an extended camping trip. All three are now presumed dead.

Search parties have been unable to find any trace of the family or most of their camping equipment. Authorities now believe the Gather family drowned when their raft came apart at a particularly fast and treacherous point in the river . . .

THE SUN
September 27, 1989

An American boy found wandering the forests of Khao Luang National Park in Thailand has been positively identified as William "Billy" Gather. Gather, his father James, and sister Beau, vanished in a white water rafting accident five years ago in the United States. The family's disappearance led to a twenty-three-day search and rescue effort.

Gather was disoriented when found four days ago by hikers, not knowing where he was, or even the year. Doctors determined the boy has suffered from shock and long-term malnutrition.

Authorities from the US embassy have attempted to question Gather as to the whereabouts of his father and sister, and how he arrived in Thailand, but as yet the boy has been unable to give coherent answers. One hospital staff member, speaking on condition of anonymity, says Gather has clearly suffered a severe mental trauma . . .

THE WASHINGTON POST
October 2, 1989

Authorities now believe James Gather and his family were the victims of a criminal attack.

Gather, a Massachusetts contractor, vanished five years ago with his daughter Beau and son William. While their disappearance and presumed death was ruled an accident at the time, federal investigators now believe an international crime ring may have been involved. Agent Wesley Coleman of the FBI says William "Billy" Gather's reappearance in Thailand last week has led authorities to reopen the case and pursue new directions, with several departments contributing to the investigation.

An anonymous source says the younger Gather has suffered a severe break with reality, most likely brought on from systematic abuse. Gather claims his family spent the past two years living in a cave but cannot account for the other three years he has been missing. He has also told authorities his father, James Gather, died over a year ago, but insists his father was killed by a Tyrannosaurus. The carnivorous dinosaur known as Tyrannosaurus Rex has been extinct for over sixty-five million years . . .

FROM *DINO BOY: A TRUE STORY OF SURVIVING TRAUMA IN AN ELABORATE FANTASY WORLD*
Crown Publishing, 1993

Billy Gather described so many unbelievable things during his years of interviews, talk show appearances, and publicized therapy sessions. The countless wonders of his magic valley (all discussed in later chapters) included a robot who cooked, cleaned, and told bedtime stories; an aggressive tribe of Neanderthals; a shape-changing alien castaway; shipwrecks; castles made of ice; and so many, many dinosaurs.

Indeed, Billy's fantasy world was so complete, so densely packed with details, one has to assume some adult—perhaps his father and/or older sister—were feeding him elements of the story to spare him the horror of what they were actually going through as prisoners of the Far East sex trade. A masked kidnapper bringing them food becomes a robot. Violent criminals become angry cavemen. Even his father's death becomes part of the story—although one has to wonder what horrific events Billy witnessed that imagining his father eaten by a T. Rex was the *better* version of things for his young mind to process . . .

FROM THE *ROLLING STONE* ARTICLE
"A DECADE OF DINO BOY"
Issue 821, Sept. 16, 1999

Fifteen years ago Billy Gather vanished with his family. He reappeared five years later, almost to the day, on the other side of the world. While his story of a mysterious and magical valley populated by fantastic creatures captured the attention of media, celebrities, and authorities, the sad reality was that it caused a desperate coping mechanism to become Billy's only identity. He wasn't a survivor, he was just Dino Boy. He wasn't a victim, he was the kid who thought he grew up with an android butler serving him dinosaur eggs for breakfast. The trauma he went through became a joke, and the joke was too good—too lucrative—to just fade away.

So it wasn't a surprise to some people when Gather took his own steps to end the ongoing joke—legally changing his name on his 22nd birthday and vanishing yet again, this time perhaps forever . . .

1

OLIVIA

The air brakes hissed, the bus swayed to a stop, and Olivia pretended to wake up. She rolled her neck until it made a loud pop. She'd kept her eyes firmly on her tablet for the first two hours of the bus ride, feigned sleep for a lot of the next two. A way to get caught up on a ton of reading and avoid any awkward conversations with Logan. Gave him an excuse to do his own things. Which he needed to get used to doing.

Most of the undergrads were already on their feet and packing the aisle. At least supervising them didn't extend to getting them off the bus. Over four hours, two state lines, and only one stop to enjoy food and a bathroom that didn't crowd your shoulders. They leaned and shuffled and tried to gather whatever belongings they'd brought onto the bus with them, desperate to get out into the open air.

Olivia had spent last night at Logan's—her *last* night at Logan's if things went as expected—since he still lived on campus in grad student housing. It cut twenty minutes off her travel time this morning, and what the hell, he deserved a goodbye bang. They'd bumped into Kyle on the way to the bus, and Kyle could be an ass but having him there kept the morning conversation from going in directions she didn't want to deal with.

As if on cue, Kyle whapped the headrest of her chair three times.

He'd stood up as soon as the bus pulled into the rural parking lot. Kyle was one of those guys who spent an hour or so every morning making himself look like he hadn't spent any time getting ready. Hair just a bit too long and artfully messy, stubble that somehow never got past about a day's growth, clothes rumpled but not wrinkled, but still tight on his lanky bod. She thought of him as the tech bro version of an astronomer—niche-smart, loud, kind of fun, but ultimately not doing half as much groundbreaking work as he thought he was.

He leaned over her to look out the window, shaking his head. "This is ridiculous. We're in the middle of fucking nowhere."

Olivia pushed him back into the aisle. "It's an imaging class. No light pollution."

"There's places without light pollution that aren't three-hundred-plus miles away."

Logan worked his way up the aisle like a salmon fighting its way upstream. He slipped between two undergrads, wedging himself alongside Kyle and Olivia. He let one foot drift into her leg space, his knee settling between her knees. Intimacy through proximity. She managed to not sigh or roll her eyes again.

"But seriously," asked Logan, leaning into Olivia while he looked at Kyle, "why are you here? Do you even have a lab with Dr. Barnes?"

He tried to give her a kiss. She managed to dodge most of it, made it seem like bad timing, like she'd been reaching for her coat and tablet on the seat beside her. He brushed it off with a smile. Too confident about where things stood to be bothered.

Kyle shrugged. "No, but I need to earn a few points with Hideko. She owed Barnes a favor, he needed people who knew the telescopes and the camera rigs to make sure some dumb undergrad didn't destroy them."

"Hey!" said one of the undergrads with a glare.

"Not you," he said, waving the young woman away. She shot him another look and pushed her way down the aisle. He turned back to his friends. "Yeah, absolutely her. I think she's broken half the equipment she's touched. Keep an eye on her."

Logan looked toward the front of the bus. "We should probably go out and help unload the equipment."

"No rush," said Olivia. "Let everyone get off, get all their stuff out from underneath."

Logan's brow twisted up. He had one long hair on his eyebrow, almost twice the length of all the others. It had been gnawing at her since yesterday.

A lot of little things about Logan had been gnawing at her lately. If Kyle was the Seattle tech bro, Logan was the Clark Kent. The glasses, the farm-boy body—okay, she'd definitely miss the body—the way he quietly did better work than most of the people around him. Too earnest for his own good, though. It was cute at first.

But "at first" had been a few months ago.

Kyle sighed, turning to the side to let another student slip past him. "I still say this is fucking dumb. There are closer locations we could've done this."

Logan shrugged. "Maybe he knows something cool about this particular site."

"Maybe he's trying to hide from some donors this weekend."

"What's that supposed to mean?"

Most of the undergrads had shuffled toward the front of the bus. Kyle lowered his voice anyway. "I mean, you've heard all those rumors about Barnes burning through his grant money?"

A quick nod from Logan. "Yeah."

"Well, they're beyond true. He's broke. Completely broke. Spent two years of donor funding in eight months."

"Yeah, everybody knows. It's not some big secret scandal."

"Drug habit? Hookers?"

"Nothing that interesting," said Olivia. She looked out the bus window at the top of Noah Barnes's head. "Better computers, more telescope time, all the usual stuff. Everybody does it. He just, y'know, kept doing it. For all of last semester and over the summer."

"Dumb," said Kyle.

"He's brilliant when it comes to orbital mechanics," said Olivia, "just not big on money management."

"At university level, that means you're dumb."

"Stop saying dumb," Logan interrupted. "It's ableist."

"You're ableist."

"What are you, ten?"

"No, I'm eight. I'm just really well hung for my age."

Olivia spit out a laugh. "Oh my god."

Kyle shrugged again. "Point is, he's got nothing."

"Until his next grant comes in."

"If he had another grant coming in, he wouldn't've needed to beg the department to fund this trip."

The last few undergrads bounced down the steel bus steps. Logan moved toward the front. Glanced back at Olivia. She gave him a little wave. "Want to make sure I've got everything."

"I'll grab your pack from down below." He launched himself down the steps and off the bus.

Kyle moved toward the front of the bus, leaned his head to make sure Logan was gone, and then swung around, grabbing a chair on either side of the aisle. "Why'd you even sign up for this if you're dumping him?"

Olivia let out a long sigh. Let her shoulders slump. "It was a surprise. He signed us both up without telling me. And I'm not dumping him."

"Yeah?"

"No." She finally stood up. Slung her coat into her armpit. "Dumping implies we're in a relationship."

"Aren't you?"

"No."

"He thinks you are."

"Having sex a couple times a week isn't a relationship. It's just having a workout buddy you see naked sometimes."

"So it's not working out anymore, I guess?"

She stepped out into the aisle. "He wants more. I don't. And that's the end of it."

"So you're saying you're on the market?"

She pushed past him. "No, I'm not on the market because I'm not a fucking box of Cheez-Its."

"Sorry."

"Just stop talking, okay?"

"I said I'm sorry."

"And I said stop talking."

"Sorry."

She gave him a warning glare as she reached the steps and he held up his hands in surrender, throwing her a quick smile that was the perfect mix of apologetic, sympathetic, and flirty. How the hell did he pull that off? Something else he probably spent an hour in the morning working on.

She took a deep breath and stepped off the bus.

Two sides of the mostly empty parking lot were lined with trees. A ranger station—or maybe a gift shop or a rustic restaurant or something—stood on another side. A large noticeboard hung between two posts, decorated with a few announcements and faded posters. Decades of sun had turned the blacktop pale gray, even inside the random little potholes. The lot was big enough to hold forty or fifty cars, easy. She wondered how many years since it'd been even half full. The dusty cobwebs, so many she could see them from across the parking lot, hinted that the wooden ranger station hadn't been open in maybe a year.

Olivia stared into the forest. Big, solid trees with coarse, rugged bark and at least a century of history behind every one of them. Trees after trees after trees, the ground around them dotted with rocks and broad swaths of dried needles and red-orange leaves.

Probably beautiful, if you were into that kind of stuff.

Dr. Barnes and the bus driver discussed something a few feet away, near the front of the bus. Most of the other students already had their packs. A few were doing half-assed jobs of attaching sleeping bags or tents that Barnes had requisitioned from some department. Logan already had a tent and was strapping it to the side of his backpack.

Crap, did Logan think they were sharing a tent? Of course he did. He had sleeping bags for both of them. How had she not thought of this until right now?

The only other vehicle was a shiny green BMW on the far side of the lot. The man standing next to it looked shiny and out of place too. Olivia put him in his mid-thirties, with a skinny build that only came from genetics, not any kind of diet or exercise. The man frowned at his phone, texting away. He glanced over at the grad students, went back to his phone, then looked at them again.

Olivia looked around at the crowd scattered around the bus. Almost all sophomores and juniors. She recognized most of them from classes she'd assisted with.

Logan appeared in front of her holding their backpacks. "You want to keep an eye on these? I was going to help Parker unload the telescopes."

"Yeah, of course."

He smiled, set the packs down, and headed back to the bus. A trio of undergrads moved to the side and gave Olivia a clear view of the bus's luggage compartment with its big door raised up to reveal the cave-like space beneath the bus. And right next to said cave, staring at her—of course she was staring at her—was Parker. Their gazes met like a low-speed car collision and left Olivia with the same feeling of dread.

She didn't think of herself as the type of person who had a nemesis, but if anyone asked her to guess at one, Parker Sangthong would've been the first name on her tongue. Ever since they'd met, she'd pretty much been a one-woman mean girls squad, sidelining and diminishing Olivia every chance she could. She'd never felt the need to explain why. Olivia'd never bothered to ask. Some people were bitches and that's all there was to it.

Olivia turned away. Picked up her pack. Slung it over her shoulder and wrestled her other arm through the strap. The backpack didn't sit quite right, probably because she'd overpacked. She hadn't been camping since she was eleven and hadn't been sure what to bring. Or not bring.

She stopped fidgeting with the straps. Logan would be back soon with their share of the equipment. The bus ride had been tough but she needed to pull it together. She could fake it for one more night. End things when they got back home. She hated stretching things out any longer than they needed to, but she also hated drama.

She looked back at the bus. Logan had all the plastic tripod cases. Kyle had one of the bulky, suitcase-like telescope packs at his feet. Parker had one of the camera bags. Sam, their last-minute add, stared at the other two telescope cases while he traded words with Parker.

Sam piqued her curiosity a bit. Olivia knew the guy from around the department. Maybe thirty, buzzed-short hair and beard, always seemed a little rushed and short of breath. Short and squat to the point of almost being round, but he wore baggy clothes so she wasn't sure if he was chubby or all muscle. Working on a dark matter project for his doctorate. They'd talked three or four times. Nothing deep and personal, but long enough she got the sense he wasn't a creep, probably, and maybe a little bit on the spectrum.

But he'd shown up at the bus minutes before they were supposed to leave, basically desperate to come with them. Not sad-desperate, more like urgent-desperate. He hadn't signed up, but after a few minutes of pleading—and Parker pointing out they could use another grad student for wrangling equipment and undergrads—Barnes had let him join their little expedition.

Which, Olivia realized, was the subject of the bus-side discussion. Parker had divvied up the equipment and stuck the short guy with two of the telescopes to carry. Sixty extra pounds while they hiked up the small mountain, on top of his own pack.

Granted, Sam didn't have a full-sized backpack. He had a little cranberry-colored thing that looked even smaller against his broad shoulders. Not much more than a glorified book bag. It looked stuffed, but Olivia felt pretty sure the guy didn't have a tent and a sleeping bag stashed away in it.

Parker turned on her heel, her thick braid swinging out like a whip. She'd had her brown-blond hair in a single tight braid for the entire three years Olivia had known her. Every minute of it. She couldn't recall ever seeing the leggy woman with her hair in any other state. She'd probably figured out a way to shower with it. A psychologist would probably have a lot to say about the relationship between the tightly wound woman and her tightly wound braid.

She walked away, which was Olivia's cue to join the other grad students by the bus.

". . . can trade," Logan was saying to a beaten-looking Sam. "We'll each have a telescope and a tripod. It won't be that bad."

Sam shook his head. "It's okay."

Olivia stepped a little closer. "God, you're both bad at this." She turned to the scattered undergrads, pointed at a random guy. "Hey—you want a bonus five points on your next test?"

The guy hesitated, but a buzz-topped kid in a Bruins sweatshirt stepped forward and raised his hand. "I do."

"Cool." She took one of the tripod cases from Logan, swung it over to the kid. "Danny, right?"

"Yeah."

"You're carrying this up the mountain. Drop it, bang it against anything, damage it in any way, the offer's null and void. I might even feel resentment when I'm grading tests. Got it?"

Danny hefted the tripod by its strap. "Got it."

"Great. Anyone else?"

"Me," said a skinny girl with an undercut.

"Thanks, Allison." Olivia handed off another tripod. The girl swung it up onto her shoulder, wobbled, gave them a thumbs-up before rejoining her friends. A third went to a bald, waify kid who pulled the strap over their head and set the case against their chest like a marching band instrument before heading back into the crowd. She got rid of the last three camera bags the same way.

"And voila." Olivia gestured at the three telescopes. "Less for all of us to carry."

Kyle chuckled. "Parker'll throw a fit if she sees undergrads carrying the big expensive stuff."

"It's a fucking tripod in a padded case. They'd need to throw it off a cliff to damage it."

Sam picked up one of the telescope cases. Slung it over his shoulder. "Thanks."

They all headed away to find Dr. Barnes.

He stood at the edge of the crowd, looking around like he'd lost someone. Parker stood at his side like an overeager assistant. Which she was, yeah, but she didn't have to lean into it so hard.

As Olivia's little group reached him, Dr. Noah Barnes shouldered his own pack—a monstrous thing that looked like it probably had supplies for a family of four—and started across the parking lot toward the stranger with the green BMW. Parker followed. Some people thought she had a crush on him, but Olivia didn't believe Parker would bother with mundane, human things like emotional attachments.

Granted, Barnes was pretty crushable. She'd kind of crushed on him a little bit when she first met him. For a week or two. Maybe three. Super smart, just the right amount of absent-minded, good lecturer, liked to include people and make everyone feel smart. He didn't mind the grad students calling him Noah, although Olivia never did. Chronically single, married to his research, by all accounts. Bit of a mid-forties dad bod, but you could still see he'd been in shape for a long time before that. Enough silver in his hair to give him those Doctor Strange stripes above his ears.

Olivia, Logan, and Kyle followed them across the parking lot. So did a few undergrads.

"Hello," called Barnes. "Skip?"

The man looked up, reached to put his phone into the pocket of a coat he wasn't wearing, then awkwardly slid it into his dark, immaculate jeans. "Yes," he said, smiling, "that's me."

"You look a lot different in person."

The man smiled again. He had super white teeth, like a news anchor, or a spokesman for some dental procedure. "It's an older picture on the website, when my hair was darker." He reached up and scruffed his head.

His hair flexed and then settled right back in place. "It gets a lot lighter when I spend time outside."

Olivia couldn't see Barnes's face, but she registered the moment of hesitation from the professor. "You know where we're going? The trail we need?"

Skip nodded. "It's not exactly a trail, but I know where you want to be. Hiked up there a bunch of times. Beautiful view."

"We're not going for the view. I mean, the daytime view."

"No, of course not." He walked around, pulled his own pack from the BMW's trunk, and waved a hand at the bus. "You need a little time or are you ready to go?"

Barnes checked the time on his phone. "We're ready to go. We can make it in three hours?"

"Yeah, absolutely. A little fast, but doable if we take the less scenic route up—"

"Less scenic is fine. We just need to be there before sundown."

"We'll be higher up. There'll be plenty of light for a while, don't worry."

Barnes glanced at his phone again. Put it away. "Not worried at all."

"Then let's go." Skip's smile stretched a little wider, and he tugged a green baseball cap down over his durable hair. He gestured at the forest off to the right.

Barnes turned back to the group and clapped his hands three times. "Let's go, people. Still on a schedule. Planetary motion waits for no one!"

"Bathroom?" called out someone in the small crowd.

Skip pointed at the structure across the parking lot. "Bathrooms and water fountain around the backside."

"Be quick," called out Barnes. "You've got five minutes and after that you'll have to catch up." He nodded at Skip and the two of them started toward the edge of the parking lot.

A handful of people broke off for the bathrooms. A few more fell right in behind the two men. Parker led that group.

Olivia adjusted the backpack's strap on her shoulder. "We should probably get going."

Logan jerked his head at the far side of the parking lot. "I think I might hit the bathroom."

"Better be quick," she told him, "or we'll have to leave you here."

"We're not in a rush." Kyle shook his head. "So fucking dumb."

Logan shot him a look. "Seriously, stop saying dumb."

"Whatever. You both know we don't need to be there exactly at sunset. It's not like the universe is going anywhere."

Olivia shrugged. "Maybe the part he wants to show us is."

2

SAM

Half an hour into the woods and Sam was painfully aware he had inadequate shoes for hiking. He'd been wearing a beat-up old pair of Nikes when he headed out the door and he hadn't bothered to pack anything else in his equally inadequate backpack. The cross-trainers had been showing their wear back on campus, and out here he could feel every stone and exposed root. A few spots of uneven ground made the lack of ankle support clear, too.

Granted, nothing about his body was remotely suited for hiking.

Truthfully, he hadn't prepared for this trip at all. When he'd remembered the departmental email from Noah Barnes, he'd sprung into action. No planning at all, he'd just seen the opportunity and leaped at it. Some clothes thrown in his pack, not even good clothes, all things considered, and he'd been out the door of his apartment and running across campus.

He just had to get through the next few hours. And the next few after that. And then maybe he'd wake up and everything would be different.

The forest seemed nice. Spacious trees, high canopy. The uphill slope was obvious but not harsh. Lots of fall foliage starting to overtake all the green. Did it still count as foliage on the ground? He kept letting his gaze drift, then realized he was trying to let his mind wander, and then he was back in his head and not *not* thinking about goddamn Gabe.

He glanced around at a few of the other students hiking alongside him. Passing him. Watched a few of them pair up as they walked. Some had sneakers, but in much better condition than his. At least half of them wore some sort of boot. Hiking boots, two pairs of cowboy boots, and one pair of combat boots. The combat boots were on Olivia, who kept half-stepping away from an oblivious Logan anytime he walked closer to her. Dr. Barnes had a good pair of boots with a few years of wear on them. Skip, their well-manicured guide, had . . .

Skip was wearing boots, but they were, well, dress boots. The barely ankle-high, soft-leather things someone would wear in an office or a retail job. Maybe two steps above dress shoes.

In fact, Skip's whole outfit was odd. He had a nice, well-used backpack and old ball cap, yeah, but past that . . . Dress boots, dark jeans, an ivory shirt with the sleeves rolled up. The black coat looped through one of the backpack's shoulder straps looked like a wool blazer, not a fleece pullover. Less forest guide and more unexpected office teambuilding weekend. Like he hadn't had much more time than Sam to prepare for the trip.

Then the sole of Sam's shoe flexed around a rock, pulled tight across the top of his foot, and threw off his stride physically and mentally. He half-stumbled, quick-stepped, and realized nobody had seen him stumble because his slow pace had already let him drift close to the end of the line.

He let himself walk a little slower. Even the dozen or so students who'd lagged behind at the bathroom had caught up and passed him. He stopped hiking altogether and watched the uneven line get farther ahead of him. Maybe an hour out from the bus now. Well, the bus was probably gone. The parking lot, then. He'd heard stories about people getting lost in the woods even though they were less than an hour from landmarks and civilization. It was mostly downhill, granted. Hard to miss the parking lot and the road. But it could probably happen. Getting lost out here and never being seen—

"What are you doing?"

His mind snapped back to the present and Parker loomed a few feet to his left, almost behind him. Had she been behind him the whole time? How'd she end up last in line?

"I was just—I was looking around."

"At what?" Her brows furrowed closer together. Not her usual three-degrees-too-serious intensity, she seemed . . . annoyed. Suspicious.

He felt his breath quicken. He'd already been breathing hard from the hike, but any kind of excitement always made him pant a little. "Just at—looking. Trees. Nature. Thinking about stuff."

She huffed a little air out through her nose as her face pressed tighter into a scowl.

His words logjammed on his tongue, trying to phrase and rephrase things while he talked. "Why are you—what are you doing back here? I thought you'd be up near—at the front of the line with Noah. Dr. Barnes." He glanced at the retreating line, back to her, then somewhere that wasn't her glare.

"I had to stop," she said.

"Why?"

"I have a small bladder." The edge on her words could've cut glass.

His eyes were aimed past her elbow, half focused on a pair of largish, shrub-looking plants a few yards off the rough path Skip had led them along. Maybe small trees that had spread their leaves and branches low. And then all at once he realized where he'd been looking and why her tone was so sharp.

"No," he said. "No, no, absolutely not. I don't—I didn't even know you were back here. I thought I was the last one in line. I was staring off into space and thinking about—" He closed his mouth. The only way to cut off the stream of words.

"About?"

"About not being—about getting lost in the woods."

Parker judged him. Almost a full minute stretched by of her staring him in the eyes. "What are you doing here?"

"I'm serious. I swear, I wasn't looking at—I was just letting my mind wander while I—"

This time she cut him off. "Why are you on this trip?"

He stumbled again. This time, just mentally. "I needed—it was open to anyone in the department."

"Until the sign-up was full. Two days ago."

He kept his mouth shut.

She waited.

Sam took a breath. Forced his thoughts and his tongue to slow down. "I was staring off into space. Thinking of something else. That's it."

Air hissed out through her nose again. It made him think of a steam engine. "I don't understand why you needed to be here so bad."

For half a second, he considered telling her. Trying to explain it. He knew enough about Parker from random department chatter to know she'd sort of understand. Maybe.

Or she'd laugh at him.

The half second passed. He readjusted the strap of the telescope case. Shrugged the strap of his inadequate backpack up until it sat firm on his shoulder. "I don't—there's nothing to understand."

Sam turned away and lumbered after the line, now fifty yards farther through the sloping forest. He heard her start after him, made a point of not looking at her when she passed him. He wanted to slow down, but she glanced back a few times as she worked her way back up to the front of the line. So he kept striding across the uneven ground, feeling it in his thighs and calves and the arches of his feet. Twenty minutes of uphill hiking later he'd caught up with the line, passed some of the other students, and brought himself alongside Logan, Olivia, and Kyle.

Olivia gave him a half nod of acknowledgment. Logan's phone was out, and he skimmed through search results. Somehow he managed to do it without looking up, avoiding random fallen branches, exposed roots, and ankle-twisting dips in the ground. "Yeah," he said. "Check this out." He handed the phone to Kyle.

Kyle looked at the phone, glanced up to the front of the line. "What the fuck," he said with an uneasy smile.

Sam didn't say anything. Didn't want to talk with any of them.

Didn't want to deal with any awkward questions about why he was here.

Olivia looped him into the conversation anyway. She jerked her chin at the front of the line. "Kyle tried to ask our guide there, Skip, about campsites at the top. Was it just dirt, are there facilities, another ranger station, or what."

Sam waited for something more. "Yeah?"

"He didn't answer me," said Kyle.

"Oh."

Kyle handed the phone over to Olivia. He met Sam's eyes as they walked. "I mean, I said his name two or three times and he didn't even act like I was talking to him. I thought maybe he had pods in or something, tried one last time, and he kinda jumped. Told me his real name's Josh. Skip's the name they use for the website so he's not used to it. He said it's a marketing thing, comes across more casual and friendly."

"Ah. Okay." Sam wondered if he could start slowing his pace again. Would it seem rude? Rude enough to draw attention? He just wanted to be invisible. No small talk, no questions, no distractions.

Logan shook his head. "The guy's already kind of sketch. Did you see his outfit?"

Sam glanced forward. Caught a glimpse of the ivory shirt, remembered the dress boots. "Yeah."

"He's definitely not the guy from the website," said Olivia. "It's not just his hair being lighter. It's a whole different guy."

She passed the phone on to Sam. They'd zoomed in on the web page so he couldn't see much more than a sky-blue background, a few broken words, and a photograph captioned HENRY "SKIP" GALE, FOUNDER. The man in the picture stood next to a large tree and wore the same bright green baseball cap as their guide. The two men had similar builds and smiles. But the man in the photo had darker eyes, a narrower nose, black curls poking out on either side of his cap, and a complexion that could easily mean some strong Latino or Native American heritage.

Definitely not the guy leading them up the mountain.

Sam felt his fingers come together, the tips tapping against each other two-three-four times. A weird habit he'd developed years ago. Something he'd copied from a TV or movie scientist he couldn't remember. In theory, it made him look smarter, and it also gave him time to think and try to stop his tongue from spilling a dozen words at once.

"I'm thinking identity theft," said Logan, lowering his voice. "He looks like the type."

Olivia rolled her eyes. "What's that supposed to mean?"

"It's white-collar crime. He's wearing nice clothes."

"You know," said Kyle, "when people steal your identity, they usually don't show up at your job and hope nobody notices they're a different person."

Sam laughed. Couldn't help himself.

Logan bit his lip, but he grinned a bit, too. "You have a better idea?"

Kyle shrugged. Tugged the telescope case strap higher onto his shoulder. "He's clearly the point man for some cannibal hillbilly clan, leading us out into the woods so they can eat all of us."

Now Olivia laughed. Logan grinned, and Sam felt his own mouth twitch again. "Well-dressed cannibal," he said.

"Hollywood perpetuates a lot of ugly stereotypes. They don't all wear masks and aprons."

The three of them laughed some more and Sam's smile lasted a few beats longer than he thought it would. They kept hiking and quietly shared other theories about their guide. Sam's mind drifted in and out of the conversation, unsure if it was the distraction he'd been hoping for.

The slope got steeper as they continued through the woods. One or two students fell further behind, and Kyle fell back to offer encouragement or teasing as needed. Sam took an odd pride knowing he was still trodding along in his beat-up sneakers. Now he'd made it halfway through the line, maybe even closer to the front than the back.

Whoever "Skip" was, he knew his job and the forest. He pointed out better stepping points, flatter ground, and easier routes around boulders and fallen logs. A few times he stopped to show off the view between trees, but Barnes waved them on, urging them toward the top.

"You know," Not-Skip announced at one of the scenic points, "this is Bigfoot country. The legendary Sasquatch."

Parker sighed. "No, it's not." Like Barnes, she didn't stop to look.

"How can you be so sure?"

"Because I'm a scientist," she called back over her shoulder, "and because Bigfoot's not real."

A couple of the undergrads chuckled.

"Don't listen to her," Not-Skip told them. "People have been seeing ape-men in these hills for decades."

It got a few more laughs and an over-the-shoulder glance from Barnes.

The sun got lower, the ground got rockier, the trees thinned. Sam felt himself calming as they went higher and the air cooled a bit. They'd been hiking for over two and a half hours now. He felt pretty sure he'd regret the uphill hike in the morning, maybe regret a lot of things, but for the moment, for the first time in the past twenty-four hours, he felt . . . centered. Ready for the future.

A phone alarm beeped and Barnes slowed down in a clearing of broad stones and patchy grass. He looked at the screen. Let his backpack slide from his shoulders and pulled out a heavier, more industrial-looking phone and checked that. It took Sam a moment to recognize it as a dedicated GPS device.

Parker and Not-Skip took a few more steps and turned to look back at him. The line of students spread out around Noah, forming a rough circle. Olivia and Logan stood across from Sam. Olivia still leaned ever so slightly away from Logan. Not-so-secret rejection.

Not-Skip shrugged and pulled out his phone. A few of the grad students let their packs drop and did the same. Sam checked his. No texts or voicemails or missed calls. Still two solid bars. He looked around, wondering if one of the trees around them was a carefully camouflaged cell tower. Did they disguise them out in the middle of nowhere? Maybe they were high enough nothing blocked the signals, giving them better range? He was doing it again. Pretty much forcing his mind to wander.

Barnes took a few long strides, then a few more in a different direction, and then one last one. Stared at his GPS. Pulled out his phone again. Took in a deep breath.

Then he became aware of all the students around him. "Sorry. Nothing important." He turned his attention to Not-Skip. "How much farther?"

"Not far at all. Thirty minutes, tops." He gestured at the trees beyond the rough clearing. "Once we're past these, you'll get a much better view of the sky."

Barnes nodded enthusiastically. "Great. Everyone go on, get your tents set up. I'll catch up in a little bit."

Not-Skip put his phone away and waved for the group to follow him. The students sighed, grumbled, readjusted bags and backpacks. They drifted away from Barnes, headed after Not-Skip.

Sam watched them go, debated following them. He could see indecision working its way through the other grad students. Kyle finally turned and headed up the hill. Olivia hesitated, then slowly followed. Another trio of undergrads stood a few yards away going through the same calculations. Two more stretched and headed up the hill through the trees. Another one sighed and followed them, her pack hanging on one shoulder.

Parker went against the slow tide and moved closer to the professor. "Can I do anything to help?"

He shook his head. "This is where we part ways. Go on with the others. You know the drill. Make sure everyone's got their tents set up, then get the imaging gear ready. Walk them all through it."

"Are you sure?"

"Absolutely. This is just a bunch of really boring measurements. Double-checking some calculations I made a few weeks ago."

"For your mysterious side project?"

Barnes looked at her and Sam watched half a dozen emotions flit across the man's face. "Yep. For the mysterious side project."

"Fine."

"I just . . ." Sam could almost see the man weighing his words. "Thanks, Parker."

"For what?"

"For everything." He waved his hand up the hillside. "For taking care of them. For all your help over the years. I never said thank you enough times. You've been great."

He went to hug her, then stuck out his hand instead.

She looked down at the hand and chuckled awkwardly. "Are you okay?"

He laughed too. "Sorry. Random emotional moment. I'll . . . I'll see you later."

It crossed Sam's mind that he'd been standing here through what should've been a private moment. And then, as if they'd heard his thoughts, Barnes and Parker both glanced over at him.

Barnes cleared his throat. Parker gestured at his backpack, then at the retreating students. "Want me to have someone take your pack up to the site?"

Another glance made it clear Sam was the hypothetical "someone."

"No." Barnes held out a hand, waving the GPS device at her like he was warding off a geographic vampire. "It's fine. Just get up there, take charge, get everything ready for tonight. They can't do anything until the telescopes are set up."

"Right. Of course."

"Thanks again, Parker."

She nodded and turned, her braid slashing the air. She marched up the slope past Sam. "Come on," she told him, tipping her head at the telescope bag. "You heard him. We need that up at the site."

Sam fell in behind her. He took a last look over his shoulder. Saw Barnes pull something else from his pocket. Check the big device again. Scratch a big chalk X on the expanse of flat stone directly in front of his feet. The man straightened up and stared at the pink-streaked sky.

And then Parker barked at Sam to keep up.

It took them five minutes to catch up to the last of the straggler students, another ten to rejoin the core of the group, and ten more before they all reached the big plateau. Sam's calves ached at the sudden shift in angle. The front of his thighs, too. It hadn't felt like a rough hike until they'd stopped on flat ground.

The plateau spread over an area a little bigger than a lecture hall. Some scrub brush cast long shadows. A fallen tree trunk had been stripped of its branches and turned into a long, rough bench, already being used by half a dozen undergrads. Not quite the top of the mountain, but the plateau gave them a solid view of the sky. Far below he could see the thin ribbon of a road going through the trees, maybe the road they'd driven in on.

He looked around for the best place to set the imaging gear. Saw Logan, still wearing his backpack, standing with two of the telescopes, waving down undergrads with tripods. Sam added the case he'd been carrying to the pile and drifted away while Kyle and Parker talked.

Maybe a third of the undergrads were setting up tents across the plateau. A few were already up, colorful little domes of blue and green and neon orange that caught the setting sunlight. A few formed small groups, others tried to maintain a bit of distance. Not-Skip had set his own pack down and strolled through the scattered students, pointing out better spots for tents, answering questions, offering help.

Once again, Sam thought about how maybe he shouldn't've charged out of his apartment as soon as he had a chance. All things considered, he didn't plan this out at all. Not even slightly. Maybe he could just disappear into the dark. Nobody would notice. Nobody would bother him. Nobody—

"Hey," said Not-Skip. "Need any help getting your tent set up?"

Sam shook his head. "I'm good, thanks."

Not-Skip's gaze drifted to Sam's inadequate backpack. "Roughing it. I can respect that."

Sam debated how to respond. The sun had sunk a third of the way below the horizon now, and the air had cooled a few more degrees. He hated that he'd drawn attention to himself, and then realized taking so long to answer drew more.

"I think they need my help setting up the imaging gear," he said, and walked away from Not-Skip.

Parker gave Sam another suspicious look as he approached. Logan showed a group of undergrads how the cameras mounted to the telescopes. Kyle and Olivia opened cases and did quick inventories. Olivia glanced at Sam. "Did you see Professor Barnes?"

"He's not joining us," said Parker. "He's working on another project while we run the imaging exercises."

"Seriously?" Kyle let out a sigh.

"Yes," she said, glaring at him.

Olivia pointed Sam at one of the tripod cases. He unfastened the straps holding it shut, unsure if he should be doing it himself or handing it off to an undergrad. He really had no clue about the parameters of this exercise. There'd been some information in the departmental email, but he hadn't read much past "overnight" and "out of town."

"No, this one here," Logan said to one of the undergrads, pointing at a connection point on the camera.

"So he just took off?" Kyle asked Parker, although it sounded a bit more like a statement.

"He didn't take off," she said. "He's using this trip to work on another project."

"What?" asked Olivia.

"Something else."

"Yeah, but what?"

"A side project of his."

Kyle laughed. "You've got no idea what he's working on, do you?"

Parker glared at him. "He's just trying to be efficient. We can teach this class, he can work on his own—"

"He's trying to save his ass, isn't he? Piggybacking his project onto this field trip."

"No."

"Is it true he's living out of his car?"

"No!"

"He's—" Sam started to say, then shut his mouth.

All the grad students turned to him. Logan glanced at the undergrads and gestured them back toward the tents. Parker gave Sam an icy stare.

"He's what?" Olivia asked.

Sam sighed. "I saw him—I think he's been sleeping in his office, maybe. I went into the lab early a few weeks ago and found him there. He told me, he made a joke about couch-surfing wipeouts. That wasn't quite how he—it was funnier when he said it."

Various expressions crossed their faces. Even Parker looked a little shaken. "I knew he'd maxed out a few credit cards working on things," she said, "but I didn't know it was that bad."

"A *few* credit cards?" echoed Logan.

"He's really dedicated to his work."

"So am I," said Olivia, "but I'm not sinking myself into debt over it."

"Except student loan debt," Kyle deadpanned.

"Well, yeah."

Parker made an annoyed sound and went off to instruct some undergrads.

The rest of them stood around the empty cases as the last sliver of sun slipped beneath the horizon. A few phone lights flicked on across the plateau, and two flashlights with red lenses in place to preserve night vision. "I guess I should set up our tent before it gets too dark," said Logan.

"Yeah." Olivia nodded. "Yeah, that'd be great."

Sam could see Kyle making an effort not to say something and decided to save Logan some embarrassment. "I have a—does anyone know what we're doing for, well, food?"

Kyle's eyes relaxed. So did Olivia's. Logan nodded. "There's a pair of coolers. I think it's all hot dogs and bottled water. Maybe some veggie burgers. And we can all trade whatever snacks we've got. I brought some chips."

"Barter," said Kyle. "Like in the olden times."

Sam looked around the shadowy plateau. "Do we have a fire pit?"

"Maybe we're supposed to make one?" suggested Olivia.

Kyle peered toward the tents. "Where's our fake guide?"

"I think he's helping people get their tents set up."

A random memory crossed Sam's mind. His earlier thought of getting lost in the woods. "Is Professor Barnes coming up here to sleep?"

Logan glanced at the trees, then at Sam. "What?"

"Is he just—is he staying back down the hill? He's got his pack with him, but does he—do we need to take him a tent or food or anything?"

They all exchanged looks. Kyle straightened up. "Parker!"

"What?" It had gotten dark fast, and Sam wasn't 100 percent sure where her voice had come from, but it sounded maybe halfway across the plateau.

Kyle waved his arm in a "come here" gesture.

A few moments later Parker was in front of them. "What?"

"Is Barnes coming up here to join us?"

"He's . . . I don't know."

"Is he setting up a tent up here or down wherever he's doing his secret project?"

"I just said I don't know."

"Do we need to take him food?" asked Sam.

"I . . ." She made a sound that could've passed for frustration or anger. "I don't know. You were there. You heard him. He said goodbye and that was it."

"He said goodbye?" echoed Olivia.

"Not like that."

"It sounded pretty goodbye-ish," Sam said.

"Son of a bitch," said Kyle. "He's leaving us up here while he goes and sleeps on the bus."

"I think the bus left for the night," Logan said.

"A motel then."

Olivia rolled her eyes. "How's he going to get to a motel?"

"He's not leaving us," Parker declared. "Besides, he'd be walking all the way back in the dark."

"I mean, he's probably—I'm sure he's got a flashlight."

Kyle sighed. "Well if he's not leaving us, where's he going to . . . fuck."

"What?" asked Parker.

"How much money does he owe?"

"That's his business, not any of ours."

Kyle shoved his hands in his pockets. "I'm just saying, deep in debt, in trouble at work, he wanders off into the woods . . ."

There was silence for a moment and then Parker vigorously shook her head. "No."

"Oh shit," said Olivia. "You think he's going to—"

"No, he isn't," said Parker.

Sam wanted to not care, but Barnes had always been a decent guy. *Was* a decent guy. "I'm sure he's okay."

"He's fine," Parker agreed. "And I'm going to go check."

She started for the trees and Logan held out a hand. "Wait."

"I'm not going to—"

"It's already dark. It'll be darker in the trees and none of us know the way." He raised his voice. "Skip!"

"Fake-Skip!" added Kyle.

"Josh," yelled Sam.

A flashlight wandered out of the dark and dropped down to aim at their feet. "Hey, guys. What's up?" He had on his black coat and it *was* a blazer, making him look even more like middle management.

"We need to get back to where we left Professor Barnes," Parker said. "Right now."

The guide glanced around. "Yeah, sure. We were just about to start a little fire, do you want to wait until—"

"Now," said Sam.

"Sure. Now it is." He stepped past them, veered a bit to the left, and headed for the tree line, keeping his flashlight pointed at the ground. "This way."

Parker followed him. Sam fell in step behind her. Kyle came too.

They went down into the dark trees.

Everything looked different at night. Studying astronomy meant Sam was used to moving around in the dark, but the forest still had so many shadows and dark shapes. The flashlight bobbed and weaved ahead of them. Behind him Kyle had turned on a red-lensed flashlight, but the same properties that made it great for stargazing made it crap for wandering downhill through the woods.

Heading down went faster than going up, and maybe fifteen minutes of stumbling brought them out of the trees and back to the stone clearing. Barnes still stood there, his pack on and his phone held with both hands. The white chalk X sat between his feet, almost glowing in the dim forest.

He looked at Parker. At the guide. At Sam. He looked . . . worried? Had Kyle been right? Had they caught him in the middle of something?

"What are you doing here? You should all be up at the camp."

Sam glanced back. They'd all followed along. Kyle. Logan and Olivia.

Parker glanced over at Kyle. "I . . . we were worried about you. Nobody knew if you needed a tent or food or—"

Barnes shook his head. "You don't need to worry about me. I'm fine. Really. You can all head back to camp. I'll be right behind you."

Kyle looked down at the X. Up at the sky. "What are you doing?"

"It's a side project." He glanced at his phone again before dropping it into his pocket. "And I really can't afford any distractions, so if you don't mind . . ."

"It's just kind of weird," said Parker. "You being off here all alone."

"I know. I can explain it all at length on the bus ride home. Or maybe once all the imaging equipment's set up and—"

"It's set up," Logan said. Still wearing his backpack. Had he forgotten he had it on? Sam glanced down at the straps of his own tiny pack, still hanging off his own shoulders.

Olivia nodded. "We need to know what you want them aimed at."

"Pick something. You've all done this before. It's about getting them familiar with the equipment. You don't need me for that."

A harsh beeping came from his pocket. An alarm.

Barnes looked anxious. "I don't want to be the guy pulling rank," he said, "but get back up there and get them started on the imaging. Now. You all know the drill. One of you at each telescope."

"Are you sure everything's okay?"

"Yep. I'm just . . . this is very time sensitive, Parker. I'm only going to get one shot at this and I can't afford any distractions. So you all need to go. Please."

Sam looked at the others. Was about to announce he'd go back to the camp when he realized Barnes's phone was still beeping. And the beeps were speeding up.

Barnes knew it, too. "I'll explain later, but right now you all need to get out of this clearing." The casual tone had vanished from his voice, replaced with sudden urgency.

Confusion spread across Parker's face. "What are you—"

"Now!" He put a hand on her shoulder and gave her a push—almost a *shove*—toward the tree line, waved hard at the rest of them with his other hand.

"Hey," snapped Logan. He rolled his shoulders and his pack dropped, freeing his arms up. "Don't push her around."

"What the hell's wrong with you?" added Olivia.

"Get out of here," shouted Barnes.

Sam took a step back from all of it. He got out "Maybe we should—" and realized nobody could hear him over the raised voices and the harsh . . .

The countdown beeps from the phone had become an electronic drum roll. One after another after another after another. And even as Sam registered it, recognized the implication of it, the urgent beeps blurred into a single, sharp tone that cut across the argument.

"Goddammit," muttered Barnes.

The hillside vanished beneath their feet, and they plunged down.

3

KYLE

Kyle fell.

He screamed, terror overwhelming him. It'd happened so fast. His stomach lunging up into his throat, the sudden absence of weight, the feeling everything was rushing past him.

And the fall kept going. Hundreds of feet? At least four or five seconds now. Long enough for him to grab impressions if not complete thoughts. He'd fallen into a cave. Or a mine shaft.

Holy fuck it was cold. And dark, like falling through black smoke. But somehow he saw Olivia a few yards away. Parker, still in his line of sight, her braid sticking out from the back of her head like a handle. Past them was the fake guide, Josh-not-Skip, screaming with his arms wide and mouth wide.

And they were still standing. All of them. He could feel . . . something under his feet. Not as solid as the hillside had been. Or maybe not as connected. Like one of those old cartoons where the whole cliff drops and the Coyote drops with it, riding it a thousand feet down into the canyon.

A thousand feet. Ten seconds. Terminal velocity at twelve and a half seconds. Was the whole mountain hollow?

They were going to die. Their bodies would explode on impact. He knew the math. No saving any of them.

Josh-not-Skip kept screaming. Olivia too. Kyle realized he hadn't stopped, either. He heard other voices, but maybe it was the wind in his ears.

Fifteen seconds now? Twenty seconds of plunging through the void? Enough time he was thinking more than reacting, organizing his thoughts. A chance for the idea to cross his mind that maybe he was just dreaming he was falling. It had the unreality of a dream, so maybe any minute now he'd start flying or get caught by Spider-Man or end up in an airplane having sex with the redhead from the gym or please anything that wasn't exploding like a watermelon.

And then the plunging sensation vanished, the not-quite-ground under his feet solidified, and his arms dropped to his sides. The idea flew through Kyle's mind they hadn't hit or crashed but *landed*, and as it did the ground found its final form, shifting beneath his feet into a slope his balance and posture weren't prepared for. He stumbled, reached out for anything, and fell. His arms took most of the impact, but then his hand slipped, and he rolled down the slope like a little kid going down a hill in a park. A rock hit him in the gut, and another one scraped the back of his neck. Grunts and yelps echoed in his ears, not all his. He turned over three times, maybe four, before something heavy caught his thigh and held him in place.

He blinked. Climbed to his feet. Shook his head clear. A few more blinks got his eyes adjusted to the dark. Nighttime dark. Starlight. He could see trees and the sky and . . .

Still on the hill. *Outside* of the hill. He'd tumbled back down into the forest below the small clearing.

"Hey?" he called out. "Anyone? Everybody okay?"

He heard a grunt and saw something moving a few yards away. Someone sat up. Olivia. There was enough light to see the scratch on her face and the tear in her sleeve. Darkness and confusion had spread her eyes wide open.

"Ouch," muttered someone else. The short guy. Sam. He knelt, rolled his shoulder. And a few yards past him Logan pushed himself up onto his feet.

Kyle turned the other way and Barnes was in his face.

"GO," roared the man, pointing. "BACK UP TO THE TOP, NOW!"

Kyle stumbled back. Sam grabbed his arm, caught him before he could fall again. Olivia staggered to her feet.

"RUN! GO NOW! RUN!!!"

They ran.

They flung themselves up the hillside, fighting the slope and soreness and confusion, moving as fast as they dared in the dim light. A figure staggered out of the darkness near Kyle—Parker! He grabbed her arm, dragged her along with them.

They ran through the trees, their feet thudding against the hard-packed dirt. It wormed into Kyle's mind he didn't know what they were running to—or *from*—but the look on Barnes's face had left zero doubt running was the only response. He glanced back at Logan limping behind them, dragging one leg. The guide, Josh, too, looking scared and confused, his ivory shirt smeared with something dark.

He ran another ten yards. Then twenty. And then he broke through the tree line and staggered to a stop. Parker wobbled next to him and he put out an arm, half catching her as she slumped against him. He looked to either side, behind them again, and at the swath of rock ahead of them, a sheer cliff.

"Was that an earthquake?" asked Josh, looking around. His baseball cap was gone and he had blood on one ear.

Olivia shook her head. "It wasn't an earthquake."

Kyle looked around. Tried to get his bearings. "Where the fuck is the plateau?"

Another sloped clearing of stone, more than twice the size of the one they'd found Barnes in, stretched out where the plateau had been. Rocks and small boulders covered the far side of it. And at least one massive slab the size of their bus. The pile of rubble led up to the cliff, a vertical wall of stone stretching up so high Kyle lost sight of it in the night.

"Where's everyone else?" asked Logan, his eyes wide in the dark. "Where's the camp?"

"Oh, holy fuck." Kyle looked around. "Was it . . . was it a landslide?"

Josh shook his head. "Can't be. We weren't that far from the top and it wasn't . . . it wasn't that steep."

Olivia took a few more steps. Peered at the massive pile of rubble. "They could all be hurt."

"We're hurt," Kyle said.

"They could be hurt worse," she snapped.

Logan looked around. A white crack ran across one lens of his glasses. "But where are they? Where did all the tents go?"

A light flared. Josh had his cell phone out. Kyle pulled his out too. Cracked screen, but it still responded. Logan and Olivia added their mini-Maglites with the red lenses. The clearing got brighter, but not enough.

"Hey," Kyle called out, panning his light back and forth across the rubble. "Can anyone hear me?" He called out a few names, people from his lab he remembered seeing on the bus and the hike.

Olivia looked up at the sky. "Where's the damned Moon?"

Logan craned his head up. "Behind a cloud?"

"You okay?"

"Yeah. Smashed my knee on a rock when I fell down the hill, but I think I'm okay other than—"

"Oh, crap." Josh pointed his phone at Parker. "She's bleeding pretty bad."

All their phones swung in, and Kyle let Parker slump against him even more. Her head rolled against his shoulder. The side she'd had away from him was dark and sticky. A gash up by her hairline, between her ear and her eye. "I'm fine," she said. "Just a little dizzy from running."

Kyle tried to hold her up and also get a better look at the wound. "She must've hit her head when we landed."

"Check her eyes," said Logan. "People's eyes look messed up when they've had head trauma." He shined his phone's flashlight in her face.

"Messed up how?"

Parker raised a hand and tried to wave the light away, shielding her eyes.

"I don't know. Dilated, maybe?"

"I think her eyes look okay," said Kyle.

"I said I'm fine."

"We're just making sure," said Olivia.

Parker made a rude noise with her lips. "Sure you are."

Olivia sighed. "She's fine. Stupid bitch."

"I heard that."

"Good."

"Has to be a landslide," said Logan. "It swept everything off the plateau."

Olivia shined her flashlight across the clearing. "Where's everyone else then? Shouldn't someone besides us be calling for help?"

They all went silent. Kyle counted to five, then to ten. He heard wind, the rustle of leaves and grass, but nothing else. No voices.

"I don't hear anything," whispered Logan.

"Me neither," muttered Parker.

Sam panned the light from his phone around the clearing. "Why isn't there—shouldn't we hear *something*? I mean, a couple—a few hundred tons of rock and dirt just slid down the side of the mountain five minutes ago."

"It couldn't've," said Josh.

"Shhhhhhh."

Another few seconds of silence as they listened.

"I don't even hear an echo," said Olivia.

"Why did you say landed?" asked Sam.

Heads turned. Kyle realized the question had been directed at him. "What?"

Sam tipped his head at Parker. "You said she—said Parker hit her head when we landed. What'd you mean?"

"When we . . . we fell, right? We fell and then we landed."

He saw their faces. They'd all felt it. He'd just been the one to say it.

"We've got to get help up here," said Logan. "Rescue teams. Maybe a helicopter or something."

Olivia pulled at her phone. "Shit, I'm not getting a signal."

Sam held his phone up. "I had two bars, but I've got nothing now."

"You didn't make it."

Kyle turned toward the voice, swinging Parker with him, tightening his grip around her waist.

Barnes stood maybe ten yards down the slope. Even in the half-light from their phones and flashlights, Kyle could see the man's posture was looser. More relaxed. The nervous tension was gone from his face, replaced with . . . sadness? Disappointment?

"Make what?" asked Logan.

Barnes sighed. "I'm so sorry. So very sorry."

"We've got to get help," said Kyle. "Parker's hurt. We think lots of other people might be too."

"Do you know what happened?" asked Logan.

"I'm pretty sure everyone else is fine," said Barnes, hiking up to them. "Really."

Olivia looked around the clearing. "So where are they?"

"They're back at camp. Some of them might be looking for us by now."

"What do you mean?"

"I'm still not—I can't get a signal," Sam announced.

"Is *anyone* getting a signal?" asked Kyle, not taking his eyes off Barnes.

"You're not going to get a signal," the professor told them. He shoved his hands in his pockets. "There aren't any antennas in range."

"There was one earlier," said Sam.

"It's long gone. So to speak."

"Are we dead?" asked Josh. "Ohmigod we're dead, aren't we?"

"We're not dead. We're fine." Barnes tapped Olivia's phone, pointed at Parker's head. She lit up the wound while he examined it.

Logan swept his flashlight around the clearing again. "Where's all our gear?"

"Back wherever you left it."

"It's not. There's nothing anywhere on the hillside."

"This isn't the same hillside," Barnes said. He gave Parker's shoulder a gentle squeeze. "I'm sorry about shoving you earlier. You should be fine by morning."

"It's okay," she mumbled. "You're forgiven."

"That's a pretty nasty gash," said Sam. "Maybe a concussion. And head wounds bleed a lot."

Barnes straightened up. "Trust me. She'll be fine."

Kyle looked up at the towering cliff. "It couldn't've *all* gotten swept away," he insisted.

"Nothing got swept away," Barnes told him. "Not exactly."

"Then where *is* it?" demanded Olivia. "What happened to everyone?"

Barnes took a breath. Looked at each of them in turn. "We've made a lot of noise," he said. "We should head back into the trees, make the best camp we can, try to get comfortable for the night. And then I'll explain."

4

LOGAN

Barnes led them back down into the forest below the clearing. Logan's knee throbbed, but it didn't feel broken. Just a good whack that was still echoing back and forth through his nervous system.

They found his backpack propped against a jagged tree stump as if it'd slid down the slope and gotten caught. They couldn't find any other packs or equipment anywhere. Kyle pointed out it could all be a few yards away and look like stones in the dim starlight.

They found a spot between three trees without too many lumps or rocks. Barnes unrolled his sleeping bag and had Parker sit down on it. Then he unzipped his pack and slid out a higher-end first aid kit. Logan held the light while the professor took a few gentle passes at Parker's face with some alcohol wipes. She flinched as the wipes brushed the gouge, but she didn't fight. It looked like a long stripe of road rash on her temple, the size of a business card and deep enough that Logan wondered if he might be looking at a bit of exposed skull.

While they cleaned her up, Josh, the questionable guide, gathered a few small stones from around the site and made a rough ring. He piled some sticks and pine needles in the center and Barnes waved a hand at him. "Don't."

"It's okay," said Josh. "It's not my first campfire."

"We don't want to attract attention."

"Actually, yes we do," said Kyle. His perfectly messy hair had a slant to it now, and it made his head look lopsided. "We want to attract as much attention as possible because we're lost in the woods with no phone signal and there was a fucking landslide!"

Barnes pulled an oversized Band-Aid from his kit. "Not exactly."

"Then *what* exactly? What the hell is going on?"

"I'm going to tell you. I'm just not sure where to begin. I didn't expect to have anyone with me on this trip. Sorry."

"We know," Olivia said. "It was last minute."

Barnes chuckled, but he didn't smile. "Not really."

Logan sat down on the ground near Olivia and she shuffled a few inches to the side to give him room. She went far enough it left a gap between them. It felt like that'd been happening a lot lately. On a couple levels. He knew she'd mostly agreed to this trip to humor him, and well . . . now they were all a little distracted.

Barnes turned around, settled on the ground near Parker. He folded one leg beneath himself. Looked at each of them. A glance at Parker, sitting with her chin almost touching her chest.

"We're in the past," said Barnes.

Josh glanced back up the hill. "Past what?"

"*The* past," said Barnes. He swung his bulging pack in front of him, unzipped a pocket, and pulled out half a dozen PowerBars. "About a hundred million years. Prehistory. Although I'm not sure that's the best term for this place."

Kyle rolled his eyes. "The fuck are you talking about?"

"Like . . . time travel?" asked Logan.

Barnes nodded. Tossed him a PowerBar across the unused fire ring. Another one went to Olivia. Josh snatched his out of the air with one hand.

"Bullshit," said Kyle, fumbling the bar thrown to him.

"It's not," said Barnes. "You all know physics allows for it. We just don't know how to do it. Well, not practically."

They stared at him. Sam checked his phone again. Josh looked back up at the dim, towering cliff. They could still see it through the trees.

"That's a bad place to start," said Barnes. "Okay, the whole story. I wasn't always Noah Barnes. The name I was born with was Bill Gather."

"Is that supposed to mean something?" asked Olivia.

He shrugged. "It did for a lot of years."

"Wait." Sam looked up from his phone and Logan saw his face change, almost lighting up. "Bill Gather like *Billy* Gather? Dino Boy?"

Barnes sighed. "Yep, that's me."

"No way?!"

Josh tapped a finger against his chin. "You were a fifteen-minutes-of-fame celebrity, right? No offense. Back in the early '90s?"

"None taken."

A memory tickled Logan's mind. Some sort of pre-meme joke he'd seen a few times. "You were that kid forty-something years ago who had a mental break when you were kidnapped. You thought your dad was eaten by a dinosaur?"

"It was thirty-three years ago, I wasn't kidnapped, and I didn't have a mental break. My father was killed by a T-Rex. Right in front of me and my sister."

"Holy crap." Sam stared at Barnes, starstruck, slowly tilting his head, examining the man's face. "You're really him. It's really you."

"Yes it is."

"Could someone fill me in?" asked Josh. "Pretend I'm an idiot."

"Something tells me that doesn't involve a lot of pretending," said Kyle.

"Hey!"

"Kyle, seriously, give it a rest," Logan said.

Barnes raised his palms. "Please . . . keep your voices down."

Olivia rubbed her hands on her arms. "Why?"

"Like I said before, we don't want to attract attention."

Logan looked off into the dark woods. So did Olivia and Josh. They all listened quietly for a moment. There wasn't a lot of sound. No crickets or owls or anything. Just distant echoes, too muffled to be identified.

Barnes laced his fingers together, and Logan thought it looked like he was in therapy. Ready to talk, relaxed, but still defensive on some level. Like he already knew how the session was going to go.

"A few weeks before my tenth birthday," said Barnes, "my father took my sister and I white water rafting in Maine. It was the anniversary of our mom's death and he didn't want us to be sitting at home upset about it. We'd been on the water for two hours, went over a big group of rapids, and our raft . . . kept falling."

Logan looked back into the woods. Remembered the sensation of plunging down through the darkness.

"We'd encountered a wormhole," Barnes continued. "An actual, honest-to-God stable Ellis wormhole. And it dumped us a hundred million years in the past."

"Bullshit," said Olivia, rubbing her arms again. Logan could see goose pimples in the dim light. It wasn't cold, but he wondered if she might be in shock.

He wondered if *he* was in shock.

Barnes shrugged. "Well, I've never been exactly sure how far back, to be honest. We didn't have any way to check. But my family . . . I was lost there for two years."

"Five years," said Sam. "I read all the books. Dino Boy was—you were gone for five years."

"Please don't say 'Dino Boy.' And it was five years back in the present. For me, it was barely twenty-six months."

"How?"

"Time dilation. My gut says it's from the wormhole, but I've got nothing to back it up."

Logan tried to map out a wormhole in his head. He knew the basics, but they really weren't his specialty. "That only works when you're going through it, though. If you made it to the other side you wouldn't keep getting time dilation."

"Maybe. A lot of things work differently here."

Blue light spilled over them as Josh held up his phone, searching for a signal.

"You're wasting your time," Barnes told him. "And your battery. There's not going to be any cell phone towers in range for a long time."

Logan slid his hoodie off and draped it over Olivia's shoulders. "I thought the whole thing was trauma," he said. "A coping mechanism."

"It wasn't. It was real. Two years living with dinosaurs and Neanderthals and our robot, Ross."

"Your robot?" echoed Olivia, sticking her arms into the hoodie. She looked up at Logan, gave him a quick, neutral smile.

"I mean, we found him stuck in the mud by the watering hole. It's not like I built him out of coconuts or something."

Kyle snorted. "Dinosaurs and cavemen didn't exist at the same time."

"Like I said, the rules are different here." He reached out and plucked a twig from the ground. "Any of you have a junk drawer in your homes growing up? A drawer in the kitchen that collects all the little odds and ends that don't fit anywhere else."

"I did," murmured Parker, raising a hand.

Logan raised a few fingers. Olivia nodded.

"I've got one now," said Josh.

Barnes nodded with them. "My dad called this place God's junk drawer. Things from all across time end up here. Things that don't fit anywhere else in the cosmos, for one reason or another. This is where they all accumulate." He held the twig by the end, waved it back and forth, then tossed it into the circle of stones.

"Wait," said Kyle. "Are you saying that's where we are now? We're in magical dino-land or whatever?"

"It's not magic," Barnes replied, "but . . . yep. We're in the valley."

"Bullshit."

"Sorry."

Sam mouthed a silent *whoa* and stared at Barnes with fanboy awe. "You're saying it's all true? All the stuff in the books?" His voice hadn't been this lively all day.

"Well, not everything," Barnes shrugged. "A couple of them exaggerate on points, and some of them take the angle of debunking everything I said. And a few of them are pure nonsense. One reads like a Saturday morning kids show."

Kyle coughed into his shoulder. "You'd think if there was a wormhole on a white water rafting route, somebody would've noticed it."

"Exactly," said Barnes. He pointed a finger, singling out the clever student. "For years I thought the same way, that the wormhole was in a specific location. Once I was back, I went down that river so many times. Twice a day, three times if I could manage it. I must've done it two hundred times, trying to cover every inch of the rapids, think of every variable. Speed, weight, materials, weather, time of day. Then I spent a year in Thailand, in the forest where I reappeared. Tried to find the exact location I got out."

Olivia cocked her head. "Why?"

Barnes didn't hear her. He was in lecture mode, giving the class information with a story. "Then I started investigating other disappearances. I knew other things ended up in the valley. Maybe I could find a pattern to the disappearances and where they happened. Start predicting where they were going to happen."

"I'd guess there are a lot of unexplained disappearances," Logan said.

"You have no idea. Especially when you start figuring the ones with accepted explanations. Plus, when random objects go missing, there's usually less of a record." Barnes waved a hand at the dark forest around them. "All sorts of stuff ends up here. Animals. Plants. Vehicles. Statues."

"You found—there was an Egyptian riverboat," Sam said. "And a giant sundial, right?"

Barnes let out a little chuckle. "You really did read all the books."

"I really . . . it was a phase. When I was twelve. Not, like, a recent thing."

"Anyway, spend two decades studying wormholes and eventually you get a doctorate, and then you're an associate professor. It meant I had more resources, I just needed to teach an undergrad class now and then."

"Plus help out with the occasional graduate project," said Logan.

"Well, yes, but that came a little later."

"I still say this is all bullshit," Kyle said.

"So one day I was teaching the orbital mechanics class for the fourth or fifth time," Barnes continued, "walking everyone through geosynchronous orbits, and I realized my problem, the wormhole, *was* all about location. Just not a location on Earth."

He pointed up at the sky.

Olivia got it first. "You're saying the wormhole's somewhere else in the solar system?"

"It's orbiting the sun," added Logan, close behind her. "An orbit that sometimes intersects Earth's orbit."

"Almost," said Barnes. "If my calculations are correct, and, well, current evidence seems to show they are, there's a stable Ellis wormhole at a fixed point in Earth's orbit."

"It's at one of the Lagrange points?"

Barnes shook his head. "No, it's fixed at September twenty-second, currently at . . . well six fifty-eight Eastern Standard Time."

"Currently?" echoed Kyle.

"Leap days. Earth's orbit is almost six hours longer than a year, so we're not always at the same point."

"But this hypothetical fixed wormhole is?" Olivia asked.

Barnes gave a half smile, almost a smirk, and gestured at the forest again. "It's not hypothetical."

"So it's a fixed point in the orbit," said Logan, "but it's not a Lagrange point?"

Josh finally lowered his phone. The screen winked out, and they were in near darkness again. "Excuse me, could someone explain what a La Range point is?"

"Lagrange," corrected Barnes. "And it's not important."

"They're points in an orbiting system where things stay put," Kyle said, sounding annoyed he had to explain it. "The gravitational forces between the Earth and the sun balance out with the centrifugal force of the orbit, so if you get something to one of the points it stays there."

"But the points move as the system moves," added Logan. "For example, one of the Lagrange points is on the other side of the sun, directly across from Earth. But it's *always* directly across from us. Earth moves around the sun and that point moves to keep the same relationship."

Josh's face lit up. "Oh! So it's like Counter-Earth."

"What?"

"In the comics, there's another Earth on the opposite side of the sun, and we never see it because it's orbiting as fast as we are. They changed it in the Marvel movies, but that's what it was originally. They did the same thing in some old *Doctor Who* episodes, too, but they called it Mondas."

"I . . . yeah, that's actually it."

"Really dumb," said Kyle, "but basically it."

"And not what we're talking about," Barnes said, a hint of irritation in his voice.

Olivia rolled a twig between her fingers, then flicked it into the unlit pile of leaves and sticks. "So what *are* we talking about?"

Barnes shrugged again. "I've been calling it a heliostationary point. To be honest, there isn't a term for something that behaves like this."

"Because nothing behaves like that." Kyle blew air out of his nose.

Barnes stared at him. "This wormhole does. And once a year, Earth's movement brings them together. Depending on the exact point of contact, the intersection can be extremely minor or it can be . . . larger. And whatever's at the intersection gets transported here."

Sam tried to throw a leaf into the stone circle, but it spun in the air and landed at his feet. "Like you, like you and your family did."

"Like *all* of us did." Olivia crossed her arms.

"Sorry." Barnes picked up another twig. "I tried to warn you all away."

Josh looked up at the trees. "Could've been a little more specific."

"I'm pretty sure if I'd said, 'Back up or you'll get sucked into a wormhole,' it would've led to more questions."

"So why bring all of us out here," asked Logan. "If there was a risk of other people getting sucked in, why not come alone? Why bring all of us?"

"And a few dozen undergrads," Sam added.

"Really, the only one I needed was him." Barnes pointed a finger at Josh. "Or the guy I originally hired. I just needed to get to that exact spot. But the truth is, by the time I'd gathered all the information, made all the calculations, triple-checked them . . ."

Logan remembered their discussion back on the bus. "You were broke."

"Yep."

Olivia shook her head. "But this is . . . it's maybe two tanks of gas to get here from campus. And how much can this guy really cost?"

"Hey!" said Josh.

"I was *really* broke," Barnes said. He patted his bulging backpack. "Associate professors aren't rolling in money to start with, and this has been my life's work. I'd spent my departmental budget, my savings, everything. I sold my car, went about sixty grand into debt, and I've been couch-surfing for the past three months. If I wanted to travel through time, I needed the department to approve me traveling a few hundred miles and hiring a guide."

"This is all fucking bullshit," snapped Kyle. "We're not a million years in the past. We're in the forest on the side of a mountain, right now, in the present, in New York, and this whole trip's turned into a disaster so he's trying to cover his ass."

Logan rolled his eyes. "How, exactly, is this covering his ass?"

"He's trying to confuse us."

"Why?" Olivia asked.

"So he doesn't get the blame for all this. So we don't call for help."

"There's no phone signal," said Josh. "We can't call for help."

"Not down here," Kyle said. "Why do you think he led us down the hill?"

They all looked at Barnes.

He shrugged. "You're welcome to go back up the hill and try to make a call."

"Yeah?" Logan and Kyle said at the same time.

"Yep. I'd almost be glad if you got through." He pulled something from his coat pocket. Turned it on. Looked at the screen. Tossed it over to Logan. "You're not going to, though."

Logan spun the GPS device right side up in his hand. The screen was blank except for one line at the top.

UNABLE TO ACQUIRE SATELLITES

He showed it to Olivia, then held it up for Kyle to see. Kyle scowled. "It's bullshit," he repeated. It didn't have as much force this time.

Logan glanced up. Imagined the sky completely free of satellites and space junk and the words spilled out of his mouth as soon as they formed in his mind. "Wait, are we stuck here?"

He glanced at Olivia, saw her eyes open wide. "Oh fuck."

Josh glanced around at the dark forest. "We're trapped?!"

"But you got out," said Sam. "You got out before."

Noah shook his head. Raised his hands like he was calming down a classroom. "We're not stuck. Not trapped. I knew how to get here, I know how to get back. I told you, I've spent years figuring out exactly how the wormhole works."

Olivia didn't look confident. "Are you sure?"

"Absolutely sure. You're all going to get home."

Logan and Olivia passed an uneasy look between them. Then he shared it with Kyle. Josh looked uneasy, but something about it seemed a little off.

"So you, you've spent your whole life trying to prove all of this was real?" asked Sam.

"No," said Barnes with a shake of his head. "I've spent my whole life trying to figure out how to get back here."

Logan blinked twice "What?"

"Why?" Josh asked.

The air shifted around them. Not a breeze, but a pulsing rumble, a shockwave that pushed against Logan's chest and arms and cheeks. Like a sound pitched so low he felt it more than heard it. His mind called up the image of a shark roaring deep underwater. Olivia shifted, and he saw Kyle and Sam look around.

Logan glanced over at Josh. "What the hell was that?"

"Something . . . big," said their guide.

"Yeah, no shit," Kyle said. "What was it?"

"A bear?"

"Sounded like a chainsaw and a tuba having sex in a pool," murmured Olivia.

"It sounded like Fang," Barnes said.

"Fang?" echoed Logan.

"The tyrannosaurus that killed my dad. That's what we called him. He had two oversized canines that stuck out of his mouth."

"Fang," Sam whispered with awe.

Kyle laughed awkwardly. Uncertainly. "No, seriously . . . what was that?"

"Seriously," said Barnes. "It was a tyrannosaurus."

Josh peered off through the trees. "Like, someone's watching a loud movie."

"Nope."

"Where's the bear?"

Past Barnes, Parker stared straight up into the night sky. She pointed with a shaky hand. Shaky, or trying to take in a lot of the sky through the trees?

Barnes leaned closer to her. "It wasn't a bear."

She shook her head, winced, ran her words together. "Ursa Major. The Big Dipper. Where's it?"

Logan looked up. So did Olivia. And Kyle.

"Is . . . are the trees blocking it?" she asked.

Kyle stood up and leaned to the side. "Where's Polaris?"

Logan leaned back, tried to find a spot between the trees wide enough for him to see . . . anything. "Where's Vega?"

"I don't see . . . what are these stars? Where is everything?"

Olivia pointed up. "Is that . . . Jupiter?"

Kyle snorted. "How could it be Jupiter?"

"Well, what is it, then?"

Logan let his eyes drift. A simple stargazing trick called averted vision. Easier to find faint objects by looking from a different angle rather than looking right at them. A faint thrill danced in his chest. Seeing a new sky excited and terrified him all at once.

He stared at Barnes across the circle of rocks. The man looked tired in the starlight, but his weariness had a touch of satisfaction to it.

"We're in the valley now," Barnes told them. "Things are different here."

"Meaning what?" asked Kyle.

A branch snapped in the forest and they all spun. Logan raised his flashlight, painfully aware of how much the red lens cut the range. He aimed at one tree, then another, and another.

One of the trees moved.

Logan's brain immediately leaped to *BEAR* because it stood upright, but even in the dim red light he could see the animal's fur was too light and patterned. And he was pretty sure it was too small. And the proportions were wrong. And it had a big tail. And the fur was more . . .

The animal stepped forward and . . . it had to be someone in one of those inflatable suits. The bouncy, head-wobbling suits people wore to cons and street fairs and marathons and . . .

"What the actual fuck?" whispered Kyle.

"Oh my Godddddd," wheezed Sam.

The dinosaur took another step forward and stretched its spike-covered head up to grab one of the low-hanging branches in its jaw. It slowly exerted pressure, staring at all of them as they stared back at it, and the branch bent, cracked, twisted off to show white wood that looked like bright blood in the red light. The branch swung loose and the creature caught it in its front paws. Claws? They reminded Logan of bird feet. It blinked once, a fast flick of the lids over a round, black eyeball, then lowered its head and started to munch on the leaves.

Logan put it at maybe six and a half feet tall—taller than any of them, but not drastically so—and maybe twice as long counting the heavy tail. There had to be maybe a dozen spikes on its bare snout, but the top of its head was a prominent mass of fur—it wasn't fur but his mind wasn't working much past basic observation—a mass that almost looked like a pompadour.

It kept staring at them while it munched leaves. Was it staring at him? Its eyes were big and dark, and in the red light of two or three flashlights it looked like a bad found footage monster.

Parker's voice came from behind him. "Everyone else is seeing this, right?"

Someone moved into his peripheral vision. Barnes. "It's a pachycephalosaurus. Pretty much harmless."

"How much is pretty much?" asked Josh.

Barnes shrugged. "Don't try to take his food. Watch out for the tail if he turns around fast. Probably shouldn't stick your hand in his mouth."

Josh leaned slightly back. "Meat eater?"

"Nah. Nothing our size, anyway. But he can still give you a nasty bite."

Kyle let out some air. "It's a dinosaur."

"Yep, he is."

"It's a *dinosaur*!" said Sam. His eyes were wide with excitement.

"Yep."

Olivia leaned forward and aimed her flashlight between its legs. "How do you know it's a he?"

"The feathers on his head."

"The what?"

Barnes gave her a quick smile, stepped forward, and raised his hands over his head. The dinosaur dropped its leaves and pulled its head back in a very birdlike motion. And then the pompadour on its head straightened up and splayed open like one of those big feather fans dancers used in old movies. Even in the red light, Logan could see three or four bands of color across all those feathers.

Josh yelped. Logan realized he'd taken a step back himself. Almost bumped into Olivia. He glanced at her. Back at the dinosaur.

At the friggin' *dinosaur.*

Barnes let his arms drop, and the packy . . . the dinosaur relaxed. The crest of feathers settled back down. It reached back up and grabbed another leafy branch with its mouth, still watching them as it did.

A real live dinosaur. Right in front of them. Eating leaves.

Barnes stepped back across the little fire ring. "It shouldn't bother us," he said, settling down next to his monstrous backpack.

"Shouldn't?" said Kyle.

Parker still sat on the ground, gingerly holding the side of her head. She stared at the dinosaur with an expression that rolled back and forth between awe and confusion. Probably wondering if she had a concussion.

The dinosaur reminded Logan of a squirrel, holding its food in both hands and munching away. Sam had inched closer and stared at it in awe. Josh still looked nervous. Olivia's eyes stretched wide and her lips trembled, like she was still deciding how to react but it was going to be extreme when she figured it out.

Logan tried to keep his flashlight on the dinosaur and looked back at Barnes. The professor had settled back against his pack. "We'll be safe here in the trees as long as we don't draw attention to ourselves. Get some rest. Tomorrow's going to be a big day. I'll figure out exactly where we are and we can get going."

"Going where?" asked Logan.

But Barnes just crossed his arms, closed his eyes, and relaxed into his pack.

5

BILLY

Billy's backpack bounced against his hips as he trotted after Dad through the leafy forest. He clutched his sleeping bag under one arm, and the bag of snacks tugged at his other elbow. He felt a little clumsy and off-balance, but he'd tried switching hands and arms a couple times now and this was the least annoying way to carry everything.

The worst part was, with both hands full, he couldn't push leaves out of the way. A lot of the plants stood a bit shorter than him, enough that their soft green branches flopped against his chest or neck or face as he pushed through them. Every now and then Dad would bend one aside and it would spring back a little too fast, giving Billy a gentle slap. He tried to block them with the snack-laden arm, but the cans of Pepsi were heavy and awkward. Then he'd tried using the sleeping bag as a plow, but then a little thorn had caught the fabric and almost torn it.

Mom had bought him the sleeping bag. His first full-sized one. Too big, but he'd grow into it, she'd said. He'd rather have branches hit him in the face than damage it.

And he couldn't complain because Dad and Beau were both carrying more than him, and she'd tease him about being a wuss.

So when another big fern leaf slid across his face, he sighed in the loud, exasperated way only a nine-year-and-nine-months-old could and shifted the sleeping bag so it sat a little more on his hip.

"Wuss," Beau said from behind him.

"Jerk," he responded.

"Double-wuss."

"Triple-jerk."

"Hey," said Dad. He stopped, looked back at each of them. "Not now, okay?"

"Sorry," Billy said.

"Trying to lighten the mood," said Beau.

"I think I've still got us heading south." Dad glanced up at the sun. "We should run into the river again any time now."

"That's what you said half an hour ago," Billy said, trying hard not to sound like a wuss. "Are we lost?"

"We're not lost. Just a little off course."

"Like, South America off course," murmured Beau. She got closer, rested her elbow on Billy's head. He smacked it off and she grinned at him.

Dad raised an eyebrow. "What's that supposed to mean?"

She sighed. The why-won't-you-get-out-of-my-room sigh. "This isn't a forest, Dad. Not a regular one. It's a jungle. Like, a real in-the-tropics jungle."

Billy thought it looked like a jungle from the movies and TV shows he'd seen. It smelled like a jungle, too. The forest usually had a woody smell, like old bark, but this one smelled . . . green. Green and wet, a little like a mowed lawn. Or maybe the produce section of the grocery store.

"We're not in the tropics," Dad said. "We're in Maine."

"It's at least ten degrees warmer."

"Because we're not on the river anymore."

Beau waved her hands at the trees and tall plants around them. "There is no river, Dad! It's gone!"

"It's not gone. We got . . . we got turned around a little, that's all."

But Billy didn't like the look on Dad's face. He'd had that look a lot right after Mom died and always tried to cover it up for them with fake smiles and happy words. Like now.

Dad gave them a weak smile, a thumbs-up, and turned back to the forest.

Beau sighed again and gave Billy a little push to get him moving.

Billy thought back to being in the raft a little while ago, bouncing on all the waves in the river. A wave had splashed him right in the face, and then . . .

He remembered thinking the raft had gone up into the air, like a bike off a ramp. It did that sometimes. A few seconds and then it came crashing back down into the water. Dad could even make it happen sometimes.

But then the raft had gone down and *kept* going down. Like being in a dream where you fall and your stomach goes up and you jump awake. Except Billy didn't wake up no matter how far they fell. Beau had grabbed him, wrapped her arms around him, pulled him tight . . .

And they'd lurched to a stop, falling back into the raft. He'd stayed in his sister's arms for a moment, breathing hard, feeling her breaths on the top of his head, making sure he hadn't peed his pants. Then he'd wiggled free. "Dad?"

Dad had already sat up, looking around. He didn't look hurt. Just a little confused. It took Billy a moment to realize why.

Their deflated raft sat on land. In a forest. This forest.

And like Beau said, it didn't look like any Maine forest Billy'd ever seen before.

Once they were sure nobody was hurt, Dad had scouted around, trying to figure out how they'd been thrown so far from the river. While he was gone, Beau checked out the remains of the raft. The front three feet of it were gone. Like someone had cut it off with a lightsaber. The little anchor and rope were gone, too, and the bag of climbing equipment Dad always brought when they went camping "just in case," even though he hadn't gone climbing in years, since Mom had first gotten sick.

They'd packed up everything they could carry and headed into the woods. They'd left one of the plastic oars stuck wide-end-up in the ground like a bright yellow flag so they could find everything else later. Dad insisted they'd find the river, get to the campsite where their friends were waiting, and laugh all night about how far inland they'd managed to crash their boat.

Half an hour later, they hadn't found the river.

Hadn't even heard it.

Dad pushed another branch out of the way and held it long enough for Billy to get his hand up. Billy caught it, looked back to make sure it would hit Beau when he let go, and ran into Dad's backpack.

"What the hell?"

"Sorry," said Billy.

Dad didn't answer. Billy waded into the tall grass next to him to see what he was looking at. Beau came up behind them and put a hand on Billy's shoulder. "Whoa."

Mom had loved this one big photography book about abandoned places. Houses and malls and factories people had left for some reason, and then nature came in and grew over everything. Grass and moss and sometimes even trees. One time they'd been visiting family and Beau and Billy had found an old car like that in the woods, wedged between two trees that had grown up around it. "This is how people used to throw some stuff away," she'd told him. "They just took it out in the woods and dumped it."

Billy figured that's what they were looking at now. A big display from a minigolf course or maybe an amusement park. There was one of those they kept seeing signs for when they drove to see Grampa—Maine's Largest Zoo and Amusement Park!—and Dad kept saying they'd stop someday. Maybe the amusement park had taken this out into the woods to get rid of it.

Although Billy couldn't understand why anyone would get rid of a perfectly good dinosaur statue.

It stood on all fours, surrounded by the leafy plants, and had to be at least twice the size of Dad's truck. The same blue-gray, too, although white dust covered the statue and Dad liked to keep his truck shiny clean. As Billy stared, he saw a faint pattern of stripes on the statue, too, like a faded zebra. It had a tall, round back with diamond-shaped fins sticking out of it, like Godzilla. Billy couldn't remember the name of this one—he'd never been into dinosaurs like some other kids—but he recognized it enough to know it'd have a spiked tail and a little head. Although the head would still probably be as big as him.

Then the head came up out of the grass like a dog looking up from its bowl, and for a brief moment Billy thought it was an electronic statue-robot like he'd heard they had at Disneyworld.

Beau's hand slipped off Billy's shoulder. She dropped the other bag of groceries she'd been carrying, and the strap of the first aid kit slid off her arm. The grass rustled as it caught both of them.

"Oh my god," said Dad.

The dinosaur stared at them, munching on the big fern in its mouth. Not really a mouth but a beak, like a big bird. The fern got shorter, shorter, shorter, and then the last of it vanished into the beak. The dinosaur looked at them, shuffled its feet, and bent its head to tear up another beakful of frilly leaves.

Beau took a step past Billy. "Is that . . . is that real?"

"I . . . I mean, it can't be."

"It's a dinosaur," said Billy.

"It's a stegosaurus," Dad told him. "A real live stegosaurus."

Beau took another step forward. Billy followed her. They were next to Dad now, staring at the huge animal. Its head—as big as Billy's body—came up again. It sucked down another fern and gazed back at them. It had dark eyes, like a parrot or a crow. The beak opened and let out a quick, deep hiss, almost a squawk.

"Is this . . ." Beau gazed up at the trees, over her shoulder. "Are we in some kind of . . . animal sanctuary? Or a . . . a zoo?"

"I think we would've heard about a dinosaur zoo."

"Can I touch it?" asked Billy.

"No. Maybe it's one of those . . . you know, a leftover. It's managed to survive all this time and nobody noticed. Like the Loch Ness Monster."

Beau sighed. "Really, Dad?"

"Do you have a better idea?"

A low rumble echoed through the jungle. Billy thought it sounded like when a truck drove by a few streets over and you felt it through the ground. But the noise was more like . . . breathing? The only thing he could say for sure was it sounded . . . it *felt* big.

The stegosaurus turned its head at the not-sound. It grabbed another fern in its beak and started walking. Billy felt the ground shake a little every time it took a step, like something heavy dropping on the floor. It plowed through the grass close to them, and Billy could see all the muscles moving and sliding under its powdery skin. It wasn't fast, but it was big enough that every step covered five or six feet. The long tail followed it like a snake, ending in a bunch of spikes the size of Billy's arm.

Beau stared off into the woods, looking toward the sound. "Dad?"

"Yeah, honey?"

"Do you think there could be . . . other dinosaurs here? Wherever here is?"

"I . . . I don't know."

"Maybe dinosaurs that one doesn't want to run into?" She jerked her head after the stegosaurus.

Dad turned his head to follow the path of crushed grass and ferns the stegosaurus had left as it plodded away. Then he looked into the woods. Toward the sound. Nodded. "We should probably get out of here."

Billy hugged his sleeping bag. "What about the campsite? Everyone's waiting for us, right?"

"We might not make it there tonight, pal. We're going to have a little adventure. Camp out in the woods."

"In the woods?" echoed Beau.

Dad shrugged. "Maybe we can find somewhere a little more sheltered. A cave or something. Come on, pick up everything and let's get going."

Billy picked up the bag of snacks he didn't remember dropping.

Beau swung the first aid kit over her arm and swept up the plastic sack of groceries. She gave Billy a nudge. "You doing okay?"

"Yep."

The low sound rippled through the jungle again. And this time Billy was pretty sure it was an animal. Like a bear. Or maybe a lion. But still definitely big.

"Let's go," said Dad. "You guys in front now."

"Why?"

"So I can poke you to move faster." He smiled, but it wasn't one of his real ones.

Beau considered the flattened grass. "Are we following the stedge . . . the dinosaur? Or do you want to keep going the way we've been going?"

Dad rolled his shoulders. Looked back toward the sound. "Let's split the difference. A little bit the way we're going, a little bit the way the stegosaurus is headed."

"Away from whatever made it leave," said Billy.

"Exactly." Dad smiled again. Still not a real one.

Beau slid her arms between two ferns and pushed the big leaves out of her way. She glanced back at Billy. "Come on, twerp."

He caught the fern leaf before it landed on his face. "Loser."

"Double-twerp."

"Triple-loser."

"Quadruple-twerp."

"Infinity-loser."

"Infinity plus one twerp," she said without even looking back.

"Dad, she's cheating on infinity."

Dad laughed. Not a big laugh, but a real one. "How about we try to keep it quiet? Inside voices, so we don't tell anything where we are."

Beau gave him a thumbs-up. Billy looked back, zipped his mouth, and threw away the key. Then he remembered he hadn't mimed locking it shut and wasn't sure what to do next. But Dad gave him an approving nod anyway.

They marched through the forest for another ten minutes. They didn't hear the sound again, and Billy watched the stegosaurus through the trees until he couldn't see it anymore. Some more wading through the grass and ferns and then they reached the edge of the trees. And in front of them stretched . . . an old, weedy parking lot? In the middle of the jungle.

The rough concrete had the faded look that said it'd been out in the sun for years. But Billy couldn't see a school or an office building or *any* buildings. Just an open space covering an area the size of his Little League baseball field. Stones, not pavement, he realized. Big ones, the size of tables. Flat, but not smooth. Tufts of grass and a few flowers squeezed up between them.

A few yards away, maybe the distance from home plate to the pitcher's mound, a dark triangle stretched up out of the patchy weeds like a shark's fin. Billy thought it looked as tall as him. He pointed. "What do you think that is?"

Dad scuffed his foot on the ground. "These are like big pavestones."

Beau pointed too, taking a few steps out onto the stones. "Dad? Do you recognize those?"

Billy followed her finger, up past the treetops on the far side of the clearing. Off in the distance, a wall of rock stretched up over the trees, easily ten times taller than any of them. The cliffs stretched off in both directions, and Billy felt pretty sure they were curved. Like a big fence surrounding the jungle.

"I've never seen anything like this," said Dad. "Never even heard of it."

"It looks like the mountains in New Hampshire." Beau took a few more steps, walking slowly across the stone parking lot. "The big cliffs where the Old Man of the Mountain is? But they're the wrong color, aren't they?"

"Yeah. Definitely not in New Hampshire."

"I don't think we're in Maine, either, Dad."

Billy took their walking as a sign he could stride ahead and check out the big fin. It was a lot easier to move without leaves hitting him in the face every couple of feet. He got to the big triangle in a few loping steps.

The triangle sat on a big circle of white marble, half covered with dirt and grass. Someone had smoothed this piece of stone a lot more than the others. If Billy stretched his fingers up, he could just touch the top of the triangle. Maybe as tall as Beau then. Not as tall as Dad. Up close he could see the metal fin had turned green and rusted—or corroded, maybe—but he could still see lines and symbols scratched into it. Carved into it. It looked like there might be lines carved on the big marble circle, too, under all the dirt. And then he recognized the whole thing from history class.

"Hey," he yelled back to them. They were still looking at the cliffs, talking while they walked across the stones. "I think this is a sundial."

Beau took a few quick steps over to join him. She reached up and rapped the edge of the fin. The clang echoed through it.

"Be careful," said Dad.

"It's a big piece of metal," she said.

Billy kicked the dirt, dead grass, and old leaves away from the marks in the stone. The marble was a lot smoother than the big paving stones around it. He scraped some more and revealed a triangle the size of his foot. Then he twisted his head around and smiled. "It's a V," he told them. "Roman numerals."

Dad scuffed his feet on the other side of the big metal fin while Beau cleaned around its base. "How old do you think this is?" she asked.

"I don't know." Dad looked at the space he'd cleaned, then out across the open space. "It's some kind of plaza. These stones are rough, but it might just be a design choice."

"Yeah, but all this grass and stuff . . ."

"I don't know. I've seen some construction projects that went on hold and they got overgrown pretty quick. This might only be a year or two."

Beau sighed. "Do you ever remember hearing about a place like this?"

"No, but . . ." Dad's voice trailed off. "No, I haven't."

"That's got to be pretty old though, right?" Billy pointed at the big metal fin.

Dad shook his head. "Copper can last a long time, but it gets that patina after a couple of years. Maybe less depending on the weather. It could be three or four years old, or over a hundred."

"Cool." Billy went back to kicking dirt away with his foot. He'd uncovered an IV and a III, plus some more lines.

"Hey." Beau dropped to her knees and started sweeping at the ground with her hands. "Hey, I think I found something."

Billy ran to look. He dropped to his knees next to her. Dad crouched on the other side of her.

The plaque was the size of a school cafeteria tray. The flat ones the older kids got, not the ones with all the little spaces. A thick border ran around the edge and held in a lot of dirt. Beau swept it away with her hands, and Billy saw metal letters appear. They both dug at it with their fingers, working dirt and stones and grit out of the spaces around the letters.

"It's in English," Dad said. He leaned back to look at the whole plaque while they kept cleaning. Then Beau sat back on her heels. Billy bent low, blew hard on the numbers at the bottom, and he leaned back, too. There was still a lot of dirt in some of the spaces, but they'd cleaned enough of it to read the message.

Beau got quiet. So did Dad. Billy thought they were being respectful until he read the plaque for a third time.

WE WILL REMEMBER

THOSE LOST HERE

FOR ALL OF TIME

APRIL 8, 2315

"Dad," said Beau, "where the hell are we?"

6

PARKER

The sun was high in the sky when Parker blinked herself awake. She had fuzzy memories of the night before, as if she'd had one too many drinks. Falling. Hitting her head. Noah saying he had another life. Staring up at the stars and being too out of it to find anything. And then . . . a dinosaur?

No headache, though. That was a plus.

The night had left a chill in her bones. She'd fallen asleep on top of her sleeping bag instead of inside it. She didn't even remember unrolling it. Hell, why hadn't she set up the one-person tent she'd borrowed for this weekend?

This wasn't her sleeping bag.

She'd been using Noah's folded-up fleece as a pillow. And this was *his* sleeping bag. He'd had it in his office a few days ago. She was out in the woods away from the camp and oh fuckfuckshit what had she done last night?! Had she—had *they*—her clothes were all still on and how drunk had she been?! She didn't remember drinking anything, but every memory was confusing nonsense, waving around in her head like a handheld camera.

Why was she here alone?

Something croaked above her. A big crow, maybe a raven, crouched on a branch, looking down at her. Watching her sleep? It twisted its neck—it had a long neck—and opened its beak to hiss quietly at her. The serrated beak looked like it was filled with little teeth. It tapped its talons against the branch, then threw itself into the air and turned into a little whirlwind of wings, flapping away through the trees.

"Hey, you're up."

Parker whipped around and saw Logan, Olivia's current boyfriend. What was *he* doing out here in the woods with her? With his own sleeping bag? Over there?!

He finished rolling up the sleeping bag and slipped an elastic loop over either end to keep it tight. "How are you feeling?"

"What?" she blinked again, and this time she felt the resistance, the faint pull on the side of her forehead when her eyelids moved. She reached up, felt the slick tape over her skin, and pressed gently against it. Sore, but not painful. She peeled it off as Logan stepped closer to her.

"Wow," he said, looking above her eyes. "Guess it wasn't that bad after all."

"What wasn't?" Her fingers brushed the skin between her eye and ear. Some dried blood flaked off at her touch. The skin had the coarse, leathery feel of an older scab, not fresh but not quite faded away either.

Logan leaned back on his heels, giving her some space. "What do you remember? From last night?"

She tried to arrange things in her mind, but there was so much chaos. "We . . . fell?"

"You fell. Well, we all fell. Sort of. And you hit your head pretty hard. There was a lot of blood, but he said you'd be all right."

"Noah?"

"Yeah."

But he *wasn't* Noah. That fact stuck out. He'd been hiding another identity from her—from everyone for years.

He'd given a lecture. Or told a story? Something about orbits and wormholes and . . . had he been talking about dinosaurs? Why did she have such a vivid memory of a dinosaur?

Parker stood up, caught her balance as more chunks of memory fell into place, and looked around. It was just the two of them, a circle of stones holding some unburned wood, and a few backpacks. "Where is he? Where is everyone?"

Logan pointed up the slope. "He's up there getting his bearings. Everyone else kind of scattered in the woods for, y'know, morning stuff."

"Oh, hey, you're up," said a voice behind her. Sam. The last-minute addition. He looked happy. He leaned close to her for a second and a low whistle slipped out between his lips. "He said it'd heal fast but it's still something to see it."

"Get away from me. What do you mean?"

Sam nodded at her. "Your head got gashed open last night when we fell. Like, probably six or seven stitches gashed."

"It wasn't that bad," said Logan, although his expression told her he'd thought it had been.

Sam shook his head. "My little sister, she fell once, cut her head. She got four stitches and this looked a lot worse."

"It was a lot of blood."

Parker reached up and felt the rough spot along her temple again. It didn't feel like it needed more than four stitches. Then again, she'd never needed stitches, so maybe she wasn't the best judge.

He'd said something about healing faster. The man she'd thought was Noah. People healed faster here.

Sam gestured up the slope. "Noah said he needed to—he was going to get his bearings and then we'd be on the move. Probably want to get that rolled up, do whatever you need to do."

"What was his name?"

"I—sorry, what?"

"Noah. His real name. You knew it. You'd heard of him."

Sam nodded and a grin spread across his face. "He's Billy Gather. Dino Boy."

A few more memories of last night fell into place. Time travel. The heliostationary object. The unknown sky.

The dinosaur.

While Parker rolled up the sleeping bag, Olivia came wandering up from the trees behind Logan. She'd changed into a T-shirt that looked more his size than hers and carried yesterday's shirt balled up in her hand. They locked eyes, Parker shoved down something dark and bitter, and then Noah came bounding down the hill with Kyle and the guide behind him.

Noah looked . . . young. He still had the silver streaks above his ears and the darker swaths below his eyes, but excitement and energy came off him in waves. He met her eyes. Smiled at her in a distracted way. "You're awake. Excellent. Let's get going." He turned to the small group. "You're all going to like this."

Noah tugged the sleeping bag out of Parker's hands, swept up his backpack, and headed down the slope. Sam and Logan swung their packs over their shoulders. Parker looked at each of them, still trying to sort out what the hell was going on, and then instinct took over. A few quick steps moved her in front of Olivia and Logan, right behind Noah.

The hillside leveled out quickly, nowhere near as tall as Parker remembered it from yesterday's hike. The forest was different, too. She remembered lots of leafy trees, but now it looked like mostly evergreens. The ground was carpeted with needles. The air smelled . . . sharper? Cleaner? A whiff of ozone, faint but definitely there. She'd never been one for camping, so maybe this was what the forest always smelled like.

"I thought I knew this forest," said Josh, "but I don't recognize any of this."

"How do you recognize a forest?" Kyle asked.

Josh looked around. "Certain trees. Rocks. Smells. Little landmarks. I know one hike near here I've done maybe twenty times, and there's a boulder that looks like a big engine block when you look at it from the southwest. We called it the engine rock."

"I told you," Noah called back, "it's not the same forest."

Kyle snorted.

Parker picked up her pace. Got herself alongside Noah, a little ahead of everyone else. He shot her a quick, familiar smile. She waited for him to say something.

He didn't.

"You lied to me," she said after a few minutes of walking.

He glanced at her. "What?"

"About who you are."

"No, I didn't."

"You didn't tell me you're some time-traveling child celebrity."

"I never told anyone. I've been Noah for almost thirty years. It's my name."

They walked for another two or three minutes before she spoke again. "I thought you trusted me."

Noah sighed. "I didn't trust anyone. Believe me, you came closest. But I just . . ."

"What?"

A handful of expressions slipped across his face before it settled into his lecture look. "I spent seven years getting laughed at. My entire teen years, I was either on television or in a magazine being mocked for thinking I saw dinosaurs, or I was . . ."

She waited, then prodded. "Or you were what?"

His stride got heavier. "Or I was back in some kind of hospital being treated for my delusions. That's what telling people who I really was got me. Seven years of being a punchline or a patient. I spent what should've been my senior year of high school heavily medicated and being told almost everything I remembered about my dad and my sister was a figment of my imagination. It's why I became Noah. It's why I've never told anyone I was Billy."

"I'm sorry."

"Thanks."

They hiked for another ten minutes before the trees abruptly ended at a broad swath of sand, like a beach. The type of pristine beach you saw in commercials for Hawaiian vacations. It even had a faintly cool, briny scent, but with no ocean in sight. Someone had found a big, wide clearing in the woods and covered every inch of it with sand. No trees, no bushes, nothing but white sand.

Almost nothing.

A dozen yards into the beach-clearing stood a miniature Washington Monument made of gray-brown stone and twenty-three feet tall, by Parker's eye. It didn't look like it sloped in, either. A straight, square pillar, about thirty inches across on each side, with a pyramid at the top. A herringbone pattern covered big swaths of the thing, and from this distance she couldn't tell if the pattern was part of the stone or something carved into it.

Noah walked out into the sand, glanced back, waved them closer. He looked happy but distracted. Energized. Like a little kid riding a sugar high.

"Definitely don't remember seeing that on the hike before," said Josh.

"It's the granite obelisk," said Noah. He waved a hand up the hill. "I saw it through a break in the trees."

"Obelisk," repeated Josh.

"Fancy word for pointed column," said Kyle.

"I know what it means."

Parker took a few steps forward. The sand felt . . . deep. It shifted a little under her feet. It wasn't sitting on top of leaves or grass or anything. It was sand all the way down. She took another few steps until she was next to Noah, then realized everyone else was moving with her. They approached the pillar of stone.

Sam looked . . . excited. Gleeful almost. "These are in the books. They're all over the valley, right? Six of them?" He looked back at Noah.

"Yep." Noah'd already forgotten the stone monument, looking around the clearing, pointing back the way they'd come. "If we're here, and the wall is that way, then the castle should be right around—"

"Are these runes?" Logan crouched close to the obelisk.

"Yep," said Noah. He looked up over the trees, clearly trying to find some sort of landmark. Parker's instincts kicked in, wanting to help him, wanting to ask questions about the castle, but . . .

She stepped closer to the strange obelisk. The herringbone pattern resolved into strings of tiny symbols carved into the stone. Circles and hexagons with lines coming off them in different ways. To her eyes it looked more like Thai than runes, and she briefly regretted not paying attention when her grandmother'd tried to teach the language to her.

"It looks like the Matrix code," said Josh. "All the streaming letters and numbers."

"Except there's no letters or numbers," Olivia said.

"That we recognize," said Kyle. He reached out a finger to touch the engraved symbols. Hesitated. Pulled his hand back. Stretched his finger out again. Stopped again.

"What's wrong?" Parker asked.

"I can't touch it."

"What do you mean?"

Kyle glanced at her. "I mean . . . I can't touch it. I can't get close enough."

Olivia rolled her eyes and went to put her palm on the obelisk. She halted two inches from it. "What the hell?"

"Is it an optical illusion?" asked Josh.

Parker reached out her own hand and felt . . . resistance? It reminded her of trying to push magnets together, feeling them gently deflect away from each other. "I think it's some kind of . . . force field?"

Logan put out his hand like a claw, trying to touch with all his fingertips. "It's like the air gets thick around it. Like a barrier."

"So . . . a force field," Parker said.

"Yeah, I guess so. Sorry."

Kyle took a step back and leaned forward, putting both hands on the obelisk's face. Trying to anyway. He dug his heels in and pushed. Parker and Logan both moved in close, watching the narrow gap between Kyle's palms and the stone. He grunted, pushed harder, and his feet slid in the sand.

His hands never got any closer.

"There are six obelisks all around the valley," said Sam, nodding back at Noah. "All made out of different materials, but they're identical other than that. They had all these weird rules and conditions about touching them."

"Rules?" asked Parker.

"Like, some you could touch during the night or day, but not the other way around. Some you could never touch. There's one that glows in the dark and one that knocks you out and another one shoots lightning or electricity or something like that."

Josh reached up high and tried to press his hand against one of the less-engraved spots with no success. "How do you know which one's which?"

Sam shook his head. "I don't remember. Sorry."

"I thought you read the books?"

"When I was twelve."

"The books got half of it wrong anyway," Noah called out to them. "Come on, we need to get going."

"Hang on," said Parker. "What is this?"

"It's the granite obelisk."

"Yeah, but what *is* it? Where did it come from?"

He shrugged. "No idea. They were here when my family arrived. Watch this."

Noah stepped back toward the trees, scanned the ground, and picked up a thick chunk of gray bark the size and rough shape of a paperback book. He took a few steps forward and spun it at the obelisk like a frisbee. It hit the stone with a soft thud and bounced off, scattering a few bits as it fell to the ground.

"Did that hit?" asked Logan. "Like actual contact?"

Noah nodded. "But if you try to touch the obelisk while you're holding the bark, it won't work."

Kyle scooped up the fallen chunk of bark and held it toward the obelisk. It moved closer, then tilted and twisted in his fingers. He tried to hold it tight and the bark trembled a few inches from the stone surface.

The idea of repelling magnets swam through Parker's mind again.

Kyle pushed hard and the piece of bark crumbled apart in the air. He held onto the back half, then tossed it. The bark made a scratching noise as it hit the stone and slid down to the base of the obelisk. "What the fuck," he murmured.

Olivia traced one of the lines of tiny shapes and lines in the air. "Does anyone recognize the symbols? Any of them?"

Most of them shook their heads. Josh tilted his head to look at one set. "Are they even a language? Or is it just fancy decoration?"

"Or pictographs," said Sam. He had his phone out, snapping picture after picture of the engraved stone. "Less a language and more of a comic book, sort of."

Kyle smirked. "You think this is a record of when the mighty hexagon people conquered the squiggly lines?"

Sam leaned back and lined up another picture. "Sure, why not."

Parker looked at Noah.

He shrugged. "I just know I spent a lot of time throwing stuff at it when I was a kid."

She looked back and forth between the towering column and the professor. "And you've got no idea what it is?"

"None."

"Is it from the future?" asked Josh. "Or is it some sort of, like, lost civilization thing? From Atlantis or Lemuria or something?"

Noah shrugged again. "It doesn't matter." He started across the white sand.

Parker recoiled like she'd been slapped. "It doesn't matter?"

"Not to me. I didn't come back here to study the obelisks."

"But aren't you curious? Don't you want to know?"

"Nope." He pointed at the far side of the sandy clearing. "We want to go this way. Lookout Hill should be a little over half a mile."

"Lookout Hill?" Parker called after him, trying to catch up. She glanced back. The others were following too, reluctantly leaving the obelisk behind.

"It's a gigantic rock," he explained, not looking back. "But it's almost a hundred feet up, higher than everything else in this part of the valley. We can get our bearings again, see everything, send signals."

"Signals?" Josh had almost caught up to them.

"When my family was here, we all carried little round mirrors. Well, the tops of cans we polished until they were really shiny. If we got lost or separated, it was the easiest way to signal each other."

"Fascinating," sighed Kyle.

Noah glanced at him. "If you like, we can leave you behind and see what you come up with on your own."

"No. Sorry. Look, I'm just . . . this is all a bit much, you know?"

"It's a lot to take in." He looked ahead. "I wish none of you had to."

"Yeah. Well . . ." Whatever Kyle planned to say, he swallowed it. He gave Parker a look, then slowed his pace.

Parker glanced over her shoulder. Josh was almost next to her. Sam and Kyle were close behind. Logan and Olivia lagged, looking back at the granite obelisk. "Keep up," she called to them.

Logan waved in acknowledgment. So did Olivia, but she only used one finger.

Parker shoved down more angry thoughts that swelled up in her mind. Her scalp itched along the scab, and she brushed her fingers across it. Focus on helping Noah. He knew this place. He knew what he was doing.

They walked back into the trees and traveled in relative silence. Parker listened to the sounds of the forest. Faint sounds drifted through the trees, and it gnawed at her how many she couldn't identify. Animals? Birds? The forest was alive, but . . .

She stopped and looked around. *Can't see the forest for the trees* flashed through her mind, and it seemed the inverse of that held true. She hadn't looked at the individual trees as they'd been walking. Really, she'd been following Noah and not looking around at all. At some point the evergreens had been replaced by palm trees. Dozens of them, at least. Maybe over a hundred. Even the ground cover was different. Suddenly they were walking in a rainforest.

Logan let out a squawk. They all jerked to a halt, and Parker turned in time to see something dark bounding over a fallen palm frond and off through the woods in broad leaps. The ground crunched with each contact, and then the shape vanished behind a tree. They heard a few more rustling leaps and then nothing.

"What was it?" Parker asked.

Olivia shook her head once, still staring after it. "I don't know."

Logan slapped his chest twice to calm himself. "I saw a shape by that rock, and then I saw eyes and realized it was watching—"

"It was a cat," said Kyle. "Just a stray cat out in the woods."

"Probably," said Noah. "There were at least a half dozen cats here when I was a kid." He stared after it, then continued through the woods.

"You kept one as a pet, right?" Sam phrased it as a question, but Parker knew the tone from helping with so many undergrad classes. Less a question, more confirmation.

"Yep. Dad told us not to name them. That I shouldn't get too attached to anything out in the wild. But one kept showing up at the edge of the Boneyard and we ended up adopting him."

"Charlie."

"Yep." A faint smile crossed Noah's face.

"Should we go after it?" asked Logan. "The cat? If it's lost here, too . . ."

"It probably grew up here," said Josh. He had something in his hand, a transparent rectangle with a compass ring on it. "Might be a whole feral cat colony."

"So it's not dinosaurs we need to worry about," said Olivia, "it's getting eaten by cats."

"Come on," said Parker. "We need to keep up with him." She pointed after Noah. He'd already gotten a hundred feet ahead of them and didn't seem to notice they weren't behind him.

She hurried after him. So did the others. The group stayed a little tighter.

"Just pointing out," Kyle said quietly, "this could all be some kind of super-elaborate prank or something."

"We're in the valley," said Sam.

"That doesn't really mean anything."

"It does, you just don't like it."

Kyle waved a dismissive hand. "I'm just saying, I haven't seen a damned thing that couldn't just be New England woods."

"Palm trees," Logan said, pointing up.

"Set dressing."

"And that obelisk," added Olivia. "With a few hundred tons of sand all around it."

"Somebody's weird art project," Kyle replied. "Remember during the Covid lockdown when those chrome-metal monoliths showed up all over the world and went viral?"

"The obelisk none of us could touch," Parker added.

Josh coughed. "The dinosaur?"

Kyle paused. "It was dark. Are we all really sure about what we saw?"

"Yes," said Sam.

Olivia nodded

Josh tilted his compass back and forth as they gained on Noah. Held it up. Tilted it again.

"You need help with that?" asked Logan.

"No," said Josh. "Must've broken it in the fall."

"How do you break a compass?"

"I don't know. You can break anything, can't you?" He pointed a finger at Logan's cracked glasses, then held up the clear rectangle. "The needle just spins back and forth."

"You need to let it settle," Kyle said.

"Gee, thanks. I've never used a compass before."

"Have you?"

"Yeah."

Parker shot Kyle a look. "He's the guide, remember?"

"No he isn't," Logan said. "The guy on the website's completely different."

"What?"

"It's a franchise thing," Josh explained. "Like Santa Claus."

Kyle shook his head. "He's a fake. Maybe he's in on all of this."

Parker bit her lip. She'd been so focused on the mystery of Sam during their hike up the mountain, she'd only half registered all the oddness about Josh, even after he said to call him by a different name.

The guide shoved the compass back in his pocket. "I'm a friend of Skip's. The real Skip. We've known each other since high school. I was visiting, he came down with a bad case of food poisoning, and I offered to come out here with all of you."

"Why?" asked Parker.

"So he wouldn't lose the job. Even giving me a cut, this was a good gig for him. He didn't want to cancel."

"So you're not really a guide," said Olivia.

"Well, no, I'm not licensed by the state or anything. But Skip and I have done this hike more than a dozen times together."

Kyle shorted out a laugh. "It ever go like this before?"

Josh managed a faint smile. "Not exactly like this but . . . we did see a bear once."

"I've been on a dozen planes," said Olivia. "Doesn't make me a pilot."

Parker bit back a sigh. "Are you complaining about his qualifications as a guide?"

"I'm just saying."

"It's no big deal," Josh said. He tipped his head toward Noah, a few yards ahead. "But for what it's worth, I know we've walked further than half a mile. And I don't see a hill anywhere."

They all looked around. Parker took a few quick steps and put herself next to Noah. "I thought you said it was only half a mile to your lookout point?"

He glanced at her, and she recognized the faint wrinkle over his left eyebrow that meant confusion. "A little over. I remember my dad telling me that at least twenty times. I always whined about walking and he'd say it's only half a mile."

"Maybe he was lying to you."

Parker and Noah glanced back. Logan had caught up with them. Olivia still hung back, closer to the end of the little group.

"Not maliciously, I mean," Logan explained. "Just, y'know, how parents lie to kids sometimes to get them to be quiet or keep them happy and stuff."

"White lies," said Parker.

"Right."

"My dad didn't lie to me," said Noah. "And I walked this route a hundred times, easy."

"Maybe it's because you were a little kid," said Sam, ambling a little closer. "You know, everything seems bigger, then you come back and it's all shrunk."

"But it doesn't seem smaller." Parker waved a hand at their rough route through the trees. "It seems further."

"We may be a little off course," Noah admitted. "It's been a while for me, okay?"

She slowed her pace. Logan took the hint. Sam didn't, so she grabbed his little backpack and pulled. "Give him some space," she said. "He's trying to figure things out." Kyle walked past them, oblivious to their created distance and Parker's glare.

"Hey," said Josh. "Look at those guys." He pointed up into a tree.

Two black birds clung to the side of a palm tree, watching them. Just like the long-necked one that had hovered over Parker when she woke up. The pair hunched on either side of the trunk, watching the people with gleaming, gold-green eyes.

"Do they have . . . tails?" asked Olivia, stepping closer.

"Yes, birds have tails," Parker said with a sigh.

Logan tilted his head. Leaned closer to the tree. "Not like that."

Parker looked at the birds again.

Half-camouflaged by the dozens of vertical shadows stretching behind them, a long, straight tail hung from each bird. Each was maybe as wide as her thumb and a foot long, more like what she'd expect on a cat than anything she'd ever seen on a bird. They even had a tuft on the end, like a lion. While she looked, one of the birds swished its tail stiffly back and forth.

"Are those crows?" asked Kyle, suddenly back with them, his voice a little too loud, as usual.

The first bird took off in a frenzy of flapping wings, throwing itself up off the tree trunk and flying away. The second, the braver one, glared at the group for a moment longer, tapping its oversized talons against the palm tree's wood-like husks before it spread its wings. The tuft of its long tail fanned out into a wide triangle of feathers.

Then it leaped into the air, spread a second set of wings, and soared off through the forest after its mate, all four limbs stretched wide.

They watched it fly away.

Parker pointed after the bird. "Did . . . everyone else see that?"

7

KYLE

Kyle liked to think of himself as professionally skeptical. It was a good attitude in the sciences. And it sounded better than "asshole."

Once the initial shock had worn off last night, long after the . . . the animal had wandered away and everyone else had passed out from exhaustion, he'd sat there awake. Trying to poke holes in this "time travel" story Barnes had fed them. Trying to rationalize some of the things they'd seen. It wasn't easy. But it also wasn't impossible.

He reminded himself of this as the four-winged bird vanished between two distant trees.

Just a regular bird. A crow or something. The extra wings had been an illusion created by the movement. And all the shadows coming down from the treetops.

Everyone else chattered away. He could see they'd already convinced themselves they'd seen a four-winged bird instead of approaching the whole thing logically. Because a four-winged bird was nonsense. All of this was nonsense.

But the packy-dinosaur last night had looked pretty damned real. If it had been a guy in a rubber suit, it was a really expensive, Hollywood-level suit. And Kyle hadn't been able to pick out any constellations he recognized through the gaps in the trees. And that obelisk had something around it. Magnetic field? Maybe some sort of pressurized air curtain?

The bird sure looked like it had four wings.

"But what was it?" Parker asked again. Her voice had a demanding edge to it. Kyle didn't deal with her a lot, but he'd heard stories about how annoying she could get when she didn't get answers.

"Some kind of mutant," said Josh. "Maybe from toxic waste."

"Toxic waste mutants aren't a real thing," Logan said.

"Maybe it was just a bird," said Olivia. "Are we sure it had extra wings?"

"Thank you," Kyle said.

"It had four wings," Parker declared. "No question."

"There's definitely a question," countered Olivia.

"No, there isn't."

"It was a microraptor." Professor Barnes had doubled back to see what they were looking at. He looked after the weird bird. Glanced at them. "Not a mutant," he added.

"Microraptor like . . . velociraptor?" asked Logan.

"Yep. Same family. Weird little evolutionary offshoot. Their front and back legs both formed wings."

"Are they dangerous?"

"If you're a mouse or a frog."

Josh looked up at the tops of the palm trees. "They won't team up and eat you?"

"Nope. Well, maybe if you were already badly wounded."

"Microraptor," repeated Parker.

"Yep." The professor shrugged and turned back to the path.

Kyle quick-stepped after him. "So it was . . . another dinosaur?"

"Yep."

"A four-winged dinosaur. With feathers."

"Lots of dinosaurs had feathers," said Sam. "People've known that for years now."

"I didn't know it."

"That doesn't mean it's not true."

Kyle huffed air out of his nose.

"Funny thing is," said Barnes, dropping into lecture tones as they walked, "I told people about the microraptors when I ended up back in the present, and they used it as more evidence I was making the whole thing up. Four-winged birds? Nonsense. It was maybe ten years later, '97 or '98, they found the first fossilized ones in China. I don't think anyone ever connected them to what I'd said."

"Somebody must've," said Sam.

Barnes shrugged.

They fell into a rough line as they walked. Parker pushed her way to the front, dedicated ass-kisser determined to be near her boss. Olivia settled next to Kyle without saying anything. He was pretty sure she was making space between her and Logan. Poor bastard. All this crap going on and she still seemed determined to dump him. Logan hung in the back with Sam and Josh, all of them looking around like Times Square tourists.

They hiked another ten minutes. The forest got dark up ahead of them, suddenly way more dense. A few more steps and they were back in a classic northeast forest with pines or spruces or whatever they were. When Kyle was a kid his parents had taken him to a Christmas tree farm once. It'd been like this. Tons of one kind of tree, take a few steps, and now you were surrounded by completely different trees.

He glanced back at the jungle behind them. Just like the farm. A straight line where one ended and the other began. On this side, the ground covered with a mat of needles. On that side, woody palm fronds, ferns, and plants with huge, upright leaves the size of—

Wait.

His eyes slid back, focused where he'd seen—half seen, really—the face watching them. He'd only caught a vague impression of it between two big leaves. A kid with dark, stringy hair and dark eyes. Round face. A big, upturned nose. Covered with dirt. Like, filthy. Or maybe just tanned. Maybe brown skinned.

He couldn't see the face now, though. The leaves drifted back and forth like someone had brushed against them. Or he'd imagined the whole thing and they'd just caught a breeze.

And wow, had he really seen brown skin and immediately assumed filthy?

"What's up?"

He managed to not jump. Found Logan next to him. Still wearing his glasses, despite the big crack through one lens. Kyle looked over his shoulder, and realized the rest of their scraggly line had moved on without him.

"I just . . . thought I saw something."

"Another dinosaur-bird?"

He looked back at the tall leaves. "A kid."

"What?" Logan turned his attention to the jungle. "Seriously?"

"Maybe. Watching us through the plants over there. I don't know. Probably a trick of the light."

"You sure? If there's a little kid out here—"

The dark-haired kid exploded out of the plants, hit the ground in front of them, and leaped again, swinging one of his arms. Kyle stepped back, put his hands up, felt something hot slash across his forearm. The kid snarled, shuffled his feet, pulled back with his knife to swing again, and Logan slammed into him, shoving him to the ground.

"Son of a *bitch*," yelled Kyle.

Logan glanced at him. "You okay?"

The kid spun around and somehow was back on his feet in a low crouch. The knife pointed at Kyle, then Logan. He glared, showed off some yellowed teeth, then dove back into the underbrush.

Logan took a few steps toward the mass of ferns and thick leaves. "What the fuck was that?"

Sam crunched through the pine needles behind them. "Was that—are you okay?"

Kyle looked past Logan. "Is he gone?"

"What happened?" asked Josh. "Oh, crap, you're bleeding, man."

Even as Kyle heard the words he registered the ongoing burn in his forearm, and the wetness on his fingers. He twisted his arm and got a good look at the slash. Diagonal across his forearm, four and a half, maybe five inches. Not that deep, but a lot more than a scratch. No pulsing blood, though, that was good. He flexed his fingers and didn't feel any serious pain. He wondered if he'd need stitches, then remembered Parker's quickly healing head wound.

Logan whacked at the ferns with a stick. "I think he's gone."

Kyle tried to press the edges of his wound together. It made a fresh swell of blood run down his arm. He flicked it off his fingertips, then looked around for a rock or leaf or something to wipe his hand on.

The others made their way back through the trees. Barnes looked at Kyle's arm. "What happened?"

"Some crazy little feral kid tried to stab us. He cut me and Logan shoved him down."

"What do you mean, 'feral kid'?" asked Olivia.

"Little kid, five foot nothing. Long messy hair. Dressed in furs."

"A fur skirt," said Logan. "And sort of sandal-boots."

"Yeah."

Sam's mouth formed an amazed O. "Was it—was he a Neanderthal?"

Kyle felt his own eyes open a bit. "Maybe?"

"Could've been," agreed Logan.

Barnes walked over to the ferns, looked back the way they'd came. "He was probably out hunting and stumbled across us."

Kyle squeezed his arm again. "A little kid?"

"He might've been full grown. A really tall Neanderthal might be five five."

"So you're saying we just fought off a caveman?"

Barnes nodded. "Yep. You probably startled him. Doesn't take much for them to go to fight or flight. You weren't in any real danger."

"Could've fooled me," muttered Kyle, squeezing his arm.

Sam went to peer through the ferns. "Do you think it was . . . could it've been Zock?"

"What the hell is a Zock?"

"A Neanderthal kid I knew when I was here before," Barnes explained.

"Hell of a reunion," said Josh.

Barnes nodded at Kyle's arm and let his pack slide off his shoulders. "We should clean that up. Fresh blood attracts too many things."

Ten minutes later Kyle's arm was bandaged and Barnes got them moving again. It didn't take long after that for their hike to end. Or for the forest to end, anyway.

Another steep wall of stone stretched up above the trees, although this one looked like it was maybe a hundred feet tall. Thick moss streaked the sides. A few small plants grew out of cracks in the surface.

Barnes turned to them, smiling. "Lookout Hill."

"There's no way I can climb that," said Sam.

Parker shook her head. "Me either."

"I probably could," Josh said, stepping forward, "but it'd take a while."

"We don't need to climb it. There's an easy slope on the other side." Barnes gestured for them to follow him.

They walked between the trees and the mass of stone. Kyle kept watching the trees for faces. He saw another one of the weird crows—the microraptors—watching them, but didn't point it out to anyone.

Barnes led them around a moss-covered boulder the size of one of those tiny houses and, like he said, there was the easy slope. Mostly bare rock, spotted with some more small plants. A little steeper than the grade they'd hiked up yesterday, but Kyle thought it still looked like an easy climb. The top half of it stretched up past the treetops.

Barnes didn't say anything to them, just started up the rock. Parker followed without a question. Josh was a few strides behind her. Kyle watched them go.

Olivia took a step forward, looked back at him. "You coming?"

"Rather not."

Logan stepped up next to Olivia. "Ready for another incline?" he asked her.

"Yeah, sure."

They headed up the stone hill.

Sam settled next to Kyle. "Come on," he said. "The view's fantastic."

"How would you know?"

"It's in the books."

"You're way too excited about all of this."

"Well, yeah. It's all real. It's right here in front of us."

Kyle shook his head.

"Come on. Maybe we'll see another dinosaur from the top of the hill. Or, y'know, you can wait around—stay down here and see if the Neanderthal comes back."

He sighed. Looked at the surrounding trees. "Fine."

Sam smiled and headed up the hill.

Kyle waited another few seconds, just out of sheer stubbornness, and then followed.

He left Sam behind pretty quick, caught up with Logan and Olivia and passed them as well. Only five or six minutes to the top, but it felt like he'd gone up a dozen flights of stairs. He yawned and stretched. Had to be close to noon, going off the sun. It'd already been high in the sky when they woke up.

He stretched again and looked out at the valley.

The first thing that popped to Kyle's mind was *crater*. Three years back he'd gone with a group to Meteor Crater in Arizona. It was mostly closed off except for the little observation platform and glorified gift shop, but their professor had known someone, made arrangements, and they'd been allowed to go to the crater floor. Standing down there, Kyle had been struck by the high walls around him, by the fact he couldn't see anything except the crater and the sky.

The valley stretched out farther than that crater, but it had the same high walls. The same sense of blotting out everything else. All he could see in every direction was the valley. No distant mountains. Not even trees up at the top of the surrounding cliffs and peaks.

But, damn, there was plenty to look at in the valley.

Lookout Hill reached a good fifty or sixty feet over the surrounding treetops, although in the distance Kyle could see a large swath of what looked like redwoods standing at least twice as tall as anything around them. In fact, the longer he stared out at the valley, the more he noticed distinct areas. Another expanse of palm trees. A wide swath of pines. One nearby area that looked like . . . oaks? Maples? Something lush and leafy. Off to their far left was a massive green meadow, and to the right a stretch of prairie like in a western. A shimmer of water in the distance looked like a large pond, or maybe a lake?

The patchwork landscape stretched out to the distant, hazy side of the valley. He'd thought of a Christmas tree farm before, but seeing it from a little higher made him think of a zoo, or maybe a theme park, divided up into different zones and areas.

"It looks . . . big," said Sam.

"Yep," said Barnes.

A few miles away, a jagged white lump of ice, or something crystal-ish, stood up above the forests, at least twice as tall as the distant redwoods. Maybe taller. It looked like the oval skyscraper in London, the Gherkin. Or maybe like someone had tried to make an ice sculpture of the Gherkin, halfway through decided to turn it into the Disney castle, and then just gave up when it was clear the thing was going crooked. The whole structure reminded Kyle of prehistoric knives and axes, chiseled into their crude, multifaceted shapes.

He pointed at it. "What's that?"

"The Ice Castle," said Sam, a huge smile breaking across his face. He turned to stare at Barnes like some fanboy meeting Mark Hamill.

Barnes nodded.

"The what?" asked Olivia.

"The Ice Castle." Sam took a few quick breaths. "It's the—it's where the Castaway lives."

Kyle took a deep breath. "Will you please stop saying things like we all know what you're talking about?"

"Which part?"

"All of it."

Sam looked at Barnes, as if asking permission. The professor gave a little half nod. He was staring across the valley. Looking a little uncertain, but definitely looking for something.

Sam interrupted Kyle's thoughts, the prize student taking over the lecture. "The Castle's more or less the center of the valley. Billy—Professor Barnes and his family called it the iceberg at first because of the shipwreck near it."

"Shipwreck?" echoed Logan.

"Yep," said Barnes. He gestured out toward the silvery lines of the lake. "A big riverboat, half rusted through and tipped over in the shallows of the swamp. My dad thought the writing on it was Arabic."

Parker raised a hand to shield her eyes from the sun. "That's made of ice?"

"No, that's just what we named it at first. It's made of some kind of crystal. And then we explored it and . . ." Barnes looked at Sam.

"And then you and your family discovered someone lives in it," Sam said.

"Yep."

Josh held up two fingers. "And when you say 'someone,' you mean . . . ?"

"An alien," said Sam. "The Castaway."

Parker looked doubtful. "An actual, outer space alien?"

"Yep."

"You were friends with an alien when you were a kid?" echoed Kyle, sure that Barnes couldn't be serious.

"Yep."

"The Castaway's ship crashed and they got stuck here," said Sam, leaping in to share his fanboy knowledge again. "They built—they made the Ice Castle. And they can change shape."

Noah waved a hand at Sam. "They don't change shape. They appear to change shape because we can only see so much of them."

Parker's mouth pulled to one side. "He's really big?"

"They're six-dimensional. That's what my dad said. And it's they."

"They?" echoed Josh.

"Yep. The Castaway was my first experience with nonbinary pronouns. Back in the eighties."

"Cool." Parker gave an approving, only slightly ass-kissing nod.

Kyle sighed. "Great. Woke aliens."

Logan scowled at him. "Dude, seriously?"

He waved Logan off and gazed out at the valley again, hoping to spot some power lines or a cell tower or maybe a ranger station. Those were usually up on stilts or something. Something that would be proof this could all still be some big, elaborate prank.

Barnes gave his attention to Josh. "Have you ever seen examples of a three-dimensional being encountering a two-dimensional world?"

Josh managed to look thoughtful for a moment. "I think maybe on *Cosmos*?"

"They can only interact within that plane, so even though the three-dimensional being is bigger, the two-dimensional beings can only see this thin slice of it." He held up his hand, then made a claw of it with all his fingers pointing down at the ground. "Think of it like reaching into a sink full of water, but the two-dimensional people can only see the part of you in line with the surface. Nothing above or below. So as I reach in they'd see five circles appear from nowhere, and as I went further they'd see a sort of curved oval—the cross section of my palm. And then something closer to a circle around my wrist. Make sense?"

Josh nodded in a way that told Kyle it only barely made sense to him.

Parker, the ever-supportive kiss-ass assistant, stepped over a large outcropping of rock, moving a little closer to Josh. "Think of it this way. You've made a shadow puppet before?"

"Yeah."

"Your shadow looks like a dog or a rabbit or whatever, but your hand doesn't, right?"

"Sure."

"It's because your shadow's the two-dimensional outline of your hand. If I understand Noah correctly, when we see the Castaway we're seeing a three-dimensional shadow puppet."

"Exactly," said Noah. "Again, looking back on it with wiser eyes. And an astrophysics degree. Sometimes they make themself look more or less like a person, and sometimes they get distracted and become . . . a thing."

"Like a monster?" asked Olivia.

"No, just a weird shape. A modern art sculpture or something like that. If you stop thinking about making the shadow look like a rabbit, your hand tilts and now the shadow's just a random shape."

Josh gave another slow nod packed with so much thought and reflection Kyle was certain the man still had no idea what they were talking about. "So he—they, sorry—exist outside of three-dimensional space, but you could still see their three-dimensional shadow."

Kyle re-estimated the fake guide.

"Yep," said Barnes. He looked a little surprised, too.

"And you talked to them?" asked Parker.

"A lot of times, yep. Sometimes with my family. Once alone." Barnes looked out at the crystal tower. "Once we figured out what they were, and that they weren't going to eat us or something, the Castaway would tell us all sorts of useful things. But always in this weird, happy-stoner, seeing-the-whole-picture way, because they could see through time."

"It could see through time," said Olivia, and it gnawed at Kyle how she phrased it more as a statement, not questioning any of it.

"Yep. The Castaway can look across time the way you or I look across distance." Barnes swung an arm dramatically at the valley. "But it meant if you asked if something was poisonous, for example, you had to ask them if it was poisonous to *your* species at *this* point in its life cycle."

Sam's eyes opened a little wider, like a teenage girl at a K-pop concert. "That's in one of the books. Beau got sick because the Castaway told you some berries were safe to eat, right?"

"Yep."

Kyle pounced on a detail. "If he can see across time, did you ever ask him how to get out of here?"

"They," murmured Logan.

"Whatever."

Barnes nodded. "All the time. They told my dad it wasn't safe to leave. Told my sister she'd get out. Then they told me I'd just accept this place was my home."

"'No, Billy Gather. Someday you will call this place home,'" quoted Sam.

Barnes shook his head. "A little flattering, a little creepy."

"Sorry."

"Well," said Josh, "hopefully they didn't mean now."

"I always figured it was more their way of saying I'd come back."

"For that matter," said Kyle, "if it . . . if *they* exist outside of three-dimensional space, how were they stuck here?"

"What?"

"You said their ship crashed here. But if they exist outside of space-time, how can they be trapped somewhere? Hell, what would they need a spaceship for?"

"What does God need with a starship?" Josh murmured.

"That's a good point," said Olivia.

"I never thought about it, to be honest," Barnes said. "The Castaway told us they couldn't leave here after their ship crashed and we never questioned them. They were always painfully honest with us. In their own way."

Kyle spotted another flaw. "Why did they tell your dad it wasn't safe to leave? I mean, you got out, right?"

"Right. But that actually ended up being a big clue for me. We'd been here in the valley maybe six months when my dad asked them. Earth wasn't anywhere near the wormhole then. It was on the other side of the sun. So it wouldn't've been safe to leave—we would've returned out in deep space."

"Ahhhhh . . ."

"Wait a minute." Parker's voice almost scraped on the rocks. "The wormhole only lines up with Earth once a year?"

Barnes's jaw shifted.

Kyle realized what Parker was saying. "We're stuck here for *A YEAR*?!"

Barnes tried to do his quieting-the-class thing again with his hands. "I'm sorry. It's not ideal, I know, but I can still get us all home. Don't worry."

Parker glared at him. "I'm not worried, I'm *pissed*."

Kyle pictured his home, imagined what'd it be like after a year, and another realization crashed home. "I'm going to lose my apartment."

"Oh fuck," said Logan, running with the realization. "People are going to think we died. We're going to be declared dead."

Kyle threw his hands in the air. "Jesus fucking Christ! We're going to lose everything. My sisters are going to . . . Jesus." He glared at Barnes as consequences kept snowballing in his head.

"I told you all to go back up to the campsite."

"I don't know," said Josh. "Some good things could come out of getting declared dead."

"Like what?" snapped Kyle.

He shrugged. "Probably a lot of debts get forgotten."

Olivia looked ready to punch him. "You're thinking of your credit cards?"

"Not just credit cards."

"Credit cards, student debt, who cares? Everyone's going to think we're dead. My parents are going to have a breakdown."

"Goddamn it." Parker tried to set the rocky ground on fire with her stare. "That bastard Colin's going to take credit for all my work."

Barnes slashed a hand through the air. "Can you all just be quiet! We don't want to make a lot of noise. Sound carries in the forest."

Josh gestured at the rocky hillside. "We're not in the forest."

"The forest is right there."

"You've ruined our lives," said Kyle. "Our homes, our careers, our . . . everything. Gone."

"And again, I *told* you to go away. I told you to go work up at the camp, I tried to make sure none of you would be anywhere near the intersection point, and you all came back anyway."

"Because I was worried about you," said Parker.

"And then I told you to get away and you still didn't listen."

"So it's our fault?"

Barnes bit down on his reply. Swallowed it. Let it settle. "You're all going to be famous when we get back. It'll be worth it."

"You told me you were famous for being a joke," said Parker.

"Olivia." Logan stared off the other way, pointing up at something. "Is that . . . what I think it is?"

Kyle found himself looking up at the massive valley walls almost two miles behind them. It took him a minute to spot the oddity, a triangle of charcoal gray set against the tan-and-brown streaks of the cliffs, maybe halfway up. It looked to be maybe four or five inches across from here, so it had to be huge. Maybe the size of . . .

"It's a fighter jet." Olivia had both hands cupped over her eyes, blocking the sun. "I'm not one hundred percent positive but I think it's an F-35 Lightning II."

Sam glanced at her. "Beg your pardon?"

Barnes pulled a pair of compact binoculars from his own pack and held them out to her. She took them, found the triangle again, adjusted the focus. "Definitely a Lightning."

"How do you know that?"

She handed Sam the binoculars. "The tail fins, and it's a single engine. It's state of the art."

He focused on the jet. "No, I mean *how* do you *know* that?"

"Some little girls wanted to ride horses. I wanted to fly fighter jets. Higher, further, faster, baby. Still hoping I might get on a NASA mission someday."

Sam passed the binoculars to Logan. He peered through them for a moment. "The windshield's gone."

"Canopy," said Olivia. "The pilot probably ejected before they hit the cliff."

Kyle took the binoculars next. "Would there be that much jet left if it hit the cliff?"

It took him a moment to find the plane through the lenses. It definitely looked like a cutting-edge fighter jet. It also looked like someone had pressed it into the rock, like a toy into soft Play-Doh. Aside from the missing canopy, it looked undamaged. Dusty, like it'd been up there for a while.

In fact, it looked like it had been buried in the cliffside thousands of years ago, like a dinosaur skeleton that got exposed by a landslide.

"I never found any records of a fighter jet disappearing," said Barnes. He had a square something in his hand that he tilted back and forth near his chest. A little mirror. "Might've been classified if it's top of the line. Or maybe it hasn't ended up here yet."

Kyle felt his jaw tense. "Sorry, what?"

"It could be from the future. Like Ross."

"Ross the robot," said Logan.

"Yep."

"Holy fuck," said Parker. She stood a few yards away, still looking out at the valley. One hand shaded her eyes while the other one pointed. "Look."

A cloud of maybe fifteen or twenty shapes swooped and circled in the sky. They looked like birds, maybe hawks gliding on thermals, but Kyle had trouble guessing their size and how far away they were. He kept looking down, trying to get a sense of what part of the valley they were above, then looking again because the perspective didn't make sense unless—

"Those are huge," said Logan.

Josh shielded his eyes with both hands. "Got to be, what, a fourteen- or fifteen-foot wingspan?"

A rattling screech echoed across the distance. Another one answered it. And a third.

As they watched, one of the shapes went into a wide banking loop, swinging closer to them. Even this far away, Kyle could make out the dark, narrow wings and the long head. As he watched, two or three members of the group—the flock?—soared down toward the trees.

"Is that a . . . pterodactyl?" Olivia asked. Not a real question, Kyle realized. She knew what she was seeing, she just wanted confirmation.

"Probably," said Sam.

Logan tugged the binoculars out of Kyle's hands.

"Technically, only the big ones are pterodactyls," said Barnes absently. He stared across the valley, not even looking at the distant creatures. "If it's smaller, it's probably a rhamphorhynchus. You can tell by the tail."

"Holy shit." Josh pointed at another flock on the far side of the redwoods. "There's a bunch of them."

"Those could be . . ." Kyle wanted to be the voice of reason. Professionally skeptical.

He looked back at the jet embedded in the valley wall. Two of the flying things swooped between him and the cliff as he did. The rhamphorhyncuses. Rhamphorhynchi? The *dinosaurs.*

"Holy fuck," he said.

Sam looked over at him. Smiled. "Yeah."

"A biologist would have a field day here," said Olivia.

Barnes finished looking at whatever he was looking at, reclaimed the binoculars, and packed them away. "We need to get going."

Parker turned away from the soaring dinosaurs. "Where?"

"Across the valley." He pointed quickly, then slung his pack over his shoulder and headed down the slope.

"Why?"

The cynic in Kyle saw the rest of her question. "Last night you said you were trying to get back here. Deliberately. So why? What the fuck are we doing here?"

Barnes turned, and Kyle saw the casual confidence in the other man's gaze. "What do you think? I'm here to rescue my sister."

8

OLIVIA

"Hang on," said Olivia. She felt like she'd been playing catch-up all day. Waking up a hundred million years in the past, finding out they were stuck here, realizing they were going to be missing for a year, and *god-dammit* Logan's too-big shirt annoyed the fuck out of her. "Your sister who was here with you forty years ago?"

"Thirty-three years ago," said Professor Barnes.

"Beau." Sam looked like he'd developed a hard crush on Barnes. "She's still alive?"

"Yes."

Olivia spat out her first thought without thinking. "She can't be. Not after all this time."

Barnes gave her a small, slow smile. "It hasn't been thirty-three years here in the valley."

Logan made a little sound in the back of his throat. "The time dilation."

Barnes nodded. "Here it's been thirteen years, two months, and twelve days. Beau hasn't even turned thirty yet."

Sam made a little sound, almost a squeak.

"But is that . . ." Parker's gaze kept going back and forth between Barnes and Logan. "That's not how time dilation works."

Another dismissive wave from Barnes. "Time dilation's the simplest term for it. There's a number of possible causes. What matters is it's been a lot less time for Beau than it was for me. For us."

"Not to be the harsh voice of reason," said Kyle—and for once he honestly sounded a little reluctant—"but if even half the stuff you've told us about this place is true, it still doesn't give her great odds. Or us." He gestured back at the distant swarm of flying dinosaurs.

"She'll be fine. She's smart and resourceful. And she's got Ross with her."

"Even so . . ." started Olivia.

Barnes pointed across the valley. "Our cave's over there."

Sam squeaked again. "Really?"

"Yep. I still remember all the landmarks." He tapped his foot on the ground. "Lookout Hill. The Redwoods. The Ice Castle. We've got a four-and-a-half mile hike to the cave."

Josh stared out at the valley. "Your cave's on the far side?"

"Yep. It's right by—"

"That's—sorry to interrupt—that's a lot farther than four and a half miles."

"No, it isn't."

"Yeah, it is. Sorry." He pointed out at the gleaming pillar near the center of the valley. "I'd say *that's* four and a half miles, the big tower. Closer to five, really."

Barnes shook his head. "No offense, Josh, but don't quit your day job."

Josh shrugged. "I'm just telling you what I'm seeing."

Olivia stared out at the tower, then at the far side of the valley. It had the pale haziness that came from looking through too much air. "I don't know. That looks pretty far."

"It's not," said Barnes. "Trust me."

She took a few steps. Gave Josh a nudge. "How far do you think it is? To the far side?"

Josh stretched out his arm and raised his thumb. It made Olivia think of art students taking measurements. He closed one eye, then the other. "The perspective's a little off. It gets harder the farther away things are. We're up high, we don't have an actual horizon to work off, the air's a little—"

"I can save you the time," Barnes interrupted. "The valley's only six miles across."

"It's not."

"It is."

Josh's face and tone shifted. "With all due respect, I don't know the place you grew up, but wherever we are now it's fourteen, maybe fifteen miles to the far—"

"Dude!" called out Kyle. He turned away from the view, pointed at Barnes. "Fuck, you almost had me hooked."

"What?"

"All this back-in-time, magic-valley-rhamphodactyl stuff."

"Rhamphorhynchus," said Sam.

"Whatever. Look right over there." He pointed across the valley.

Olivia took a step forward and felt Logan's shirt flap around her. She tugged at the shoulder, trying to readjust it as she followed Kyle's pointing finger. Off to the right side of the big glass tower. Patches of forest, a few clearings, more trees. She couldn't figure out what he'd seen. Logan stepped in next to her, trying to find it too. She looked over at Kyle's smug face, tried to follow his line of sight again, saw even more trees and there it was.

Three lines of smoke curled up beyond the distant trees, dark enough to stand out against the cliffs. Even so, they were so thin, so far away, she never would've spotted them if not for the faint hint of movement. She squinted, tried to get some sense of a source, but there was too much forest blocking it.

Logan had his hands over his eyes again. "Are those campfires?"

"I think they're chimneys," said Olivia.

"No," said Barnes. "They can't be."

"It might be a small camp," Parker said to him in a calming tone. "Or maybe, I don't know, a farm with a few—"

"No. It's probably just a few small fires. There's lightning sometimes when it rains."

Josh looked down at the ground. Scuffed the dusty rock with the toe of his shoe. "Hasn't rained here in a while."

"Maybe it's the Neanderthals," said Sam.

"The Neanderthals don't live on this side of the valley. They're all over that way." Barnes waved his hand to the other side of the tower.

"What's the problem?" Kyle's voice had regained its doubting, annoying edge. "Chimneys mean homes and people. It means we're not a hundred million years in the past."

Sam pointed at the swooping flocks. "I thought you were a believer now."

"I'm not a believer. I'm a scientist." Kyle looked at all of them. "I thought we all were."

Olivia felt a little curl of doubt in her gut. She wasn't sure if she should ignore it or not. Instead she gave Josh another nudge. "How far to the smoke?"

He squinted. Judged. "I'd say ten miles. Give or take."

Barnes chuckled and shook his head.

"Closer than the far side," Kyle said.

Now Barnes straightened up, shedding some of his dad-bod posture and looking more like an authority figure. "We're going to the cave."

"You're going to the cave," said Kyle. "We don't have to go with you."

"I don't think you want to be finding your way here without me."

They glared at each other.

Parker stepped forward. Not between them, but close enough to get their attention. "It's been thirteen years, Noah. Maybe your sister moved."

"She wouldn't leave the cave."

"What if something happened to her?"

"Nothing happened to her."

Olivia sighed. The only thing worse than backing up Logan would be backing up her nemesis, but if it ended all this stupid dick fighting . . .

"It doesn't matter. The smoke's pretty much the same direction as your cave, isn't it? We make a small detour, see what it is, and then keep going if we need to."

"Not a small detour," murmured Josh. "Maybe three miles out of our way."

"Give or take a mile?"

He shrugged. "Maybe?"

Barnes stared out at the valley. At the flock of flying shapes. At the thin curls of smoke. At the faraway cliffs of the valley wall.

"Let's go," he said. "We should be able to go there and still be at the cave before night." He turned and headed back down the rocky hill.

Parker started after him without a word. Kyle went two steps before he called out, "Wait, what?"

Barnes clapped his hands. "Like you said, there might be someone there. Let's go."

They all fell in line behind him again. Olivia's boots slid a little bit on the downward slope but caught quickly. Sam wasn't as lucky. Fell on his butt twice. Josh seemed to know what he was doing. His fancy boots slid, but he kept his balance and made each slip almost look deliberate.

The trees rose back up around them. Barnes reached the bottom of Lookout Hill, oriented himself, and headed into the forest. They all followed.

Olivia tugged at her borrowed shirt as they walked. She'd worn a few of Logan's shirts before, so she'd accepted it this morning when he offered. She'd had it on for maybe half an hour when she realized she usually wasn't wearing anything else when she wore them over at his place. Hell, most of the time they didn't even stay on that long. After a few minutes of trying to make it sit right, she grabbed a handful of fabric, twisted it tight, and tied it into a knot.

A few quick steps carried her back up toward the front of the line. Away from Logan, closer to Barnes and Kyle. And Parker.

"I admit," Barnes said, "some things seem a little off. Not quite how I remember them."

"You were a little kid," said Sam.

"Not that little," Parker said. "I have a niece who's ten. She's sharp as hell."

Barnes nodded. "Exactly. Thing is, I *know* the valley's six miles across. I remember when we mapped it out."

"Maybe it's changed," said Parker. "Landscapes change all the time. Erosion. Forest fires. Landslides."

"He said it's only been thirty years," Olivia pointed out. "It's not going to change this much in thirty years."

"It could."

"Meteor," said Josh. "Or maybe a bomb? Maybe someone set off a nuke and we're in the crater?"

Parker rolled her eyes. "And all this grew back in thirty years?"

"It could."

"It hasn't been thirty years," Noah said. "Not here. It's been thirteen."

"Still could've been a meteor," Josh insisted. "That's what killed the dinosaurs."

"Except the dinosaurs here aren't dead," said Sam.

"And what about everything that wasn't destroyed?" asked Olivia. "The castle-tower-place or the monuments and the other landmarks."

"What about them?"

"If there was a meteor or a bomb, how are they all standing? Did they grow back too?"

"Hey, did you forget the force field around the obelisk thing?"

"It only stopped people," said Parker. "Or things people were holding. Wouldn't stop a meteor."

"You don't know that."

"I don't, but it fits what Noah's told us."

Josh shrugged. "Look, I'm just trying to brainstorm, okay? Isn't that what scientists do?"

"You're not a scientist."

Kyle cleared his throat. "What are you, anyway, Mr. not-a-real-guide?"

Olivia glanced back, saw Josh fiddle with his Adam's apple in a familiar way as he walked. Reaching to adjust a tie he wasn't wearing. "I'm in marketing. Sales and marketing."

A few groans passed through the group. "Are you a telemarketer?" asked Sam.

"What? No. I'm in charge of regional marketing and sales for a pharmaceutical start-up."

"Start-ups have regional marketing?" asked Logan.

"Some do. Mine does."

"So why are you out here?"

"I needed some time off. Job stress. All that."

"You got fired," said Kyle.

"No, I didn't. It's more like . . . unpaid leave. I needed to get out of town for a few days, so I filled in for Skip, like I told you. That's it."

"Why did you need to get out of town?" asked Sam.

"Some folks I work with . . ." Josh waved his hands in the air to erase his previous words. Found a new starting place. "Okay, I'm part of a speculative business venture, a sort of partnership. They're the manufacturing side of it, I'm sales and marketing. I made a few risky decisions I thought would open up new revenue streams for us and the risk didn't really pay off. I ended up losing all the product the manufacturing guys had entrusted me with. The head of manufacturing wasn't happy. He forwarded his displeasure to the complaints department and there's a conflict resolution team looking for me right now. The situation called for a certain cooldown period, Skip was sick, and so I covered for him and led all of you out into the middle of nowhere. Which seemed perfect at the time. And here we are."

Olivia spun all the words around in her head. "When you say lost, you mean . . ."

"I was scammed."

"Uh-huh. And when you say *product,* you're taking about drugs?"

"In simple terms, yes."

Sam tapped his fingers together. "So you're a drug dealer on the run."

"No!" Josh straightened up and wagged a finger in the air. "I am not a drug dealer. Drug dealers are guys who wait on street corners and do their business through car windows. I offer a designer pharmaceutical experience to a select, high-end clientele."

"I see," said Parker, looking back over her shoulder. "And how many designer pharmaceuticals were you scammed out of?"

Josh twisted his lips. Tried to look casual. "About seven hundred and fifty thousand dollars worth."

"Holy shit!" gasped Kyle. "Seven hundred and fifty?"

"Yes."

"Seven hundred and fifty thousand? You owe someone three-quarters of a million dollars?"

"Well, of course it sounds like a lot when you say it like that." He frowned at their expressions. "It's a tough business. Ever since they legalized pot, designer pharmaceuticals have taken a real hit."

"Thanks for coming clean," said Olivia.

Josh nodded. "No real point in keeping it secret, I guess."

Another cat dashed through the trees, rustling leaves as it sprinted across the forest floor. A big black one. It ran alongside them for a moment, then veered off deeper into the trees.

"I think it was chasing something," Olivia said.

"Anyway," said Josh, "I dropped in to lay low with Skip for a week or three. He was sick, told me he had this gig, I offered to fill in for him. And then, you know, hike, fall through time and space, dinosaurs."

"Is that why you've got the tuxedo jacket?"

He tugged the lapels. "It's a casual business blazer. You want layers at night and this was the only coat I had handy."

No one responded, and they walked in silence for a few minutes.

Olivia looked up through the trees. Every now and then she'd catch glimpses of the valley walls. On her left they were soft and blurry with distance, but they loomed on her right. She was pretty sure their path took them away from the massive cliffs, but they were so big it was hard to get "away" from them. She studied them whenever she could, wondering if she'd spot another jet or who knew what embedded in the wall.

"Hey," she said. "Can you climb the valley walls? Is that a way out?"

Barnes glanced back at her. "No."

Now Logan peered up through the trees. "No, you can't or no, no one's ever tried."

"Beau tried climbing it once. The Castaway told her she'd get out of the valley, and she figured maybe that's what they meant."

"How far did she get?" asked Josh.

"Maybe six hundred and fifty feet. Close to halfway. Our dad was pissed. Didn't realize until later how worried he must've been."

Olivia looked over and up at the valley wall. "That's kind of badass."

"She is. It wasn't a brutally hard climb, lots of ledges and handholds, but it was still over six hundred feet."

"Too exhausted to go further or . . . ?"

"Exhaustion. Too much wall. After a certain point she said it felt like the top never got any closer."

"That's a solid climb," said Josh. "She did it with no equipment?"

"Yep. Just barehanded. Six hours up, three down."

"Badass," Olivia said again.

Kyle shrugged. "I used to do climbs like that."

"What about the flying dinosaurs?" asked Parker. "Do they ever fly out?"

"No idea. Maybe? I've never seen one fly over the edge."

Sam took a few quick steps, put himself alongside Barnes. "Do you think we might see any of the lizard people?"

"The what?"

"The lizard people. They're nocturnal, right? Don't like sunlight or bright light."

Noah sighed. Kicked at an oversized pine cone. "There aren't any lizard people. Whatshisname made them up for his book."

"Oh."

"You read that one, too?"

"I read all of them."

"You didn't think lizard men in ancient temples sounded a little odd?"

"I mean, yeah, I thought it was weird they didn't show up in any other books, but he said he'd talked with you a lot when he was working with you at the, while you were at . . ."

"The psych hospital."

"Yeah."

Olivia's stomach dropped. She glanced at Logan and Kyle. They both had the same expression, and she was pretty sure it was the one she had.

Barnes looked back at them. "It's not like I spent six months in a straightjacket or anything. It was trauma care to get over my 'kidnapping.' Daily sessions to talk through stuff after I got back."

"Oh."

"And if you look the guy up, he wasn't even a doctor there. He was a janitor."

"Seriously?"

"Yep. He got fired for eavesdropping on group sessions. Fell down a big conspiracy hole ten years ago. Nowadays he rants online about stolen elections, vaccine microchips, the deep state, and, well, lizard people."

"Wow. I didn't know any of that."

"Sorry to be the bearer of bad news."

"Oh yeah," muttered Kyle. "We're stuck a few million years in the past, our lives are ruined, but the real tragedy's finding out the dinosaur book you read as a kid was all made up."

"Shut up," said Sam.

"You shut up."

"Both of you shut up," Olivia said.

They walked in silence for few more minutes. Then Parker slowed her pace slightly to walk alongside Sam. "So how many books are there about him?"

"Seven. Two of them are complete nonsense. Worse than the one with the lizard men. Even as a kid, it was pretty clear they were real Discovery Channel–type things. They try to tie Billy—Noah's story to every pseudoscience theory out there. Alien wildlife preserves, Stonehenge, ley lines, mokele-mbembe, all that sort of stuff."

Olivia rolled the word on her tongue. "Mik-coley . . . ?"

Sam nodded, looking back and forth between them. "It's an early twentieth-century urban legend. Basically a bunch of old white guy explorers insisted they'd found that there were still dinosaurs living in Africa. Brontosaurs, or maybe apatosaurs, hanging out in the jungle. One of the Dino Boy books tried to say there was probably an entrance to the valley somewhere in the Congo River Basin and the dinosaurs could wander back and forth. That's why they kept getting seen, but also how they could vanish if you went looking for them."

Parker smirked. "Quantum dinosaurs. Only there when you're not looking for them."

"Pretty much." He looked ahead at Barnes, dropped his voice. "One of the other ones goes deep into the idea the Gathers were kidnapped by some Southeast Asian gang they claimed his dad was involved with. Crime and construction, bribery, permits, that sort of thing. Plays up the sex-trafficking angle about him and his sister." Sam waved a hand at the forest around them. "How he imagined all this as some mental escape from reality."

"Fuck," said Olivia.

"Yeah, it's pretty messed up. I didn't realize how much until I was . . . until years later."

She looked at the back of Barnes's head. He'd pulled a bit ahead of them. "You remember a lot of this stuff."

"I was really into it. You have no—as a kid the idea of vanishing from the face of the earth was appealing."

"Why?" asked Parker as she ran into Barnes's backpack. Sam weaved to avoid hitting both of them. Olivia looked up in time, sidestepped, and found herself next to the professor.

"That's odd," said Sam.

Three rocks, maybe small boulders, sat in a rough line in front of them. One the size of a beach ball, one a little bigger than her desk back at her apartment, the last one a few feet away and maybe the size and shape of a really big suitcase.

Past the three rocks, the forest was all palm trees again. Big, solid trees, with scaly trunks a few feet around. The pines all stopped right at the line of rocks. Even the ground past the line was different, fewer needles and more knee-high grass and ferns.

Sam crouched by the middle stone. Touched it. Turned his head to look at the suitcase-rock. "Check this out," he said.

"What's up?" asked Kyle. The stragglers had caught up and gathered around the line of boulders.

All three rocks had been cut flat, all along the same vertical plane. Olivia crouched at the far end, closed one eye, and lined them up. A perfectly straight line, like someone had taken a giant sword and cut through all three boulders at once. She tried to get closer to the edge and it was so goddamn straight they all blurred together. Logan moved to the far end of the line. Closed one eye. Stared back at her.

She touched the stone plane. It felt like glass. Like her granddad's tombstone, all polished and glossy.

"Is it me," said Parker, "or does the whole forest change on either side of the line?"

Olivia looked at the ground. The division did seem to run right along the flat edge of the boulders. Not as clean, but it did seem to be the same line.

"It's not you," Kyle said.

"Is this the cut rock?" Sam asked Barnes. "That's real, right? It's in most of the books."

"Please stop," said Barnes. "And I don't know. These look like little versions of it. The cut rock's huge. And it should be closer to the cave, between the mushroom forest and the swamp. It marked the start of Neanderthal territory."

"So many fucked-up things in that statement," Kyle said.

Logan let his fingertips slide back and forth on the smooth surface of the middle stone. "What's the cut rock?"

Barnes glanced at Sam, but the younger man had his mouth shut tight. "There's a rock here in the valley, a landmark. It's this big boulder. Perfectly flat on one side. Size of a garage door and smooth as glass. And no sign of the other half of it."

He waved a hand at the ground. Parker dragged her foot in front of one of the stones, looking for anything buried. Logan brushed aside some pine needles. Neither of them found anything.

"Okay," said Olivia. "So, your rock broke apart into little rocks."

"Maybe when the meteor hit," Josh added.

"Jesus, dude, give it a rest."

"And all the pieces fell in a perfectly straight line?" Parker shook her head.

Logan made a chopping motion with his hand. "Force fields, maybe?"

Kyle pressed both hands to his head. "Jesus fucking Christ, not you too?"

"This isn't the cut rock," said Barnes. "They're the wrong color and they're in the wrong place."

"So what are they?" asked Olivia.

He looked at the three boulders. "I don't know. Rocks."

"I mean, it's some kind of boundary between parts of the forest. Clearly."

"Maybe, but I don't know what they are. I never saw anything like this before."

Logan brushed the smooth surface again. "You said the other one marks the start of Neanderthal territory?"

"Yep. But not like this. It's a landmark, not a . . . not an actual line." Barnes waved them on and they headed into the palm trees.

"So, there's a whole tribe of Neanderthals, right," said Sam. Less of a question, more looking for eager confirmation. So much eager fan light burning in his eyes. "The Pakka."

"Yep," Barnes said. "Five of them when I was a kid, but who knows how many there are now."

"At least one," said Kyle, touching his bandaged arm.

Parker appeared on his other side, matching his pace. "Could you communicate with them?"

"Sort of. Beau figured out a hundred or so words of their language, but it took months. They weren't very friendly."

"Hostile?" asked Josh.

"I'd say so," Logan murmured.

Barnes shook his head. "No, just . . . not friendly. They helped us a few times, when they had to, but even as a kid I got the sense they didn't like anything that wasn't another Neanderthal. Sort of like a broad, inherent xenophobia. There's been some study of their skulls and brain impressions recently—back in our time—that back it up."

"So they're stupid," said Kyle.

Barnes shook his head. "Not stupid. More like really, really set in their ways. Think of anyone you know who says, 'We do it this way because we've always done it this way.' Now imagine them taking that attitude with everything. Food, clothes, tools, relationships, all of it."

Olivia nodded. "I've known some folks like that."

"Well, imagine a whole species like that. You do everything the way your parents did it and your grandparents and your great-grandparents. That's what Neanderthals are like. The Pakka had never dealt with anything like us before, so most of them just didn't want to deal with us."

"Sounds a little limiting," said Parker.

"It could be, sometimes."

"Also, they're matriarchal," added Sam. "There's a woman who led, who leads the tribe here. Scarnose."

"Yep. Although we were never sure if it was because she was a woman or because she was the most vicious one."

"Cool either way," said Olivia, picturing herself decked out in a fur bikini and cloak. Maybe with a big bone club. Something she could hit Parker over the head with.

"Cavewoman," said Kyle with a nod. "Is she hot?"

Olivia's vision of barbarian power vanished. "Seriously? That's where your mind goes?"

"Half her nose had been ripped off," Barnes said. "Most of her left cheek, too. Some kind of animal attack. Almost half her face was just a mess of scar tissue. First time I saw a Freddy Krueger movie, it made me think of her. My dad said it'd probably been one of the bigger raptors. Beau tried calling her Scarface but I changed it to Scarnose. Dumb little-kid name for something I was scared of." He reached up and brushed his temples. "She had white stripes, too. I considered dyeing mine when they went gray. It was weird to see in the mirror every morning."

"One of the *bigger* raptors?" said Josh.

"How'd she survive an injury like that?" This from Logan, walking half a step behind them. "I'm guessing Neanderthal medicine didn't involve a lot of sutures or blood transfusions."

"Same way Parker recovered from hitting her head last night. Like I said, people heal faster here. You can still die or be killed, but a lot of wounds that should be dangerous just . . . aren't."

Barnes looked over at Parker. So did Olivia and Logan. She flinched a bit from the attention, then reached up to scratch at the scab on her brow.

"You healed from a broken arm once in fifteen days, right?"

He sighed. "Sam, there's a lot in those books, but there's a lot that's *not* in them too. And a lot they got wrong."

"Can we get back to the part about bigger raptors?" asked Josh. "Like, *Jurassic Park*–sized?"

"A couple of them," Barnes said. "They're not quite as scary as the movies make them out to be."

"Not exactly reassuring."

"Holy fuck," said Kyle. He took a few running steps ahead. Ferns rustled around his knees and thighs. "Holy fuck!"

Logan took off after him, jogging a few yards and then pausing to stare up into the trees. Olivia followed them. She didn't have to go far to see what Kyle had found.

"Is it another dinosaur?" Josh called out.

Olivia put the robot at fifteen feet tall. What she could see of it, at least. The section of it above ground was roughly human-shaped, which implied another fifteen or twenty feet beneath the surface. It was buried at an angle, one arm disappearing into the ground, while the other stretched out across the forest floor like a fallen tree. With all the moss, she probably would've mistaken it for a tree if Kyle hadn't seen it.

"What the hell?" said Barnes.

Sam let out a little squeak of air that wasn't quite a whistle.

A cluster of recessed lenses made up the face, ranging from baseball-sized to one bigger than a bowling ball with a Y-shaped crack running through it, like Logan's glasses. Two of the antennas on top were bent, and a third was broken off, leaving a stubby pole with a frayed tip. More tubes pointed from the sides of the head that could've been . . . guns? Sensors? Fire extinguishers?

Broad shoulders, and the higher one had what looked like a rack of missiles mounted on it. Orange and yellow cones stuck out from maybe a third of the miniature silos, while the others were visibly empty. Olivia followed the shoulder down to the overgrown arm and realized one of the thick speed-bump mounds along the forest floor was a half-buried cannon mounted to the robot's forearm. A scaly palm trees had grown up between the arm and torso, reaching up to the forest canopy, swelling to fill every space it could.

Large yellow and brown triangles covered most of it. Camouflage meant to confuse rather than conceal. Olivia remembered seeing an article about similar patterns on battleships to hide their outlines at sea. She wondered where the machine had been that it needed these colors. Mountains? Deserts?

Kyle reached up and ran a hand across the angular chest. He rapped it twice with his knuckles. "It's not metal. I don't think so, anyway. Maybe some kind of ceramic plating? Or maybe a plastic composite?"

"Is it a robot?" Josh asked.

Olivia snorted out a chuckle. "I'm pretty sure it's not a dinosaur."

"No, I mean is it a robot as opposed to, like, a mobile suit?"

"A what?"

"A mechsuit. Battlemech. You know. Is it a big, self-controlled android or is it a walking tank somebody's piloting? Or was piloting, I guess."

Kyle looked up at the mechanical frame and jumped. His fingers grabbed an edge and he pulled himself up onto the robot's shoulder. He tilted his head and stared down at the top of the machine's chest. "I think this is a hatch," he said. He thumped his hand on a panel.

Olivia took a few steps forward. Glanced back in time to see Sam lean toward Barnes. "Is this one of the things that's not in the—"

"I've never seen this before."

"Really?"

"I'm sure he'd remember it," said Parker.

"Okay," said Sam, "so maybe it's new."

Barnes glanced from the robot to Sam. "What?"

"Well, it's been a couple years. Maybe this thing fell into the wormhole too."

Olivia moved closer to the half-buried giant. Logan, half listening to the conversation, pointed at the ground. "This has been here for a while," he said. "The ground's all gone flat and there's stuff growing in it."

"How long does that take?"

Logan shrugged and batted a tall fern with his hand. "I don't know. I had an undergrad roommate who had a fern—"

Olivia snickered. "A fern."

"—and it didn't get anywhere near this big in one semester. Maybe a couple years?

"Still fits," said Sam.

"Except it doesn't answer where it came from," Parker pointed out.

"Japan," said Josh. "They love Jaegers and mobile suits in Japan. There's a life-sized Gundam in Tokyo."

"None of those words mean anything," Kyle called out. He'd found a lever, and his arms strained with effort as he pulled at it.

Olivia looked at the lower shoulder. Saw some markings behind some of the moss and vines. Black and red lines running in different directions. And a stenciled letter E? She scraped at the moss with her fingers.

"It makes sense," Barnes said with a nod. "The wormhole throws things back in time to the valley, and in the future it's still throwing things back in time. That's how we ended up with Ross."

"Ross?" Parker asked.

"Their robot butler," explained Sam.

"Right."

"The point is," said Barnes, "this could've fallen into the wormhole two or three hundred years from now and arrived the same day I left. It could've been sitting here for over a decade."

Olivia swept her hand back and forth over the lower shoulder, knocking away the last of the moss and breaking a few of the thinner vines. "Check this out," she called to the others.

An American flag decorated the shoulder, like the patch on a soldier's uniform. Below it, *042* was printed in blocky black numerals. She tapped the blue corner of the flag. "It's got fifty-four stars. Six by nine."

"Future America," said Sam.

"At least there's still a future America," said Parker.

Olivia pulled some more overgrowth away from the massive block of the shoulder, revealing smaller letters and numbers. "It's a Cerberus-16, whatever that is."

"Maybe it's the pilot's call sign," said Logan. "Like Maverick or Goose."

"Or Avenger," Josh added.

Olivia shot him a thumbs-up.

"We should probably get going," Barnes told them. "We want to get to the cave before dark."

"You don't want to check this out?" asked Logan.

"It isn't going anywhere and I—"

Something hissed loud, almost a whistle, and Kyle shouted in triumph. "Got it!"

The lever folded back, and the top half of the metal figure's torso swung forward. The dappled sunlight hit two chrome pistons. Olivia watched Logan grab the edge and pull himself up and oh yeah she was going to miss those arms. Sam waded through the ferns, moving in closer.

"Definitely a cockpit," said Kyle, peering down into the machine. "Don't recognize half this tech, but I'm pretty sure that's a pilot's chair."

"Looks more like a saddle," Logan said, looking over the edge of the torso hatch. "What are those?"

Kyle turned his head. "Arm braces? Controllers, maybe?

"Very *Pacific Rim*," said Josh.

"Is there a pilot?" asked Olivia.

"Nothing," said Kyle. "Looks like a lot of stuff's been stripped out. Lots of loose wires."

Logan let go of the hatch, pushed off the giant arm, and landed on the ground near Olivia with a soft thump. He grinned at her. A random thought passed through her head—*what happens in the prehistoric valley stays in the prehistoric valley*—but she didn't want to deal with any of it right now. She turned back to the robot's shoulder and wiped off some more moss, determined to find more words.

She felt a second thump in the ground, and a smell hit her nostrils. Dusty and oily at the same time, with a sour meat undertone. And then she heard a third thump and, wait a minute, who else jumped down from the robot?

Olivia turned. Saw Logan and Kyle looking around. Felt the fourth thump in the soles of her feet.

Parker touched Barnes on the arm. "What's wrong?"

Another impact. Something big hitting the ground. Josh turned. "Did anyone else feel that?"

"I did," said Olivia. And then she saw Barnes staring past them. His face unnaturally still. Trying hard not to react.

"Hide," he whispered. "Hide now."

9

LOGAN

Logan sighed, looked casually in the other direction as Olivia turned back to the big robot, and watched Noah's eyes go wide. He glanced up at Kyle, halfway into the robot's cockpit, then over at Josh standing on the half-buried arm. Everything looked fine.

"Hide," Noah stage-whispered. "Hide now." He trembled, and Logan's first thought was to comfort the professor the way you'd talk to a little kid who'd woken up from a nightmare and needed to be convinced a monster wasn't real.

As the thought went through his mind, Logan felt the pulse in the ground. A wave of pressure.

Noah took three eerily calm steps to the side. He had an iron grip on Parker's wrist and dragged her with him. He wedged them between two scaly palms that'd grown close enough together they might've been a single plant with two trunks. Then he crouched, tugging Parker down with him, letting the ferns and tall grass surround them.

The whole time his gaze stayed locked on the forest behind the giant robot.

"What's going on?" asked Josh.

Another low thump echoed up through Logan's boots. And another. Getting stronger.

Getting *closer.*

Another heavy impact paired with the noise of breaking wood. The horror movie twig breaking in the forest, but to Logan it sounded like a full tree branch. Maybe a thin trunk.

Something brushed his arm and he flinched. Olivia. Their eyes met and he saw the same fear and worry sparking there, waiting for the kindling that'd create a full fire.

She looked back over her shoulder. He followed her gaze and saw the nook beneath the robot's shoulder, right where it connected to the torso. It wasn't deep, but it was shelter. Hopefully concealment. He nodded and they slipped back into the small space, wrapped their arms around each other, sank in another few inches.

He could barely see Noah and Parker. Just the tops of their heads from this angle. At the edge of his vision, he thought he could see Sam pressed tight against a tree.

No, not against. Behind. Sam shuffled a few inches to the side, keeping the swollen palm tree between him and something else.

Then the something stepped into view and the ground trembled again.

When Logan was little, his parents had taken him to a zoo while on some family trip to upstate New York or maybe Canada. He'd looked out at the crocodile pen from the safety of the walkway and seen the big lizards sunning themselves in the man-made swamp. He'd been staring at one as it drifted along through the water when he noticed the people next to him gleefully pointing straight down at the big log inside of the fence.

A moment later little Logan had shrieked—half joy, half terror—when he realized the log was another crocodile, maybe the biggest in the whole pen. Its sheer size had hidden it from him, his brain unable to process something so large it stretched out of his field of vision in two directions. He hadn't been able to take his eyes off it until his parents picked him up and carried him away.

The dinosaur was like that. So big it didn't seem possible. Too real to look away from.

It loomed over them as it moved into view, coming out from behind the robot, out from behind *them*. At least as tall as the half-buried machine, maybe taller if it wasn't bent low. As it was, some of the lower palm fronds scraped and scratched against a head the size of a small couch.

Its glossy black eyes took in everything. Triangular ridges—or maybe horns—sat above the eye sockets, like the angry eyebrows on a cartoon villain. Its jaw hung open and the warm stink of its breath rolled out. Bad teeth and meat and blood. Sunburn-red splashes spread across its gray-blue jaws and shoulders and down its sides. So many jokes about little arms, but those arms were longer and thicker than Logan's legs.

Someone started to scream, just the squeak at the start of it, and Olivia pressed her hand over his mouth. Hot air rolled off her palm. He'd been screaming. Him. Oh Jesus it was so fucking big.

It marched between the palms and the robot, and each taloned foot hit the ground like a falling tree. It slowed, sniffed the air with wet, glistening nostrils bigger than its eyes. Moved that giant head side to side. Never stopped. Another big sniff and it lumbered past, its sheer size making it eerily fast. Logan's whirling, chaotic mind threw out the image of a hockey-masked killer that always walked but couldn't be outrun.

It was only in sight for fifteen, maybe twenty, seconds and then its tail vanished. Logan took two more frantic breaths through his nose, two calmer ones, then reached up and moved Olivia's hand away from his mouth. He took a deep breath. Tasted urine in the air. One of them had pissed themselves, and he was pretty sure it hadn't been Olivia.

Logan started counting to ten—no, make it twenty—to give the dinosaur as much time as possible to move on. On eight he stopped squeezing Olivia. At fifteen he leaned slightly forward out from under the robot's arm. He could see Noah and Parker, still crouched between the two palms a few yards away, watching him through the ferns. Probably doing a count of their own.

A beat later he heard a thud, two clunks, and Kyle landed on the ground in front of the robot. He turned to them in their little nook.

Smiled nervously. "Holy fuck," he said. "Holy. Fuck. Did you see the teeth on that thing?"

Parker's eyes were huge. Noah made small, desperate gestures. The ground pulsed again. Faster.

They felt the roar more than heard it. The armor plates of the robot *buzzed* with it. Logan screamed. Olivia screamed in his ear. Kyle screamed and kicked up loose dirt as he launched into a run.

The other dinosaur stomped after him, its massive legs jackhammering into the ground. Logan had half a second to think how it ran like a chicken, almost wobbling side to side, and to register the white streaks on its big haunches. Then its head darted down like it'd grabbed a worm but the worm was Kyle and he screamed as it tossed him up into the air and slammed its jaws shut on his body again. Blood sprayed out of his mouth and out of his chest and thighs and then he was gone as the dinosaur's momentum carried it another dozen yards into the forest. Kyle fell to the ground, still screaming. The dinosaur's foot came down on his flailing body, pinning him in a patch of ferns. Its head dipped again and yanked up and Logan heard a ripping sound and Kyle stopped screaming.

Kyle had . . . Why had he stopped screaming? What . . . what had . . .

The dinosaur bent down again, yanked its head back up, moved its jaws back and forth. It ate four, maybe five bites, prodded at the ground with its snout, and then wandered off into the trees. The first dinosaur, the bright red sunburned one, joined it. They huffed at each other as they stalked away.

The urine smell was much stronger now.

The dinosaurs lost their shape and became motion in the distance, and then the motion blurred into the forest.

Kyle still hadn't moved from where the dinosaur had dropped him. Probably . . . probably not moving to confuse it. Like in the movies. Its vision was based on movement, right?

Something shifted behind Logan and he tried to throw himself away from it. Olivia whispered to him to calm down. Just Olivia. She had her hand over his mouth again. When had she done that? Why had she done that? Had he been screaming again?

Noah and Parker stood up. Noah looked after the dinosaurs. Parker stayed glued to his arm, not holding it, but standing close enough that their elbows touched. Sam appeared from somewhere, his eyes wide.

Something moved under Logan's nose. Olivia, taking her hand away. She put her hands under his arms and lifted, pushing him out of their safe nook under the robot's arm. He pushed back, tried to grab the edges of one of the big armor plates, tried to keep them where it was *safe*. She slid past him. "Just . . . just stay here," she told him. "It'll be okay."

"No!" He tried to pull her back under the robot's arm but his fingers slid off her arm, ignoring his command to hold her.

Outside the nook a figure moved close to Olivia and Logan yelped, but it was only Josh. Noah walked over to them, Parker pressed to his side. "Is anybody else hurt?"

They all gave each other half glances, shook their heads. Olivia looked back at Logan. "I think he . . . he might be in shock."

Logan wasn't sure who she was talking about. Why wasn't anyone heading over to check on Kyle? Sam kept looking toward the ferns, but he didn't move, didn't go to help.

"I . . . I think we all might be," said Parker. "In shock."

"No, I mean, he's *really* in shock."

Noah stepped closer, crouched a little to look at him. "It's understandable."

"Understandable?" echoed Josh. "A dinosaur *just ate Kyle*!"

Logan pushed the words away. Pushed himself a little deeper beneath the giant robot's arm. Stared at the distant patch of ferns. Some bugs were circling around them now. Their wings buzzed in the forest.

Olivia and Noah and Sam kept talking. Logan had trouble hearing them. Maybe trouble paying attention? Maybe he'd hit his head? If he'd hit his head he might not be remembering things right.

Something moved in front of him and he jumped back, definitely hitting his head on the underside of the robot's arm. The pain stopped his whirling thoughts for a few moments, made things clearer. He'd never liked the movie bit of slapping someone to calm them down, but maybe there was something to it.

Olivia crouched in front of him, holding her hand out. "Come on. We're going."

"What about Kyle?"

"Come on." She took his hand in hers and pulled.

He let her guide him out from beneath the robot's arm. Sam had stepped a few feet away to throw up in a bush. Parker still hadn't moved away from Noah. Logan looked at the ferns off in the forest. "But what about Kyle?"

"We . . . we're." Olivia swallowed like something hot was stuck in her throat. "We can't help him."

"Logan?" Noah peered at him. "Are you going to be able to walk?"

"Yes."

"We can't stay here. The scent of . . . the smell's going to attract things."

Logan's arm shook, and he made a fist to stop it. "More dinosaurs?"

"Probably. And other things."

Olivia pulled his hand again. Logan took a step forward. Another tug and another step, and then he was walking next to Olivia, a little bit behind Noah and Parker and Sam.

Noah steered them around the ferns, never getting closer than a few yards, but Logan could smell something tangy in the air that hadn't been there before, and something dark had splattered on some of the fronds. One of the four-winged blackbird dinosaurs swooped down as they passed, flailing at the air as it landed.

Nobody talked. Logan counted steps. It felt like a safe thing to do. Olivia held his hand. He thought about holding her hand and counting steps and all the plants around them and not at all about Kyle screaming as the dinosaur carried him off into the woods.

Twenty-three steps so far.

"Was that . . . was one of those Fang?" asked Sam.

Noah didn't look back. "No."

"Are you sure?"

Parker glared at him. "Jesus, Sam, not now."

"That wasn't Fang," Noah said. He sounded annoyed, like something had gone wrong. "Those weren't even tyrannosaurs."

"What?"

"They're too small."

"Too *small*?" said Josh, coughing. "Are you serious?"

Noah turned to glare at the man. "I know what a tyrannosaurus looks like. These are too small and their heads are all wrong. Did you see the horns? I think they might've been allosauruses."

He marched forward and backhanded a big leaf out of his way. Parker caught it as it swung back. Logan worried about how much noise the rustling leaves made. And the voices.

Forty-two steps.

"I didn't know there were allosauruses in the valley," said Sam.

"There aren't any," snapped Noah.

Olivia looked back over her shoulder, past Logan. "Then what were those?"

10

SAM

Sam knew he shouldn't be excited. Somebody had died. I mean, Kyle had been mauled right in front of him less than half an hour ago.

Ripped apart by an allosaurus.

Kyle could be a dick sometimes—a serious dick—but he was still a person. And Logan and Olivia's friend. His death had pretty clearly messed up Logan. Olivia was holding it together a little better, but she looked a little pale.

What did it say about him that he kept sliding back into excitement? Someone dead, lost a hundred million years in the past, and he felt like they'd arrived at Disneyland. Every time he got too excited something kicked over in his gut, twisted in his stomach, tried to remind him this wasn't fun or fantastic or good in any way.

And then . . .

He was in the valley! The. Valley. The actual valley he'd read about as a kid. Written fan fiction about. Probably shouldn't tell Noah that one.

Noah was Dino Boy! The actual, real Dino Boy. Even if he didn't like the name, it didn't change who he was. Sam kept sneaking glances at him, seeing the familiar features peeking out from beneath the man's face. It was so obvious now that he knew to look for it.

The forest shifted again as they walked. They'd crossed another invisible line and the jungle had given way to a long stretch of huge trees, so tall their lowest branches had to be twenty or thirty feet up. Not redwoods, but maybe supersized maples? Had Neil deGrasse Tyson talked about giant ancient trees on a *Cosmos*? Maybe? How they related to carbon storage and global warming.

The guilt-ridden worm turned over in his gut again. Seriously, what was wrong with him? Kyle's body was probably still warm, what was left of it, and he was getting excited about trees. And dinosaurs.

Dinosaurs!

This had been his dream for so long as a kid. To escape to *the valley*. To get away from everything. Angry, disapproving mom. Fighting parents. And then, when he was desperately trying to get away as an adult, when he wasn't even thinking about this place . . .

A screech echoed between the trees. It reminded Sam of a hawk shrieking. An answering sound called back, then two-three-four more. The distant noise swelled up for a moment, then faded away. Josh and Parker both stood with their arms half up, ready to ward off attacks. Logan's eyes had gone super wide.

"It's just microraptors," said Noah. "They can get loud when there's a flock of them."

Parker looked up. Shook her head. "How did you survive here?"

Noah looked at her. "We were careful. I didn't realize how much of our lives was being careful until I was older. My dad figured out how to deal with so many things, made Beau and I follow so many rules. I knew it was tough, but I didn't realize *how* tough until years later. I hit that age where you look back at things and see it all through new eyes. Pick up on all the subtext you missed earlier."

"It must've sucked," said Josh.

"It didn't. I was young enough I just accepted a lot of it. And it's not like I had tons of distractions."

"I would've been so distracted here," Sam said.

Olivia shook her head. "I couldn't've dealt with so many rules."

"Sure you could've," said Noah. "We all do, all the time, every day.

Don't run indoors. Eat your vegetables. Keep your clothes on. Wear a mask. You have to pay for that. We all grow up with tons of rules. I just grew up with different ones."

Olivia gave Logan's arm a tug. "Big jump from 'eat your vegetables' to 'watch out for the T-Rex.'"

"And yet, we got used to it. And we survived."

"Kyle didn't."

Noah shot her a look. "I've told you all at least half a dozen times now to keep your voices down. He kept being loud."

Josh coughed hard. "Are you saying it's his own fault he got killed by a dinosaur?"

In the corner of Sam's eye, Logan shuddered.

"No, no, of course not," said Noah. "What happened to Kyle was horrible. A really horrible accident. But I hope from here on out you'll listen to me and trust my experience."

"Experience from thirty years ago," said Josh.

"And assuming we've even landed in the same place," added Olivia.

"It's the valley," Noah said. "There's a few minor differences, but it's still the place I remember."

"Didn't you say your memories were all skewed?"

Noah huffed a little air out of his nose. The professor dealing with a student who wasn't right but still wouldn't back down. "It's still the valley. Do you think there could be two places like this?"

"If you'd asked me yesterday," said Olivia, "I'd've told you there couldn't be *one* place like this."

Sam stopped himself from saying he'd hoped for this place. He was pretty sure he'd started repeating himself in his excitement. It was hard not to be excited. Even with . . .

Kyle hadn't even been dead an hour. Ripped apart right in front of them and it bothered Sam that he kept forgetting. Then the screams and the tearing sound and that hot smell all flooded back into his mind.

He realized Noah's casual attitude made it easy to forget. The professor seemed focused, but relaxed. At home.

He wondered if Noah felt guilty about Kyle's death.

The giant trees stopped, and oversized pines became the forest's tree of choice. Not as clear-cut as the line before, but still a definite here and there. The ground even felt different under Sam's feet, more hard-packed dirt than the soil between the massive maybe-redwoods.

He slowed to look at the carpet of needles and moss. Olivia came up alongside him. Passed him. She still led Logan by one hand, not dragging him as much as guiding him along. He kept touching trees, as if he was trying to drain some stability out of them. Sam felt pretty sure if Olivia let go of his hand, Logan would just stay here with his hands pressed against bark.

Another thought flitted through his mind and out past his lips before he could stop it. "Do you think the Castaway's still here?"

Noah puffed a little bit of air out his nose. "Probably, yep."

Parker's face brightened a bit. "Can I . . . can we meet them?"

"Maybe. They're not my priority right now."

"How is visiting an actual alien not your priority?"

"Because I'm here for Beau."

Sam watched Parker's lips twitch as she bit down on her response.

They walked for another half hour before Olivia asked about lunch and they stopped to divide up some food. Noah handed out more bars. "I've got supplies for two weeks," he told them, "but we'll be able to find food long before then."

"You sure?" Josh looked around.

"There's lots of food here. Trust me."

Sam remembered the descriptions of meals the Gather family had eaten. Dinosaur eggs. Mushrooms. Berries. Some fruit little Billy—Noah—hadn't been able to identify past family nicknames.

He took a bite and managed to chew three times before the image of Kyle in the allosaurus's jaws filled his mind. He managed to swallow what was in his mouth. Wrapped up the rest and shoved it in his pocket.

Olivia tried to feed Logan. The guy was still deep, deep in shock, like most of his brain had shut down. Almost sleepwalking. Sam wondered how long it'd take him to get over it. And what would happen if they had to run again.

A pair of microraptors dropped down and stalked around while they ate. Sam thought they looked like little dragons on the ground, their wings jutting up at awkward angles. After a few moments they climbed the trunk of a tree, moving like cats now, and then threw themselves back into the air from a lower branch.

They all traded a few looks, silently agreed they were done eating, and got moving again.

They hiked silently, but the forest made noises for them. Distant screeches and growls. A loud noise that sounded like . . . an elephant? Sam didn't remember there being elephants in any of the books, but maybe they were new arrivals. Or maybe some of the different book writers thought elephants would sound boring in a valley filled with dinosaurs and left them out.

The space between the trees got brighter, and a few more minutes of walking revealed a clearing up ahead. A few steps later they were standing at the edge of a wide open area the size of a baseball field.

Dozens . . . no, hundreds of dark, flat stones covered the ground. Flagstones? Paving stones? Whatever they were, they'd been here for ages, taking on the dull colors of years in the sun. The soft edges of who knew how many decades of wind and rain and paws and hooves and feet. Generations of grass and weedy flowers pushed up through every gap between the stones like an abandoned strip-mall parking lot, and all at once Sam knew where they were.

He looked across the wide expanse of flagstones and saw the green wedge of the sundial rising out of the grass. The sundial the Gather family had seen on *their* first day in the valley. The one they'd found after running into a stegosaurus and avoiding Fang, the T-Rex.

Noah stepped forward. Looked up past the trees toward the distant high cliffs of the valley's edge. Then he stuck his arm out straight, pointing to the right of the sundial with his whole hand. "We got off course. Whatever's making the smoke is that way."

"I thought it's more that way," said Josh, tipping his head to the left.

"It's not. Directions can be weird here. You need to go off landmarks and ignore your sense of . . ."

Noah's brow furrowed as he stared across the wide, flagstone plaza. Sam followed his gaze. It took a moment for his eyes to find the thing that'd caught Noah's attention.

Maybe a dozen yards past the sundial, almost lined up with it perfectly, stood another obelisk. Size and shape-wise, it could've been a twin of the one they'd seen a few hours ago. But this one was transparent, a collection of white, highlighted edges in the sunlight. A gray-white haze hung in the air between those edges, and it took Sam a few seconds to realize he was looking at the lines of glyphs and symbols decorating each side.

There'd been a clear obelisk in the books. Glass or crystal, depending on which account you were reading. But that one sat between a trio of black boulders in the middle of an old lava flow, a mile from the sundial. If you averaged all the distances given in different books. Not that Sam had ever made his own maps of the valley.

Noah took a few steps out into the plaza. He looked confused and was doing a bad job of hiding it. He kept looking at the obelisk, at the far trees, the sundial.

Parker stepped closer to him. "Is something wrong?"

"No. Maybe. I don't . . ." He shook his head and pointed across the plaza, taking a few more steps as he did. "This shouldn't be here."

"The big triangle?" asked Josh.

"It's a sundial," Sam and Parker said at the same time.

Noah took a few more steps into the plaza. He looked down at the flagstones, then at the far trees again. Past the trees, at the high, distant cliffs.

Sam leaned to the side, trying to get a better look at the obelisk. There'd been a point when he could name all of them by material and their different, specific quirks. "The glass one . . . puts you to sleep?"

Noah glanced at him as they continued across the plaza. Shook his head. "No, that's the marble one. Knocks you out cold for an hour or so."

Sam reshuffled the obelisks in his mind. He'd thought the marble one was the one with the glowing runes. "So what does this one do?"

"It . . . I'm not sure. There's not supposed to be an obelisk near the sundial."

"Maybe someone moved it?" suggested Olivia.

Noah shook his head.

Josh pointed at the big metal triangle as they trudged across the plaza. "Maybe they moved the sundial?"

"And all the stones around it?"

Josh shrugged. "Some people have strange hobbies. A friend of mine knew this guy who built giant movie spaceships in his garage. Like, the size of cars."

Another head-shake from Noah, much more adamant this time. "Beau wouldn't touch the glass obelisk, and even if she did she couldn't've moved it alone."

He glanced ahead. "So it's *not* the glass obelisk?"

"No. It looks like it, but that's about three-quarters of a mile over . . ." Noah turned, raised his arm to point, then looked at the sundial's big fin again as he walked past it. Up at the cliffs. At the distant white tower of the Ice Castle poking up above the trees. Another frown crossed his face.

"What?"

Noah's frown deepened into a scowl. "The sundial's pointing the wrong way. Somebody messed it up." He tugged on the straps of his backpack and kept marching.

Sam's heart bounced in his chest as they approached the sundial, like leaning in for a first kiss. The books had described it as somewhat patinaed, but that seemed to be another instance of young Noah's—of Billy's childlike view of things. The sundial's big fin—something Gabe would know the actual name of, because he knew all those odd trivia-worthy words—the big fin looked like an archaeological relic. The greenish-gray corrosion coated the whole thing like a thick, crusty coat of paint.

He stopped to gaze at it. Couldn't see any disturbance in the stones around the base, so whatever had moved it had been careful. Or had done it a long time ago. And there was the creepy future plaque! He debated grabbing a few quick pictures with his phone—him and the actual sundial from the valley—and then Parker moved past him. Noah hadn't slowed his pace, still heading for the far tree line.

"Can we stop for a second?" Sam called after Noah.

"No."

Sam sighed. Pulled out his phone. Got a few quick shots of the sundial and the base and the plaque.

Josh tapped his knuckles against the metal triangle and made a low noise in his throat. Their eyes met for a moment. Josh pushed his lips together.

"What's wrong?"

Josh looked at him. "Nothing."

"He knows what he's doing."

"Maybe."

"Maybe? He's Dino Boy."

Josh gave a half-shrug. "Look," he said. "I'm a people person. I know people. My whole job is keeping them happy and getting them to buy product, right?"

"I guess."

"I haven't known him long, but I've got good instincts. Your professor . . . he's a tough-sell guy, because he's never going to admit he's wrong. Even when he knows he's wrong."

Noah and Parker were almost forty feet away now, passing the obelisk. Noah gave a quick glance over his shoulder. "Probably shouldn't touch that. Just in case."

Josh gave a semi-acknowledging wave to Noah.

"What do you think he's wrong about?" asked Sam.

"I don't know. Maybe nothing. I just know he's got that never-budge, tough-sell vibe."

Noah and Parker continued on across the overgrown plaza. Josh followed. Sam took a few strides after Josh, tried to space himself between the front and back of their loose line so Olivia and Logan wouldn't feel like they were getting left behind. Although he wasn't sure Logan would even notice. He was still just plodding along, reaching out to run his fingers along the sundial.

Jesus, why weren't they all in the same condition? Kyle'd been ripped apart right in front of them by a dinosaur. Close enough to right in front of them, anyway.

Maybe that was it, Sam told himself. Maybe it wasn't so much that he was a bad person, just that the whole situation was so surreal. His brain had shoved Kyle's death into a place where he could walk away and not have to deal with it right now.

That sounded like him.

The glass obelisk gleamed in the sunlight next to him, looking like the kind of thing you'd find in the courtyard of some big corporate office. He pulled out his phone and snapped a few photos as he walked past. All the engraved runes looked just like the ones on the granite obelisk, but it'd be good to compare them.

Ahead of him, Noah pointed up at the cliffs as they approached the trees. "See that knobby peak up there?"

Parker matched his steps, shaded her eyes from the overhead sun with her hand. "The one with the reddish stripe?"

"Yes. We want to be to the right of it."

The battery bar at the top of the screen read 16 percent. Sam hadn't charged his phone on the bus. Not since yesterday morning. Probably not going to find an outlet anytime soon, either. He held the button to power it off. If they were stuck here for a while, maybe they could make some kind of generator or battery out of prehistoric potatoes or something to keep their assorted devices . . .

Battery.

Electricity.

The glass obelisk.

His memories fell in line, he turned his head, and the sound hit him like a slap. The flash burned his eyes, brighter than the overhead sun. So much light there were no shadows. Too clear. Too sharp. Olivia, caught in mid-step, her eyes wide. Logan, one hand holding Olivia's, the other stretched back to graze the surface of the obelisk as they walked past. His fingertips were hidden in the blinding arc of electricity surging over them.

By the time Sam turned fully around the lightning crack was echoing away and Olivia and Logan crumpled to the ground.

He ran back. Reached for Logan's shoulder, stopped himself, looked over at the obelisk. Logan had tipped to the side as he fell away from it and he'd—*Jesus*, his hair was on fire! Sam dropped and his knees thudded against the flagstones. He patted the man's head with his palms, crushing the little licks of flame.

"Oh my GOD," shouted someone. Josh? Parker? In the corner of his eye someone checked Olivia.

"What happened?"

"They touched the obelisk," shouted Noah. "I said they shouldn't touch it."

Blood streaked Logan's face. Under his nose, out of his mouth, out of his eyes and ears. Like he'd sneezed blood and spit up blood and cried blood all at the same time, so much blood Sam couldn't see his eyes and holy fucking Jesus he still had eyes, right? Had his eyes burst? Burned up? They were just covered with blood. They had to be. Where were his glasses? Had they been thrown off when his eyes—

"Olivia?" Definitely Parker. "Olivia, say something. Olivia?!"

"She's breathing. She's got a pulse."

Pulse. Sam reached for Logan's wrist and saw the charred fingers. Hot dogs burned black at a cookout. Smoke, or maybe steam, curled up from the tips, out from under the cracked fingernails. Sam froze, just for a moment, then set his fingers against the other man's wrist. Then his throat. He looked at the bloody face again. At the scorched fingers. At the unmoving chest.

Someone was next to him. Josh. "Is he . . ."

"He's dead," Sam croaked. "He's dead."

"No," said Noah. "No, no, no."

Josh checked for a pulse too. Wrist. Throat. Dropped his ear down low, close to Logan's mouth. He sat back on his heels.

Sam looked at Noah. "The glass obelisk. It gives lethal shocks, like lightning. You saw it kill a raptor once."

"I told them not to touch it."

"You said we *shouldn't* touch it," yelled Josh.

"It's the same thing!"

"The last one had a fucking force field!"

"Olivia's not waking up," said Parker. "She's breathing but I can't wake her up."

Sam tore his eyes away from Noah and crawl-shuffled across the stones to Olivia. A thin line of blood ran from her nose, and a drop beaded up on the corner of her mouth, but nothing like the torrent that'd boiled up out of Logan. She might've been asleep, if not for the fact that she didn't open her eyes as Parker kept shaking her shoulder.

Sam looked back at Logan. At the smoke curling off his head and fingers. The thought of cookouts crossed his mind again. The smell. The plaza smelled like a backyard barbecue now.

He turned his head and threw up for the second time today. Mostly sharp, bitter stomach acid. And then the image of Kyle in the dinosaur's mouth slammed through his thoughts and the guilt worm twisted in his stomach and he threw up again.

Sam turned his back to the obelisk, to the body—to *Logan*—and Olivia, and took three deep breaths. He spat all the liquid out of his mouth, wiped his lips on his sleeve, then spat again. He leaned back and stared up at the sky and tried not to think about the two people he'd seen killed in as many hours. A shape soared by up above, its long tail stretched out behind it. Rhamphorhynchus. Two more joined it, and the three of them swooped off to the left and vanished above the treetops.

Parker stopped shaking Olivia. Josh checked the unconscious woman's face in a surprisingly professional manner. Her cheeks rested in his hands, his fingertips settled around her eyes, gently moving her eyelids and spreading them open. Sam could see little shifts as Josh did his examination. Tiny spasms and tics worked their way back and forth through Olivia's body, like someone about to wake from a dream.

Sam counted to ten, but she didn't wake up.

"She's out cold," Josh said. "Totally unresponsive."

"What does that mean?" asked Noah.

"It means she's unconscious and I don't know when she's going to wake up."

"But she's going to." Noah phrased it more like a statement, but Sam heard the question beneath it.

"No idea. I think Logan took most of the, the shock, but that doesn't mean she didn't get enough to fry her brain."

"It's enough to kill a dinosaur," said Sam. "That's in two of the books."

Noah looked at the ground. "It's a lot," he agreed.

Parker stared at the obelisk. Back at Olivia. "But she's moving. She's not brain-dead, she's just . . . asleep."

They all watched Olivia twitch, waiting for her eyes to flutter open. Sam knew part of it was that nobody wanted to look at Logan. The breeze had carried away the worst of the smells, but it still lingered in the air, making Sam's stomach churn every time it struck his nose.

Olivia still didn't wake up.

"We . . ." Noah stopped. Cleared his throat. "We need to get moving."

Parker stared at him with wide eyes. "What?"

"We need to find Beau . . . and the source of the smoke. And we don't want to be out in the open at night."

"We were out in the open last night," said Josh.

"We were higher up then. On the valley floor . . . it's less safe."

Parker snorted out a laugh with sharp edges. "Less safe?"

Sam tried to block them out. Tried not to think about things. Played to his strength, and that strength was avoidance. If he remembered right, Olivia stood four inches taller than him. He guessed she was maybe fifty or more pounds lighter. Less than he could bench press on his irregular trips to the gym. "I can carry her," he said.

They all turned their attention to him.

"I mean, I'm not going to be able to—to sprint or anything, but I'm pretty sure I can carry her for a little while."

"I'm not sure we should move her," said Josh.

"We can't stay here," Noah said.

"And we can't leave her," said Sam. "So I'm carrying her."

Josh shook his head. "We should make a . . . a stretcher. Something so she'll bounce around less."

Sam thought about it. "Yeah. Yeah, okay."

Josh pointed two fingers at Noah's massive pack. "You've got to have some rope or something in there, right? Maybe a heavy poncho or something?"

"I've got zip ties. And a small tarp."

"Fantastic."

Parker's hands twitched. "What about . . . Logan?"

The distant trees made a quiet whisking noise as their needles brushed back and forth against each other. Noah broke it with a deep, sighing breath. "We may . . . we'll need to leave him."

"Jesus," whispered Josh.

"We can't," said Parker. "I mean, Kyle was . . . we can't."

"We don't have a choice," Noah said. "We can't carry both of them. I'm sorry."

Parker stood up. Brushed at her knees. Stared at the obelisk.

Sam tried to control his breathing. "We can't—we're not leaving him sitting out in the open like this. For things to—to get at."

Parker nodded. "Yeah."

"We don't have time," said Noah.

"We've got to," Sam said.

Noah opened his mouth again. Shut it. "You're right. I'm sorry. You're right."

Josh kicked at one of the flagstones. "I don't think we're going to be able to dig. Unless you've got a jackhammer in that pack, too?"

Noah shook his head.

"Rocks then." Parker looked at the trees around them. "Should we move him closer to the trees? Or would he be better off here?"

They all waited for Noah to answer. He shook his head. "I think . . . as I remember, the smaller animals tend to avoid the open spaces, but the bigger ones might be able to knock the stones away and . . . well . . ."

Parker nodded. "We'll move him away from this thing," she said, waving a hand at the obelisk, "but not all the way into the trees. Maybe far enough into the clearing to make some things cautious."

"I think I saw some good-sized rocks on the way in," said Sam, remembering the trek through the woods. "And some fallen branches. We can probably circle the tree line and find . . . enough."

"Should one of us stay with Olivia?"

"Nothing should bother her," said Noah. "If one of the big ones shows up . . . well, there's not much we could do."

"Great pep talk," said Josh.

"Sorry."

They spread out to the edges of the plaza, gathering every stone they could easily lift. On his sixth or seventh stone, Sam realized he was piling them next to Logan, not on him. Not on his body. The others were doing the same. It took them half an hour to build four piles of stones, most of them somewhere between a softball and a watermelon in size.

They all stood around Logan—around the body—for a minute.

Josh cleared his throat. "I know I'm the outsider here but we shouldn't . . . we should keep his backpack."

Parker let out a sigh.

"We're going to be here for a year, we need every advantage we can get."

Sam looked at him. "You want to take his boots, too?"

"I'm just saying . . ."

"He's right," Noah said. He took in a breath like he might say more, but he left it at that.

They rolled Logan onto his face, slid the straps over his shoulders and down his arms. They spent another moment looking at the back of his head, and then Parker pressed her lips together and pulled on his arm, flipping him onto his back again. "We shouldn't leave him face down."

Sam nodded his agreement.

Another minute passed. Josh crouched, picked up a football-sized rock, and set it against Logan's thigh. He propped another one next to it, then set a third so it sat on top of the other two, resting against the leg.

Sam picked up one of the stones from his pile and placed it on Logan's wrist. Parker did the same across from him, putting her rock near the elbow. They placed eight more stones before Noah moved his first one into place.

There was a word for a pile of rocks like this, a stone grave. Sam couldn't remember it. Another clever word Gabe would know.

It took them ten minutes, once they got going. Sam didn't want to place a stone against Logan's head or neck. He kept hoping Logan would cough or blink, would miraculously be alive.

But Logan never coughed. Never blinked. Never moved. There was no other part of him left to cover, and Parker ended up being the one who placed the first stone against his neck. Josh set one by the top of his head. Sam put a larger one on the other side of his neck. It only took eight more gently-placed stones and Logan was gone.

Once he was out of sight, they placed the remaining rocks much faster.

Putting the stretcher together didn't take long. Josh selected two long pieces of wood from the four or five they'd gathered. Broke another one over his knee. It took him maybe ten minutes with Noah's zip ties and the tarp. Sam got an arm behind Olivia's shoulders and, with some help from Josh, moved her onto the stretcher. They used a shirt from Logan's pack to brace her head.

Sam traded looks with Josh. Picked up the end by Olivia's head. Josh lifted the other end, then carefully switched his hands so he was facing the other way.

Noah gave them a moment to get settled. "Got her?"

Sam adjusted his arms. Olivia was a little heavier than he expected. Less soft, more muscle. "Yeah."

Noah double-checked the distant cliffside, and they headed back into the forest.

11

PARKER

Parker wanted to walk alone, but the guide guy, Josh, kept slowing his and Sam's pace to make sure she didn't get left behind. She wasn't sure if it was some honest chivalry-safety thing or a half-assed attempt to flirt. He struck her as the kind of person who did a lot of things half-assed.

Noah still had the lead. He'd go a little faster through the woods, remember the others behind him, and slow back down. His mood reminded Parker of when he sometimes had to teach undergrad classes. Understanding people couldn't keep up, but still annoyed he had to slow down.

Parker rolled her shoulders, adjusting Logan's pack. It was a little heavier than she'd expected and didn't sit great on her narrow shoulders, but it wasn't too bad. She figured she could carry it as long as they needed.

Sam and Josh seemed to be doing okay with the stretcher. Josh seemed to be struggling with it the most, although he was trying hard to keep it level and steady. Parker wouldn't've guessed Sam for the strong one, but he had thick arms and legs and she didn't know much about him.

They kept walking. Half an hour after they buried Logan beneath the stones, the forest ground became rocky. Parker was pretty sure most of them had noticed it, even though nobody'd said anything. Then again, this was all familiar to Noah. And Sam didn't seem surprised by it, either.

It annoyed her that Noah had this whole secret life she didn't know about. She'd worked with him for over three years and never even suspected. She'd heard of Dino Boy, sure, but she'd heard of pogs and the Macarena, too. Things that'd been big enough of a phenomenon to be dimly remembered and heard of years later, even by people who hadn't even been alive at the time.

It bothered her that Sam knew things and she didn't.

The patchwork forest bothered her, too. It had to be planted like this, groves of assorted types of trees that had slowly grown together. But why? Why such a wide variety? And why was the ground different? She could maybe understand someone planting groups of different trees, but why change the ground?

Unless . . . had all of it ended up here by accident? Just a big quilt of random locations? Noah had fallen through the wormhole by accident. Maybe over the years it had sucked up whole sections of forests from all over the world, with the soil and rocks under them.

They walked for another ten minutes before Josh kicked at a long, low rock. It made a low, hollow thump, almost a clang. He glanced over at her, opened his eyes wide and raised his brows, but kept walking forward with the stretcher.

She slowed to look at the rock and recognized it as the back bumper of a car. The bumper, part of a half-rusted trunk, cracked brake lights, and holy shit was there a whole car here, buried nose down in the ground?

A deep impression marked the ground maybe two feet from the car's taillight. Parker thought maybe someone had lifted a rock away, which made her think of the mound of stones they'd left back in the clearing. This would've been a big one, though, going off the size of the hole.

Then she registered the flattened pine cone in the bottom and the toe divots on one side. A footprint, crumbling on the edges, but still big enough for a basketball to sit in it. She turned her head, could see a few more prints in either direction, half hidden with old needles and twigs.

Dinosaur? Elephant? Shit, were they the tracks of some future animal that hadn't even evolved yet from their point of view?

She took a few quick steps across the uneven ground and got caught up with the others. It didn't take long. Noah had moved ahead, but Josh and Sam had slowed down again to wait for her.

Another change in the forest. Palm trees again. Huge, thick ones, at least fifty or sixty feet tall. She had no idea how long it took palm trees to grow that big. Waist-high ferns dotted the ground. She looked for a clear line where the new trees began, the stitches in the patchwork forest, but couldn't find it. Just a long stretch where the trees changed from one type to another.

What time was it anyway? Almost an hour since Olivia . . . since the obelisk. Parker realized she hadn't looked at her phone once today. She wasn't even sure if the time it told her would mean anything here. According to Eastern Standard Time, it might be one in the morning right now. She looked up through the trees, trying to get a sense of the sun's position in the sky, but palm fronds blocked her view.

More walking. Josh slowed the stretcher and asked if they could rest for a minute. Parker checked her phone out of curiosity. Four twenty-three in the afternoon. Back in the present, anyway. Also, her battery was at 21 percent, even though she'd fully charged it on the bus. Probably roaming, trying to find a signal. She thumbed the menu down and flipped on airplane mode. Then she shut it off. Probably a good idea to save as much life as she could.

Another half hour of walking and the light got brighter. The faint fireplace smell of wood smoke tickled her nose. Ten more minutes and the trees stopped at another clear, distinct line. Ahead of them stretched a field of tall grass, and beyond that even taller, stalky plants. A little over a hundred yards to the dense grove of trees on the far side.

Five dark lines curled up from beyond the grove. Maybe six sources, with two of them close enough that their smoke curled together into one thin column. Whatever was burning was past the distant grove. A big campground? Had Noah's sister built a whole homestead, maybe, in the years he'd been gone?

Josh coughed into his shoulder. Nodded at the field. "You said the big ones aren't scared of open ground, right?"

"Yep. When I was little we had a few close calls and tried to avoid all the open spaces after that. We stuck to the forests and the cliffs."

"So this was a big no-go zone, I guess?" Parker tried to make it sound lighthearted.

Noah stared out at the field.

Sam and Josh slowly lowered the stretcher, setting Olivia gently on the ground. Sam adjusted the shirt under her head. Parker thought about helping too, but it'd be weird now for all of them to be clustered around her.

Instead, she let the backpack slide off her shoulders and moved to stand by Noah. His gaze swept back and forth across the field. A sound echoed across it, like a giant parrot letting out an epic belch. It happened again, at a higher pitch, then a third time in a weird, overlapping harmony that made her think of whales.

She glanced at him. "Any idea what that was?"

Noah glanced at her. "Triceratops, I think. Maybe two of them."

"Really?"

"Yep. They sound a bit intimidating, but they've got the personality of cows. Maybe more stubborn."

"Huh."

The grass looked like wild wheat, maybe, and stood as tall as Parker's neck. She could see brighter green leaves standing up farther into the field, even taller than the grass. Technically not open ground, but they'd be almost blind if they walked into it.

She looked at the tall grass again. At the heights and lines and rows. "Is this . . . a field? I mean, a farmer's field? Like, grain or something?"

Josh looked at the tall grass, down at the base. "It . . . it does look pretty regular. Like someone spaced it out."

Noah shook his head. "It's not."

Parker crouched to peer at the grass. It didn't grow in rows, like she pictured fields on a farm, but there seemed to be a flow to it, like wood grain. "Are you sure?"

"Positive."

Sam grunted, stretched his arms over his head. "Didn't you and your sister have a garden?"

"We did," said Noah, "but the whole thing could've fit in a two-car garage. Nothing close to this."

"Maybe," Parker said, "the wormhole scooped up somebody's farm and it grew wild."

Sam let out a pair of gasps that might've been a laugh. "A farmer in Kansas walked out one morning and thought somebody had stolen his wheat field?"

She shrugged. "Maybe. Or in Siberia. Or India. It had to come from somewhere."

A slow, twangy *wowl* echoed across the field, pitched low enough Parker felt the sound bounce off her skin. Noah twitched as a second *wowl* washed over them. The third one stretched out long and stopped abruptly.

Parker waited a moment for another note. "What the hell was that?"

"I know that sound," said Sam.

"That's close," she said. "I could feel it."

Noah stretched up, trying to see over the tall grass. "Is it some kind of horn?"

Sam wobbled his head. "Maybe? It sounds like—"

"Australia," interrupted Josh.

"Yeah." Sam nodded in agreement.

Parker looked at each of them. "Australia?"

Josh shrugged. "Every movie or commercial I've ever seen about Australia has that same *wohh-wohh-wohhh* sound in the background. That's what it sounds like."

Her mind put the sound in context. "Goddamn. You're right."

"We can figure out what it is later," said Noah. "Let's go straight across."

Josh coughed. "I thought we just said open ground was bad."

"It's not open ground. And it'll be a lot faster to go straight through than to go around."

Sam glanced down at Olivia. "Maybe?"

"It looks pretty open to me," said Josh. "Definitely open to those T-Rexes."

Noah waved a hand at him. "They weren't T-Rexes."

"Not really my point."

"We'll be fine. Fifteen, maybe twenty minutes of walking through the grain."

"'Beware he who walks behind the rows,'" said Josh.

"What?"

"From a movie. About how safe cornfields are."

Noah nodded. "Great, then."

Parker lifted Logan's backpack. It felt like someone had slipped a few rocks into it. She got it over her shoulders again while Josh and Sam got Olivia's stretcher back up. The two men murmured quietly to each other as they balanced Olivia between them.

Sam met Parker's gaze. "How long have we been walking?"

"All day or since . . ." She gestured at Olivia.

"Since."

"A little over an hour and a half, I think? Maybe two? Why?"

Josh shook his head, gave a quick nod upward. "It's only a little after noon."

Parker glanced up at the sun, almost directly overhead. "Fuck," she muttered.

"Yeah," Sam said in agreement.

She held out her hand, looked at the shadow on the ground. "How's that even possible? It feels like hours since we woke up. Hey."

"What?"

She glanced up again. "If the sun's that close to directly overhead, we're near the equator."

"Everyone ready?" asked Noah.

"We're near the equator," Parker said. She wiggled her fingers, watched the shadow-digits move, then waved the hand up at the cliffs. "This valley's in South America or Africa."

Noah shrugged. "Maybe."

"Maybe?"

"The sun acts weird here."

"The *sun* acts weird?" echoed Sam.

Noah turned, reached out, and spread the tall grass with his hands. They headed into the field.

Moving through the tall grass turned out to be a challenge. Parker tried using one hand to hold the backpack in place, grabbing both straps in a fist on her chest, while the other hand went up to protect her eyes and nose from the swaying grass. The grunts behind her meant Sam and Josh were probably having the same problem. Maybe worse since they had to keep both hands on Olivia's stretcher.

Another seedy tassel tapped Parker's cheek and the smell danced across her nose. She had no idea what a grain plant smelled like, but one scent overwhelmed everything else here. The grass might not be a crop, but it dominated the field.

Noah pushed more stalks aside, stepped through the V he'd made, and lurched to a stop.

Parker pushed after him, battering the grass away. "What's up?" she asked, even though she saw what was up before the words were done.

The red figure loomed over them, arms spread wide, a large gray hood covering its head. Parker felt her stomach churn at the thought of someone crucified out here in the field, but just as quickly she realized the outfit was empty. A big orange-red jumpsuit of thick cloth—thick enough it still had some heft, even with nothing in it. The dangling cuffs were frayed and torn, she could see ragged, off-color squares where pockets, or maybe patches, had been torn away, and a few slashes across the torso. A heavy, rusted zipper ran down the front from neck to crotch. The post it hung on had been driven into the ground off of a narrow path of hard-packed dirt. It divided the possible-grain behind them and the bright green stalks ahead.

She looked into the stiff, empty hood. "It's a scarecrow."

"It's a *spacesuit*," said Sam.

And as quick as it had gone from body to scarecrow, Parker saw the tattered, out-of-context outfit for what it was. The heavy red bodysuit with vents for hoses. The small, white helmet with a thick layer of dust on it, the visor gone and the seals rotted to thin threads. Something old-school, from early space exploration, when the goal was just to get someone into orbit and bring them back alive.

Noah took a slow step forward, stretched up on his toes, tried to reach the brim of the helmet, but couldn't. Barely touched the top of the suit.

She heard feet shuffle behind them. Sam and Josh trying to pivot in the grass with the stretcher. Sam craned his neck to look at the scarecrow. "There's letters above the visor, where it should be. Pretty faded and covered with crap. Looks like . . ."

"Coop," said Josh. "Maybe it's another call sign?"

"C-C-C-P." Sam relaxed his neck. "It's Russian. A cosmonaut."

"Soviet," Parker clarified. "Somebody's using a Soviet-era spacesuit as a scarecrow."

Josh let out a dry laugh. "You think this scares those little raptor-birds?"

"It's making my skin crawl a little, so maybe?" Parker reached out, touched it. The fabric had the look and slick feel of old nylon. "How do you think it got here?"

"They probably put the pole in first. It'd be too awkward to stand it up with the suit on it."

"No, I meant . . . y'know, never mind."

Sam cleared his throat. "I remember reading an old conspiracy theory that the Soviets sent up a bunch of cosmonauts before Gagarin, then hushed it up when things went wrong."

"Wrong how?"

He managed the best shrug he could while holding up one end of the stretcher. "Nobody knows. Assuming any of it's even true."

Parker looked up at the old-fashioned suit. "Gagarin went up in . . . April?"

"Yeah."

"So if they'd tried someone eight months earlier, the previous September, they would've launched them into space just as Earth passed by the wormhole."

"One small step for Mother Russia," Josh murmured.

Parker checked to see Noah's reaction to the idea. He didn't seem to have registered any of it. He kept staring at the spacesuit.

Parker touched his arm. "Noah?"

He snapped out of whatever rabbit hole his brain had been in. Looked at her. At the others. "This is wrong. None of this should be here."

"Beau could've put it up while you were gone," said Sam.

Noah shook his head. He started to say something, shook his head again, and marched down the path, more or less in the direction they'd been heading.

Josh sighed and murmured something to himself.

Sam looked after Noah, then to Parker. "What are we doing?"

"We're going after him." She shrugged the backpack higher up on her shoulders. Someone had packed more stones into it. Was she this out of shape? She wasn't a gym rat or anything, but she never thought she would've gotten tired this fast. Sam and Josh looked beat, too.

They headed down the path after Noah.

Now Parker could see the tassels at the top of the bright green stalks, and the tight, coarse leaves curled into cylinders and topped with silk. "It really is a cornfield," she said over her shoulder as they trudged down the path.

"Dinosaurs, electric obelisks, scarecrows, evil cornfields," wheezed Josh. "We're all gonna be dead by tomorrow."

"Why is it an evil cornfield?" asked Sam.

"Well, one, it's a cornfield at the dawn of time. Two, it's a cornfield. They're all evil. It's why they make mazes out of them."

Up ahead, Noah had reached an intersection in the rows of corn. He stepped back, peered through the stalks at the distant cliffs, and turned left. The corn immediately hid him from sight.

"You know what else is weird?" Josh tossed out.

Parker fought the urge—the *need*—to roll her eyes.

"I think this is modern corn. Like, corn on the cob. Not, y'know, early, precrossbreeding corn."

"How would you know?"

"Because it looks like corn from the grocery store?"

Parker turned the corner after Noah. The corn fell away a few dozen yards ahead to show a field of mud and low plants that stretched at least two hundred feet to the grove of trees. She could see the dark lines of smoke drifting up into the air from beyond the trees. This close she could also see how tight together the saplings were, more like a dense grove of bamboo than regular trees.

Then her vision shifted and once again she saw past the optical illusion and mentally kicked herself. She was supposed to be better than this at seeing things for what they were. Everything about this place messed with her brain.

They weren't trees, they were logs, chopped smooth and straight. The greenery she'd thought topped them belonged to much taller trees in the distance. Most of the logs stood upright, about sixteen feet tall, and formed a wall like an old western frontier fort, complete with the pointed tops. A few of them stood out at angles, like massive spikes pointed out at the field.

"What the hell," said Sam behind her.

Noah staggered forward, his head looking from one end of the wall to the other. Parker caught a glimpse of his face. Saw the confusion. The anger in his clenched fists.

Sam and Josh sidestepped up to her, Olivia swaying between them. Josh gaped at the wall. "Do you think they built that to keep the dinosaurs out?"

"Or King Kong."

Josh shook his head. "Kong's huge now. He could step right over that."

Parker felt the overwhelming urge to respond swell up in her chest and fought it back down.

People moved at the top of the walls, but they were too far to make out more than general shapes and spots of color. And what looked like spears. Neanderthals, maybe? A tall, off-white banner stood up on a pole, hanging slightly to one side and almost looking more like a sail.

"This shouldn't be here," Noah said.

"What do you mean?"

He shook his head. "This. All of this. These fields. The spacesuit. This . . . this wall. This is all wrong."

"Hello there," called out a voice with a thick accent.

A tall, lean man stood off to their right, maybe a dozen yards away, his hands behind his back. The first thought that danced through Parker's mind was stranded Tom Hanks standing on the shore of his little island. The second was the man wasn't hiding anything behind his back. He stood—what did the military call it?—*at ease.* His clothes had the soft shape and faded colors that came from years of use, and his stubbly beard spoke of months away from a good razor. He wore a round, pointed straw hat, a lot like the one her grandmother used to wear when she was gardening. Tucked into his belt was a long pale stick of what looked like bamboo.

Not a Neanderthal. She didn't think so, anyway. In fact, she was pretty sure he was white under all that tanned skin.

"English, yeah?" he said to them.

"Don't answer," said Noah.

"Yeah," Josh replied with a big nod.

"I said not to answer."

"And I ignored you. Don't worry, I'm a people person." Josh took in a breath, raised his voice. "We're damn glad to see you, man. To see anyone."

The man gave them a slow, over-polite nod. "When did you arrive?"

She noticed he made no effort to move closer. And his accent gnawed at her. German, maybe? Soft, but definitely there.

"Yesterday," Josh answered. "Last night. We . . . we've had a bad day."

Another slow nod from the man. One hand came out from behind his back, then the other. Not hiding anything, like Parker had guessed. In fact, he moved like he was trying to keep them calm. Like he was dealing with a group of unpredictable, potentially dangerous animals.

A little chill danced up her back, and she fought the urge to look behind them, to assure herself a dinosaur wasn't looming over them.

The man pointed at the stockade wall with two fingers. "We have food, water, and shelter. You will be safe inside. But we should be quick. We were preparing to lock down for the night."

Sam looked up at the sun. "Already?"

Noah made a little sound Parker couldn't identify. A snort? A laugh? "Give us a moment," he called out.

The tall man raised an eyebrow.

Noah leaned his head back, still looking at the man. Lowered his voice to whisper. "I'm not sure we should go with him."

Parker took a breath. Tried to use her best please-explain-it-to-me voice. "Why not?"

"Because this shouldn't be here. This is all . . . wrong."

"Noah!"

"My cave isn't far from here. We should go there."

"I'm trying to be positive," said Josh in a salesman-ish tone, "but you haven't had the best track record today about where things are."

"I know every inch of this valley," Noah said.

"Except the giant robot. And the weird rocks. And the evil cornfield. And this big-ass fort which apparently has several people in it. One of whom might be your sister, for all you know."

"None of which were here before."

"Thirteen years ago, right?"

"Noah," said Parker, "we're all exhausted. Even you. And they can't keep carrying Olivia."

"Yeah," agreed Josh.

Sam said nothing.

Across from them, the tall man took a few steps toward the stockade. Big, obvious steps. Not trying to sneak away from them. He locked eyes with Parker for a moment, and the overwhelming sense she got from him was concern.

Of course, she thought she'd had a good sense of Noah for the past three years and it turned out he had a whole secret life.

One of the figures up on the wall—definitely a man, wearing a sky-blue shirt with long sleeves—waved to them.

"I say we go with him," said Parker.

"I agree," said Josh. He looked over his shoulder, across Olivia's unconscious body to Sam.

Sam didn't meet his eyes. Or Parker's. "I think we should do whatever Noah thinks. He's the expert here."

Parker looked at Noah. They all did. Noah looked at each of them in turn. At the wall. Back at the field and the forest beyond it. Back at them. At Olivia.

"Fine," he said. Frustration dripped off the word.

Parker gave him a moment to sulk. "Do you want to lead us over there?"

Noah turned without a word. The tall man watched them come closer and then turned and continued toward the big fort. He kept the same distance. Again, Parker got the sense of someone dealing with nervous animals, trying not to alarm them.

They followed a zigzag, single-file path through the low plants to the wooden wall. Parker wasn't sure, but the plants looked like they might have some kind of beans, or maybe peas, on them. She heard a huff of breath, glanced back, saw Sam and Josh maneuvering Olivia's stretcher through the bean plants.

They came out of the gardens to open ground. Maybe fifty feet from the stockade wall now. All whole logs, Parker noticed. Not a single plank or board. It's how it had confused her at first. She saw a few metallic glints here and there. Nails? Spikes? The whole thing looked solid as all hell.

Two faces peered down at her from the top. A woman, maybe Japanese, a couple years older than Parker. A slightly younger black woman. They followed Parker and the others as they walked along the path.

The tall man led them around the corner of the wall. A greater-than-ninety-degree corner, Parker noticed, which made her wonder if the wall was shaped like a pentagon or hexagon or maybe just turned with the terrain. And then she saw the doors. Bare wood, with rough boards across it, like old barn doors. Or big castle doors in fantasy movies.

Two people stood outside, a man and woman, waving them forward. The white guy looked to be as old as the one leading them, with a ratty, gray-streaked beard, and matching hair tied back by an old red bandana. He wore patched jeans, a green military vest like something from a Vietnam movie, and held a thin walking stick. The woman looked Latin, maybe, with dark wavy hair. She wore a ragged sundress, also patched.

Noah took it all in. Parker glanced at his face. Awe? Denial?

The soldier-looking man exchanged nods with their escort, then gestured them closer. "Come on, people. Let's move!"

"What's the rush?" she asked, slowing down.

"Lady, these doors are closing in five minutes and they're not opening again until morning. Which side of 'em you're on is up to you."

The woman stepped forward, looking past Noah and Parker. "Is your friend hurt?"

Parker followed her gaze to Olivia on the stretcher. "We don't know. She touched a . . . a monolith and got some kind of shock."

"The glass obelisk," said Sam.

The woman's eyes went wide, and she turned back to the open gate. "Someone get Monique!" she called out. "They've got wounded!"

Another figure stepped through the gate with the sort of awkward pace of someone who'd been moving quick and then tried to slow down and look casual. Chinese, maybe. At that point in life where he could easily be anywhere between forty or sixty, like Tony Leung. His weathered clothes had been restitched and patched so many times they looked like they'd been made from an old quilt.

"They're being slow," the soldier said without looking at the other man. "Got to close up."

"It'll be fine, Em." The man in the patchwork clothes looked at

Parker, at the rest of them, and smiled. "Welcome. Please come inside and we can explain everything."

"Who are you?" demanded Noah. "Who are all of you? What are you doing here?"

The man's smile shifted a little. Parker recognized the new expression. A patient smile. "My name's Qiang. I'm the village elder. Or mayor, if you prefer. Welcome to Roanoke."

12

JOSH

Josh's mind had been racing for a few days now. Granted, falling a billion years into the past through a wormhole had spun his concerns in a new direction. After watching someone get eaten by a dinosaur and seeing two more people get struck by magical lightning, though, he felt like he'd maxed out his norepinephrine reserves for the day.

Then Qiang had casually dropped the name of the little fort or village and Josh's heart was racing again. He hadn't heard the story of the lost colony since high school, but it'd left an impression. It had on the professor and Parker, too, going off their faces. He felt Sam's grip shift through the poles of the stretcher, like he'd almost dropped his end.

Noah looked like he was almost choking, really, and then spat out, "Roanoke?"

"Please." Qiang stepped aside and raised a hand, directing them through the big wooden doors. "Em can be a little overenthusiastic, but he's right. We need to close the gate."

The old soldier guy snorted. Flexed his fingers on the long wooden shaft he held. A spear or maybe a javelin? Was there a difference? Probably. Not Josh's field of expertise.

He looked at Noah. Realized Sam and Parker were, too. Noah looked at the wooden wall. Sighed. Nodded.

They walked through the gate into a small crowd of people.

Parker let the backpack slide off her shoulders. The wavy-haired woman caught it before it hit the ground. Josh and Sam staggered forward and another figure appeared, a brown-skinned woman a foot taller than Sam with an oversized, glossy eye patch. She scooped Olivia up off the stretcher, hefting the unconscious woman up with the energy of someone who hadn't been carrying a person for . . . however long it had been. "I've got her," she told Josh in a husky voice. "It's okay."

He glanced back at Sam. Made an effort to straighten his stiff fingers and let go of the stretcher. Someone else stepped forward, a bearded, burly man in ren faire clothes, and gathered it up under his arm. The woman with the wavy hair had Sam's backpack now as well as the one she'd gotten from Parker. It felt like a good neighbor thing, helping you with your luggage. Or maybe porters at a nice hotel offering to take your bags. The wavy-haired woman said something to Noah, gestured at his well-stuffed backpack but he didn't seem to hear. Or maybe he just ignored her.

Inside the wall smelled like firewood and sawdust. Dirt paths—almost dirt roads—stretched off in three different directions from the gate, and Josh could see at least two dozen buildings made of logs, bamboo, rough planks, and piled stone. It was like a hundred architectural styles from all through history had a wild, monthlong orgy and the houses here were the resulting children. He could see cottages and large sheds and holy crap a windmill? He'd seen one of the big arms from outside and thought it was some kind of flag or banner.

About thirty men and women stood around them, but not in a creepy way. Less a crowd and more like a half dozen small groups. Most of them kept back a few yards, giving Josh and the others plenty of space. Curious onlookers trying hard not to look *too* interested. They all wore various levels of threadbare, sun-washed clothes. Two or three had baggy hoods, and the high sun put dark shadows across their faces.

Behind them, the middle-aged soldier guy, Em, grabbed a loop of thick rope with his free hand and dragged one door shut. Then he stepped back out and pulled the other one closed. Josh watched as another man lowered a bar across the doors, and Em helped him drop a second bar as well.

Qiang still stood close, still smiling reassuringly. The tall woman holding Olivia stayed close, too, and the wavy-haired woman now holding their backpacks. It all felt a little rehearsed to Josh. A sales routine—a script—they'd used a few times before. He guessed it was supposed to reassure them. Em looked like the only person with a weapon, that tall spear, but Josh had noticed some people up on the wall who probably . . .

The woman holding Olivia didn't have an eye patch. The skin around her eye was made of dark blue plastic. The eye inside the glossy socket shined a little brighter and more vividly than the one on the other side of her face. One of her hands curling up under Olivia's shoulders wore a skintight glove made of the same dark blue material. Or maybe the woman's whole hand was made of it. Her whole arm, actually, now that he looked.

A figure pushed through one of the groups of people. A petite woman no older than Parker or Olivia. Smooth skin, gorgeous face, a fountain of tied-back curly hair coming off her head. The wide skirt and tight waist of her clothes felt . . . colonial? Same with the boxy leather bag slung over her shoulder. She made the whole thing work, though.

"Someone touched the glass obelisk and survived?" she asked. Her accent was almost comically French, like something from a movie.

Noah came alive and cleared his throat. "Her boyfriend touched it. He'd seen the granite obelisk earlier and thought the glass one had a force field, too."

"Yeah, why'd he think that?" murmured Josh.

Parker shot him a look.

The French woman carefully opened Olivia's eyes. "He touched it, but she received the jolt?"

"They were holding hands," Noah explained. "He's . . . he died. She got shocked through him."

She nodded while checking Olivia's pulse and leaning in to listen to her breathe. She looked up at the woman with the plastic eye socket. "Can you take her to my rooms?"

"Not a problem."

The thin crowd made space for the two women as they walked away with Olivia. Parker moved to follow, but Qiang held out a gentle hand. "Don't worry," he said. "Monique is our doctor. Your friend's in good hands."

Parker looked like she had something to say but decided against it.

Josh tried to get a sense of the people around them, looked for the little physical and verbal cues that usually guided him through deals. They were still keeping back, but he still had this sense of . . . anticipation? Not in a dangerous way, but more like a crowd waiting for the doors to open at a concert. They were eager, almost excited, but trying not to show it.

Then he realized Qiang and the others were doing the same thing. Sizing up him and Parker and Noah and Sam. Studying them. Looking for clues.

"Well then," said Qiang, focusing on Parker. "Let's get some names."

"Parker. Parker Sangthong."

"Sam."

"Josh. Josh Redd. Pleased to meet you." He held out his hand. Qiang smiled. Shook it. Again, that same sense of being rehearsed. All the usual formalities and small talk before everyone sat down to talk business.

Qiang turned his attention to Noah, but the professor ignored him. Staring out at the village. Or maybe at the cliffs behind the village? They looked a lot closer. Had they crossed most of the valley?

Qiang waited a few more polite moments before accepting Noah wasn't going to talk. He focused on the others, gestured deeper into the village, took a few steps. "I'm sure you have many, many questions about where you are and how you got here. We've got food waiting in the main hall. We can sit down, talk, and—"

"I've got a question."

All eyes went to Noah. He looked . . . annoyed. He raised a hand and pointed past one of the small groups of people. Josh followed the pointing finger.

In the middle of one of the dirt roads—the center road of the three—maybe forty or fifty feet past a quartet of villagers, stood another obelisk. This one looked . . . steel? Chrome? It reflected enough of the buildings around it to blend in, but once you knew it was there you could see it. Like the camouflage force field the Predator used.

Noah's finger jabbed twice in the air. "That's the platinum obelisk. What's it doing here?"

Qiang's brows furrowed for a moment. "It's always been here."

"No, it hasn't. It's supposed to be on the savanna. Why is it here?"

A low murmur crawled through the villagers.

"How would you know that?" asked Qiang. "When did you arrive here?"

"Last night," said Noah. "We arrived over by Lookout Hill. Where are we?"

"You're in . . . well, we just call it the valley." He took a few more steps, heading into the village, clearly trying to get back on his prepared script. "I know this may sound unbelievable, but this place is millions—"

"A hundred million years in the past, somehow disjointed from time." Noah waved the man's words away, then widened the gesture to take in the buildings spread out in front of them. "What is *this*? Where did all of this come from?!"

Josh could feel the uncertainty in the air. The mood shifted. Noah had shifted it.

"I . . ." Qiang's smile grew a little wider. A little more forced. "I must admit, I'm not used to being the confused person in these conversations."

"Who are you?" asked the wavy-haired woman holding the backpacks.

"Noah Barnes. My father and sister and I lived here when I was younger."

She looked over her shoulder. "In Roanoke?"

"In the valley. Our valley. And it didn't have any of this." His voice was getting a manic edge Josh recognized. Someone failing to adjust, getting close to a full freakout.

A new murmur danced through the crowd. "Your father and sister?" repeated Qiang. "The three of you lived in . . . a place like this."

"Yes."

"What was your name again?"

"Noah Barnes."

"Back then he was called Billy," added Sam.

A few wide eyes. Sounds of disbelief. Even more murmurs. They stared at Noah in awe.

Parker leaned in closer to Sam and Josh and lowered her voice. "What's going on?"

"I don't—I have no idea."

Qiang took a slow breath. Studied Noah's face. "Billy . . . Gather?"

"Yep," said Noah. "That's me."

"Son of James, brother of Beau?"

Noah straightened up and his eyes opened a little wider. "You know my sister?"

Josh looked at the crowd. A new mood rolled across their faces and hit him in the gut. The unmistakable realization you'd said the wrong thing, that damage control needed to happen fast.

"You're Billy Gather?" asked a woman in the crowd.

"He is," said Sam.

Qiang shook his head. "No, he's not." A lot of the friendliness had drained out of his voice.

Josh felt the confidence roll off Noah. How was this guy not reading the room? How could he not see the reaction he was getting from these people? The whole village was maybe ten seconds away from demanding to speak with a manager.

Noah set his hands on his hips. "Yes, I am. I'm Billy Gather."

"Billy Gather," Qiang said icily, "was murdered four hundred years ago."

Noah's face crumbled.

Josh raised two fingers. "I'm sorry . . . how long?"

13

SAM

"Four hundred years?" repeated Sam.

"No," Noah said. "That's not possible."

Qiang gestured past them. "Warwick? Emerson? Perhaps you should join us at the main hall?"

Sam glanced back, saw the Vietnam-vet guy in the combat vest lower his spear and step forward. Another movement caught his eye and he saw another black man—no, he realized, an Aborigine—wearing what looked like a Civil War uniform. Cowboy-ish hat, knee-high black boots, a leather sash slung over one shoulder, Klingon-style, and a ragged coat under it. He had a spear, too. And a knife shoved in his belt. The two of them kept moving forward until Sam and the others started moving away from them.

The murmuring crowd parted and Qiang led them into the village. They walked right past the tall platinum obelisk, and Sam could see all the runes inscribed across it. Again, just like the others, but a different material. The little group didn't slow at all and they passed by before he could do more than give it a few quick looks.

He was pretty sure the books said the platinum obelisk was on a savanna of tall grass. One of them noted little Billy choosing that particular word—not a field or a plain, but a savanna. And that savanna was supposed to be a mile or so from the Gather's cave.

"Is this maybe a misunderstanding?" asked Josh as they headed down the dirt road. "Like, a metric-to-American thing? How long are your years?"

Parker sighed.

"Three hundred sixty-five days," said Qiang.

They passed what looked like an old English cottage with a bamboo front porch. The building after it was mostly bamboo with heavy posts at the corners and a few rough planks stretched between them to make a framework. It looked like the most common style of building, from what Sam had seen so far, although the one next to it had a foundation of stones, but otherwise looked like a log cabin.

Then the guilt worm twisted in his stomach again because he was checking out random houses and he'd let these people take Olivia. And Logan was dead. And Kyle.

He wondered if anyone had seen him happily studying buildings, but the others all had their own things going on. Noah still looked stunned. Josh looked worried. Parker looked . . . well, she looked like she was waiting for someone to pause in their lecture so she could ask a question.

The road turned a corner and led them to a larger building. A few quick looks around made Sam think it might be the center of the little village. Close to it, anyway. It felt a little church-like. The kind of church you imagined missionaries making with whatever logs or rocks they could find.

Sam leaned back, shaded his eyes, but didn't see a cross on the roof. Or any other symbols. Same with the double doors and the thick, rough-hewn frame that wrapped around them. Off to the side he caught Parker looking up too. She'd had the same thoughts.

Josh sighed. "Weird church at the center of the long-lost village in the middle of the evil cornfield at the dawn of time."

Sam managed to stop most of his nervous laugh.

Parker glared at both of them.

Qiang walked up three big slabs of rock that served as steps, and turned at the double doors. "Em, could you go ask the Timekeeper to join us? He should be able to clear this up."

The middle-aged soldier gave a quick nod and headed back into the village.

Qiang pushed one of the doors open. "Let's all sit down and talk a little more about your claims."

"They're not claims," said Noah.

"We'll see. The Timekeeper has a bad leg. It will take him a little while to get here."

"It might be more time dilation," Parker said, turning to Noah. "Maybe the effect's greater than you thought."

Noah shook his head. "That's not how time flows here."

Qiang gave them an odd look. Noah walked past him into the big structure, Parker following close behind. As Sam walked up the steps Qiang turned to the Aboriginal man. "Warwick . . . perhaps you could stand watch out here?"

"Yeh sure?" His accent was thick and Australian. Sam wondered if he knew about the sound they'd heard out in the fields. Probably not the time to ask.

"For now."

Despite the churchy feel outside, inside the big building felt like the bastard child of a log cabin and an island resort. The open space, relatively low roof, and all the wood reminded Sam of an old-fashioned town hall. A big table, not much more than a massive log split down the middle and propped up on a dozen stout legs, filled half the room. Lots of chairs surrounded it, all from rough-hewn wood. A handful of dish-like lamps sat along the length of the table, a flame the size of Sam's thumb dancing on each one. A fireplace of mismatched stones, big enough for him to crouch in, sat against one wall.

"It's like some big mead hall from a ren faire," said Josh.

Sam wandered to the wall across from the fireplace, where a set of shelves held a few dozen books. There didn't seem to be any order to them. Fiction and nonfiction. Several languages. A handful of them were so old and decrepit the pages had been tied together with coarse string.

Two were shiny new, with spines that looked like nylon and titles he didn't know by authors he'd never heard of.

Mounted on the wall around the bookshelf was . . . all sorts of stuff. Random trinkets and tools and accessories. On one level it reminded Sam of a theme restaurant, trying to fill space and look hip and deliberately eccentric. But something about the placement felt more . . . careful? Reverent? Less decoration and more of a display.

His breath started to quicken.

A few feet away Parker moved into his field of vision, also looking at the assortment on the wall. She moved closer, looked at the bookshelf, back up at the wall. "What's all of this?"

"I don't—I have no idea."

"It wasn't in all your books?"

"None of this was in the books," Sam said. "They were mostly about him and his family and what he remembered."

Qiang stood by one of the chairs, waiting for them all to drift over to the table. Josh had already flopped in a chair, resting his head in his arms. A new person, a man with shaggy black hair, had appeared through a back door with a tray of wooden cups.

Sam dragged one of the chairs out to sit on. It was heavier than it looked. The wood had an odd smoothness to it. Not polished with effort, but by years and years of use. Oiled by thousands of touches.

He sat down and his legs ached with the sudden relief. How long had he been standing? He'd only been carrying the stretcher for . . . a little more than an hour? Two hours? They'd been in the trees for a lot of it, but it seemed like the sun hadn't moved much.

Time could be strange in the valley.

Noah hadn't moved far from the door. Parker went back to him. Took his arm. Guided him to the table. Sam couldn't figure out if the man was in shock or denial or some weird combination with a few other emotions thrown in.

Noah dragged one of the heavy chairs out and sat down.

Sam sniffed the wooden cup. Water. And . . . berries? He sipped it, tasted the thinnest juice he'd ever had. Loved it. He hadn't realized how dry his tongue was.

"Well. Normally this is when I say something calming and reassuring to newcomers." Qiang looked at each of them in turn, settled on Noah. "I've had this talk with people over a dozen times now, but, as I mentioned before, this is the first time I'm the most confused person at the table."

"It hasn't been four hundred years," Noah responded. "It can't be."

"Four hundred and thirty-four, since the Gather family first arrived here. Four hundred thirty-two since Billy was killed by the Pakka."

"Killed by the . . . the Pakka? What?"

"But this is where they—this is the valley?" asked Sam.

Qiang nodded. "It is. Which raises my big question. How do you know about this place?"

"Because I grew up here," said Noah.

"Billy Gather's been dead for centuries."

"No, I haven't."

"It's really him," Sam said.

Josh pushed his head up off the table and raised a finger. "Although yesterday we all thought his name was Noah Barnes."

"Yesterday we thought your name was Skip," said Parker.

"Fair point."

The man with shaggy black hair reappeared from the back. He had a larger tray filled with bowls and plates. Sliced fruit and vegetables. Big knots of bread, like over-inflated pretzels. A bowl of yellow, clumpy jelly that smelled like . . . scrambled eggs?

The tray went down. Josh grabbed one of the bread knots. Sam and Parker looked at Qiang and he waved them to eat.

"The Gather family were the first known people here in the valley. Most of us here owe our lives to their legacy."

Noah leaned back in his chair and crossed his arms. "You're welcome."

"As such, the idea of an impostor doesn't sit well."

"I'm not an impostor."

"So you . . . went into hiding? For four hundred years?"

"He got out," said Parker.

Qiang stared at her. "What?"

Sam was suddenly aware he could hear everyone's food in the big room. Josh chewing. The crust breaking on Parker's bread. The iron knife scraping egg-jelly softly across his own bread. Noah swallowing a mouthful of the fruit water.

Noah set the wooden cup down. "I got out."

Qiang shook his head. "You're lying. No one gets out of the valley."

"I did."

"How?"

"I don't know. Didn't know, for a long time."

They all waited. The shaggy-haired man watched and listened from the doorway to the back room.

Noah let his eyes drift down to the tabletop. "I was back down at the watering hole, standing on the rocks. It'd been a year since our dad was killed. Only about five months since Beau and I started splitting up and doing chores alone again. I'd been there at least a hundred times before. Not a big deal."

Sam leaned forward. He knew the story by heart, but to actually hear it from Dino Boy—Billy—himself, in his own words, not filtered through a biographer or a late-night host or a child psychiatrist trying to prove some theory. Then he tried to rein in his glee. Reminded himself that Logan and Kyle had both died. That Olivia was pretty much in a coma.

"I set one of our gourds down, but as soon as I straightened up it felt like the rocks vanished out from under me. I lost my balance and fell. Hit my head on the other gourd, the one I was still holding, and landed in the deep end of the watering hole. Not the first time that had happened, either. But when I stopped splashing around and got my head up above the surface again . . . I was somewhere else. A big pond in the middle of a jungle."

"Thailand," said Sam.

Noah nodded at him. "That was almost thirty-four years ago. On Earth. And unless I really miscalculated the time differential, it should only be thirteen and a half here."

Qiang nodded slowly. Picked a slice of something green and shiny off one of the plates. "Let's say I believed you. I don't, but for the sake of argument, let's say I did. People end up here completely at random. You're claiming you found a way out . . . and then somehow ended up here again?"

"I chose to come back here."

"It's not that simple."

"It's not," Noah agreed. "But with thirty years of work and access to a bunch of astrophysicists, I managed to do it."

Qiang's gaze slid around at each of them again. Sam thought the man was starting to look angry. "Now you're saying you can leave and enter the valley at will?"

Noah shrugged. "Not quite at will. But I know how to calculate when and where you need to be on both sides. I got us here. I can get us back."

"Technically," said Josh, "he got himself here and all of us sort of got pulled along for the ride."

"You're lying. All of you."

"He's not," said Parker.

"I won't have you giving my people false hope."

"It's not false hope," said Noah. "I came back for my sister. To bring her home."

"Your sister?"

"Yes. Beau Gather. My sister. Now where is she?"

Qiang's face ran through a variety of emotions. Confusion. Almost-hidden annoyance. A bit of pity. "It's been four hundred years. The Gathers are long dead. All of them."

Sam watched expressions cycle across Noah's face, too. "No. She's supposed to get out, not end up stuck here alone."

"She wasn't alone, Master Billy Gather," said a new voice. "She had me."

A cloaked figure hobbled into the meeting hall through the open door. Sam noticed the village outside had gone dark. Not shadowy sundown but full-on middle of the night. It didn't seem like they'd been talking that long. Half an hour at most. His sense of time had been completely shot since they'd arrived in the valley.

The new arrival had a wooden walking stick, almost a staff, and what looked like a mechanical leg, barely more than a pole or pipe with a rectangle of hammered metal for a base. Their other foot swung forward and that one was mechanical too but sculpted to have more organic curves. Years worth of dust and grime covered its dull plastic, and even from here Sam could see the cracks and crumbled sections all over the limb.

Then the man turned his head to look at each of them and Sam saw the round blue eyes glowing beneath the cloak's hood. He'd imagined them a hundred times as a kid. Drawn pictures of them.

Noah stood up. "Ross?"

The narrow head tilted one way, then the other, then back up to center. "Hello, Master Billy."

The professor crossed the room, wrapped his arms around the android, and hugged it hard.

"It's nice to see you again as well," said Ross. He awkwardly patted Noah on the back with a skeletal hand of metal and plastic. "Qiang-Shizhang, I can confirm this is Master Billy Gather. He matches nine of the fourteen biometric datapoints I have on file, and four others are within acceptable parameters when I account for aging."

Sam knew he was staring. Couldn't stop. His heart bounced like a little kid meeting Mickey at Disney World. Ross, the robot butler, live and in the flesh. So to speak.

Noah's hug had knocked the android's hood down, and Sam could see the smooth, cylindrical shape of its head. The casing had dulled from white to yellow-gray, and there were cracks in every molded plate of the android's body. With the cloak out of the way, Sam could see the fractured, twisted section where one leg had been torn loose and the crude replacement bolted in its place. One of the eyes had a definite flicker to it, never going out but notably dimming. The robot looked old. Decades easily.

Maybe centuries.

Sam couldn't stop staring.

Noah and Qiang had been talking with the android for a minute, at least, and Sam had been so thrilled at the sight of it he hadn't registered a single word. Now Qiang stared at Noah with a mix of awe and . . . fear? Sam wondered what he'd looked like when he realized who Noah was. He tried to calm himself. Stop fanboying and pay attention.

Which he did in time to hear Noah ask the big question.

"Ross . . . where's Beau?"

The android jerked its head to the left and back. In the books, Ross's quirks sounded charming and human. In person he came across more like a creepy animatronic, a *Five Nights at Freddy's* reject unable to make any subtle movements. Another electric spasm shook its fingers as it tried to make a casual gesture in the air.

"Miss Beau was distressed when you vanished, Master Billy. For nineteen days she stayed convinced you were lost, and she and I went on many trips throughout the valley looking for you. Then she believed you'd been killed and eaten by some of the local fauna. After two months and three days, she shifted blame to the Pakka tribe."

"Why blame them?" asked Parker.

Ross's head swung to face her, and one of the glowing eyes rattled in its socket. "She did not share her chain of reasoning with me, Mx."

Noah closed his eyes. "So what happened?"

"Two years, sixteen days after your disappearance, on her twentieth birthday, she left the cave and did not return."

Qiang, Sam noticed, didn't add anything.

Noah didn't catch it and stayed focused on the android. "Did you go looking for her?"

Ross cocked his head slightly to the side and back. "As you know, such independent decisions aren't within my operating parameters, Master Billy."

"It's . . . I'm Noah now."

"Of course, Master Noah Billy."

"Just Noah."

The android's hand shook in the air. "Of course, Noah."

"So you didn't look for her at all? You did nothing?"

"I waited seventeen days in the cave before I moved to the ledge, which offered the more direct solar exposure my internal batteries needed, and also a greater view of the valley. I stayed on the ledge for four years, eight months, fifteen days, watching for any sign of her."

Noah's shoulders dropped a little more. "And you never saw anything? She didn't signal you or say where she was going?"

"I'm afraid not, Noah."

"Did something get her?" asked Parker.

Noah's lips tightened.

"Such speculation is not within my operating parameters, Mx."

"Parker," she said. "I'm Parker."

Ross nodded its head. "Of course, Mx. Parker."

"Miss."

"Of course, Miss Parker."

"And I'm Sam," he said, instantly aware of how eager he sounded. "Just Sam."

"Of course, Sam."

Qiang cleared his throat. "Timekeeper, could you tell our . . . new friends how long it's been since then."

"It's only been thirteen years," Noah said. But Sam saw him looking up and down the old robot as he said it.

Ross looked at the village elder, then back to Noah. "I'm sorry to correct you, but it's been four hundred thirty-two years since your death."

"I didn't die."

"I'm glad to hear that, Noah."

Sam managed to bite back most of his laugh. Couldn't help it. It was just a funny response. A robot's response. Noah shot him a desperate look that cut off the rest of the laugh and made the twisting guilt worm flip over in his gut.

"It can't've been four hundred years. I did all the calculations. I spent decades on this. My whole life! It . . . it has to be thirteen."

Ross's featureless round eyes somehow managed to look ashamed. "I'm sorry, Noah. It isn't."

14

NOAH

Noah'd long since accepted the valley probably wasn't the place he remembered. Like any childhood memory, he knew it was colored by a degree of innocence and a general lack of knowledge. It hadn't been as fun, and some of the horrors were, no question, far worse than he recalled. He'd been back in the present for over a year before a therapist—unknowingly—helped him realize so much of his trouble readjusting was post-traumatic stress from all his time in the past.

But after all this time, after decades of study and research and calculation . . . he *understood* the valley. He knew how it worked. The basic mechanics of it weren't a mystery to him. Those he knew absolutely.

He looked at the big crack running across Ross's faceplate and wondered if the old android—his old *friend*—had taken some kind of mental damage. Processing damage? Maybe a corrupted database or memory file or . . . something. He understood computers a lot better now than he had then but still didn't really know how Ross worked.

"You have to be calculating the time passage wrong," he said out loud. "Or remembering it wrong or . . . something. It hasn't been that long."

Ross looked at him. Turned to gaze at the students. Parker and Sam sat quietly, watching the discussion. Josh poked at the tray of food, picking up one thing after another and dropping them back down. Noah'd been so wrapped up in this, so confused with figuring out why all these people thought so much time had passed, he'd almost forgotten they were here until Sam had chuckled.

Qiang stared across the table at him. Noah knew the look in those eyes. He'd seen it from so many doctors and therapists and counselors. The so-controlled, so-faint glimmer of hope and pity and frustration.

He's so close to a breakthrough.

"Over my decades at Roanoke," Ross said, "I have been given a title. Many here refer to me as the Timekeeper. There's no way to accurately measure time here, so I've become, to play off a phrase your father once used for me, a walking, talking clock and calendar. I've also kept track of numerous historical events."

Noah rolled this back and forth in his head. "But there . . . there isn't any history here."

"I've recorded four hundred thirty-five years in the valley."

"Excuse me," said Josh before Noah could say anything else. He held his hand up with a piece of green fruit in it. "Can't they build an hourglass or use the stars or something? Like people used to do?"

"Or just make marks on a tree or something," Sam added. "That's what you did back in your cave, right?"

"You can only make so many marks on a tree."

"The technologies needed to build an hourglass haven't been rediscovered in the valley," Qiang said. "We have only the barest of metalworking and ceramics. Stellar timekeeping isn't possible because the stars don't move."

"Since the what don't what?" Parker straightened up in her chair.

"The stars don't move," Noah said. "I told you things were different here."

Sam's lips mouthed the start of two or three words before he settled on, "That's not in any of the books."

"Because everyone said it wasn't possible."

"But they were all cool with dinosaurs and robots and aliens?" asked Josh.

Noah shrugged. "Sometimes even the crazy kid says something too crazy to believe."

"If I may continue?" asked Ross, sounding more like an aggrieved professor than a machine.

"Sorry," said Noah. He'd forgotten Ross could imitate so many emotional tones with his voice.

"Your beliefs about the valley and its history are based on your father's flawed hypothesis that everything entering the valley arrives close to the same point in space and time, no matter what time period they originated in."

Something low in Noah's chest twisted. "What?"

Ross shifted his feet, the signal a lecture or lesson was about to begin. It crossed Noah's mind that he did the same thing. Odd teaching habits he'd learned decades ago from the android.

"The space-time anomaly absorbs individuals and objects from various locations and time periods on Earth," Ross began. "However, my long existence here has let me observe these items also appear at random space-time points within the valley itself, and not in any linear fashion. Just as all of you have arrived here now, more than four hundred years after Noah's original time here."

Noah shook his head. "No, that's not right."

"You and your family believed that the valley was a patchwork made up of numerous life-forms, objects, and locations from throughout Earth's history. What you didn't realize, because of your limited window of experience, is that this is the valley's ongoing, dynamic state. It's expanded several times over as creatures, places, and objects continue to appear. Since your time the valley's acquired new fields, forests, water, hillsides, and a glacier."

"How does that work?" asked Parker. "One day everyone goes out and there's a forest outside the gate?"

"Yes," said Qiang.

"Really?"

"There's a large grove of cypress trees to the right as you exit

Roanoke's main gate. About three and a half hectares. They appeared there twenty-two years ago. Just after lunch."

"Along with approximately one-point-three megaliters of water," added Ross.

Noah shook his head. "This doesn't make sense. If things were appearing throughout the valley, we'd know. We'd've seen it."

"How would you know if something had appeared before you arrived here, Noah?"

"Because we'd see it."

Sam did that thing where he tapped his fingertips like an overcaffeinated Bond villain. "It . . . sort of makes sense."

"No it doesn't," said Noah.

"It kind of does," Parker admitted. "Things get pulled from any time in history, but then get dropped anywhere in the valley's smaller subset of history."

Ross's electric-blue eyes flickered. "That's my understanding as well, Miss Parker."

Again, thousands of facts spun and collided in Noah's head. This time it took him longer to sort them out, to get it all to make sense again. He knew Ross was still talking with the others, but he didn't register any of it as more than sounds in the room.

Four hundred years.

It couldn't be true. It made horrible, perfect sense. It explained some of the things he'd seen as a kid and some things they'd seen since yesterday. But it also meant he'd been wrong about so many things.

It also meant he'd made some huge mistakes.

It couldn't be true.

Qiang was still watching him. Still waiting for that breakthrough moment.

"You believe . . ." he started. "You're sure about this?"

Ross's cylindrical head leaned forward. "I have recorded forty-seven instances of it happening."

"You've actually seen it?"

"I've directly witnessed sixteen events in the four hundred twenty-seven years since the first one. The other thirty-one I became aware of through indirect but immediate means. As the valley's become larger over time, it's become less likely for events to happen within range of my senses. It's likely there have been others I was unable to register."

"What was the first one?" Sam asked.

"A statue, seven meters tall, surrounded by approximately one-quarter hectare of white sand appeared. The outer edge of the area was two hundred and six meters from the base of the cliff where the Gather family's cave was located."

"And you just happened to see it?" Parker asked. Noah heard the skeptical edge in her voice. Good for her.

"Yes. I was on the ledge outside the cave, watching for Miss Beau. This event happened four years, three months, twenty-nine days after her disappearance."

"What did it look like?" Sam had turned his chair to face the conversation, and now he leaned forward. "When the statue appeared? Was there a light or a sound or anything?"

"No. One moment the statue wasn't there, one-thirtieth of a second later it was. The only notable effects were the shift of several tree lines when the landscape changed and a minor atmospheric pressure wave radiating out from the statue."

"Like something expanded in the air."

"Yes, Miss Parker."

"Could we go with just Parker?"

"Of course, Parker."

Noah bit his lip. "And this statue . . . it landed on top of, what, the mushroom grove?"

"No. The statue and its surrounding landscape appeared between the mushroom grove and the edge of the area you and Miss Beau called the Boneyard. The grove at that point was forty-five meters further away from the cliff."

Josh propped his head up on one hand. "Like a landslide?"

"No, Mx. There was no movement through intervening space. The grove was simply in a new location."

"Josh is fine."

"Of course, Josh."

Noah kept processing, kept trying to reconcile this new version of the valley with the one he knew. "How?"

"I don't know, Noah. It's the nature of the valley. As I said, since that first event, I've seen numerous other locations appear across the valley, expanding it to its current size. It's also made the creation of maps difficult as most landmarks don't maintain the same relationship to each other for more than a few years."

Sam's fingers continued to tap against each other. He looked at Noah. "You thought Lookout Hill should've been closer."

"It's supposed to be closer." Noah fought the urge to press his hands over his eyes. Almost none of this had gone as he'd planned. As he'd *calculated*. He pushed all the potential mistakes and repercussions out of his mind, focused on the important thing. "If you didn't know what happened to Beau, why did you stop waiting for her? Why'd you leave the ledge?"

"The appearance of the statue so close to your cave agitated the Pakka tribe. Three weeks after it appeared they made their first attempt to approach it. Two days later the one you called Scarnose touched it. Over the next two months they made several attempts to vandalize the statue. They became bored with this and began approaching the cliff face where your cave was. And also the ledge where I stood. I was struck five times over four weeks with stones and once with a spear." The android reached up and pulled its cloak aside, revealing a dirty gouge in its chest plate close to the shoulder. A trio of cracks radiated out from it, black with centuries of dust and grime.

"They knocked you off the ledge," said Noah.

"They didn't, but thank you for your concern. The severity of the attack activated my self-preservation subroutines and let me retreat from the area when the Pakka began their next wave of attacks. I moved to a safe distance away and stayed there for another two years, eleven months, nineteen days until I was found by Miss Amelia and her partner, Mr. Fred, on their third day in the valley. I remained with them for the rest of their time here."

"What about the Castaway? Did you ever ask them? They'd know where Beau was."

"I didn't. As you know, such independent decisions aren't within my operating parameters. In addition, the Castaway made it clear several times living things were their priority. I'm not alive, and they rarely acknowledged me."

"Sounds like a jerk," said Parker.

Josh yawned.

Sam turned to him. "Dude, seriously?"

"It's been a long day," Josh said. "How are you not exhausted? We were carrying Olivia for half the day."

"It wasn't that long."

"Pretty sure it was."

"Many people suffer from disorientation when they arrive here," said Ross. "The nature of the valley doesn't align with natural biorhythms, and it's normal for people to lose track of time. It takes several days to adjust, but the feeling will subside."

"I remember," said Noah.

"We have a guest house across the road," Qiang said, gazing at each of them. "Several rooms. Beds. It's yours for as long as you want it. Most people find the first few days here a bit . . . exhausting."

"Yeah," Parker said, "you could call today exhausting."

Josh swallowed the last of his bread knot. "Nothing a few weeks of meditation and some quality pharmaceuticals won't take care of."

"What about Olivia?" asked Parker. "Should we check on her? Where's she?"

"Your friend is with Monique, our physician," Qiang assured them. "She'll be well cared for."

"They're not going to drill holes in her head or put leeches on her or something, are they?"

Ross's head squeaked side to side. "There are no leeches in the valley, Parker."

"I meant . . . she's a real doctor, yes? She practices modern medicine, not, like, Middle Ages medicine?"

"Madame Cadieux was born in 1726. However, while she lacks in some resources, the past nine years have advanced her medical knowledge considerably, including techniques and medical knowledge from the late twenty-sixth century."

"So . . . no leeches."

The cylindrical head moved side to side again. "There are no leeches in the valley, Parker."

Noah watched them all get up. Stretch. Pick up useless smartphones. They shuffled around the room for a few moments. All ready to head home and collapse into their beds.

Home.

Numbers and theories and calculations that he'd been pushing away came crashing down in his mind, impossible to ignore any longer. He stared at the wooden tabletop. At the old, well-worn wood. "I was wrong about everything."

"About the valley?" asked Sam.

Parker moved a little closer to him. "About your sister?"

"Everything. All my work, all the calculations I made, I assumed things were stable on this side. That the wormhole deposited things at more or less the same point in space-time, in a valley with set internal coordinates. But I didn't . . . my understanding of all of it was so wrong. There's so much variance on this side of the wormhole, and it means all my work's off by several orders of magnitude. It's just . . . it's all wrong."

Noah let himself drop into one of the chairs. Felt the impact shudder up his back. Stared at one of the oil lamps. Felt the heat of the fire on his eyes.

"I don't know how to get us home."

15

BILLY

Billy followed Dad through the forest. It was a forest now, even though it'd been a jungle ten minutes ago. Palm trees, then pine trees.

"When are we going to go home?"

"Soon, bud," Dad told him. "But until then, this is still our big camping trip."

Four days here now. Dad called this place a lost world. Beau called it the valley before time. On their first night, as they stretched out in their sleeping bags, Billy suggested calling the place the Savage Land, but Beau had told him that name was copyrighted and lawyers would find him if he called it that. Billy had cleverly pointed out they *wanted* someone to find them, so calling it the Savage Land was clearly the best thing they could do. Beau and Dad had both laughed and then she'd said he didn't understand copyright law.

They'd started the hike this morning, right after the sun had appeared in the sky. It was the first time out of the cave for Billy and Beau. Dad had gone out yesterday to get the last of their supplies from the raft. He'd made it back and told them he thought they could move through the valley as long as they stayed quiet and stuck to cover.

So here they were. Day four. Hiking through the jungle-forest. Dad. Billy. Beau.

She bonked his butt with the big water jug. "You're slowing us down."

"No I'm not."

"It's your tiny legs."

He looked over his shoulder at her. "You're not that much taller than me."

"I'm closer to Dad than you are to me." She swung her arm and the empty container bonked Billy again. He swung his back at her and she blocked it with her own. They clunked together, so he swung again and she knocked his attack away with another dull *bonk*.

"Hey," said Dad. "What did I say about no extra noise?"

"Sorry, Dad."

"She started it."

"Shut up."

"Both of you shut up or I'll take you back to the cave."

"I'll pull this valley over right now," murmured Beau. Billy laughed and smothered it with his free hand.

Dad had bought four gallons of water for the raft trip. One jug had burst when they . . . landed. Or maybe got stepped on by a dinosaur right afterward. Either way, they only had three left and they'd drank the last of their clean water yesterday. Which is why they were hiking through the jungle toward the center of the valley.

Old pine needles crunched under their feet for a few more steps and then the trees stopped. They were on the edge of a field of waist-high grass. On the far side, maybe two hundred feet away, Billy could see something that looked like an old, rusty school bus. And past the school bus, almost touching it, stood the iceberg.

"If it looks clean," Dad said, "it'd be all the water we need. There might even be some runoff around it. Maybe a little stream we could fill the jugs at, like a fountain."

"Unless it all melts first," said Beau.

"That's a lot of ice." Billy gazed up at the tall lump. "It'll probably take a hundred years for it to all melt."

"Well, hopefully we'll be home before then," Dad said. He looked across the field. Closed his eyes and listened. "I don't think the big one's close by. I don't hear anything."

"We should stick close to the trees." Beau's finger swept a path around the edge of the field. "We can hide quicker if he shows up."

Billy blew some air out between his lips, making a fart sound. "Unless he comes out of the trees close to where we are."

"It's still better," said Dad. "We'd hear him coming sooner. Good thinking, Beau."

She smiled, then stuck her tongue out at Billy. He made another fart noise at her. She waggled a finger at him. "Hey, Dad said no extra noise."

"It's not extra. It was a special one just for you."

They made their way around the field, pushing through the tall grass. Billy tried to look around Dad to get a better look at the school bus. He could see long rows of windows, but as they got closer he realized it was a lot bigger than they'd thought. At least twice as big as a bus.

They got closer and closer, and then Beau made a little sound behind him. "Ohmigod," she said. "It's a riverboat."

Billy didn't see it at first, but then he realized seeing it tilted over on the ground away from the water gave it a different shape. It looked like some of the boats at Niagara Falls that went close to the waterfalls. But the windows were all broken and the whole thing had rusty holes all over it. The brown, rough railings looked more like wood than metal. A thick rusted chain came out of the boat's side—its *hull*—and Billy followed its zigzag path through the grass. About ten feet away a big anchor hook curved up out of the grass. He'd seen it before and thought it was a branch.

"Is that Arabic?" Beau pointed up at the front of the boat. Below the railing, some curvy dirty-white lines peeked out from beneath the rust. They reminded Billy of cursive writing, but they didn't make any actual letters. None he knew, anyway.

"Maybe?" said Dad.

They walked around the boat. None of it was crushed or bent. Aside from all the rust and broken glass, it still looked mostly in one piece. It looked like it had tipped over on the ground.

Billy wondered if it had fallen here like they did, and if there'd been people on it when it happened.

They passed the two big propellers. He stopped to stretch his arms out and grab the far edges of one, grunting as if he'd stopped them whirling with his bare hands. Beau rolled her eyes and gave his shoulder a little shove.

The iceberg loomed on the far side of the boat. If the rusted shipwreck had been bigger than they'd expected, it was because they'd misjudged how huge the iceberg was. It had to be at least thirty stories tall. Dad had worked on some tall buildings, and the thick tower of ice was at least as tall as all of them. Maybe even taller.

Dad placed his hand against the iceberg. "Huh."

Beau stepped next to him. "What?"

"It's cold. It's just . . . it's not as cold as you'd think."

She put a hand on it. Billy pushed in between them, dropped his water jug, and put both hands flat on the wall of ice. It was cold, but can-of-soda cold, not like holding a piece of ice.

Beau looked at her fingers. "It's dry."

Dad lifted his own hand away. Flicked his fingers a few times. "Yeah."

"It's got to be close to eighty degrees in the sun. How is it not melting?"

"I don't know."

"Why isn't there any condensation on it? The air's moist and it's cold enough. Shouldn't it at least have a few drops running down the side like a cold beer bottle or something?"

Dad shrugged. "You'd think so, yeah."

Billy craned his head up. "It doesn't look like a real iceberg."

"How so, bud?"

He waited for them to keep talking and realized Dad and Beau were both looking at him. It hadn't been a random acknowledgment, they really wanted to hear what he thought. He straightened up a little taller, leaned back, waved his hand up and down the wall. "It looks like how people draw ice in comics or cartoons. Like when Iceman freezes something. Lots of long, straight lines, like a big diamond. But real icebergs are rough and snowy and cloudy."

Beau stared at the wall. "I hate to say it, but the little twerp's right."

"Hey!"

She gave his shoulder another shove, but this time it was gentler. "Good catch. Seriously."

Dad ran his fingers back and forth across the wall again. "It doesn't feel like ice, either, does it? It's too . . . glassy?"

"What's that stuff they make big windows out of?"

"Tempered glass?"

"Yeah. No, not that. Remember when you showed us the bulletproof windows?"

"Lexan?"

Billy picked up his jug, stepped around Beau, and walked along the base of the iceberg, sliding his fingers along it. His sister was right. It felt more like plastic than glass, but it wasn't either of them. It definitely wasn't ice, even though the cold kept making him think it was.

He plodded off a few more steps through the grass, counting them off. He wondered how long it would take to walk around the iceberg. He could see the rough curve of it, tried to picture in his head how big that would make it. He looked up at the height again and tried to think of some of the tall buildings Dad had helped build and how big they'd been at street level.

He glanced back over his shoulder and realized he couldn't see Dad or Beau anymore. He kept walking forward as he tried to listen, to get a sense of how far back they were. How far around the iceberg had he walked?

Then he turned his head to the front again and jumped.

The not-ice stretched out in front of him, coming out of the iceberg like a big arm, sloping down to the ground. His brain made half a dozen leaps in as many seconds. Was the iceberg a giant ice tree, with roots stretching down from its trunk? Was it a giant ice monster, reaching down to scoop Billy into its mouth? Was this one of those things Dad pointed out on old buildings, a buttress? Was the iceberg a *building*?

Then he took a good look and realized what it was.

He turned and ran back. Twenty, thirty, forty long strides through the grass, a little over a minute, and there was Beau. Her face relaxed as soon as she saw him. "You little asshole. You had us worried."

Dad stepped into view, trying to shift his worried face into a neutral one. "You can't run off like that, bud. We're still figuring this place out."

Billy nodded. "You guys have to come see this."

"See what?"

"There's a way inside!"

They followed him around the iceberg and he showed them the not-ice ramp sparkling in the noon sunlight. It went up at least twelve feet. Twice as high as Dad was tall.

Beau stepped closer to the foot of the ramp. Dad nudged Billy to follow her, to stay together. The ramp looked narrow edge on, but it was as wide as their driveway back home. At the top of the walkway, a jagged, lopsided opening led to the interior of the looming iceberg.

Dad set his boot against the ramp. Leaned into it. "Feels solid."

Billy took two quick steps onto it and then a little hop. The not-ice didn't even tremble. "Solid."

"Take it easy, twerp."

"You take it easy."

"It might be cooler inside," said Dad. "We might get some condensation in there, maybe find some pools of water."

Beau crossed her arms. "Really?"

"We're here. We might as well look."

Billy looked up at the crooked opening in the iceberg's side. It was a cave. A deep, not-ice cave in the not-iceberg. "Do you think something lives in there?"

Beau looked at him. Looked out at the trees across the grassy field. "He's got a point. Again."

Dad took a few steps up the ramp. Pointed at the entrance. "It's too small for any of the big ones to get in. We can deal with any of the little ones."

"The ones we've seen so far," she clarified.

He shrugged. "It's this or we hike blindly through the forest looking for a spring or a stream."

She sighed. Looked down at Billy. "Come on, twerp. You can go first and find all the monsters for us."

"Found one!" he cried, pointing at her face.

"All together," said Dad.

They walked up the ramp. Through the crooked opening. Into the iceberg.

Inside was cool and quiet, and the not-ice cave turned out to be a long tunnel. The walls flowed into the ceiling and had ripples all through them like dozens of arches. Or ribs. It was wide enough for them to walk almost side by side. Dad stayed in front, Billy and Beau behind him on either side. Sunlight still reached through the not-ice and gave everything a bright edge.

"It smells clean," said Billy. "Not like our cave."

Beau sniffed the air. "It smells fresh. Like water."

Dad took a deep breath through his nose. "Maybe nothing lives here."

The tunnel forked and they went left. Some smaller tunnels split off, and a few small chambers. It forked again; this time the other branch went up on a slope and curved away out of sight.

Dad leaned into both tunnels. "Go up or stay on this level?"

"Water's going to run down," Beau said.

"Good call."

Billy pointed at the floor. "It's really clean."

"You said that already," she told him.

"No. It doesn't just smell clean. There's no dirt or leaves or little pieces that broke off the walls or anything." He waved his hand at the tunnel. "There wasn't any in the little rooms, either."

Beau looked at Dad. Dad shrugged again. "Maybe it all gets washed out in the rainy season."

"There's a rainy season here?"

"I don't know."

They walked a little farther and the tunnel opened up into a big space, almost thirty feet across and at least that high. Big pillars of glassy white-blue stretched up the walls and then reached out to hold up the wide expanse of not-ice above them. The whole room reminded Billy of big underground caves, but also of old churches and castles. He couldn't tell if it was something that had happened or something somebody'd made.

He pointed up. "It's a cathedral ceiling."

Dad patted his shoulder. "Technically, this one's a vaulted ceiling."

"Yep. That's what I said."

Everything sparkled in the big room. Little spots of brightness decorated it like the glow-in-the-dark stars in Billy's bedroom back home, except these seemed to drift up and down the walls. More hallways stretched out between the thick pillars, and a few little spaces sank into the other openings, like small cave closets.

Almost a quarter of the floor was raised up like a low, almost round stage. Again, like in a church. Or the school auditorium, but without any seats. At the center was a tall, bright purple column reaching up to the ceiling, maybe as wide around as Dad's leg. It shimmered in the light, like it was holding up a lot of weight and trying not to move. Billy thought it looked like it was made of grape jelly. Or blueberry pie filling.

Beau took a few steps toward the purple column, looking up and down it. "What the fuck is that?"

"Language," said Dad, but he was staring at it too.

"Sorry."

Billy walked to the edge of the stage. "Can I touch it?"

"Let's hang on a minute, bud."

Then the pillar grew a dozen tentacles and reached for him.

Billy shrieked. Dad grabbed him by the collar and yanked him away. Beau grabbed them both, and they all stumbled back a few feet. Dad pushed free of their grips and put himself between them and the tentacles.

The purple column collapsed down from the ceiling, getting thicker and shorter until it formed a big ball as tall as Beau. Half the tentacles pulled back into the ball while the others rolled together into a pair of long arms with an extra elbow. The ball stretched up, the top pinched in and became a little ball, and that ball had a chin and a nose.

"Salutations, Gather family," said the shimmering grape-jelly man.

"What the FUCK?!" shouted Dad.

"LANGUAGE," yelled Beau, and Billy laughed despite being scared.

A ripple ran through the purple figure. It stayed up on the little stage, away from them. "Forgive me, Beau Gather. My attention was on other matters and I did not note your arrival. Is there a problem, James Gather? Do you require my assistance?"

They all stared at the shape. It didn't have eyes, but Billy felt pretty sure it was staring back at them. He also felt pretty sure it wasn't a mean stare.

Dad stood a little taller. "You know us?"

"For almost two years now," said the purple figure. The thin-groove mouth didn't move, the words just came out of the air around the creature. The voice sounded . . . bubbly. Like a bunch of people all saying the same thing at the same time. "Since the three of you first arrived in the valley."

"Two years," repeated Beau.

The jelly-face flattened out and became smooth, like an egg. "Yes, Beau Gather. As your perception of time is measured. Not in that manner, no. My vessel encountered an unexpected conflict in this location and was destroyed."

"What?"

"I see the cause of your confusion," said the purple figure. "I am what you would call a multidimensional entity. My perception of what you refer to as *time* is nonlinear. While I have known you and your family for twenty-one months, you view this as our first encounter. They have no effect on stegosaurus biochemistry."

Billy realized it was still talking to them even though it didn't have a mouth anymore.

Dad took a step forward. "You can see through time?"

"This is a correct interpretation of the facts, James Gather."

Billy stepped forward to stand by Dad. "Did you fall through time like we did?"

"Not in that manner, no. My vessel encountered an unexpected conflict in this location and was destroyed. While I escaped destruction myself, I cannot leave this place."

"Your vessel?"

"Yes, Beau Gather."

"You . . . you're an alien. Like, an outer space, different-planet alien."

The purple figure dropped its arms to its sides and they melted into the simple shape of its body. "'Alien' is a concept that does not consider the interconnectedness of the cosmos. I am life, as are you. We are merely life with different origin points."

"Whoa," said Billy. "We're talking to an alien."

Beau snort-laughed.

"So you're another castaway here?" asked Dad.

"Yes, James Gather. That is the name you assigned to me when we first encountered each other."

"We're meeting for the first time right now."

Billy snickered.

"Salutations, Gather family. I am, as always, pleased to make your acquaintance again. You may refer to me as the Castaway."

16

PARKER

The sun had already risen when Parker stretched herself awake in her little room. The mattress—more like a futon—was a roughly-knitted sack stuffed with straw or grass, but it'd still been a lot more comfortable than the ground the night before. Truth was, she'd been so exhausted last night it had felt luxurious.

She looked over at the window. A couple shafts of light close to the wall. No shadows she could see. Crap, how late had she slept? It'd barely been two days, but this place, the valley, was already messing with her internal clock.

Parker stretched again, slid out from under the heavy quilt, grabbed her underwear from the lone wooden chair. Nothing else to wear, so she'd shaken out her clothes, left them hanging to air out overnight, and gone to sleep in her T-shirt. She knew she should've aired it out too, but she always felt weird sleeping naked, especially in a place she didn't know.

She examined the room in the daylight while she buttoned her shirt and tied her boots. Like a lot of the buildings they'd seen yesterday, the guest house was mostly wooden planks and bamboo. Not even broken up into rooms as much as divided with thin walls. Someone had snored like hell all night. Probably Josh or Noah since Sam had slept on the other side of the house. He'd offered her the far room, but she'd felt a little safer being close to Noah.

No decorations anywhere that she'd seen. More like a barracks or a hospital ward than an Airbnb. It felt like temporary housing.

It was *supposed* to be temporary housing.

They'd argued with Noah for almost another hour last night. Half berating him for dragging them through time and getting them trapped there. Half encouraging him to figure out the flaw in his calculations and fix it. Not quite half and half. Josh didn't seem that upset about being away from all his problems in the present. She and Sam had been more determined to get back.

They'd all been upset, though. Enough so that they stayed up arguing until all of them almost dropped from exhaustion.

And even then, she'd spent twenty minutes last night studying the quilt in her room by lamplight. Lots of squares and triangles and rectangles of all different fabrics, bound together with dull, heavy thread. Cotton. Polyester. Wool. Linen. Denim. Nylon. One red triangle of spandex. A black rectangle that gleamed like silk but felt like . . . metal? One of the cotton panels looked like it might be part of a faded concert T-shirt in Spanish. There didn't seem to be a pattern to the quilt, like other ones she'd seen. Just someone trying to piece together all the fabric they could without wasting any of it.

Parker liked that. Someone trying to find the right place for everything. Trying to bring some order to chaos.

Was the valley like that? All pieced together? Maybe with an underlying order?

The guest house had a back door that led out to the . . . outhouse? Privy? Whatever it was, maybe half a dozen of them were clustered together, surrounded by the different buildings. There was more modern design inside than she'd expected, and it didn't smell as bad as she'd worried.

Better get used to that, too.

Back in the guest house, she wandered out to the common room.

More wooden chairs. Something probably wide enough to count as a couch. A stone fireplace. A nice place, but it had the same temporary vibe.

Noah and Ross, the old android, sat across from each other. Noah had his thinking face on, and she could see the wrinkles between his nose that meant frustration was creeping into his mood. The android's hood hung down on its—his?—back, exposing all the cracks in his can-shaped head.

"What about the orchard? All the pear trees?"

"The original trees died off," said Ross, "but the orchard grew wild for several decades until a trio of giant sloths took up residence there and ate all the fruit and then a large percentage of the trees themselves. Seventeen years after that several hectares of tundra appeared and shifted the remains of the orchard deeper into Klaa territory. Approximately seventy meters of a Roman or possible Etruscan road appeared forty-four years after that, and shifted the orchard again, closer to the Ice Castle this time. It's remained there since."

Noah's jaw shifted. He glanced up at Parker, gave her a little nod of acknowledgment, maybe wondering if she was going to pick up where they left off last night. "I'm just trying to get caught up on what happened to my sister. And the valley."

"Oh."

The android turned at the waist with a squeak. "It's good to see you again, Parker."

"Um . . . thanks."

"A lot of this is kind of personal," Noah said. "I'd like to just talk with Ross by myself."

Parker briefly thought about how personal having her whole goddamned future ripped away was and maybe that should be his priority right now. Then she remembered when one of her undergrad roommates learned that a friend had died and Facebook algorithms had hidden the news from her for almost a year, and how much it'd devastated her. But then Parker also remembered that Noah had been lying to her for years about who he was.

And then out loud she just said "Sure."

"You're free to go anywhere in Roanoke," Ross told her. "It's safe within the walls. If you wish to go outside, you may want to ask a warden to go with you."

"What about the big statue of Anubis we found in the cliff wall?" Noah'd already turned his attention back to the android, and Parker knew she'd been forgotten. Again.

She crossed the room. Pushed the door open into the eye-blinkingly bright sunlight. Three steps carried her down the rough steps and almost right into Sam, who squatted on one knee in the dirt path between houses.

"What are you—"

"I just—sorry—dammit!"

A few feet away one of the black-feathered microraptors let out a rattly hiss and awkwardly threw itself into the air. Its flurry of wings carried it to the far side of the path, where it perched on something that looked a lot like a mailbox made of bamboo. The little dinosaur's claws scraped on the mailbox for a moment and then it hurled itself upward again, flapping and fluttering until it was on the roof of a cottage.

Parker watched it settle. "It's like when chickens try to fly."

"I was trying to lure it closer."

"Is that smart? They probably bite."

"Yeah, but I'd—how many people get to say they'd been bitten by a dinosaur and lived?"

She sighed. "I'd guess a lot more than we'd think."

"Fair point."

Parker looked around. After a night's sleep, she noticed more details about the little village. The guest house had two big patches of wildflowers growing in front of it, or maybe they were gardens that'd been left to do their own thing. Looking at the other small cottages around her, she could see decorations hung on doors and a few windows with curtains. Some had simple bamboo blinds hung in them. A few other buildings had flowers. One down at the end of the wide path, closest to the big wall, had a little waist-high fence made of bamboo.

She didn't see as many people wandering around as there'd been when they'd arrived yesterday, but maybe they were all at . . . work? Did people have jobs here? Was there a schoolhouse full of kids somewhere?

Sam glanced up at the sky. "What time do you think it is?"

"No idea. Why? Do you have to be somewhere?"

He snorted out a laugh. "No. No, definitely not. Just weird. I almost never sleep late."

Parker shrugged. "We were exhausted. And didn't you and Noah say everything's different here twenty or thirty times?"

"I only said it fifteen."

She let out a little laugh of her own. Looked around. Waited for him to say something else. Realized he was waiting on her. "We should go check on Olivia."

Sam's face danced through a few emotions. "Oh. Okay."

"What?"

"A little confused, I guess."

"About?"

She got the distinct sense Sam was deciding the best way to phrase something. "I know you and I—we don't know each other that well, but with some of the talk around the department, I had the sense you and Olivia aren't—you don't like each other. Much."

A handful of memories and responses bubbled up in Parker's mind. "It's all her. I try to be professional about it."

"About . . . ?"

She looked up and down the path, tried to get her bearings and remember the path they'd taken last night. "Let's just both be professional and go check on our colleague who's in the . . . hospital. Doctor's office. Whatever."

He took the hint. "Okay."

Parker looked back and forth on the street. Big wall one way. Big building the other. "I have no idea where that is."

"Me either."

"Retrace our steps to the front gate? Ask someone along the way?'

"Yeah, I—that sounds good. I'm pretty sure we came from that way last night." He pointed toward the big two-story building.

As they approached, Parker realized why the big structure looked so utilitarian. Small, scattered windows. Two big doors. It looked a lot like a barn. Or maybe a warehouse.

One of the big doors was open a little bit.

"Do you . . . what do you think's inside?"

Parker shook her head. The silver obelisk loomed off to the right, and the main gate past that. Definitely the way they'd come in. Had the bionic-looking woman carried Olivia this way, too? Was one of the surrounding buildings the doctor's?

Sam nudged the big door open a little wider. "Smells like plants, maybe, or grain. And dirt."

"Dirt?"

"Yeah, it sort of . . . it smells like a barn, I guess."

Parker sighed. Moved a little closer. Sam pushed the door a bit wider.

It did smell like a barn. Parker'd never even been on a farm, but if you'd asked her to name the combined smells of dried grass and leaves and fresh dirt and dust, she probably would've gone with *barn*. The door was almost halfway open now and she could see bundles and baskets and bulging sacks everywhere. Fruit, vegetables, a wooden rack of what looked like basketball-sized eggs. Bolts of coarse fabric, coils of rope, a small lizard-bird thing gnawing on a potato, a whole shelf of—

The lizard was maybe the size of a cat and looked like a blue-green cartoon version of a T-Rex, with an overly rounded head, stubby beak, and plump legs. A crest of green and yellow feathers ran over its head, down its back, and thinned out on its stubby tail.

"Shoo," said Sam. He stepped forward, waved a hand at the lizard, and it leaped out of the basket. Landing jarred the potato out of its mouth, and its head lunged down twice trying to grab it again. Sam waved his hand again and the little dinosaur dashed behind a stack of baskets.

Something hit the ground behind them. "Can I help you two?"

A woman about their age had come from . . . somewhere? She had dark, wavy hair, tanned skin, solid shoulders, and a wide smile. A bulging sack sat by her feet, dust settling around it.

Parker waved into the warehouse. "There was a . . . a little dinosaur eating something. A potato."

The woman's smile faded. "Chubby little blue-green thing? Feather mohawk?"

"Yeah."

She shook her head. "Three or four of them snuck in here and I can't ever get them all out. Doesn't help when *Geoff keeps leaving the storehouse door unlatched!*" She shouted the last words to the sky, or maybe to somewhere else in Roanoke, but there didn't seem to be much anger behind them. Then her gaze fell back to Parker and Sam. "So, hey, what's crackin', newcomers?"

Sam's eyes bugged a little. "You remember us?"

"Well, y'know. Small town, we don't get a lot of strangers."

"Of course," said Parker.

The woman stuck her hand out, half gesture, half offering. "I'm Marissa."

"Parker." She shook the hand. The woman had thin fingers, but a solid grip.

"Sam."

"Nice to meet you."

"How long have you . . . been here?" asked Sam.

"Four years. Up until last night, I was the newest person in Roanoke."

"Jesus."

"Yeah." Marissa's clothes reminded Parker of the quilt in the guesthouse. Enough denim to recognize the heavily-stitched-together bell-bottom jeans. The wide sleeves and deep V-neck that might've been lightweight and silky a dozen patches ago. *The clothes of Theseus,* she thought to herself.

"So is it, I don't know, rude to ask where you're from?"

Marissa shook her head. "Nah. I'm from New Jersey, but I was in Queens when I ended up here."

"Queens as in New York City?"

"Yep. Right out of the Big Apple. Makes you wonder about all the people who disappear, doesn't it?"

Parker gave a slow nod. "And when was this?"

Marissa gave her another smile. "September of '73."

"1973 was four years ago?"

"For me, yeah. Freaky-deaky, right?"

"Wow," said Sam.

"Speaking of which . . . people have been talking about you all morning. And, y'know, the guy you're with."

Her gaze settled on each of them. Still friendly but waiting for them to speak.

"You mean Noah," Sam said, filling the empty moment. "Billy Gather."

The smile never flinched, but a whole collection of emotions rolled through the woman's eyes. "So it's really him?"

Parker shrugged. "Well, we only found out two days ago."

"Oh?"

"He's Billy Gather," said Sam. "Really."

"So he did it? He got out and came back?"

"Sort of."

"And does he . . . does he know how to get out again?"

Parker's mood sank again. "No."

Marissa's mood sank, too. "Oh."

"Sorry," said Sam.

Marissa shook her head. "My own fault. Should've known by now."

"Do you think maybe you could help us, though?" Parker asked. "We're trying to find our friend Olivia. They took her to the doctor last night. Where's that?"

The woman shifted her feet and jerked her thumb over her shoulder, gesturing down the path toward the main gate. "See the house over there with the yellow flowers out front? Right across from the obelisk?"

Parker found it. "Yeah."

"That's Madame Monique. She's the doctor."

"That's her office?"

"Her everything. Office. Clinic. Home. Hospital."

"Right. Of course."

Marissa sighed. "So you're all from the . . . what, '90s, if Billy's all grown-up now? 2000-something?"

"2023." Parker looked for a red cross or a barber pole or something that implied a doctor's residence, but apparently Roanoke was small enough signs weren't needed.

"Wild," said Marissa. "We're gonna have to have some long talks about music and movies."

"Maybe after we check on our friend."

She flashed them a two-fingered peace sign, crouched, and heaved the big sack back on her shoulder. "Back to work, then. Kill for a shopping cart, right?"

Marissa balanced the sack, kicked the door open a little more with one foot, and took a few heavy steps into the storehouse.

Parker and Sam walked down the path. As far as she could tell, this was the main road, running straight through the little village. Front gate to back wall. The whole place couldn't be much larger than two football fields.

Sam paused at the obelisk. "He was right about this. Noah. It's not supposed to be here. The platinum obelisk's on a big savanna maybe a mile from their cave."

"Maybe they built the town around it." Parker examined the tall monument. It looked like the other ones, just shinier.

"We're at least two miles from the valley wall."

"Maybe it moved. Like . . . like the android was saying last night."

"Ross. He's a Rossum Seven. Roman numerals."

She gave him a look.

"Some people memorize baseball games or Marvel movies. I memorized this place. Back then. When I was little."

She nodded at the obelisk. "So how does this one kill you?"

He reached out a hand and she reached out her own to stop him. "It should be safe," he said. "The glass one's the only dangerous one."

"You sure?"

"I mean, it did what he always said it did. He was confused because it was in the wrong place."

"Like this one is."

He still let his hand drop. Pointed at some of the engraved lines. "The runes light up when you touch them."

"Why?"

He shrugged. "They never figured out why any of them did anything. There's, well, there was a gold one on the other side of the valley that hums in sunlight. And one made of marble that knocks you out cold."

"It shocks you?"

Sam shook his head. "You just fall asleep. Instantly. His sister was the first one to touch it and she dropped so fast they thought it'd killed her."

"Jesus. And they'd just lost their mom, right?"

"Yeah."

"They must've been freaking out."

"They did. Probably saved them, though. They got *really* cautious about touching any new obelisks they found."

"Like the glass one."

He nodded.

"Or this one, maybe."

"Yeah, okay, point made."

She walked up the stone steps of the doctor's house and rapped her knuckles on the heavy wooden door. It looked like the kind of door someone would have in *The Lord of the Rings*. Rough planks and iron straps and square-headed nails.

A few moments later they heard movement inside. The movement became footsteps and the door opened to reveal the petite woman from yesterday. Parker got a better look at her now, free of shock and confusion. Not much older than her. Not much taller than Sam. Big eyes.

Curly brown hair pulled back into a messy bun. Her long skirt brushed the floor, her long sleeves and high collar ended in frayed ruffles. The cords of her corset didn't match, and they'd clearly snapped and been retied or replaced several times.

The woman smiled and looked even younger. "Ahhh. The other newcomers. Hello!"

"Hi," Parker said. "We're here about—"

"Your friend, *oui, oui*. Please." She waved them inside. "She is in the side room."

The doctor's house felt more like a home, even if it still had the island resort feel. Bamboo furniture and shelves, a few bundles of dried flowers. Something about it felt more . . . permanent.

"We were not properly introduced last night," the doctor said, gesturing at herself as she walked across the main room toward a short hall. "I am Madame Monique Cadieux."

"I'm Sam."

"Parker."

The doctor tipped her head to each of them. "Samuel. Parker."

Sam cleared his throat. "It's not—it's just Sam."

She led them into the hall, pulled aside a curtain of what looked like coarse linen, and gestured them through.

Going off her bare shoulders, Olivia had been stripped, cleaned, and tucked into the bed. Her arms lay flat on top of another multicolored quilt, and one hand had been bandaged with a ribbon of off-white cloth. Slack face, eyes closed, and for an awful moment Parker thought they were looking at a corpse. Then the quilt rose up and sank back down.

The doctor stood by the side of the bed. "I have done what I can for her. She is not responsive in any way. Her pulse is weak, her breathing shallow. She has a bad burn on one arm. Dehydration. I sat her up earlier and fed her a bit of broth. Truthfully, all we can do now is make her comfortable and wait."

Parker stepped forward. Reached for Olivia's hand. Stopped herself. "Wait for . . . ?"

Monique's hands came up, danced quietly for a moment in front of her chest.

Frustration and anger boiled up in Parker's gut.

Sam broke the silence. "She's still alive, though."

"Oui. But I do not know why. No one has ever survived for more than a few moments after touching the glass obelisk. It is possible when the electrical charge was released, her friend acted as a shield, taking the force of the strike."

"So she might live," Parker said.

The doctor raised a thin finger. "Or she merely may not die as quickly. We should not have false hope, but it would seem there is at least a possibility of hope."

"Is there anything we can do?"

Monique shook her head. "I have no other patients at the moment, so I shall continue to care for her as best I can. I shall let you know of any change in her condition."

"One other . . . can I ask an unrelated question?"

Parker and Monique both looked at Sam. "Oui?"

"The monolith outside. It's safe to touch, right?"

"Of course. If it was not, there would be a fence around it."

"There isn't a fence around the other one," said Parker.

"They have tried. It is difficult to maintain something so far from Roanoke."

She guided them back out of the house, and Parker had a gnawing, instinctive impulse to give her a phone number or email address. Something so the doctor could get in touch with them. She'd almost squashed it by the time she and Sam stepped outside and the heavy door closed behind them.

She stepped off the front step, down past the flowerbeds, and into the dirt path. Her brain spun to a new target. Sam took a few quick steps to keep up. "I guess it's better than nothing," he said, glancing back at the house. "For now, maybe we—"

"What's your name?"

Sam froze. Considered. "What's it—why does it matter to you?"

"I don't like it when things don't make sense. And you keep not making sense."

"I don't—I make sense." His voice had that nervous, sputtering quality again. Trying to rush the words out faster than his tongue could make them.

"You won't say why you joined this trip last minute, and now you won't say what your real name is. I'm already dealing with two people on this trip who were using fake names."

"Sam is my real name."

"But . . . ?"

He sighed. Took a breath. The sputter faded. "Sam is short for Samael."

"Sama—wait, what?"

"Yeah."

"Isn't that . . ." Her mind dragged out references, then went back and dragged them out again to make sure she'd heard him right. "That's like a demon name, isn't it?"

"No. Not exactly." He sighed again. "Sometimes. It's a name with a lot of mythology behind it, depending on whose version of the Bible you're reading."

"How the hell did—"

He walked past her to the obelisk. "My parents are that kind of religious where they don't actually know the Bible, just what other people tell them it says. So they heard the name somewhere and thought it was a variation on Samuel. A great name for their little due-in-five-months baby if it was a boy."

"Nobody told them?"

"They kept it a secret until I was born. Meet our new son, isn't he beautiful, we named him after the angel of death."

Parker giggled. Hated herself for it, but couldn't help it. "That must've been a hell of a delivery room announcement."

"Yeah, everyone thought they were hearing it wrong or my folks were saying 'Samuel' weird. It was over a year before somebody broke the news to them."

"Someone from the church?"

"No, a guy my dad worked with." He shrugged. "It was too late to change it without a lawyer and a court order, so they started calling me Sam. And now I get to have this conversation every time someone asks about my name for the rest of my life."

Something croaked near them, the sound tapering off into a hiss. Parker looked around. Then up.

One of the four-winged microraptors perched on the side of the monolith, maybe halfway up, its tiny claws hooking into the engraved symbols. It aimed a raspy croak down at them, then scrabbled its way up the last twelve feet to the top. Once there it straightened up, spread its larger wings, and launched. The rear wings spread once it was airborne and it sailed over a thatch roof. Parker followed it, craning her neck around as the dark shape flapped higher and then soared off over the little houses and out of sight.

She let her gaze drop, saw Sam still looking up into the sky. A few heartbeats later he noticed her looking at him. "I guess it's safe to touch."

"Looks like."

Sam reached out and touched one of the symbols. It flared to life under his finger, bright enough to be seen against the shining metal in broad daylight. He tapped three-four-five more of the glyphs, and each one lit up, only to fade a few seconds later.

Parker traced a little symbol with one finger. The metal felt . . . slick? More like polished stone than metal. And it didn't feel that warm for a piece of metal that'd been in full sun for three or four hours.

The symbol looked like a musical note, but with a loop on both ends. Or maybe a lowercase *q* and *b* stuck together. There were three fine lines under the upper loop, not much more than scratches in the obelisk's silvery surface. The whole thing was maybe half an inch tall, in a row with at least forty other characters. There had to be close to three thousand tiny runes on this face alone, more than half of them way out of her reach.

She lifted her finger away and looked at the glowing symbol. The steady, intense glow reminded her of an electric burner. But this was white light, and she still couldn't feel any heat coming from the metal obelisk. It didn't feel like fluorescent light on her eyes. An LED? Some kind of chemical reaction?

She ran her finger down the row of symbols, watched them brighten and then fade a few moments later.

"I'm touching an obelisk," said Sam, a little bit of breathlessness in his voice. His hand went up and down one metal face, leaving lines of little glowing runes behind it. "One of *the* obelisks. The platinum obelisk. From the savanna."

Parker glanced around the village, taking in the lack of open space and tall grass.

"Billy—Noah—and his sister, whenever they were near this thing, they'd race each other, trying to light up as many runes as they could at the same time."

"Did it make something happen?"

"No. Just a game. Big sister trying to entertain her little brother."

"She sounds cool."

"He thought she was the best."

Parker reached out to touch another symbol. Then her gaze dropped past her outstretched hand to the ground in front of the obelisk. "You read all those books?"

"Yeah. Pretty much. Some of them three or four times."

"Does he ever mention anything strange about time in them?"

"Besides being trapped a hundred million years in the past?"

"Yeah."

"I don't—not that I can think of. Why?"

Parker flexed her fingers and looked at the shadow on the ground. It sat directly below her hand. Maybe half an inch difference at most. "Because it's still noon."

17

JOSH

Josh's first thought when he woke up was that he hadn't slept this peacefully in a week now.

Then came the panic. Where was he? He didn't recognize the bed, or the tropical-island-themed hotel room. The smells were weird. Nature, but not the nature he knew. The distant sounds from outside made him think of a farm. Somewhere secluded, where people couldn't hear you scream. Somewhere people could . . .

And then sitting up spilled memories out over his mind, reminding him where he was. *When* he was. In a prehistoric valley with dinosaurs and killer obelisks and evil cornfields. And people who seemed to be friendly but also carried a lot of pointy sticks.

All in all, kind of a relief.

His stomach rumbled. How late had he slept? He'd eaten enough last night to be conscious of how much he was eating. How could he be hungry again?

Josh rolled off the bed. He'd slept fully dressed, like every other night for the past eight days. Never know when you might need to wake up and run. He wondered what the odds were people at the dawn of time had coffee. Or powershots. Or maybe some nootropics.

He peeled his shirt off. Swung it over his head a few times to air it out. Shook the wrinkles out and pulled it back on. Debated doing it with his pants, too, but decided they could last another day.

The little hallway of the guest house was empty. A few moments of listening convinced him the other rooms were, too. He could hear voices back by the main room, but the house had a certain stillness that told you nobody was moving.

He moved cautiously out into the room. Found Noah sitting with the android. Talking about mushrooms. Noah's eyes met his and the conversation paused in a slightly awkward way.

"I forgot you were here," said Noah. "No offense."

"None taken. What time is it?"

The android turned to look at him. "The sun's been in the sky for four hours thirty-seven minutes. We're one hour twenty-three minutes from the midday point."

"Wow."

"I guess the walk yesterday wore you out," mused Noah.

"I was running with a lot of sleep debt before this, y'know? What's up with you two?"

Noah stared at him for a moment, then pushed his fingertips up along his jawline, stretching his beard out before letting it drop back into place. "I'm not sure. Ross insists he's fine, but there seem to be holes in his memory. Things he should know, but doesn't."

"Like . . . ?"

Noah rolled his head from one shoulder and back. "A lot of specific stuff. It wouldn't mean anything to you. It's just . . . these are such precise holes, and he's got no awareness the memories are even missing."

"I don't," agreed Ross.

"It's not like damage or degradation. It almost seems like parts of his memory were deliberately erased."

Josh let the words hang in the air for a moment. "Who'd do that?"

"I don't know."

"Why would they—"

"I don't know."

Josh took a moment. Tried to get a sense if Noah was looking for ideas or just thinking out loud. The guy's ego had dropped a notch or three over the course of the night, but he still gave off *I know best* vibes that tingled Josh's salesman sense.

Josh cleared his throat. "Maybe it's a storage issue? If it's been four hundred years maybe his . . . his hard drive's full?"

Ross turned and gestured at his head with a skeletal hand. "At the moment, Josh, I have two-point-three petabytes of memory storage I'm not using. This doesn't include specialized submemories for languages, facial recognition, or standard operational datasets."

"It's not that," agreed Noah. Another few moments passed and then he nodded in that just-a-little-too-polite way people did when they had to deal with some small talk before getting back to what they were doing. "Well, you've got time to look around the village."

"Are the others still here somewhere?"

"They left a while ago."

Josh knew when to take a hint.

The sun was high and bright outside. He tried to remember if his sunglasses were in his coat pocket. The coat he'd left back in his room.

He stood in the middle of the dirt path. Alone. Painfully aware he didn't have any friends within . . . well, a few million years of here.

The little village looked peaceful and calm, but didn't they always? Then people came marching out in flowered robes and stuffed you in a dead bear or a wicker man. Or maybe into a dinosaur's mouth, in this case.

Josh wandered down to where two paths intersected. Turned left. Walked a little bit. More of these simple, cottage-ish-looking buildings. Although the ones here felt a little lifeless. He couldn't say why, but this section of the little village felt . . . deserted? Abandoned? The cottages didn't seem run-down or damaged, but he felt pretty sure nobody lived in any of them.

The path ended at a corner of the big wall. The back of the village? He was pretty sure he was on the far side, away from the main gate. The wall sections didn't come together at a right angle, and he tried to picture it from above. Was the village a pentagon? A hexagon? He'd read somewhere castle walls had weird angles for a reason. Something about defense and how attackers had to come at them.

His eyes drifted up the wall, following the lines of the heavy logs, and he realized someone was looking down at him from the walkway.

At the top of the wall thirty-odd feet away, a dark-skinned woman stood and stared at him. Her hair was all thick braids. Her clothes screamed *Egyptian* to him. Big round collar almost reaching her shoulders. Lots of gold bracelets. Skirt that went to her knees. Shin guards. Other than the big collar she was topless and Josh realized he was staring.

She stared back at him. Judging him. He remembered the low wave of hostility that had rippled through the crowd last night. Had anything changed while he'd been asleep?

The woman had a bow in one hand. Not a high-tech, Hawkeye-type bow with all the pulleys and crossbars, but a thick, squat, powerful-looking thing. An arrow rested casually on the string, held in place by her fingers. It looked like all she had to do was swing it up and she'd be ready to shoot.

Definitely staring at him. Had she been in the crowd last night? Just annoyed he was looking at her? The woman gave off serious Dora Milaje vibes with her posture and bearing. She didn't seem bothered by her own nudity, but it made him a bit uncomfortable, even at a distance.

He let his gaze slide off the woman as casually as he could. Turned his body ever so slowly. Walked off down another path between the big wall and the random buildings.

Another woman came around the bend, a heavy-looking bundle of firewood up on one of her shoulders. She wore a tank top with a square neck, and glossy blue-black boots under ragged pants. They looked at each other as they drew closer, and when they were a few yards apart he remembered the futuristic eye socket from last night.

"Morning."

"Hello," she responded.

Her blue-black boots had toes and ankle joints. Cybernetic feet. They matched the eye socket. And the arm holding the firewood.

"Old war injury."

He met her eye again. Eyes. "So sorry. I didn't mean to stare."

She waved him off with her free hand. "You're a newcomer. You're going to stare at a lot of things. Wait until you meet Thate."

"Thate?"

She nodded again. Held out her hand. Her flesh and blood hand. Well, the hand that looked more like flesh and blood. "Pyr. I'm the blacksmith."

He shook her hand. It felt real. "Josh Redd. I'm . . . well, I guess I was the guide."

Pyr gave him a quizzical look. The blue-black eye socket flexed and moved like skin. It could've been body paint, except it so clearly wasn't. The eye inside that socket was a brighter blue than the other eye.

"We were on a hike," he explained. "I was their guide. Well, substitute guide. Getting them where they wanted to be."

Her mouth twisted into something like a smile. "That didn't go well."

"I think for one of us it went exactly as planned."

"Ahhh. So. Billy Gather."

"Yeah. It's him. I mean, we didn't run a DNA test or anything. But he seems to know a lot about this place."

"Does he?"

A few random thoughts skipped through his mind. Noah being confused about distances. Where things were. Not recognizing things. "I think . . . he knows enough."

"But he doesn't know how to get out again."

"I . . . no, he doesn't. You already heard about that?"

She nodded. "Small town. Word travels fast. You can ask questions. It's acceptable."

He realized he was staring again. "I'm sorry. I've never met a cyborg before. It's . . . kind of cool."

"Not a cyborg. A person."

"Oh. Sorry." He rethought the body paint thing, then wondered if Pyr had some elaborate tattoos. Then she shifted her feet and he saw sections shift and flex and no, definitely not original parts there. He knew how badly talks could go when you messed up someone's preferred nomenclature, so he decided to avoid the topic and just nodded. "War injury. So you're . . . a veteran?"

"Technically I'm a deserter."

"Oh. Sorry? I guess."

Another wave of her free hand. "It was rough at first, but that was a while ago." She still had the huge bundle of firewood on her shoulder, as if she'd forgotten it. There had to be at least two dozen quartered logs in that bundle, held in place with a few loops of crude rope. Two hundred pounds, easy. She looked at him. At his clothes. "You're all from the twentieth century?"

"Twenty-first."

She mused on this. "Before or after the Unification?"

"I guess . . . before?"

Pyr nodded slowly.

A dozen questions flitted through his mind, but habit and sales experience kept him from asking most of them. If you can't control the conversation, at least control how people *feel* about the conversation.

"Well," he said, slipping back into casual small talk mode, "it's been great speaking with you, Pyr. I should probably . . . get going. Go find some food."

She gestured with her free hand. "Keep walking that way. The path follows the wall to the main gate, on the far side of the wood shack. You're pretty much there. Then you can go right up through the center of town and back to the main hall. They might still have some breakfast, or maybe early lunch."

"Thanks." He looked up at the bundle of firewood. "Do you need any, uhhh, help? With that?"

"I think I've got it. The forge is right over there."

She pointed at a building behind Josh. It had a large chimney of mismatched stones running up the side, with a steady stream of dark smoke snaking out of the top. He wondered if they'd followed that line of smoke to the village yesterday.

"Just trying to be polite."

"Of course." She sidestepped around him and headed for the forge building.

Josh followed the path. Went around one bend, then another, and saw one of the cottage-houses with five or six stacks of firewood. There was a big work area on one side of the building with a wooden roof over it, like an outdoor patio, surrounded by mounds of sawdust. It struck him that everything here was being done by hand. Somebody was cutting all the firewood, making all the *boards*, with an axe or a handsaw. That had to be somebody's full-time job.

After the wood shack was the square barracks-ish building. The top of it lined up with the wall's walkway. Then the main gate, and there was the windmill over there, and the big silver obelisk they had walked past when they came into Roanoke last night. Another few minutes of walking through the little village got him back where he started, standing on the path between the main hall and the guest house.

He hadn't passed anyone else. There'd been Pyr, the woman up on the wall, a guard at the gate, and . . . nobody. Roanoke didn't feel deserted, but it definitely felt underpopulated.

Granted, he didn't know how a village like this would work. Maybe people were all squirreled away in their little shops making . . . blacksmith stuff. Or cloth or food or something. Windmills were actually mills, right? For milling grain into flour. How many people did that need? Three? Four?

Still . . . Roanoke seemed a little too quiet. A little too empty.

He went up the stone steps into the main hall.

The smell of hot bread and oil hit his nose, plus some spices he couldn't name. The main hall looked brighter. Friendlier. That sense he'd had when he woke up, of being at a tropical-island-themed hotel, washed over him again.

Qiang sat at the table, speaking with the Aboriginal man, Warwick, and a woman in what looked like a quilt that had been turned into an old-fashioned coat. Or maybe it had started out as a coat and just had a dozen major repairs.

They all looked at him. No hostility. Maybe a little surprise. Of course, new faces were probably a rarity around here.

"Ummmm . . . hi," said Josh. "Am I in the right place for food?"

"You are," the woman said with a nod.

Josh looked at the empty table, followed his nose to look through the back doors. "Is it buffet style or do I just make something myself or . . . ?"

"We have meal times," said Qiang. "But we make exceptions, too."

The woman stood up. "I'll see what we've got."

"Thank you."

She headed into the back. Her stitched-up coat went almost to her knees, like an overcoat. Something about the cut made Josh think of *Doctor Who* and old BBC period shows. Warwick murmured a few last things to Qiang and headed past Josh and out the door.

"Please," said Qiang, "join me."

"Did I just break up a meeting?"

"We were almost done anyway. You just missed your friends. Parker and Sam. They were here about twenty minutes ago."

"Oh. Do you know where they went?"

"Out to the fields, I believe. Sam was very eager to see a dinosaur."

"That sounds about right." Josh dragged out one of the big wooden chairs and sat down.

Qiang let him get settled at the table. "How are you?"

Josh felt all the layers to that question. Thought about an answer. "Well . . . hungry."

Qiang smiled.

"I got a good night's sleep. First time that's happened in a while." He looked around the main hall, glancing at the assorted items decorating the walls. "Being here, in here, it almost makes yesterday feel like some kind of bad dream."

"That's common. It takes a while to get used to all of this. Where we are. *When* we are. What's here with us."

Josh nodded agreeably even as his conversational instincts kicked in. "How long did it take you?"

Qiang considered it. "In some ways, I accepted it in about a month. In other ways . . . I think it took years."

The overcoat woman came back with a wooden plate and a cup for Josh. More of the bread knots and buttery scrambled eggs from last night and a good-sized lump of what looked like soft cheese. He briefly wondered where the cheese came from, then decided he didn't want to know. "Years?"

"Yes."

"How long have you been here?"

Qiang settled back in his chair, and Josh had the same sense he'd last night. That in his own way, the village elder was a bit of a salesman. That a lot of his job was being pleasant, giving the same talks, answering the same questions. And he was back on familiar ground now. Not like last night when their arrival had messed up his script. "Almost forty years now."

"Forty?"

He nodded.

Josh scooped up some of the eggs with a chunk of bread and studied the man's face. His hair. Tried to add in rough living, lack of sunblock and other skin care products. "You must've been . . . eight?"

"Eleven. I was walking home from school in Jinshan with three of my classmates, the road collapsed under us—or so we thought—and we found ourselves here. Burn killed two of them on the first day. The other one lasted a week. I was alone for another nine days before someone from Roanoke found me."

"Who's Burn?"

"An allosaurus. He has big splashes of red on his neck." Qiang raised his hands to the sides of his own neck and mimed little explosions with his fingers. "We call his mate Gnash. They're getting old now, but they're still very dangerous."

Josh pictured Kyle bouncing up in the air. Screaming on the ground. Getting pulled in—

"I think we met them."

"I'm glad you got away."

"We didn't. Not all of us."

"Ahhhhh. I'm so sorry."

"I didn't know him that well. I'm just their guide."

Qiang nodded again. "Still an awful thing."

"Yeah. If I was home I'd probably be taking a solid dose of sertraline."

"Ser . . . ?"

"It's an antianxiety drug. Brand name Zoloft. I'm a sales rep for a pharmaceutical group."

"Ahhhh."

"You probably could've used some, too, back then."

"Perhaps."

Josh shoved the other half of the bread knot in his mouth before he said anything else dumb. He pulled apart another one and spread more of the buttery-tasting scrambled eggs on them. They had a lot of yolk, but a texture more like warm Jell-O. "These are really wonderful. What are they?"

"Styracosaurus eggs."

Josh looked at the bread knot again. Shrugged. Pushed half of it into his mouth.

18

SAM

Sam's body kept going back and forth. Almost out of breath with excitement. Almost sick with guilt about being excited so soon after they'd seen comatose Olivia. Heart pounding again as they heard the whale-like sounds. What kind of sick bastard was this happy after watching so many of his coworkers die?

The horned dinosaur marched across a field, dragging an iron plow behind it. The tall man they'd met yesterday outside Roanoke rode on the big creature's back, holding onto two of the big spikes growing out of its neck frill. Another man steered the plow. Both of them wore wide-brimmed straw hats, the kind Sam pictured people wearing in Southeast Asia. They called back and forth to each other using words from at least three languages. The man guiding the plow saw them walking, let go of the handles, and gave them a polite bow.

At least half a dozen people worked in some of the other fields. Some weeded their sections. Others gathered vegetables. Two baskets had already been filled with something leafy, another with . . . something they'd pulled out of the ground?

"Dinosaurs as farm animals," said Parker. She stood next to him, watching the rhino-sized creature lumber along.

"Yeah. It's amazing, isn't it?"

She didn't reply.

The plow team reached the far end of the field and the dinosaur awkwardly turned, guided by a few firm taps from the rider's heels and the length of bamboo he held. The big creature let out a few low, echoing notes, like someone doing bird calls with a tuba. It shuffled its big feet some more and a few sounds echoed back from somewhere around the corner of the big wall.

"So this is a triceratops, right?"

Sam shook his head. "Styracosaurus, I think. They're related. See all the horns on the neck frill?"

"Yeah."

"Triceratops have three, and they all grow straight out of the skull. They've both got a nose horn, but the one on this guy's bigger."

She nodded. Didn't say anything else. Crossed her arms and looked out at the rhino-sized dinosaur marching back across the field.

Sam watched the styracosaurus make three more passes. It didn't seem bothered by having a rider, or hauling the plow. It could've been domesticated or naturally docile or maybe a little bit of both.

He also didn't remember a styracosaurus—or even something that sounded like a styracosaurus—in any of the books. Something else biographers had left out or changed? Or maybe another sign the valley was a lot different since Noah'd last been here? Maybe that it'd never been what he thought it was?

How much was Noah wrong about?

The dinosaur lumbered by in front of them, maybe ten feet away. Sam could see all the wrinkles and creases in the leathery skin, and how the blue-gray darkened in a few places. He even saw a few patches of what looked like tiny little dark quills on the back of all four legs. Vestigial feathers, maybe? Or maybe the styracosaurus version of chapped skin?

The man guiding the plow bowed his head to them again as he went by. He didn't smile. Sam tried to guess the man's age, but his face and hands were so sun weathered he could've been anywhere between forty and sixty. Heck, they might be the same age.

They reached the far edge of the field and the rider slid off the dinosaur's back. Pretty spry for an older guy. He tapped the styracosaurus on its big armored frill with his bamboo stick. The dinosaur let out another long, low tone and settled down on its belly. He bent his knees to kiss it on the forehead like an affectionate pet owner, then gave it two more taps. It set its chin down on the ground and made a sound that might've been a deep purr. Or maybe a burp.

Sam fought a powerful urge to go hug the dinosaur.

The rider talked with the plowman, then both of them wandered back to where Sam and Parker stood. "Hello, newcomers," he called out, raising his hand.

Sam waved back. Parker didn't. He glanced, saw her staring past them at the dinosaur.

The rider tucked his bamboo stick under one arm and held out his hand as he got closer. "Diedrich Rommel. We met yesterday when you arrived."

Sam nodded. "I remember. Sam Jones."

The German had a good handshake. Tight enough to be a bully's grip, but without that aggressiveness. He shook Sam's hand three times.

The plowman gave Parker a much more formal bow. "Kim Dak Ho."

Parker pulled her gaze away from the styracosaurus and looked at him. Held out her other hand. "Parker Sangthong."

He smiled. Took her hand in both of his. He released the hand and spoke a few words in a language Sam didn't recognize. By the look on her face, Parker didn't either.

A look of resignation flashed across Dak Ho's face, hidden quickly behind another smile. "Good to meet you."

"How are the both of you?" asked Diedrich. "The first days here can be overwhelming. And disorienting."

"Yes they can," agreed Parker.

"I think it's fantastic," Sam blurted out. "You've got a—you've trained a dinosaur!"

Diedrich looked over his shoulder. "We've trained a few. That one's Gutrune. She's a good girl."

"How long did it take you? Did you raise her from when she was little? Does—"

Parker set a hand on his shoulder. "Stop. Breathe."

"Right. Sorry. Overwhelming, yeah, like you said."

"If I understand correctly," said Dak Ho, "you're from the twenty-first century, but you've been here before." The statement brushed up against a question. Sam recognized the technique from a few different professors. Casually getting something wrong to see which students correct you. And how.

"We've never been here before," said Parker. "Just our . . . professor."

Diedrich nodded. "You're students."

"Graduate students."

Another slow nod from Diedrich.

Sam took another breath. And another. "You're German?"

"*Ja*. From Darmstadt. South of Frankfort. Although at this point I have spent more than half my life here, so I suppose I am from Roanoke."

"How long have you been here?'

"Over thirty-three years, according to the Timekeeper. Qiang's the only person who's been here longer."

Parker looked at Dak Ho. "And you?"

Dak Ho gave them a sad smile. "I arrived in the valley eleven years ago."

"From . . . ?"

"Korea. A small village named Yangdong. Sometime around the late fifteenth century."

Parker crossed her arms. "You don't know what year it was?"

He gave her another small bow. "Different calendars. I was a peasant, and didn't know enough of the world to give the Timekeeper any major event to use as a common point."

"Your English is great."

"Thank you. So is yours."

"I walked into that."

"I've had eleven years to learn, and the Timekeeper is an excellent teacher."

"So how long did it take you to train her? The dinosaur? Gutrune?" The little guilt worm turned over in Sam's belly, reminding him that he should feel ashamed about being this excited. He tried to ignore it. "Did you catch her in the wild?"

Diedrich shook his head. "There've been dinosaurs here at Roanoke since before I arrived. I just give them a little direction."

"It's a *dinosaur.*"

"They're my big girls. I like them, they like me."

A dozen questions bubbled in Sam's brain and piled up on his tongue. Before he could spit one of them out, Dak Ho gestured across the field. "We should show them the boulder."

Diedrich looked that way. "I suppose."

"The boulder?" Sam managed to get out.

"One of the many oddities here. So many things have fallen into the past."

Parker looked skeptical. "Do you normally give tours when people arrive here?"

"It's better than letting people wander. The valley is a dangerous place. Even this close to Roanoke."

Sam glanced back at the wooden walls, maybe fifty feet away. He could see someone, a woman, standing up at the top. Keeping watch. "Do the dinosaurs get this close?"

"Not just the dinosaurs," said Dak Ho. "The Klaa are a—"

Diedrich coughed hard, and it took Sam a moment to realize the cough had been a word in another language. Something quick and short. He looked back and forth between the men and saw their expressions change and shift. The kind of quick, wordless conversation you can have with someone you've known for years.

Parker had caught it, too. "The Klaa are . . . what?"

"Nothing to worry about right now," said Diedrich. "The boulder.

It's over there." He slipped the bamboo stick from under his arm, pointed across the field with it, and then jammed it into his fraying belt. He walked past them and headed across the freshly plowed field.

Sam glanced at Parker. She looked back. Her eyes tried to tell him something, but he didn't know her well enough to understand what it was.

He didn't know much about farming, or even gardening, but the soil looked rich to him. Smelled rich, too. A big clump of greenish-brown caught his eye, like a basketball of wet grass had been cut in half. Probably by the plow.

"Dinosaur manure," said Dak Ho. "We compost most of it, but sometimes it goes straight into the fields."

Past the far side of the field sat a granite boulder maybe the size of a small car. Something about it looked off, and it took Sam a moment to realize it had been shaped. The top had been worn down by scraping or grinding. Not perfectly flat, but flat enough.

He also noticed the grove behind it. He couldn't identify many trees on sight, but he was pretty sure those were all cypress trees, standing up on their thick, heavy roots.

"This showed up a few months after Dak Ho," Diedrich said with a tight smile. "We came out one morning to harvest sweet potatoes and found it sitting here."

"We found it face down," Dak Ho said. "He tried to move it with one of the girls and we found the inscription."

Diedrich nodded. Gestured them to the far side of the boulder. Sam and Parker both walked around.

The far side of the boulder had also been smoothed and polished, giving it a flat face the size of a large folding table. Dozens, maybe over a hundred symbols covered that face, each two inches tall and half an inch deep. Dirt and dust had piled up along the bottom edge of most of them. At first Sam thought they might be some sort of hieroglyphs, but then he thought it might be Greek, and then he recognized some of the upside-down letters. "Is this Cyrillic?"

"Azbuka," said Dak Ho.

"It's the same thing," Diedrich said, in the tone of a person who'd said something many, many times before. "It's Russian."

"It showed up a few months after you?" Parker asked Dak Ho.

"Yes."

"Not a year?"

"You can check with the Timekeeper. It was three months and three weeks, I believe. It was all new to me at the time, but we've talked about it since then."

Sam couldn't understand a word of Russian, but he kept staring at the symbols, trying to flip the lines of text over in his mind. He went through each line until he saw a series of numbers. Realized the significance. "2063. Is that a date?"

"It is." Diedrich lifted his head and cleared his throat. "'Let mankind's great victory in this place be remembered forever, and let us remain ever vigilant that our terrible enemy from beyond time never return. April 2063.'"

"Enemy from beyond time?" echoed Parker.

Diedrich shrugged. "It's what it says on the rock."

"Some subtleties don't translate," added Dak Ho.

Sam replayed the words in his head. "Is this from . . . a war?"

"We don't know."

"An alien invasion?"

"We don't know."

"Perhaps even more interesting," added Diedrich, "is Roanoke has residents who are from years beyond this date, like the Timekeeper, and none of them have any idea what this refers to."

"So it wasn't a war?" asked Parker.

Another shrug from Diedrich. He nodded at Dak Ho. "As he said, we don't know."

Sam wrestled with it. "So there was a great victory . . . somewhere where they spoke Russian. *Mankind's* great victory. Big enough that they made a big monument about it. And then it was just . . . forgotten?"

"The sad truth of history is it does not always remember the things we want it to."

"Deep," said Parker.

Sam tapped the rock with his knuckles. "Maybe it's a movie prop."

Diedrich smiled and bowed his head. "One thing we have plenty of here is time for theories and introspection. And dinosaur shit. Plenty of that."

Sam laughed. So did Parker. And then the low, pulsing Australian wail echoed across the field.

Diedrich and Dak Ho both tensed. Diedrich looked toward the walls of Roanoke as a second and third pulse rumbled out, then back across the field as the fourth pulse faded away. "He's already back."

"He moves fairly fast out there when he doesn't have any of us slowing him down."

"Who's back?" asked Parker.

Sam shaded his eyes and looked at the figures up on the wall. "What's that sound?"

"Signal. Lets us know if something's approaching."

"No, I mean, sorry, what is it? Is it some kind of horn?"

"It's a wago," said Diedrich. "A sort of Australian alphorn. What's the other name for it?"

"Didgeridoo," Dak Ho told him.

Sam kicked himself, mentally.

"Ja. An easy instrument to make, and it can be heard for many miles."

Parker looked at the trees. Across the field. "Do we . . . do we need to go back inside?"

"No. It is a friend. You can tell by the tone. Most likely Thate, returned from his errand."

"Who's Thate?"

"What errand?" added Sam.

Diedrich's brow wrinkled, and a heartbeat later his face went slack. "Forgive me. Qiang sent him out this morning. I assumed this was why you were out here."

"We came to see the dinosaurs."

Something moved in the corner of Sam's eye. He turned and saw a glimpse of red—the spacesuit scarecrow by the cornfield. And something bright blue past it, heading their way.

A figure marched through the fields. His pants were a blur of digital camouflage, and he wore a skintight blue shirt that covered his arms and chest. The man moved along the path in wide strides. He saw them, changed course slightly, and approached without hesitation. He didn't look large, but Sam could see the swell of muscles under that blue shirt. A large pack hung over one shoulder, almost like some sort of oversized, medieval messenger bag. Carrying it didn't seem to slow him in the slightest.

Then Sam saw the man wasn't wearing a shirt.

The blue-skinned man rolled his shoulder so the bag hung behind him. "You must be the newcomers. I'm Theta Sigma-Seven. Everyone calls me Thate."

Sam stared at the blue man.

Like, *really* stared.

Then he realized he was staring and tried to casually look away, but the blue man pulled his eyes back like a little kid with a magnet dragging paper clips and screws across a tabletop. And yes, his mind went right to screwing, didn't it?

Thate stood six feet tall, maybe half that across the shoulders, and Sam couldn't see a single hair anywhere on his skin. All of his very blue, very exposed skin. His odd camo pants hung at his hips, a matching bandanna wrapped his scalp, and instead of a shirt a gray-black harness looped under his arms and across his chest. He had the lean, hard body of someone who'd worked on a farm for half his life, then joined a swim team for the other half, maybe running marathons in his spare time and, yes, Sam was definitely staring again. Because the man was blue. No other reason.

"You have everything?" asked Dak Ho.

Thate glanced at Sam, at Parker, then nodded. "All I could."

Diedrich gave a quick motion with his bamboo stick, like an officer dismissing his troops, and Thate took a few steps past them. "Good to finally meet you," he called back. "Sorry to rush off."

Sam turned to watch the man go and, yes, he looked just as good walking away as walking toward. He tried to tear his eyes away, but Thate's sculpted form heading down the path toward Roanoke was oddly captivating. Then the guilt worm twisted again and he turned to see Parker staring after the man, too. And even as he watched, she shook herself from her own fascination and said, "Noah."

Sam looked back and saw Thate had reached the walls of Roanoke. And standing just outside the big doors was Noah. The two spoke for a moment—maybe a friendly introduction—and then the blue man vanished inside the gateway. Noah looked back and forth across the fields, his gaze stopping at each group of farmers until he found Sam and Parker.

"The prodigal son returns," murmured Diedrich.

Noah took a few slow steps away from the gate, and Sam spent a few seconds overthinking if he should meet the man halfway or wait for him to come to them. Parker just started moving, and after a few quick breaths he followed her.

"I'm glad I found you," Noah said when they reached each other. A flat statement, as if they'd bumped into each other somewhere on campus. He didn't look Sam in the eyes. Or Parker.

"What's wrong," she asked.

"Nothing. Nothing's wrong. It's just that I . . ."

Sam felt his breath quicken with dread.

"I'm leaving."

19

NOAH

"I'm hoping to leave first thing in the morning," Noah told them.

He stood by the fireplace and looked at each of them, all gathered around the little table in the main room of the guest house. He didn't blame them for being upset with him, but he'd hoped for a little bit of understanding. They had to understand why he was doing this, right?

None of them said anything.

Sam stared at his feet. Josh sat back with his arms out, somehow looking relaxed and judgey at the same time. And Parker . . .

Parker looked like she'd been punched in the stomach. A lot of pain and betrayal and confusion. Again, he couldn't blame her. It couldn't be helped, but he'd hoped she'd understand.

When the silence stretched out, he decided to fill it. "I need to go see my . . . our old cave. You can come with me if you like. Both of you. All of you," he added, tipping his head to Josh. "Or stay here. You're free to do whatever you want. But I'm going."

Parker still didn't say anything. Neither did Sam. He was so still, Noah briefly wondered if the stocky man had fallen asleep in his chair. He'd barely said anything since Noah'd first announced his plans outside Roanoke's gates.

Josh raised two fingers without lifting his hand. "What are we supposed to do?"

Noah leaned back, shifted his feet, realized he was mimicking Ross again. So he made a point of lacing his fingers together and felt himself drop into lecture mode. "I talked with Ross about it. They're used to giving people a week or two to get acclimated. For now, you can all do whatever you want. Look around. Relax. Don't worry about it."

"A *week* or two?" Parker's eyes were wide. "You're just abandoning us here while you go off and—"

Noah put his hands up. "Sorry. I said weeks because that's how he put it. I should only be gone for two, maybe three days. Ross says the cave's about a day's hike from here. Apparently it's moved a bit. But after all this time I . . . I need to see it again. And I'm hoping there might be some clues about what happened to Beau. Something Ross didn't see or register for some reason."

"I'll go with you."

They all looked at Sam.

"Really?" said Parker.

He stared at his feet for a few more seconds. "Yeah. I've wanted to see this place since I was eleven. To see that cave. I'd never—I can't pass it up."

A little spark of relief lifted Noah's heart.

Josh's expression was remarkably neutral. Parker's wasn't. "This isn't Disney World, you know."

"I know."

"Do you?"

Sam straightened up in his chair and tried to make himself look taller "If you'd wanted to go to—to see Disney World your whole life, and finally you got the chance to see the park fifty years after it'd closed, wouldn't you still be interested?"

"Not if it was filled with dinosaurs, no. They made a movie about that."

"You could come too," Noah told her. "Both of you could."

Josh held up a hand. "I'm good here behind the big wall. Thanks though."

Noah would've been fine going alone, but he'd half hoped Parker would want to come along. Instead, he recognized her expression. The same one she used when they discussed experiments and research projects. She was preparing to point out the big flaw in someone's reasoning. The hole in their theory. The—

"What do we do if you don't come back?"

"What do you mean?"

"You know more about the wormhole than anyone else. If we're going to get home, we need to start working on that."

"We've got a year to figure it out. I'll be back in a few days."

"You don't know that. So what do we do if—"

"I *do* know that," he said. "I know the valley."

"You really don't, though." Josh shifted in his chair. Leaned a little more toward Parker even as he looked at Noah.

"I was here years before any of them. I've known about this place my whole life."

"Yeah, but . . ." Josh's face softened a bit even as his eyes got more serious. "Look, I don't think anyone's questioning that you and your family were here first. And I think everyone understands you really want to find out what happened to your sister. But you have to admit this place has changed a lot. From what you told us, from the things we've seen." Josh waved his hand to take in the guest house around them. "It's clear this isn't the place you expected to find. And I mean . . . I don't know about the rest of you, I've only talked to maybe half a dozen people, but it feels like everybody we've met has been here longer than you were. Qiang says he's been here since he was eleven. Forty years to your . . . two and a half?"

"What's your point?"

"My point is they all seem to think it's pretty dangerous out there. And maybe we should give a little more weight to their opinions as opposed to . . . well, some thirty-year-old memories from your childhood."

Ripples of emotion overlapped in Noah's chest. From one side came little waves of annoyance, like he was teaching a class with the occasional undergrad conspiracy theorist who just wanted to loudly declare the Earth was flat or the Moon was hollow or something equally nonsensical. On the other side, the ripples carried old emotions. All those long nights from his teens when he realized no one believed him about the valley. That people were laughing at him.

He forced it all down. Years of mandated therapy had made him very good at forcing things down. "I'll be fine," he said. "I'll be back in a few days. We'll be back. Me and Sam."

Sam beamed at the mention.

Josh cleared his throat. "About that . . ."

"Yep?"

"Are you going to share anything before you go?"

"Share what?"

"How we get home."

"It doesn't . . ." The sensation of arguing with a difficult student washed over Noah again. "My information wasn't correct. If I'm going to get us home, I need to start over."

"Right," said Parker, waving a hand at Sam "but you still know more than either of us. We'd be starting from scratch. You've already done years of work."

"Exactly. It's not something I can sum up in a few sentences. This is decades of work. And again, work based off a faulty premise."

"But it's still work. You can save us from going down dead ends."

Josh nodded in an agreeable, thoughtful way. "Maybe we should consider Parker's point. You shouldn't be going."

Noah glanced at him. "What?"

"What happens if you get eaten by a dinosaur or something?"

"I promise, I'm not going to get eaten by a dinosaur."

"You might, though," said Parker. "You could break a leg and not be able to get away. Shit, you could trip over a rock and break your neck. And then where does that leave all of us?"

He sighed. "I know this place. I understand it. I promise, nothing's going to happen to me."

Josh raised two fingers again. "Look, I know I'm not part of the cool science club, but you have to admit it's kind of risky for you to be the only one who knows how to get us home."

Noah sighed. "I'm sorry to keep saying the same thing in so many ways, but there isn't any risk."

"You're certain? One hundred percent?"

He managed to smile at Josh. "No decent scientist is ever one hundred percent certain. There's always the chance you'll learn something new that changes your understanding."

Josh nodded. "See, that's why I wouldn't be a good scientist."

"Oh?"

"Yeah. Because I'm one hundred percent certain we're screwed if anything happens to you."

The ripples crisscrossed in Noah's chest again, stirring up so many old emotions. "I know the valley. I'll be—*we'll* be gone for two or three days. We can work on a way home when I get back."

Parker scowled at him.

"What?"

"I'm just thinking how much it'll suck if a year from now we find out we need a few more days to finish doing the math."

Noah took a breath. Calmed himself. Tried to think of how scared they all had to be, finding themselves trapped here. Wished they understood why he had to know what happened to Beau.

He was forming a defense in his mind—an explanation to satisfy them—when someone rapped on the door with knuckles that rattled like a can of nails. They all glanced at each other. Back at the door.

"Do dinosaurs knock?" asked Sam.

"Come in," Noah called.

The door swung open and Ross clomped in. His walking stick echoed on the rough wooden floor. "Good afternoon, Noah. Parker. Sam. Josh."

Noah felt a surge in his heart that pushed back all the ripples. "Well?"

"Qiang-Shizhang would normally advise someone against exploring the valley so soon after arriving, but he agrees you are a special case. He will not try to stop you from going to the Gathers' cave."

"Our cave."

"Of course, Noah. I'm just using the name it's come to be known by."

"Wow," said Josh. "They named a landmark after you."

"However," continues Ross, "Qiang-Shizhang also requested certain conditions. He'd like you take a guide. Someone more aware of the valley's current geography and general state."

"What?"

Sam's face lit up. "You're coming with us?"

"I'm afraid I can't make that journey anymore, Sam. Not without slowing your group down considerably." His round eyes turned to Noah. "He's speaking with several citizens of Roanoke now to see if there are any volunteers."

"We don't need a guide," said Noah. "I'm sure I can find the cave."

"He was very firm on this point. The valley's too dangerous right now."

"Too dangerous on top of its usual level of dangerous?" asked Josh.

The old feelings roiled in Noah's belly again. People being condescending to him. Telling him he was wrong.

He shoved them back down one more time. Quieted Josh with a wave of his hand. He could feel Parker's eyes burning into him. Feel the frustration and disappointment radiating off her.

And he felt something else, too. An old instinct, freshly woken up and tickling the back of his brain. "Ross?"

"Yes, Noah?"

"How much more daylight is there?"

"Fifty-one minutes."

He almost smiled. "You can take the boy out of the valley," he said quietly.

Sam furrowed his brow. "What?"

"Who wants to see something mind-blowing and impossible?"

20

JOSH

Josh looked around as he walked past the same buildings for the third or fourth time. Big building that Parker absently identified as a storehouse. Silver obelisk thing. Was Roanoke just not that big? He'd only walked on maybe three distinct dirt roads and he was pretty sure he'd seen 90 percent of the little town. Hell, barely a village. He tried to think of how many people he'd seen and could barely come up with thirty faces or distinct outfits.

Noah and the robot were leading them to the main gate for some sort of surprise. The robot walked with a limp, leaning heavily on his walking stick, and Noah moved alongside him, taking unhurried steps. Sam was close behind them, hanging on every phrase or weird reference they passed back and forth. He'd calmed down a lot, but he still radiated pretty powerful fanboy energy.

Parker moved slower, walking with her hand out in front of her. He looked at the hand. At her eyeline.

"Checking your shadow again?"

She glanced at him.

"Seen you do that a couple times now. Studying your shadow."

"It's pretty much right under my hand. All the time."

"Should it be somewhere else?"

"Yeah."

"Okay."

She pointed up at the sky. "The sun's still directly above us. At first I thought it was just an optical illusion, maybe something created by the trees or the high cliff walls. But the sun just hangs there in the sky."

"It was yesterday, too," said Josh. "I remember thinking it was noon a couple times."

"Yeah."

"But I mean, aren't we lost in time? We went through a wormhole. Who knows what things are supposed to be like."

"I know," she said. "I know what things are supposed to be like. And this makes no goddamn sense."

The main gates were ahead of them, and Josh saw people ambling in, definitely with an end-of-the-day vibe to them. Maybe eight or nine altogether? He recognized the tall German they'd spoken to last night. Several of them carried wide baskets.

"Maybe we're frozen in time," he suggested.

"If we're frozen in time, how are we talking?"

"Maybe just the sky's frozen in time."

"The sky doesn't move in the real world. *We* move. And we're moving. So we're not frozen in time."

"Okay, quick segue. You were outside before, right?"

She glanced at him. "Yeah?"

"It's all farmland out there, right? All the fields? It's all crops of evil corn and . . . stuff."

"I guess."

He gestured at the small crowd of farmers as they dispersed into the village. "What do you think they need so much food for?"

"To eat?"

"Yeah, but I mean . . . I'm no farming expert, but this seems like a lot of food for the number of people I've seen here."

"Maybe they're storing it up for the winter."

Josh pointed up at the sun with two fingers. "You think there's a winter here?"

"Fifteen minutes until night," Ross said. The android's voice echoed inside the wall, as if he'd turned his personal volume up to eleven.

It sparked a lot of movement. Warwick pushed one of the big doors shut. The Vietnam-vet guy, Emerson, started pacing up on the walkway and shooting hand signals to someone. Sam looked up at the sky. Parker looked down at the ground, holding out her hand and examining its shadow.

"How is it fifteen minutes until sundown?" She held her hand out even further. "For that matter, how the hell is it still noon? The sun's been directly overhead for a couple hours now?"

Warwick looked at her. "Thought you'd been here for a few days already."

Noah's mouth pulled into a faint smile. "We have been, but I don't think they've seen it yet."

"Oh."

"Seen what?" Josh asked.

"The end of the day." Noah looked at Ross, then Warwick. "Are we allowed up on the wall? So they can get the view?"

"There shouldn't be a problem. Just don't get in anyone's way, and get down immediately if anything happens."

That set off little warning lights in Josh's brain. "If anything happens," he echoed. "Like what?"

"Nothing's going to happen," said Noah.

Warwick's mouth trembled for a moment, and it struck Josh the guard—no, they called them wardens, terminology matters—had resting salesman face. A sort of practiced neutral expression that leaned toward the positive. He wondered if Warwick had something he wanted to say to them. Or specifically to Noah. But the warden just nodded and turned to close the other big door.

Ross pointed out a ladder off to the right side of the gate and Noah led their little group over there. He headed up first, followed by Parker. Sam waited for them both to get to the top, rubbed his hands together, and scrambled up the ladder. Josh looked at the android and gestured up.

"I appreciate the offer, Josh, but my damaged leg prevents me from climbing." Ross turned his head to the side with a squeak. "Ten minutes until night."

Square nails held the ladder together, but it still felt wobbly under Josh's hands and feet. It stretched up past the platform, letting him climb up and onto the very solid bamboo walkway with no awkwardness. Another sign it was all better designed than it looked.

Parker stood there, her hand out, looking at its shadow. It rippled on the bamboo but sat directly under her hand. She glanced at him. "Still high noon."

Josh felt the sun on his head, tickling at his scalp.

Emerson stood a few yards away. The roof of the barracks sat even with the top-of-the-wall walkway, making a good-sized platform. The middle-aged soldier held an upright spear loosely in one hand, his fingers shifting on it like it was a musical instrument. He gazed out past the fields "First time seeing the sun go away?" he called out.

"First for them," said Noah.

Emerson nodded. "Gonna scramble your brain," he warned them, still watching the trees.

"Does it go down really fast or something?" asked Josh.

"That wouldn't make sense," said Sam.

"None of this makes sense," Parker said.

Noah leaned to the side. "Ross?"

The calm voice drifted up from the base of the wall. "Yes, Noah?"

"How long?"

"The sun will go away in seven minutes, forty-four seconds."

"Thanks. Could you let us know at the one-minute mark?"

"Of course, Noah."

Josh looked out at the valley. He was high enough to see across the tops of the trees. The big cliffs were closest behind the walled village, but still almost two miles away. If he looked the other way, he could see the—what did Noah call it?—the Ice Castle. A little hazy with distance, but taller than everything else. Maybe half the height of the cliff walls?

A set of palm trees far off to the left shook—was that the direction they'd come from?—and a sound like a distant trombone warming up hit his ears. Something big moved through the trees, and for a moment Josh had the chilling image in his head of Gnash or Burn charging the wooden wall. But then whatever it was stretched up into view, a land-bound whale just barely breaching through the treetops, and he saw dark fur and a flap of . . . ears?

"Is that an elephant?"

"Mammoth," said Emerson, not bothering to look. "Two of them hang out on this side of the valley. There were three, but the Klaa killed one about a year ago."

Noah frowned. "The Klaa?"

"It's what the cavemen call themselves. Name of their tribe or clan or whatever you want to call it."

The mammoth passed through a break in the trees and Josh got a glimpse of curling white tusks the size of tree branches and the glint of a dark eye beneath a domed head that just barely reached up over the trees. It was massive but moved with a slow grace. Now that he knew it was there, that he could see its legs move, he could feel the faint impacts in the ground when it walked. It vanished from sight again, but he could see the wake of rippling leaves and branches as it moved through the trees.

"Wow," sighed Sam.

"The Neanderthals call themselves Pakka," said Noah. "When I was little, I thought they were saying 'packet' the first few times I met them."

The bearded Vietnam vet shook his head. "They've been the Klaa as long as I've been here."

"How long's that?" asked Parker.

"Ten years."

"Well, they were always the Pakka," Noah insisted.

Emerson shrugged, kept his eyes out on the tree line.

Josh took a few steps toward the man. "Are you looking for something in particular?"

"Takes your eyes a minute or two to adjust when it goes dark. Doesn't happen often, but they've tried launching raids then."

"The Neander—the Klaa?" asked Sam.

"Yeah."

Another trombone sound bleated from the forest. Josh shaded his eyes and peered out at the trees. "Why'd they kill the mammoth?"

"To eat it. Or maybe they just wanted to kill something and it was there."

A voice called out from below. "Noah?"

"Yes, Ross?"

"The sun goes away in one minute as of . . . now."

"Thank you."

"Of course."

Parker raised her head, squinted up for a second, looked at Noah. "Why do you all keep saying it that way?"

He turned his attention to her. "Saying . . . ?"

"You're not saying sundown or sunset. You keep saying 'until the sun goes away' or just 'night.'"

Noah failed to contain a smirk. "Yep."

They all waited for him to explain further.

Parker got tired of waiting. "Well?"

Noah shrugged. "If I told you, you wouldn't believe me."

"No one can be told what the Matrix is," Josh murmured. "You have to see it for yourself."

"Something like that. Try to keep an open mind. Remember what I've told you—time works differently here."

Emerson laughed.

Parker didn't look amused.

A cloud passed across the sun, dimming the landscape. A huge cloud, because everything Josh could see in the valley had fallen under its shadow. And hadn't he looked up a couple times now and seen a clear sky?

He looked up again and the world broke apart and crumbled away.

High above them, the sun faded away, fainter every second. Josh knew staring at the sun ruined eyes, could blind people, but he stood there and stared as it dimmed like an overhead light in a movie theater. Now dusty white, now pale gray, now stars appeared in the deep blue sky around it.

"No way," whispered Sam.

The sun was a charcoal circle in the sky with a few flecks of brightness left in it. Except the flecks were other stars. Stars Josh was seeing *through* the sun because it was actually *vanishing*. Physically disappearing out of the sky.

The sun went away and left the brilliant night sky sprawling across the top of the valley. Josh absently looked for any of the half dozen constellations he could name, couldn't find any of them, and *holy FUCK the sun just vanished*. Gone. He stared at the empty spot in the sky where it had been ten or fifteen seconds ago.

The bamboo walkway seemed to shift under his feet.

He heard voices, people saying things. Someone breathing hard. Josh blinked a few times. Tried to get used to the sudden darkness. Looked around and saw Noah with a content expression on his face. Sam trying to get his breathing under control. Parker staring up at the sky like it had thrown a drink in her face and called her a bitch.

"That," wheezed Sam, "was incredible."

"Yep," said Noah.

Josh pointed up at the sky. "This happens every time? Every day?"

"Yep. The valley essentially has two times. High noon and midnight."

"But . . . how?"

"No idea. Drove my sister nuts when we were kids."

"Parker," Sam asked, "are you okay?"

Josh turned. Parker still had her head tilted back, her eyes open. She sucked a breath in through her teeth.

"What," she said. "The fuck. Is this place?"

21

BILLY

The sun went away and the big Pakka, the one Billy called Andre the Giant, pounded the ground with his stick. Billy thought it felt a little fake, like those kids on the playground who shouted a lot and caused problems to make everyone look at them. The school counselor called it an attention-getting device. Billy figured the stick was Andre's device.

He wasn't scared by it and he didn't run. Okay, maybe a little scared. Not as scared as he would've been a year ago. Now he'd lost his mom. Been chased by a tyrannosaurus. Met an alien. A stick hitting the ground a few times wasn't going to make him run away.

Also, Andre wasn't that big. He was the biggest one of the five Pakka-cavemen, and he had a thick beard, but there were kids back at school who were bigger than him. He wasn't much taller than Beau, and nowhere near Dad.

Also-also, Andre's stick wasn't that big either. Thinner than a baseball bat, even down low where you wrapped them in tape and got a grip, but not thin enough to whip through the air like . . . well, like a whip. It looked old and dry, too. Parts of it broke off whenever Andre smacked it on the ground. Billy bet if the Pakka hit him with it, it'd just snap. It'd probably still hurt, so he didn't want him to do it, but he bet it'd break and he could look tough if he didn't cry.

Also-also-also he couldn't run even if he had been scared—which he wasn't—because they'd tied his ankles with a rope made out of twisted bark. And his knees. And wrists. And then looped a rope around his neck and tied that to all the other ropes. Billy wasn't sure if they were really smart about tying people up or just kept using rope and tying knots until they ran out.

Also-however-many-alsos . . . Andre wasn't the scary Pakka.

Regardless, Billy told himself that after this he would never ever wander off into the jungle without Beau or Dad again. Not even to pee. Which is what he'd been doing when Andre and the other Pakka had grabbed him. He'd walked away from the bushes where they'd been picking berries, walked a little farther, and then one of the Pakka had grabbed him while he faced the tree.

And now here he was. Tied up next to a big rock at the Pakka camp. Which was three lean-tos like you learned how to make in Cub Scouts. These were made with more bark rope and lots of palm fronds and what looked like big pieces of leather or fur.

He wondered if Dad or Beau had seen the Pakka running off through the forest with him. Billy thought he'd made a lot of noise, even with a hand over his mouth. They'd figure it out. They'd be here soon. Hopefully before *she* got back. The scary one.

Andre got bored with smacking his little stick on the ground and walked over to the other three. They were gathered around a circle of rock, jabbing at a small fire with sticks. Billy thought two of them were maybe Beau's age, even though they were pretty hairy. Not fur hairy, but definitely Uncle-Jake-at-the-beach hairy. Even the girl had hair on her arms and legs and body. So did the smallest one, Zock.

He hadn't named the two teenagers yet. He wasn't sure if they were brother and sister or boyfriend and girlfriend, which seemed like an important thing to know. The girl had thick black hair that went halfway down her back. The boy's hair was more reddish brown, and he also had a beard, but it was a lot shorter than Andre's. The boy kept jabbing at the fire. The girl said more things to him. Billy thought she was telling him he was doing it all wrong, and it made him lean more toward brother and sister. Billy knew what it sounded like when a sister told her brother he was screwing up.

They had a lot of firewood. He wondered if they used the fire to scare things away now that it was dark. Or maybe they were going to cook something big for dinner.

Andre said words to them. They said words back. The girl looked over at Billy. Then Zock said something and they all yelled at him.

Zock was the smallest of the Pakka. Smaller than Billy, but they were the same age. He'd decided that early on, although the Pakka were all small so it was tough to be sure what age the little guy was.

Zock was also the friendliest one. When they were alone, anyway. They'd met at the swamp about a month ago and bumped into each other a few more times since then while Billy was doing chores. After the third time it happened, he was pretty sure Zock had come looking for him. The fifth time they'd learned each other's names. Or close to it, anyway. Zock kept calling him "Pilla." And the caveboy's accent was so thick, his name sounded like it might be Chalk or Shock or Zock. Billy'd decided to go with Zock, because names with *z*'s were cool and calling someone Shock sounded silly.

So he had an alien friend and a caveman friend. Cave kid? Caveboy? That was pretty cool.

It'd be cooler if Zock helped him get away, though.

Zock had said his name a few times now, since Andre and the girl had carried him into their camp half an hour or so ago. Whatever he said about Billy, nobody seemed to care. They were all focused on making the fire bigger and arguing about how to do it.

"I still need to pee," Billy told them.

Zock looked at him, but didn't say anything. He looked sad. The others kept talking. Billy wished he spoke more Pakka words.

"I really need to pee." A little louder this time. He didn't need to go that bad, but he figured if they untied him he might get a chance to run away and hide in the forest.

The girl looked up at him and grunted a few words. Andre grumbled back. He turned, pointed at Billy with his stick, and aimed a few more Pakka words at him too.

"My dad has a bigger stick than you, and he's going to kick your ass."

Something rustled in the forest as he spoke, and he regretted the word as soon as it passed his lips. Beau was old enough to get away with the occasional cuss word, but he wasn't. This'd be a bad time to get rescued and have Dad hear him swearing.

But the person who came out of the woods wasn't Dad.

It was *her*.

She held a little dog-sized dinosaur by the neck, most of it slung over her shoulder. Her other hand held a long spear with a wooden tip like a sharp pencil. Even in the dim starlight, Billy could see the dinosaur had two bloody holes in its body the size of the spear tip. She tossed it on the ground near the fire circle and growled Pakka words at the teenagers.

The boy reached for the dinosaur and she banged the end of the spear on the ground right next to his fingers. He yanked his hand away, curling up like he expected to be hit again. He was right. She hissed at him as she did it. The boy ended up with a bloody nose.

Then she turned to look at Billy. He tried to be brave. Tried not to pee.

Mom and Dad had both taught him not to make fun of people for their looks, but Billy told himself he wasn't making fun of Scarnose, just describing her. The cavewoman's nose and cheek were all twisty and pale, like someone had drawn thick yellow-white lines on her tanned skin. The lines wrapped all around her nose and stretched across her face like a spiky Spider-Man mask. It pulled the skin tight in some places, made it puff in others. The eye on that side of her face had a big red splotch in it below the pupil, like someone had dripped blood in her eye and it'd left a stain that never dried.

She moved toward Billy in her skittery, back-and-forth way. A few quick steps, almost jumping forward, then one or two back. It reminded Billy of the people who worked in haunted houses at Halloween, how they'd jump out and then slowly back up so they could jump out again at the next people.

Scarnose had dark hair and eyebrows, although a scar line split one eyebrow in half. Like all the Pakka, her hair was thick, ropy tangles that threw shadows across her face. The clumps around her ear were all gray-white, the way comic book scientists had white stripes over their ears. Or that old *Bride of Frankenstein* movie.

She grabbed Billy's foot and twisted, checking the ropes holding his ankles and knees. He yelped. He knew she'd done it quick and hard on purpose. She wanted him to yelp.

Her hand crawled up his leg like a big spider, tugging at his jeans, pulling at his shirt. It wrapped around his neck and squeezed a little. Her skin felt like one of Dad's old leather work gloves.

Her mouth dropped open, exposed her teeth. Billy could see two gaps, two yellowy-brown teeth, and an almost-black one on the bottom. Scarnose leaned in, huffed out a breath that smelled like an old trash can, and sniffed him. A long, deep sniff, the way Dad sometimes smelled things in the fridge to see how old they were. Billy could see the pores in her skin and the tiny cuts and cracks all over her lips and the glossiness of all her scars and the little bugs crawling near her hairline.

Her eyes met his and shrank down to tiny black dots. The red splotch in her left eye got bigger. He could see all the meanness in those tiny dots. She was mean and angry and didn't try to hide it at all. She wanted him to know. All he could see was her angry eyes.

Billy smelled pee.

She squeezed his neck tighter and lifted. He felt her fingers press under his jaw, her fingernails scratch beneath his ears, felt his butt lift off the ground. She dragged him to his feet and his chest felt tight like he'd held his breath for too long.

Zock yelled something. Three or four words. Scarnose shouted. Threw something at him that clattered on the ground. Zock yelped.

Billy tried to kick her, but his legs were tied together tight and he could only wiggle and swing. She pushed him away from her, back against one of the big rocks, and barked out a few more words. She talked like a teacher who hadn't been nice to start with but now she was done with all your crap.

The girl ran up to them. Scarnose talked to her. Poked Billy with a long, broken fingernail. They said a bunch of words back and forth, although Scarnose did most of the talking and Billy was pretty sure the girl just agreed with her again and again.

Something bright happened behind the girl. The boy got the fire going. A big flame, as tall as Zock. He added more sticks and broken branches to it.

Scarnose loosened the grip on his neck a little. Squeezed his arm with her other hand. Her fingernails pushed into his skin and he could feel their chipped, pointed tips. The girl reached out and felt each of Billy's fingers with her own. They talked some more.

Scarnose pulled a stone knife from somewhere and yanked him forward. Pulled him toward the fire circle. He wondered if they were going to feed him, because they couldn't, she wasn't, they weren't going to—

"*HEY!*"

Scarnose turned around but didn't let go of Billy's neck. Andre yelled something. So did Zock. Billy's chest loosened up and he took a deep, happy breath.

Dad stood at the edge of the dark forest. His face was hard under his scraggly beard, but hard the way Billy knew meant he was trying to *keep it together* and *not lose his cool*. He held the big club he'd made from a tree branch, carving it down with his knife until it looked like a cross between a baseball bat and a bowling pin. Not good against any of the big dinosaurs, but he'd whacked one or two of the dog-sized ones with it. He only had one hand on it right now, but he held it really tight.

Beau stood right behind him. She had a baseball-sized rock in her hand, up close to her head. Billy knew she could hit the catcher's glove every time.

Andre took a few steps forward, then back. Dad was a foot taller than him, the *real* giant here in the valley. Andre raised his little stick, let it drift back down. Behind him the teen boy had grabbed a rock, but he held it in both hands like he was going to smash something with it.

Dad lifted his club. Pointed it at Scarnose. “Let him go,” he called out. “Right now. I swear I’ll . . . I don’t want to hurt any of you, but I will. If I have to.”

Billy knew that Dad knew the Pakka didn’t understand him. But they knew sounds and tones. They knew he wasn’t messing around.

Scarnose didn’t let go. But she barked out a couple angry words of her own. Waved her free hand at Billy. At the girl. At the fire.

Andre took a few more steps forward and Beau’s rock hit him in the shoulder hard enough to turn him halfway around. He grabbed the spot it hit him, snarled, but she’d already grabbed another rock from her back pocket and had her arm back to throw.

The big Pakka growled and backed off.

Dad took two big, heavy steps toward Scarnose, the way you walked toward an animal to scare it off. She shook Billy by the neck, then twisted around and slipped her whole arm around his throat. He wobbled and tried to keep his balance. She yelled at Dad and it blasted in Billy’s ear.

Dad had the club up. Beau stayed right behind him, her eyes on Andre and the boy. “You okay?” Dad called out.

Billy managed to move his head up and down, then realized it was sort of going side to side because of how Scarnose was holding him. “I’m okay.” He said it loud because his ears were still ringing.

Dad let out a long breath and his face got a little less hard. But he lifted the club a little higher. Almost two feet higher than Scarnose’s head. “Let. Him. Go.”

Zock said a few words. Scarnose growled an answer. She yelled at Dad again. Then she let go of Billy and shoved him forward.

Billy tried to get his arms out, but he was tied too tight and he’d kinda turned to his side as he fell anyway. At least the ground at the Pakka camp was all soft dirt and leaves. He thumped down and it didn’t hurt much. He wiggled and tried to move toward Dad.

“Hold still.” Beau put a hand on his shoulder, squeezed once, sawed through the bark rope with Dad's knife. His legs rocked back and forth, the loop around his knees loosened, then the one at his ankles popped apart.

Scarnose spat a bunch of Pakka words at them. She took a quick step forward and Beau lifted the knife, putting it between them. Scarnose backed up, huffing out angry breaths, her eyes on the gleaming blade.

Beau helped him up and he held out his hands. "And these."

"Later. Let's get out of here. Can you still walk?"

"Yep. They didn't hurt me." He hoped she didn't notice the pee smell as they backed toward Dad. Beau put herself between him and Scarnose and kept the knife out.

Dad was still keeping Andre and the boy back. He lifted his club again, let it ease down. There was some stuff the Pakka didn't understand, but Billy thought Andre knew what Dad was telling him.

He gave Billy a quick glance. "You good?"

"Yep. But my hands are still tied."

"Beau will help you walk. The two of you get going, I'll be right behind you."

"No," she said. "All together. They'll get brave if it's only you."

Dad looked at the Pakka. At Scarnose. Thought about it. "You're right. All together."

They backed into the dark woods. Billy heard Scarnose throw some final angry words at them, got one last glimpse of her angry red eye, and then the trees hid them. He ran with his arms out in front of him. Beau stayed right alongside him, one hand on his shoulder to help him keep balance.

They jog-ran through the trees until they were in the part of the valley they called the Dead Forest, even though the trees weren't all dead. Just a lot of them. It looked even creepier at night. Dad said they could slow down and rest. Beau cut the ropes holding Billy's wrists and held the knife out to Dad.

"You keep it," he said.

"You've got the sheath."

"Keep it in your hands until we get home."

"Are you sure?"

"Yeah."

"I'll keep it," said Billy.

"Not now, runt," she told him. But she squeezed his shoulder again.

Dad leaned until he could see the cliffs looming in the night sky, got them oriented, and they headed home through the Dead Forest. He swung the club up on his shoulder and reached over to scuff Billy's head. "You sure you're okay?"

"Yep. Scarnose is a little scary, but she didn't hurt me. None of them did. I think Zock told them not to."

Beau made that sound in her throat that meant she thought he was wrong.

"What?"

"Nothing."

"What?!"

She ignored him. "Do you think they'll follow us?"

Dad shook his head. "I think we make the Pakka uncomfortable. They don't know what to make of us, but I also think that means they won't actively come looking for trouble."

Beau looked back over her shoulder. "You sure?"

"I think we'll be fine as long as there's only five of them."

22

SAM

Sam woke up early, nervous and excited. Kid on Christmas morning excited. Kid leaving home to go off to college excited. Kid who found a forest in the back of their wardrobe excited.

His room swelled with light and he realized the sun had come up. Or appeared. The astronomer in him had a thousand questions about that, about the sheer impossibility of it, but the little kid wanted to *go*. He packed his random collection of "supplies" into his backpack and stepped out into the hall of the guest house.

Noah had already left. Or maybe never came home from talking with Ross. He was probably excited, too. From his point of view, the past few days had been delay after delay, things keeping him from his actual goal here.

Sam slung his bag over his shoulder, stepped outside, and headed for the gate.

The village hadn't quite woken up yet, still stretching and yawning. A few folks gave him polite nods or waves as he walked through the town. He knew he'd met some of them—most of them, it seemed—but he couldn't remember many names.

A screech cracked the air above him, and a shadow skimmed across the ground. Then another. He looked up in time to see the third rhamphorhynchus soar by, heading out into the valley.

He passed the platinum obelisk, saw a few more people heading for the gate, and absently wondered if anyone did a morning run. Or did just existing here serve as a form of exercise? Most everyone he'd met, everyone he could see, was on the lean side. In fact . . .

He looked up and down the street. The Japanese woman with the long, dark topknot and the blue man, Thate, stood watch up on the wall, maybe fifty or so feet apart. A few houses down the doctor gathered things from her little flowerbed. Diedrich strolled twenty feet behind Sam, twirling his bamboo stick between his fingers, and Dak Ho waited just past the obelisk, wearing an indifferent expression.

Sam had met every person he could see.

His mind drifted back to yesterday at lunch. To the crowds gathered around when they arrived at Roanoke. He'd assumed they were a portion of the villagers. That other people were busy weaving or milling or something where they couldn't spare the time away for a handful of strangers arriving.

But maybe that *had* been everyone. He'd gone off the number of houses and structures, assumed Roanoke had seventy or eighty residents.

Or maybe he assumed too much. Maybe everyone else was already up and at work. Doing their duties. Whatever they called it here.

It was a quiet little village though.

Very quiet.

"Too quiet," Sam said to no one in particular.

He reached the gatehouse. And the still-closed gate. Two thick bars across it. A handful of people waited there.

Noah stood in deep debate—almost a quiet argument—with the cyborg woman, Pyr. She wore a loose satin shirt that looked like a tank top with a hood. Ross stood nearby, his own hood up over his scuffed head, both hands on his walking stick like a mechanical wizard. The Egyptian woman waited by the gate. Sam hadn't caught her name yet, but it felt like he hadn't hit the point where he should be asking people's names. Especially partly naked people. Diedrich walked to the gate with a polite nod to the woman. Dak Ho didn't seem to notice her at all.

Pyr held up a finger, pausing her emphatic discussion with Noah, and scooped something up from the ground. A solid-looking pair of hiking boots. She held them out to Sam and her eyes met his. "You should have these," she said. "You need something solid if we're going to hike halfway across the valley."

"Thank you."

She passed them off, went back to her quiet, intense conversation with Noah. It struck Sam that Noah hadn't said anything to him yet. Hadn't even acknowledged him being there.

Sam looked around for somewhere to sit, then plopped down in the dirt close to the gate. He pushed his sneakers off by the heels, tugged the first boot on. It was a little tight, but not uncomfortably so. He did some mental math about the comfort of his sneakers versus the durability of the boots, the likeliness of blisters or general irritation, and decided, yeah, the boots were the better way to go.

He reached for the second one and noticed two dark brown circles on the toes. Some kind of stain. Drops, definitely. Maybe dirty water or some tree sap or . . .

Blood.

There were two drops of blood on the boots. The relatively new but still broken-in boots that didn't have an owner. Not anymore. Not since they'd buried him under a pile of stones after blood had sprayed out of his nose and eyes and ears.

He looked up, found Thate walking the wall. Remembered the blue man coming out of the forest with his big bag. The bag that held everything he could get.

Of course they couldn't waste anything here. They weren't going to leave a perfectly good pair of boots under a pile of rocks. Not when someone might need them, like some idiot who'd only signed onto this trip because he didn't want to be home in his apartment and had all but run out the door with a backpack of useless items and wearing ratty old sneakers.

The guilt worm in his stomach flipped over and trembled, and he managed to hold it in place and tell himself it was because he hadn't eaten anything yet.

He tugged the second boot onto his foot. Absolutely did not look at the two spots on the toe.

While he yanked the laces tight, he let his gaze drift over to the guard by the gate. He hadn't been this close to her before, so it was his first good look at her clothes and jewelry. He could see wings engraved on her thick bracelets, and her skirt had strong lines he remembered from grade school history books and museum field trips. His eyes drifted up to the gold band on her arm and she moved, turning it closer to him. It had a series of long vertical lines in it, closer to scratches than engraving, as if someone had tried to decorate the band after the fact.

Then he realized she'd turned it for him to look at. His eyes flitted up and met hers. She spoke a few rolling words that felt vaguely like a question.

The walking stick thumped into the ground next to him, and two mismatched mechanical feet shuffled to join it. "Neith wants to know if you have a wife, Sam," Ross explained.

"I'm sorry, what?"

"She wants to know if you have a wife," repeated the android. "She's seeking, by her standards, an acceptable mate."

Sam looked at Neith. She crossed her arms. Stared back at him. "Is she going to stab me or something if I say I'm not interested?"

"I don't believe so, but some of Neith's customs would be considered unconventional by twenty-first-century standards."

Sam finished tying the boot. Stood up slowly, not taking his eyes off the guard. "Could you explain to her I'm not—I'm only interested in men. Usually. Not that she doesn't seem interesting, in general, it's just who I am."

Ross nodded. His head turned to Neith and spoke a series of words with the same rolling, booming quality to them. She glanced at Sam, nodded, and replied, shifting her attention from the android to Sam and back.

"She understands, Sam. She knew several men in her homeland who preferred the company of their fellows over women."

Sam stood up. Flexed his toes in the boots. In Logan's boots. Definitely tight on the sides, but his toes didn't feel cramped.

Neith said something else, and Ross responded. She gave Sam a curt nod that felt more like a salute and moved to the gate. Her arms and back flexed as she lifted one of the big bars holding it shut.

"What's her—where is she from?"

"Neith is a Medjai warrior. By our best understanding, she's from what you would consider the New Kingdom era of Egypt, somewhere between the fifteenth and twelfth century BCE. It's not possible to be more specific since she doesn't use a calendar we recognize."

"You can speak her language?"

The robot bowed his head affirmatively. "I can."

"How? I mean, she's from ancient Egypt and you're from the future. Do you just happen to—can you speak Egyptian? Or Arabic, I guess?"

"While Arabic is one of my core language files, Neith does not speak it. It took five months to learn her language to a degree that allowed simple communication."

Sam nodded. "You learned some of the Neanderthal language too, didn't you? With Beau. That was in one of the . . . I heard that. Somewhere."

"That's right, Sam. My programming allows for contextual learning of three additional languages past my core twenty. During my time here I've learned eleven additional languages. Eight have been deleted when they were no longer necessary."

He mused on that as Neith set the second bar down. "No longer necessary because . . ."

"All known speakers in the valley were deceased."

Neith pushed the big gate doors open. Something scampered away from the wall, vanishing into the field. She didn't seem bothered by it.

"So," said Noah, a little too loudly. He'd finished his discussion and walked over to Sam. "Pyr is going to join us."

He looked over at the cyborg a few yards away. She hadn't moved. He hadn't noticed her own pack before, a bulging, Frankenstein thing stitched together from three or four other packs. She gave him a quick wink with her artificial eye.

Sam turned to Noah, lowered his voice. "What's wrong?"

Noah stepped to the side, putting his back squarely to Pyr, and murmured, "She says she wants to see the cave, but I'm pretty sure she's just coming along to keep an eye on us."

"I am," she called out.

Noah turned, and he and Sam both looked at her.

Pyr reached up and tapped the ear next to her bright blue eye. "I've wanted to go see the cave again for a few years now. But, yes, Qiang asked if I could go now and make sure you two didn't get in too much trouble."

"How nice of him," Noah said.

Sam glanced back and forth between them. "I mean, this was the—this is what you agreed to, right?"

She moved closer and shrugged. "The valley's a very different place than it was when you were here. The Klaa aren't the tribe you knew back then. They're violent, short-tempered, and it's never good to run into them unexpectedly. Especially this close to tribute day. It's better to have a guide who knows the valley."

Sam saw Noah's jaw tense. His eyes hardened, just for a moment. Apparently Pyr saw it too.

"Pardon," she said. "I meant, someone who knows the valley as it is now."

Noah relaxed a little, but Sam felt the man's soreness. It kicked off his own instincts to flee from the conflict. But he wasn't sure where to run to. Back into Roanoke? Out into the fields?

Noah answered for him by making a quick gesture with his hand. "Can we just get going?" He walked out the gate and raised his hand to shield his eyes, checking the skyline.

Pyr glanced at Sam. "So he's a teacher now, eh?"

"A professor, yeah."

She made a noise in her throat.

"He's not a—he's normally not this stubborn," Sam explained. "The valley is just—being from here is a big part of who he is. It made him special."

Pyr didn't say anything. Then she rolled one shoulder and something slid off. Her big Frankenstein pack was two smaller bags smushed together. She held one out to him. "Not sure what you've got for supplies, so I made these up for us. A few meals worth of food, some water, some other stuff. And you should have this." She tugged a knife of dark metal out of her belt, spun it in her hand, and held the handle out to him.

"Thanks. My pack's . . . mostly useless stuff."

"Don't worry about it. Nobody's ever prepared to end up here."

Sam tipped his head toward Noah. "He was."

"I'm not so sure." She readjusted her own pack and headed out the gate.

Sam debated combining his two packs into one but wasn't sure which of them had more free space. The patchwork one had a few lengths of string, or maybe long loose threads, and he wondered if he could tie them together somehow and still leave both accessible. Then Noah started walking away and Sam swung both of them up onto the same shoulder. He'd figure something out as they went.

He took a few half-jogging steps, passed Pyr with an apologetic nod, and caught up with Noah on a path leading off to the right through the fields. "The cave should be straight that way," Noah said. He pointed his whole hand forward, like an aspiring politician showing the way to the future.

A few steps behind them, Pyr cleaned her throat. "If we go in a straight line, there's a lot of flat, open space between here and there. There's a pack of young raptors that've been using it as a hunting ground. It's safer to go inward and around most of it."

"Inward?" asked Sam.

She pointed. "There's only two real directions here. Inward to the center of the valley, out to the edges. Everything else is landmarks."

He looked up at the sun, hanging straight above them. "Makes sense."

Noah shook his head, never slowed his stride. "There's no open ground from this direction."

"There's a couple hectares of desert and a Roman plaza the size of a landing field."

Noah glanced back at Pyr, then pointed off through the cornfields in front of them. "The Roman plaza's that way. Used to be, anyway."

"Not for a long time. The plaza's at the edge of the valley now, against the Black Cliffs."

Noah stopped walking at the edge of the corn. Shielded his eyes. Looked up at the valley edge, looming above the nearby trees. Pointed again. "Shouldn't we go along the edge of the valley, then? Still faster than going inward. Especially if the valley's gotten that much bigger."

"We'd still have to cross the plaza. And then if the raptors show up we'd end up with the cliffs on one side of us and nowhere to run."

"I think we should risk it," said Noah.

"It won't save us any time. We can go that way and move extra slow to avoid predators. Or we can stick mostly to the forests, go around, and move at our own pace."

The idea of not seeing the Roman plaza gnawed at Sam. He cleared his throat. "What kind of raptors are we talking about? Big ones?"

"They're not full grown yet, but . . . yes?" She stretched out her dark plastic hand, and held it level above Sam's eyes. "I'd guess they weigh seventy-five or eighty kilos each."

Sam remembered Noah saying the raptors weren't as scary as the Jurassic World movies, but couldn't help but think of velociraptors hunting people through various buildings and nighttime forests.

"You've seen them?" asked Noah.

"Yes."

"But you got away."

"Barely." She lowered her hand and turned it over, showing off her forearm. A long double-gouge, maybe five inches, stretched across two blue-black panels. Sam could see scuffs, like she'd tried to clean it up or sand it down. "I promise, it won't take any longer to go around. And it'll be a lot safer."

Noah looked up at the valley wall again. Stepped aside and gestured for her to take the lead. "Okay. Let's just get moving."

Pyr stepped alongside him and pointed. They headed into the cypress trees. Sam glanced over his shoulder and caught a last glimpse of Roanoke's walls above the tall crops. Someone stood there, watching them leave, but he couldn't tell who.

Parker hadn't come to see them off. Not shocking, after last night, but it was weird to think of their little group splitting up. He wondered if it was her on the wall. Or maybe Josh. Or maybe one of the wardens.

Only a few thin rays of sunlight stabbed down through the grove, and the thick canopy dropped the temperature five or six degrees at least. Enough to chill Sam's bare arms. After about ten minutes of walking they reached the far side of the cypress trees and saw a rolling field of swaying, yellow-gold grass. Near the center of the field was a large area surrounded by a stone-and-wood fence, and they'd been back in the sunlight for almost two minutes before he realized he was looking at a very old-west cemetery. Had anyone from Roanoke mentioned a cemetery? Was it theirs? Or just something else that had appeared in the valley?

It was pretty big. Between the wooden fence rails he could see dozens of markers. Maybe over a hundred.

A lot of people had died in the valley over the years.

Pyr cut across the field and led them into another section of forest. A solid mix of trees, all old and tall enough he'd have to jump to reach the lowest branches. Leaves and needles crunched beneath their feet. She kept up a good pace.

Something moved on a nearby tree, and a section of bark the length of Sam's arm slid further up the trunk with a faint rustle. It took him a moment to recognize the giant pill bug-millipede thing for what it was, and by then it was two yards higher and twisting around the far side of the tree. He waited to see if it would come back around, but it didn't reappear.

"Be careful," Pyr called back. "They bite hard and they're venomous."

Sam stepped away from the tree.

They marched through the forest without further talk. The forest led to a stretch of unmarked, sun-faded asphalt road, not quite wide enough to be two lanes. Halfway along it was a battered, blue-and-white sign in Japanese which Pyr told them read "Ignore Navigational Guidance—Turn Right." Near the end of the pavement, Pyr led them into an area of what felt like a tropical island, with tall grass, clumps of bamboo, and widely spaced palm trees.

After a mile of feeling like he was hiking in Hawaii, they hit a new area. A concrete wall marked the border, and it reminded Sam of old World War II photos of bombed-out buildings. Pyr walked past it without hesitation. Noah only gave it a glance. Sam slowed to check it out. Most of the wall was rough and battered, with a fine layer of dust, or maybe soot.

At the edge, where it butted up against the tropical forest, the surface could've been a polished kitchen countertop.

On the other side of the wall stretched a charred forest. Black tree trunks stretched to the sky like giant needles, all their branches burned away. The crisp ground sent puffs of ash into the air with each step. No smell of smoke, though. The fire'd been long ago.

"So," said Noah, "can I ask—"

"War injury."

A few quick steps and Sam caught up with them. "Hell of an injury."

"It was more than one."

"Were—are you a soldier?"

"It's been long enough we can say was."

Noah nodded. "How long?"

"Since the injuries or since I got here?"

"Both?"

"Nine years since the first injury, seven since the last, six since I ended up in the valley."

Dust and ash swirled around their feet as they walked. Noah cleared his throat. "Not big on details then?"

"Only when they're asked for."

A sound echoed through the charred trees, a couple of grunts or maybe snorts that made Sam think of a raccoon barking. All the ash seemed to muffle the sound, knocking the edges off it. He heard a few more and tried to figure out where they were coming from. "Should we be worried about that?"

Pyr shook her head. "Nah."

"What was it?"

"Pretty sure it's a stegosaurus."

"It is," agreed Noah.

Sam's heart bounced. "Can we see it?"

She glanced over her other shoulder. "We don't have time for side trips, but we'll probably see one. There's a couple of them on this side of the valley."

Sunlight beamed up ahead, and the wind carried a dry, earthy smell to Sam's nose. The blackened tree trunks ended at a straight line, and he saw another bisected rock with a glass-smooth side. He wondered if anything—or anyone—had ever been caught on the line when areas fell into the valley.

How close had *they* been to the line when they fell? If Noah's calculations had only involved himself, had they almost lost toes or hands or arms? Did he even realize they'd been at risk?

Beyond the trees stretched a wide, warm swath of terrain, like the landscape from an old western. Lots of reddish-gray rocks, coarse-looking bushes with tiny leaves, and trees that looked like they'd used up all their energy twisting in a dozen different directions. A prairie? Badlands? A lot more open than the forest, but still plenty of cover if they needed to hide.

Maybe two miles ahead he could see an area of thicker trees. Off to his right was open enough to see the looming cliffs of the valley walls. And to his left, miles away, a shimmer of water and the sharp gleam of the Ice Castle. Winged shapes drifted around it, thin, hazy lines at this distance. Birds? Pterodactyls? Giant insects? Maybe something from the future?

Noah and Pyr had gotten ahead of him, already a few dozen yards into the coarse bushes, weaving between the chest-high plants. Sam lengthened his stride, letting his walk turn into more of a half-jog. He hopped awkwardly over a big rock and ended up behind them again.

Noah glanced back. "Careful."

"Can't help it. I feel like I'm—it's the Disney World thing. I want to see it all. Go on every ride. Meet all the characters."

Pyr snort-laughed.

"I meant look out for the cactus," Noah explained, pointing at one of the spiky bushes. "They get caught on your clothes."

"Oh, crap. Thanks."

The beaten-down trail stretched wide enough for the three of them to walk side by side, but Sam hung back to gaze at everything. It led loosely from tree to tree, as if years of travelers had chosen going from one patch of shade to the next rather than a straight line. Sam wondered if the trail had already been here when this section of terrain had ended up here, or had decades of valley-dwellers made it?

"Aren't you just a little excited to be back here?" he asked Noah.

Noah didn't slow his pace, but he looked around, taking in the cliffs and the distant tower. "Never really thought about it. For me, it's been about getting Beau home. This was just where she still was, if that makes sense."

"Sort of, I guess."

"Plus, getting laughed at for a decade made me a bit . . . numb, I guess? I may have been keeping it at arm's length, mentally. Being a lot more clinical so I could do the work I needed to get back here."

A black-winged microraptor burst out of a bush next to the path, its quadruple wings lifting it up into the air. It squealed at them as it gained altitude, then soared back down to one of the twisted trees and settled on a branch. Sam could see a few others balancing in the tree near it.

They walked in silence. The trail leaned to the left, as if it ran along the side of a hill, and the uneven ground made the rough path feel a little more like a hike. Sam guessed they were a third of the way across the badlands area. If not for the Ice Castle in the distance, it would've been easy to believe they were somewhere desert-y like Nevada or maybe Oklahoma.

"So," he said, breaking the silence. "Soldier. War injury. Super-cyborg parts. Sounds like a cool story."

"It's not that interesting."

"I'm interested."

"So am I," said Noah, after a moment.

They walked a little further.

"Can you not tell us?" asked Sam. "Is this a future knowledge-paradox sort of thing?"

Pyr snort-laughed again. "That's not really a worry here."

Noah laughed.

"I was the turret gunner on a skim tank. We got ambushed by bots. Tried to run and hit an E-mine. Electromagnetic mine. If you get near them, they jump up and latch on." She tapped her arm. "It's why so many things shifted into bioplastics."

Noah nodded. "And the bots were some kind of . . . war robot?"

"Basically. The turret got blown right off the tank. The blast threw me clear, so I didn't burn with the rest of my crew. Still managed to get shot twice. The rest of my unit fought them off and I survived long enough for the medics to find me. My left arm and leg were crushed." She reached up and brushed her cheek. "Jawbone, eye, eye socket, and three ribs. Three days later I was back in the fight."

"Three days?!" echoed Sam.

"Yeah."

Noah looked at her hand. Down at her feet. Her face. "When was this?"

"2431."

Sam coughed. "So the enemy had robots and you were sending out troops?"

Pyr glanced back at him. "The enemy *was* robots. Artificial intelligence."

"Oh."

"I remember reading some old prediction that if humanity ever developed a true AI it'd take minutes for it to turn on us. They were wrong. It took sixteen years. Almost to the day."

Something screeched up above them. Sam looked up, blinked at the sun, and saw two dark shadows in the sky. They glided along, lazily flapping their wings as they soared toward the tower at the center of the valley.

"It must've been awful for you," said Noah. "Getting thrown back into the war without any recovery time."

"I didn't need it. Cybernetics are advanced enough that these work just like my originals. They react and feel the same. I didn't notice anything different until they showed me the millexes."

"The what?"

"Military extras. A couple bonus functions they include as standard when soldiers get replacements."

Sam tried to control his breathing and wheeze-coughed again. "If the—if they're this advanced, couldn't they make the parts look like, well, you?"

"Having replacements doesn't have a stigma," she said, fixing her electric-blue eye on him. "No one cares if your hand's flesh or bioplastics."

"Sorry."

"I forgive you for your outdated view of humanity," Pyr said. She held out an arm, bringing herself and Noah to a halt. Sam looked between them and tried to see what she'd seen. The way the trail zigzagged through the brush, it took him a moment to spot the problem.

The lumpy, leather-brown boulder looked to be seven or eight feet tall and sat right in the middle of the trail. He wondered if it had fallen out of the sky since the last time Pyr had traveled this way. Could areas overlap like that? They'd dropped down in the middle of one area, so why couldn't a big rock?

Pyr looked left and right. "We'll have to go around it. Left looks . . . less painful."

Sam could see the thin cactus plants on both sides of their path. "Couldn't we go over it?"

Noah glanced back at him with a smirk. "Not a great idea."

"Why not?"

"We're at the back end. If we startle it, its tail could crush us."

Sam processed the words, started to frame a question, and then the boulder shifted side to side, like it was trying to reach an itch.

Pyr took a few more steps toward the dinosaur, then pushed herself between two less thorny-looking plants on the side of the trail. She sidestepped further into the scrub and Noah followed her. Sam stood there for another moment, staring at the dinosaur before moving after them. The plants scraped at his belly with long spines that were practically needles. One dragged across his shirt, catching again and again. He sucked his gut in as far as he could.

The dinosaur's big turtle-like back was a shell of dried leather covered with dinner plates of bone or maybe horn. The long tail shook stiffly, and he saw the massive club at the end of it, like two side-by-side watermelons. As he got further away from the trail, he could glimpse the top of its head moving back and forth, eating the bushes on either side of it.

Thus, he realized, the unusually wide trail.

"Ankylosaurus," said Noah, sidestepping between the sharp plants. "There was one here when I was a kid. Different color, though. That one was more of a rusty orange."

The head stretched up over the bushes to stare at them with a black eye the size of a tennis ball. It reminded Sam of a cockatoo. Like the bird, Sam couldn't tell if the dinosaur was curious, scared, or annoyed.

Pyr kept moving through the brush, splitting her attention between the ankylosaurus and the various stabby branches ahead of them. "We should be fine as long as we don't startle it. They're timid, as dinos go."

"That's how I remember them," Noah agreed.

The turtle dinosaur made a noise like a bored horse, the sound of a lot of air moving through a big throat, and lowered its head back to its meal.

The bushes crackled and snapped and tugged at Sam's jeans and shirt. A few cactus spines scratched across his thighs, and their points pressed through the denim. He felt a sudden honest relief for the hiking boots, imagining a few of the spines sliding through his flimsy sneakers to stab his feet and toes.

A few more minutes and they were back on the trail a few yards past the dinosaur. The path through the brush was narrower on this side of the ankylosaurus. It watched them stagger out of the scrub but didn't stop eating. Its feet shifted, scattering some dust.

Sam plucked at a few little spikes and thorns clinging to his clothes. "Do we need to worry about it charging us?"

Pyr flicked a pair of needles off her leg. "No. As long as they're not scared, these ones will barely move. You can walk right up to them."

Sam's heart bounced again. "Can we?"

Noah shook his head. "It's not why we're here."

"Oh, come on. It's a *dinosaur.* Right there. A dinosaur she says we can get close to."

"As long as you don't move too fast," Pyr added.

"Sam . . ."

"Two minutes. Just give me two minutes to look at the dinosaur."

Noah pulled one of the sharp spines out of his sleeve. "Two minutes. And then we're going on."

Sam took a few slow steps back down the trail. The ankylosaurus turned one of its ink-black eyes to watch him approach but kept eating. Its mouth looked like a broad beak the size of a football and reminded him even more of a cockatoo. As he got closer, he even saw little flat quills lying against its skin, like thin feathers.

"Hey, big guy," he said, still advancing slowly. "Or big girl. Whatever you are. Don't need to be nervous."

The beak opened, closed on a branch covered with little leaves, chomped through it. The eye facing Sam blinked. It munched the branch.

Sam was eight feet away. Six feet. Four. He could *smell* it, a scent like wet dust and bitter plants. If it swung its head around now, the beak would barely miss him.

"Look at you," he whispered. "Look. At. You."

The ankylosaurus blinked at him again. Then it shuffled its feet and stretched its head a little more to the side, baring its neck to him. No fear of him at all.

A bright red spot on its neck drew his attention. The shininess made him think it was a drop of blood, but it was the size of the dinosaur's eye and too round. A drop that big would be running down its neck. Maybe a prehistoric tick, gorging itself on ankylosaurus blood? Morbid fascination made him lean in a little closer, trying to move slowly so as not to startle the . . .

"What the hell?"

The red circle was glossy plastic, ringed with a band of metal so thin it almost vanished in the disk's shadow. Letters were molded into the disc, and a few flecks of white paint still hid in some of their corners. Sam read the text three times to make sure of what it said.

ANK MKIII 23-F

PROPERTY OF

JURASSICORP

23

JOSH

Josh got to the gate in time to see Noah, Sam, and Pyr vanish down a path along the evil corn. They hadn't waited to see if he'd changed his mind about going with them. Granted, he'd told them last night he didn't want to, and nothing had changed since then. He had zero interest in going out into dinosaur valley to be torn apart, eaten, or possibly both.

Still, it would've been nice to be asked.

The android was here, and the half-naked Egyptian warden, standing outside the gate with her back to Josh. He couldn't tell if she was watching Noah and the others walk away or just . . . on watch. After a few moments he decided she was on duty, and clearly took it seriously. She stood like a statue.

"Good morning, Josh." The android did a slight bow and waved its hand, twitching like a customer who'd enjoyed a little too much product for their own good.

"Hey." He pointed after the departing trio. "Did they say anything before they left? Leave any messages for me?"

"If they did, they didn't leave them with me. Can I help with anything else?"

"No, I think I'm . . . I'm good."

The android hobbled off, its walking stick thumping on the ground, and Josh watched it go. He wondered what the android did all day. They'd called it the Timekeeper, but he guessed that was a bonus function. Noah had said it'd been like a nanny to him and his sister. Maybe it ran the town's daycare or school or something.

Although . . .

Josh looked up each of the dirt roads leading away from the gate. People walked around, did little odd jobs, looked busy in a relaxed way. But all adults. No kids anywhere. Had he seen any kids in Roanoke? He tried to remember the crowd when they first arrived, and wandering through the village yesterday. Had there even been any teenagers?

Maybe the kids all started school early. Or had a lot of chores in their homes. Heck, the valley didn't have any child labor laws. Maybe the kids were out in the fields or churning butter or something useful and quasi-medieval.

He turned back to the gate. The warden still had her back to him, and her bare shoulders and lats would put a lot of men he knew to shame. Then he heard a deep honk, a goose on steroids, followed by a burst of loud German words, if his high school memories were correct. He took a step forward, and another one, and now he stood next to the spectacularly muscled Egyptian warden and stared out at the fields.

The German farmer guy—Diedrich, like one of the men currently looking for Josh back in the future-slash-present—led a dinosaur across the field. It was a massive, squat thing. Eight or nine feet at the shoulder, and at least twenty feet long. All muscle, like a rhino with a crown of horns. More horns than the Dinobot he'd had as a kid.

The dinosaur had a leather harness wrapped around its shoulders and belly. A few long, rough ropes connected it to a plow that Josh would've generously described as "homemade." The ropes had half a dozen knots in them. Snapped again and again, and tied back together every time. The Asian man, Dak Ho, held the plow's handles, keeping it upright and traveling in the straightest line possible behind the big beast.

Diedrich whapped the dinosaur's rump with his bamboo stick and spoke to it again. Demanding, then coaxing, then demanding again. It didn't seem to notice his words, but Josh thought it was going right where Diedrich wanted. He'd either trained it well or knew a trick to guiding it.

The German man looked over, saw Josh and the warden at the gate, and gave a casual salute from his hat brim while giving the dinosaur affectionate pats with the other hand. Then he kicked his foot up into a loop on the harness, heaved, and pulled himself onto its back. He patted it again, called something back to Dak Ho, and then tapped the sides of the dinosaur's leathery neck with his heels. It let out another deep, tuba-like honk, dropped what looked like seven or eight gallons of glistening dino manure, and lumbered forward.

Josh watched it drag the plow for a minute. Maybe two. The smell of fresh dino droppings wafted across the field and hit him in the face.

The warden finally turned her head to him and said . . . something. He didn't understand the words, but the tone felt a lot like "Don't you have anything better to do?"

He didn't know how to answer her, so he wandered back into the village.

His stomach reminded him he still hadn't eaten anything, so he found the main hall and a few warm things that could've been corn pitas. They smelled delicious, but part of that was hunger. He ate one there, took another one with him back outside, lamenting the fact that coffee beans apparently hadn't ended up in the valley.

He wandered down the dirt path, tearing off chunks of his pita and stuffing them in his mouth. Still not a lot of people out and about. He could smell wood smoke, and tried to think of things people might need fire for on a warm day. Cooking? Blacksmithing? That probably needed more than wood-fire heat, and the blacksmith had left with Noah and Sam.

"Hello."

He looked around and his brain stumbled over itself as his eyes settled on the curly-haired doctor in the patched *Les Mis* outfit. She had a rough basket with no handle, almost a woven bowl, with a collection of green plants in it. Spices? Weeds? Herbs?

After what he hoped wasn't an awkwardly long time, he managed to say, "Hi."

"Have you come to check on your friend as well?"

Her dark eyes made it tough to put things together in his head. The doctor. Gathering herbs. She had Olivia. And the doctor's name was . . . was . . .

She seemed to understand his hesitation and held out her free hand. "We have not properly met. I am Madame Monique Cadieux."

"Thank you. Joshua Redd. Josh."

"Your other friend, Parker, visited a short while ago."

"We're not so much friends as . . . traveling companions. Friendly, but not besties, if you know what I mean."

"I believe so."

Josh decided checking on Olivia and getting to know some of the locals could be his "something better to do," and said so in not as many words. Monique led him inside the house and to a small side room. She raised her little basket-bowl. "Let me set these down and I will answer your questions as best I can."

In the little room, stretched out on the bed, Olivia looked . . . unconscious. Josh's career had given him a good sense of the subtle differences between when people were asleep and when they were full-on unconscious. Little things. Sleeping people tended to breathe a little heavier, to wiggle themselves into more comfortable positions. They reacted to things, like noise or light.

With a minute of quick observation, Josh could see Olivia might be alive, but the lights were out upstairs. He'd stumbled across a client once who'd OD'd in their home and pretty much gone comatose. That's what she was like. Except he couldn't place an anonymous 911 call and slip away.

Monique returned. She brushed past Josh and did a quick exam, setting her fingers against Olivia's wrist, neck, lips. "I wish I had better news, but your friend—your companion—is unchanged. Her pulse is weak but steady. Breathing is good but slightly irregular. I give her a trickle of broth three times a day, but that will only sustain her for so long."

She gently stretched Olivia's eyelid open to reveal a blank, staring eye. Her fingers slid the eye shut again, then snapped twice by each ear. Then Monique brought her other hand up and slapped them together hard, the clap loud and sudden enough to make Josh flinch.

"Nothing," said Monique. "As I told Parker, it is amazing she survived even indirect contact with the glass obelisk. But we should be . . . realistic about her chances."

Josh had been realistic about her chances since she and Logan had gotten zapped a few days ago. He tried to think of any other tricks he'd learned for dealing with unresponsive people, but most of them boiled down to a few little smacks and then letting someone else deal with it. "I'm sure you're doing everything you can," he said.

"You are kind to say so, but I know my knowledge has many gaps in it. Pyr and Theta have told me of the miraculous medicines of their time, and whenever someone is wounded here I cannot help but wonder if their injuries would be an inconvenience if I merely knew other techniques or methods."

Josh stepped back out into the hall. "I thought . . . Noah told us people healed faster here. Something about the air or the water or something."

She stood in the doorway, holding open the privacy curtain. "Oui. Wounds that should take months to heal are often gone in a week or two. And many people have arrived in the valley with afflictions that vanished after a short time. Our miller had a . . . personal infection when she arrived. It was gone in a month, even though the doctors of her time assured her it was incurable." She looked back at Olivia before letting the curtain swing back into place. "But there is still injury here. And death."

"So when someone gets bitten in half by a dinosaur . . ."

He'd meant it as a bit of a joke, but she didn't smile. "Painful death, yes. Perhaps more painful, if the nature of this place stretches it out longer than it should be."

"Pleasant thought."

"Forgive me." She waved him back down the hall toward the front of the building.

"Do . . . so a lot of people die here, then? From dinosaurs or cavemen or whatever."

Monique gave him a weak smile, and in that brief moment Josh realized a full, happy smile from this woman would probably reduce most men to happily trembling idiots. Some women he knew, too. Not that she was secretly gorgeous in some teen rom-com way, with supermodel looks hidden behind thick glasses or a bad haircut. She just had a certain . . . well, je ne sais quoi that sparked in her eyes.

"I have seen plenty of death," she said, jarring him out of his few heartbeats of infatuation. "Most of it back in the real world. My real world. But enough here."

"I'm sorry."

"So many people die in their first few days here. Killed by the Klaa or the animals. Whichever finds them first. Qiang believes a third of the people who end up here do not last a week. And several of the rest . . ." She pushed open the front door and they stepped outside into the sunlight. "You were fortunate to find us as soon as you did."

"All thanks to Noah. He knew enough to keep us alive. Well, most of us. Some of us, I guess."

She nodded politely. Gifted him with another smile that definitely would've left anyone weak-kneed, not just him. "I will make sure you and your companions know if there's any change in Olivia's condition. I read to her last night. I will try the same again tonight." She stepped down toward her little herb garden.

"Thank you." Josh was simultaneously struck with the desire to keep the conversation going and the stark realization he'd have absolutely nothing to do if it ended. "So you . . . you take care of all the medical needs here? Comatose people. Cuts. Bruises. Broken bones. All of it?"

"For such a savage land, there is not as much for me to do as you may think. It is the one blessing of living here. Or perhaps the curse.

We all live long, healthy lives. Much better than most of us would've back home. But when we die . . . it is almost always sudden and violent."

"So, for the most part just bandages, a few shots of brandy, maybe get to deliver a baby now and then?"

It earned him one more half smile before she stepped down to her little herb garden. So worth it. "How I wish we had good brandy. Or wine. Or Scots whiskey."

"Beer, then? You must have beer. Didn't the Egyptians invent it or something?"

She shook her head.

"Ahhh, I could've made a killing here."

"I beg your pardon?"

"Nothing. Never mind."

One of the little four-winged birds fluttered by and perched on the house across the road. It stared back at Josh. Squawked. Stretched out one of its wings and started to clean under it.

Monique turned her eyes to the plants. "And truth be told, I have only ever delivered one baby, and that was many years ago back in Rouen, before I found myself here. The midwife had been detained and the mother and child were not willing to wait."

"You ended up here alone?"

"Oui, for the first few days. I thought I'd gone mad. Or perhaps died and ended up in some awful purgatory. Then Mr. Conner found me."

Josh tried to review the names and faces he'd met so far in Roanoke. "Which one is he?"

"The warden with the white beard and the splattered-green clothes."

"Oh! Emerson. Em."

"Yes."

"Did you, forgive me for asking, did you have a family? Back . . . there? Then?"

She nodded. "A husband. Chemin was the apothecary in name. In truth, we did everything together, shared the burdens of research and creation. It was why they made me the doctor when I arrived here."

"You miss him?"

"Every day. My mind tells me he's thought me long dead and moved on. My heart still hopes someday I'll escape this place and be with him again. But such hopes are dangerous here. They drive men mad."

"How long has it been? Since you . . . got here? Arrived?"

"Nine years."

"Wow."

"Oui. I was a young woman then. Now I'm almost thirty-three. All my youth wasted away in this place."

Josh laughed. "You're joking, right?"

"You mock me?"

"I mean, you're not exactly an old maid. I'd guess half the guys here would be willing to keep your bed warm if you wanted."

Her eyebrows went up, and half a dozen expressions flitted through her beautiful eyes. Shock. Scandal. A little bit of naughty happiness. A little bit of sadness. "I am a married woman, m'sieur."

He backtracked. "Sorry. I just . . . it's silly to think you're old or undesirable. Not that you should be desired. In that way."

"You flatter me, Mr. Redd."

"Just Josh. Please. Wait." His brain, already stumbling like a lovestruck teenager, caught on something and swung itself around. "Nine years?"

"I beg your pardon?"

"You've been here nine years and haven't delivered a baby?"

She shook her head.

"Never?"

"M'sieur, please. None of us here are married. To each other."

Josh looked at her. Thought of the well-muscled woman at the gate. "I may not know a lot of history, but I've got a really good grasp of human nature. I'm pretty sure there were people in eighteenth-century France who had sex even though they weren't married. One or two of them might've even enjoyed it."

Monique blushed, but he caught a little smile on her lips. "There have been several couplings here in my time. Some ongoing, some brief. I have been involved in none of them, of course."

"Of course."

"But it is a small village. Difficult to keep secrets. Or to not see things. Or hear them."

He nodded. "And no babies? In nine years?"

"None. To the best of my knowledge, from everything Ross has told me, there has never been a child born here in the valley."

"Never?"

The corners of her mouth dipped. "Never."

"Do they . . . does something go wrong?" It wasn't his area of expertise, but he racked his memory for medical terms. Clinical terms. "Do they miscarry? Are they stillborn?"

She shook her head again. "No. No woman here in the valley has ever been with child. There were two Neanderthal infants before my time here, but Qiang believed they had arrived here with their mothers, already born."

Josh tried to do a bunch of guesstimates in his head. Considered his own experiences, those of a few friends who'd tried to conceive, and a few who hadn't been trying at all. "Isn't that . . . unlikely?"

A little laugh from her. "In this place? What can we truly say is unlikely?"

"Fair enough, I guess."

"Would you like to know what I believe?"

"Yes. Yes, I would."

She looked up at the sky, off above the houses. "I have learned many things here. Things men would not know until long after my death, had I remained in Rouen. I have been told of Dr. Darwin and his theories. The true age of the world. How this planet belonged to the dinosaurs so much longer than it did to mankind. I have come to the far past and seen the far future."

"That's . . . that's kind of beautiful."

"Thank you. I do still believe in the Lord, but I believe we have come back long before he set man down on this Earth. We are here before our own creation. As such, children cannot be conceived because there are no new souls for them."

Josh bit his tongue.

She looked him in the eyes. "You wanted to know what I believe."

"I did."

"I know my thoughts may seem provincial, but it is who I am."

"Well," said Josh, "as a wise woman once said, in this place, what can we truly say is unlikely?"

She raised an accusing eyebrow, but another dazzling smile danced at the corners of her lips. "Thank you, Mr. Redd."

"Josh."

"Josh." She stood up and brushed some wrinkles from her skirt. Swept her curly hair away from her face. "And now you must pardon me. It is time for Olivia's next feeding. I must try to keep her strength up."

"Right." He stepped away, out into the wide dirt path. "Thank you for talking with a . . . a newcomer."

"Thank you as well. For the conversation."

He took another step back. "Let me know if there's any change in her condition. Or, you know, if there's anything I could do to help."

She bowed her head. "Alas, as I've said, there is little else to do. Our resources here are limited. I have no access to proper instruments or even the most basic of drugs."

Josh's mental footing shifted again. "Oh. Well . . . what kind of drugs would you need?"

24

SAM

"Is this . . . is this a wildlife tag?" asked Noah. He leaned in closer over Sam's shoulder, peering at the little red disk on the turtle-like dinosaur's neck. He didn't shove Sam into the big animal's shoulder, but it was close.

The ankylosaurus ignored them both and kept eating. Its beaky mouth latched onto a cactus paddle the size and shape of a deflated football, tugged it free, and ate it up in three quick bites. It didn't seem to notice the spines, and Sam wondered if the inside of its beak was hardened against them or if it was just indifferent to the pain.

"I don't know." Sam looked at the words again. "'Property of' sounds like somebody, well, owns it. This isn't a wild, free-range dinosaur."

Pyr stood behind them, not crowding in, for which Sam was thankful. "What's the name again? The company name?"

He double-checked the tag. "JurassiCorp?"

Her fingers snapped with a hard *crack*. "It's reassembled."

Noah straightened up and looked at her. "It's what?"

"It's not a real dinosaur. I mean, it is, but it's not prehistoric. It's from the mid . . . twenty-second century, if I remember right."

Sam stood up straight as well, realized he was crowded close to Noah again. "Reassembled?"

"It's a genetics thing. Reassembled life-forms are extinct things they've brought back for research or zoos or whatever. Assembled life-forms are all new. Usually something bred for a specific purpose. Like Thate."

"The blue guy?"

"Yes. He's an assembled human. They built him to be a soldier."

"That's very—not creepy at all."

The ankylosaurus let out a little cough, or maybe a grunt, and took two heavy steps forward. Its leathery shoulder bumped into Sam with all the gentleness and force of a slowly rolling car, pushing him into Noah, who finally took a few steps away. The dinosaur settled back down and began munching on a new cactus.

Noah shook his head. "No, I've seen dozens of dinosaurs here. I've never seen one of these tags before."

Sam glanced back at the red disk. "They're pretty small."

"Believe me, I *studied* these dinosaurs. I would've seen them."

Pyr held up a hand. "I'm not saying they're all reassembled. Just this one."

"But why is it here then?"

She shrugged. "Why is any of this here? It fell down a hole in time and here it is. Like everything else in the valley."

"But it's from the future," said Noah.

"Two hundred years in the past, from my point of view."

"I . . ." Noah stopped. Looked at the red tag again. "That makes sense. At least, it makes sense here."

Pyr snort-laughed.

"Hang on." Sam waved a hand, looked back at the ankylosaurus again. "So, in a hundred years someone's actually going to make Jurassic World?"

"JurassiCorp," she corrected.

"No, I mean . . . somebody makes a dinosaur theme park?"

"More like a zoo, if I remember right. Or maybe several zoos? It was long before my time. A meg of safety problems and animal cruelty issues. I think it got shut down after ten or fifteen years and all the dinosaurs went to zoos or collectors. Guess this one got away."

Sam set a hand on one of the big bone plates spread across the broad turtle-like back. The hard oval was warm from the sun and glaze-slick beneath a layer of dust. The ankylosaurus didn't seem to notice him. He imagined the dinosaur trapped in a cage, maybe one of those pit-like holding areas they had at a zoo, and suddenly finding itself outside in the expanse of the valley. "Lucky girl."

The ankylosaurus blinked twice and shuffled forward again. Sam managed to step out of the way this time. It found a leafy shrub and munched with a lot more enthusiasm.

"Well, then," said Noah. "We should get moving."

Pyr rolled her shoulders. Tugged on the straps of her pack. "I agree." She headed down the path. Noah was a step behind her.

Sam sighed. "Yeah, okay." He patted the dinosaur one more time—the actual dinosaur right here, inches from him—and this time it rolled an eye back to stare at him curiously. They gazed at each other for a few heartbeats, and then the ankylosaurus decided the little-leafed shrub was more interesting than a would-be astrophysicist. It bit off a whole branch and chewed it to bits.

A few quick steps put him behind Noah and Pyr, and he glanced back over his shoulder. The ankylosaurus munched away, barely aware they'd left in the same way it had been barely aware of their presence. Sam had half hoped it'd follow them.

They trudged along the rough path as it wove through the sharp bushes and cacti, stretching from tree to tree. Sam watched across the wasteland, keeping an eye on the distant trees, hoping to catch sight of another dinosaur. He saw a few distant shapes glide near the Ice Castle, heard their faint screeches, but nothing close.

They stopped twice beneath twisted trees to enjoy a few sips of water in the broken shade. Under the second tree Sam noticed a swath of birdlike tracks in the dirt, as if a whole flock had run by on the ground. Each one was smaller than his hand, and here and there he could make out the dimple of tiny claws at the end of each toe. He pointed it out to Noah and Pyr, but neither of them seemed interested.

They stepped back out into the sun and Sam tried to guess how long they'd been hiking. The always-overhead sun didn't seem as disorienting anymore—amazing how fast you could adapt to the impossible—but it still played hell with his sense of time. As an undergrad he'd taught himself to tell time off shadow lengths and now every single shadow told him it was quarter past twelve, no matter when he looked. Going off the way his feet and legs felt, he guessed it'd been . . . two and a half hours since they left Roanoke. He skimmed over the day's high points and upped his estimate to three.

They approached the tree line. A dense area with the look of a tropical rainforest in the middle of a drought. A web of dry vines hung low from the canopy, and they rustled as Pyr pushed some of them aside.

"The border of the mushroom forest's maybe another two hours from here. Another half hour from there to the cave."

Sam paused to examine a rock at the tree line, a big flat thing half buried in the ground. Once again, a smooth, glassy side facing the trees. Cut off with laser precision. He wondered if there were dozens of equally smooth-sided stones scattered through Earth's history, the leftovers of the ones that'd been swept up by the wormhole and dropped here into the valley.

As he stepped into the shade he wondered if there were bisected trees. Would they collapse? Shatter? How many mysterious "lightning strikes" in fields and deserts had been the wormhole snatching things up and leaving occasional destruction in its wake?

Long, thick tree roots stretched back and forth across the ground between the trees. They overlapped and stretched little loops above the forest floor. The random shafts of sunlight highlighted some of them like usable elements in an old video game.

Sam made it all of twenty feet before his boot snagged and sent him tumbling. He mostly caught himself, getting back up with only a small amount of wrist pain and one banged knee. Noah made it another three yards before tripping, stumbling, then tripping again. Pyr caught him before he faceplanted. Or maybe Noah grabbed at her arm and she took his weight.

Hopefully not an area they'd be required to run through.

They slowed their pace, all of them focusing on the ground ahead. Sam took a few steps, looked around, took a few more. Wondered if the roots would slow down a larger dinosaur at all. And then a few thoughts connected in his head.

"Morbid question," he said aloud. "How often does something get cut in half when it ends up here?"

Pyr looked back at him. Noah didn't. "What do you mean?" she asked.

"Well, at a lot of the edges, when we enter different areas, there's stones with sections cut off. I just wondered if it ever happened to a tree or a dinosaur or, y'know, a person. They weren't entirely within the area of the wormhole? And so not all of them shifted to here. Now."

Pyr started walking again. Stepped over a root thicker than her waist. "That is morbid," she agreed.

Sam checked the ground. Started after them. "So?"

"Yes?"

"Have you ever found half a dinosaur? Or a person?"

"Not that way, no. I mean, we've found people who didn't survive long here. A human or a Neanderthal who arrived, wandered the wrong way, and got eaten by a raptor or an allosaurus or something else."

"But nobody cut in half? Or a dinosaur with its tail clipped off or something."

"Not that I've ever heard of." She took a few quick steps over some tree roots, tapped Noah on the shoulder, and guided him slightly to the right around a tree so wide the three of them together would've strained their arms to reach around it.

"Never?"

"I'm not saying it couldn't've happened. The valley's a big place. But I've never seen or heard of anything like that."

On her last word the air shifted and Sam *felt* a noise bump on the inside of his rib cage, like somebody else's rapid heartbeat rumbling in his chest. He lurched to a halt. Pyr put up a silencing hand before they could say anything.

Far off to their left, a hundred yards away at least, something large moved between the trees.

Her arm slowly moved, slowly pointed to the nearby trees. She took three slow, cautious steps and put one of the thick trunks between herself and the dinosaur.

Another low rumble reached them. A faint tremor in the ground. A flash of red up in the branches. Something big moving *behind* the branches.

The allosaurus they called Burn.

Sam looked at the roots under his feet. At the dinosaur. Tried not to think about slipping and falling, of trying to move fast and tripping. Realized it was *all* he could think of. Took three excruciating steps to the closest tree. Got its thick trunk between him and Burn.

He heard a distant crack of tree branches. Another deep, low rumble. Jesus fucking Christ was that just its *breathing*? The scents of raw meat and dirty teeth wafted between the trees.

Pyr looked calm. Unworried. He tried to channel that calm.

The ground trembled with four . . . five . . . six slow, heavy footsteps. The air shivered with another impossibly deep breath. More branches snapped.

Another breath. This one wasn't a tremor in the air. It was a breeze. Almost wind! So close. Was it right on the other side of the tree? Could it smell him?

Then the sounds retreated. He thought about looking and immediately remembered Kyle stepping out when the first monster wandered away, only for the second one to appear from nowhere. Such a stupid, hack B-movie gimmick, the giant monster that somehow sneaks up on someone without making a sound. But he'd seen it happen and now it lodged in his head and he couldn't bring himself to peer around the tree.

"He's gone," said Pyr.

Sam exhaled. "Are you sure?"

"Yes. Passing through, and he wasn't close enough to catch our scent."

"Aren't there two of them?"

"There were two," said Noah. "Didn't you see the other one?"

"I was hiding behind the tree."

"Smartest thing to do." Pyr pointed ahead, away from the dinosaurs. "Let's go."

They started walking again as if nothing had happened. As if they hadn't just been hiding from an allosaurus. From *two* allosauruses. His mind replayed the scenario of running across the web of roots, tripping and falling. He half turned, glanced over his shoulder. No sign of dinosaurs. No ultralow growls rolling through the trees.

While they hiked Sam's brain scrolled back to what they'd been discussing before Gnash and Burn wandered by. "What about if . . . does anything ever appear halfway in a tree or boulder or anything like that?"

Pyr and Noah both glanced back at him this time. Noah wrinkled his brow. "What are you talking about?"

Sam shrugged. Gestured at the forest around them. "Well, things appear here, right? They vanish from the future and reappear here in the valley. Do they ever appear where something already is?"

Noah looked over at Pyr. "Again, not that I've ever seen," she said. "Or heard of."

"So no dinosaurs in boulders or people in trees or anything?"

She shook her head. "Sorry to disappoint you." She took four quick steps, stretching her legs between a scattering of roots.

Sam hopped up onto the next big root and stepped to the next, never setting foot back on the ground. "What about falling?"

"What about it?" asked Noah.

"Does anything ever appear one or two hundred feet up in the air? Did you ever find anything that'd been dropped and smashed on impact? Or . . . burst, maybe? Splattered?"

Noah shook his head. "Not that I can remember."

"Me, either," said Pyr. "Don't recall Ross ever telling a story about something like that either."

"What about buried twenty feet underground or inside a cliff?"

Pyr laughed. "How would we even know if that happened?"

"Okay, what about underwater in the lake? Have any bodies ever showed up drowned?"

Noah put his leg up onto a fallen tree trunk. Kicked off. Balanced on top of it. "What's with the morbid streak, Sam?"

He tossed the puzzle back and forth in his mind. "It's—if I understand all of this correctly, things can appear anywhere, right? That's why the layout of the valley keeps changing."

Pyr nodded. Noah gave a reluctant shrug.

"So if things are getting dropped here at random, isn't it odd that everything seems to end up intact and safe at ground level?"

Noah hopped off the tree trunk. Started walking across the roots again. "We didn't. We all tumbled down the hill, remember?"

"We lost our balance because our footing changed. If anything, that proves my point. Back in the present, we were much higher up above sea level, but we appeared here on a smaller, lower hill."

"We don't know what our elevation is here."

"You know what I mean."

Up ahead, Pyr snapped her fingers again. "Geoff fell into the lake."

Noah raised an eyebrow. "Who?"

"Geoff. He's the cobbler."

Sam knew the word from . . . fairy tales? A history class? "What's a cobbler?"

Pyr pointed down at her dark blue plastic feet. "He makes shoes and boots for everyone. Good at it. He used to work for some company—insurance or something—in the early twenty-first century. Tried to kill himself. Threw himself off a bridge with a two-hundred-foot drop. Instead he fell thirty feet and landed in the lake. I've heard him tell the story four or five times."

"So he had a degree of downward momentum, but he arrived in the one place in the valley where he could land without serious injury."

"I suppose so. Never thought of it that way. Everyone just considered him lucky."

Noah took that moment to catch his foot on a root and stumble, but he caught himself before falling. They all focused on the uneven ground and walked in silence for a bit. Sam took the time to toss the puzzle back and forth in his mind. He couldn't shake the feeling that he was looking at . . . something. But the assorted parts wouldn't connect in his head, and every time he felt like he got close to lining up three or four pieces he realized he'd knocked two or three others far out of place.

Something scurried out from between two roots ahead of him, leaped onto one of them, and then froze outside a shaft of sunlight. Waiting to see if it was being chased, or maybe hoping that it'd become so still it was invisible. He froze too, hoping to get a good look at it.

The creature couldn't've been much bigger than a cat, with a wide stripe of reddish-brown fur, or maybe quills, down its back. The rest of its skin was yellowy-orange, and maybe scaly. Thick tail, like a raccoon, but he wasn't sure how much of it was quills versus actual animal. Head like a tennis ball, half turned, watching him with a beady eye not much bigger than a pea.

No, not round. The head had a little frill around it, like a triceratops, and a squat beak. At this angle they helped create the illusion of roundness.

They stared at each other for a few moments as Noah and Pyr kept walking away. The little dinosaur ever so slowly lifted its front legs off the root, giving Sam a glimpse of tiny flexing claws, and stood on its thick back legs like a rabbit. Then its head twisted forward and it launched away from him, bounding over two more roots before scampering away and vanishing in the maze of the forest floor.

He realized Noah and Pyr were looking back at him. He pointed after the creature, then hop-walked across a dozen roots the size of his thigh. "Sorry," he told them. "Saw a little dinosaur."

Pyr nodded. "As long as it wasn't a big one."

Noah braced his foot against the base of a tree and stretched. "Your legs don't get tired, do they?"

She looked down and flexed biomechanical toes. Sam hadn't noticed before, but there were only four toes on each foot. "Not really, no," she said. "Do we need to take a break?"

Sam's stomach rumbled. "That wasn't deliberate, I swear."

One side of her mouth wrinkled up. "Sounds like an affirmative."

Noah sighed. Nodded. "Sure. Let's take a break."

They sat on some of the larger roots and fallen trees. Sam felt his feet and ankles relax. The uneven ground took a bigger toll than he realized. He wondered how far they'd traveled. Four miles? Five?

Pyr slung her rough bag off her shoulder, dug around, pulled out a carrot. Sam checked in his. She'd packed some basics for them. Thick slices of bread. Some fruit he couldn't name. Dried meat that also defied easy identification. A few more of the carrots.

Noah tore off a piece of bread. "I think the problem with your hypothesis, Sam, is it ultimately suffers from survivorship bias. We have no idea how many people or animals or trees have ended up in the valley. We know that the ones we encounter arrived here safely, but that doesn't mean there aren't dozens or hundreds who didn't."

"Absence of evidence is not evidence of absence."

"Exactly." He popped the bread in his mouth.

While Sam ate, he stared at Pyr's four-toed feet. Deliberate choice? More efficient design? Maybe people in the future just had four toes and her artificial limbs reflected that. No more little piggies going "wee wee wee" all the way home. He choked down a laugh, ended up half-choking on a mouthful of bread in the process.

He stared at his own feet. At the boots with the two dark drops on them. They had a lot of dust now. A cactus spine sticking out of the side like a whisker the razor had missed. They didn't feel tight anymore. Hadn't taken long for them to stop being Logan's boots and become his.

They all finished lunch. Stretched. Started walking again.

Off to the right, Sam saw light shining through the trees. He caught glimpses of a wide field of red and orange grass and low scrub. The open space they were avoiding. He heard a distant screech, closer to an eagle or hawk than the raptor sounds, but nothing out in the distance moved.

He kept throwing looks to the side, wondering if he'd see another dinosaur out there, but all it did was make him stumble.

He hopped from root to root. Walked around some. Climbed over others. They hiked and the shafts of light grew into beams, then big pools. The tree roots thinned, shrunk, vanished down into the ground. Sam looked up and saw completely different trees. Two forest areas butted up against each other. He'd barely noticed because the rainforest trees had stretched their roots into the new area.

The new trees had slick, smooth surfaces. He reached out, ran his fingers across one. It had a silky, almost thready feel. He followed the thick trunk up and not a single branch blocked his view. The tree's single shaft stretched straight up and came to a rounded, slightly tapered tip twenty feet up. He took a breath and tasted a scent like dirt and sunflower seeds in the air.

Sam let out a little laugh as he remembered a story that showed up in three of the books.

A few yards ahead of him, Pyr glanced back. "The mushroom forest," she called out.

Calm rolled across Noah's face as he set his own hand on one of the big trunks. He looked relaxed, like he had when they first arrived. "Not what Beau called it."

Sam's laugh got a little bigger. "Dickwood Forest."

Noah laughed too. He sounded . . . normal again. Back in his element.

Pyr's mouth formed a little smile. "Sounds like something a teenager would come up with."

"She was a teenager," said Noah.

Pyr's smile faded, and Sam felt his own face drop.

Noah looked through the forest, up into the sky. Sam followed his gaze. It wasn't hard to see above the limbless trees. No, not trees. Giant prehistoric mushrooms. And just past them all he could see the jagged edge of the valley.

"Look there. The top of our cliff. That's Chekhov's Rock, straight that way." He set his hand straight out, karate-chopping the air again. "I bet we can be there in half an hour if we pick up the pace."

Sam bit back a sigh. Pyr didn't. Noah glanced back at them and then headed off through the trees.

Sam and Pyr exchanged a look. Her eyes—even the mechanical one—had a sad, depressed look to them. "He's going to take this hard," she said as they fell in next to each other.

"How can you—are you sure?"

"Yes."

"Have you been out here before?"

"Once. About five years ago."

"Alone?"

"People don't go anywhere alone in the valley. Not if they're smart."

Sam tipped his head at Noah, weaving between the mushroom trunks twenty feet ahead of them. "He used to do it all the time."

"He used to be ten. And the valley used to be a nicer place."

"You keep saying that, but it doesn't seem that bad."

"I was in a war zone before I ended up here. I couldn't tell you how many people died in front of me." She turned her head to him, gestured at her eye socket with her artificial hand. "My first injury happened after five months on the battlefield. My legs were replaced three times in two years. The third time would've absolutely killed me if they hadn't already been synthetic. Smart mine. It still killed two other people in my unit."

He glanced down at her four-toed feet. "I'm sorry."

She waved it off. "It was years ago. The thing you need to understand? This place is more dangerous than that war zone. I know it doesn't seem like it a lot of the time, but people die here a lot quicker and with a lot less warning."

"But don't people heal faster here?"

"Not fast enough to recover from being trampled by a three-ton dinosaur. Or getting a spear through your chest. Or having your head torn off your shoulders."

Sam shivered at the memory of Kyle pinned down on the ground and pulled apart by Gnash. "You should probably tell Noah all of this."

She focused her gaze on the back of Noah's head. "I did. Back at Roanoke. He thought I was exaggerating."

They walked along through the mushroom forest for another few minutes. Noah didn't slow down for them. His enthusiasm, almost desperation, reminded Sam of their first day crossing through the valley.

That first day had been three days ago.

He stretched out a hand and bounced his fingers against the side of one of the mushrooms as they walked past. It felt like tapping a drum. Tight and springy at the same time. It even sounded a bit like a drum. "So, these are edible, right?"

Pyr nodded. "They're very chewy, but yes. And they've got a low-level poison, so you have to cook them first or they'll make you sick. It's something Ross let us know." She gestured ahead at Noah, "Another way the Gather family paved the way."

Sam nodded. "Why don't you grow a few of them closer to Roanoke?"

"People have moved whole mushrooms, tried growing them from spores, a few different things. It never works. It's something in the soil around here, they think. Or maybe they have some sort of population density, how small mushrooms always grow in clusters." She shrugged. "Not really my specialty."

"Right." He bounced his fingers off the next giant stalk. Looked down at her feet again.

"Left one goes all the way to my hip," she said. "Right one goes to the knee."

"Sorry. I didn't mean to stare."

"Everyone stares. Everyone asks. And I just told you about them getting blown off. Of course you'd look."

Pyr increased her pace, halved the distance between them and Noah. When they got close she called his name. Then called it again a lot louder when he didn't respond. He slowed, looked back at her. At Sam. "We're almost there."

"I know," she said. "I just want to have everything set before we get there."

"We don't need anything."

"I'd like to grab dinner now so we don't have to double back for it."

Noah's eyebrows furrowed up.

Pyr pulled a knife from her belt. She turned away from them and stabbed it into one of the giant stalks. It took her a minute to carve out a wedge the size of a Thanksgiving turkey.

Noah's look of annoyance became mild amusement. "Mushroom steak. It's been a while."

"A lot of people have it when they visit here. It saves you from having to carry too much food."

Noah nodded, turned, started walking again.

"Be careful," Pyr called after him.

He waved absently in acknowledgment. Plowed ahead through Dickwood Forest. They fell in a few yards behind him.

Another fifteen minutes and the light ahead of them lost the soft glow that bouncing off silky mushroom stalks had given it. Sam saw the cliffs a little clearer, realized the towering columns weren't quite as dense up ahead. And then he stepped between two of the stalks and there weren't any more.

The valley's cliff wall loomed in front of them. And down at the bottom, almost nothing against the sheer scale of the cliffs, sat the cave. Sam had imagined it hundreds of times. Drawn it dozens. He still froze in awe at the sight.

According to young Billy's accounts, the mouth of the cave sat thirty-three feet from the valley floor. Five stalactites reached down over the entrance, three of them meeting up with stalagmites at the bottom to form solid pillars across the opening. A natural portcullis with bars made of stone and time. Those pillars had saved the Gather family a few times, keeping Fang, the monstrous T-Rex, and other dinosaurs from reaching them.

A pile of slab-like boulders formed a rough, natural staircase up to the cave, although Sam knew distance made the steps look smaller than they really were. Little Billy'd had to *climb* up some of those steps, jumping and using his arms to push himself up. After a few months his father had run a rope of woven vines down the staircase so they could all get to the safety of the cave faster and easier.

Four hundred feet of open space stretched from the mushroom forest to the cliffs. Mostly cracked earth and drifts of sand and pebbles, like some ancient, dry lake bed. A few boulders the size of cars. He could see at least five big skeletons scattered across the expanse. Three dinosaurs, one that was scattered bones with no visible skull, and one . . . giant horse? Also a big dead tree, the whole thing withered white like old driftwood. Far off to the left, the rocky ground turned to sand, like a desert. A big statue stood there, broken off around the waist, its top half scattered rubble in the sand.

Sam couldn't see a lot of hiding places where something could be lurking, but he also didn't see any cover if something appeared moving fast. It'd be a quick decision to run to the cave or back to the mushroom forest.

Noah'd already made it a quarter of the way across the open space. Every third or fourth step almost launched him into a run. Sam could tell by the tilt of his head he was focused on the cave. He didn't look back to see if they were following him.

Pyr looked in every direction. Even up. Then she set a hand on Sam's shoulder and gave him a gentle nudge as she stepped out into the open. She walked fast. Long strides. She let her hand drop from Sam's shoulder and he struggled to keep up across the rocky ground.

Noah reached the stairs. Kicked a leg up and pulled himself up onto the first one. Half jumped, half levered himself onto the next one. Kept his eyes fixed on the cave.

The smallest of the big slabs reached Sam's hip. Pyr bent her legs and hopped up onto it. Looked back at him. He used his hands and swung himself up without too much trouble, even though his legs ached from the hours of hiking. For a moment his eyes fell on some long, brittle gray shards scattered across the top of the stone. Maybe all that was left of some vines, crushed by hundreds of years and feet.

Pyr flexed her biomechanical toes and bounced up to the next step. She reached back, extending a hand for Sam. He grabbed it, felt the fingers wrap around his, kicked off as she heaved him up. The warmth and flexibility of her fingers caught him off guard. They climbed the next two steps together.

Noah maintained his lead. He climbed slower than them but with more confidence. Familiarity made up for his lack of speed. He knew every handhold and foothold, and it got him to the top before they'd even made it halfway. He vanished into the cave, and Sam heard the man call out a name as if he expected an answer.

Sam only needed Pyr's help for three more sections of the climb, and he probably could've made it himself if they weren't in a rush. Part of him wanted to savor the act of going up these steps. But he watched her look back out over the valley a few times and thought about a dinosaur catching them on the side of the cliff, their backs turned as they worked their way up to the cave, plucking them off the steps the way Kyle had been snatched away.

It made for a good motivation to keep climbing.

They reached the top and every muscle in Sam's legs and arms had a low burn he knew would be pain soon enough. He stood on the ledge and looked out over the valley. He could see above the mushroom forest, across so many trees to the Ice Castle. Water shimmered on one side of it. A few distant threads of chimney smoke from Roanoke.

He heard something scrape. One of Pyr's feet on the ledge as she sidestepped between two of the big pillars and into the cave. She vanished from sight.

Sam looked out over the valley one more time, let his pack slide off his shoulders into his hands, and followed her in. It was a tight fit. He had to suck in his gut.

On one level, the cave was exactly what he'd expected. He'd pored over young Billy's descriptions and memories of it, studied the simple diagrams and illustrations. The fire pit made of stones and eight red bricks the family had found one day on a walk through the jungle. There were the three wide, flat sections that served as bedrooms. The shallow, natural alcove where Ross stood when he was "asleep."

But the similarity with Sam's childhood dreams stopped there.

Dust smothered everything in the cave, turning it all into shades of gray like so many washed-out post-apocalypse movies. A few bits of dull color showed here and there, faded fabrics that'd dry-rotted away or been chewed apart and used to make nests. The scent in the air left no doubt several animals had lived and died here. Decomposed leaves and twigs and maybe even a few small bones filled the nooks and corners little Billy and his sister had been tasked with sweeping out twice a week. The wooden furniture their father had painstakingly built for them—tables and chairs and simple cots for their sleeping bags—lay in crumbled, barely recognizable ruins.

Noah stood by the fire pit. Sam couldn't see anything in the man's expression. His eyes were glazed over, like his brain had been shut off. His head turned slowly, taking in the whole cave inch by inch.

He took a few quick steps across the cave. Dust and leaves and a few feathers swirled across the floor in his wake. He headed for the farthest bedroom area, deepest in the cave. His sister's. Sam took a few steps after him. Pyr stayed by one of the pillars at the mouth of the cave.

Beau Gather's simple space had been scavenged, nested in, and scavenged again. Sam could make out the rough outline of her cot in the wooden shards on the stone floor. Her backpack was a corroded frame with a single frayed strap hanging from it and some faded scraps of red nylon. Any contents were long gone.

"She wouldn't've just abandoned the cave," Noah insisted. "She would've left a note."

"She did," murmured Pyr.

Noah sank to his knees in front of a flat, dust-covered stone, roughly the size and shape of a car tire. Sam remembered reading about it. Beau's desk. It had a strange, round ridge down the center of it.

Noah lowered his head. Blew down at the stone. Dust flew up in a low cloud and churned in the air around him like a storm cloud. He blew out another long stream of air, clearing off more years of dust.

A notebook lay open across the stone. A very old notebook. The weight of the yellowed, brittle pages had broken their connection to the rusted spiral years ago. Not so much a notebook as two small, uneven stacks of paper. The gentle push of air had crumbled the edges even more. Sam couldn't believe the light wind hadn't turned the whole thing to powder. A cracked, tapered cylinder sat next to the remains, still half coated in dust, and it took him a few moments to recognize the ancient ballpoint pen.

Noah pulled a pair of reading glasses from his shirt pocket. Bent down to the page. Sam moved closer. The writing had faded to dull gray shadows on the aged yellow paper, but the words were still there. Noah tilted his head, shifting his eyes, trying to read the impressions on the page as much as the remaining traces of ink.

He read all of it. His eyes went back to the top and he read it again, shaking his head. And then a third time.

Sam had an ugly feeling he knew, but also knew he had to ask. Out loud. "What does it say?"

Noah opened his mouth to talk. His breath caught and he sniffed hard. "It, ahhh, it . . . It matches up with what Ross told me. Told us. She's been alone for over two years since I was . . . since she thought I was killed by the Pakka. It's her twentieth birthday. And she . . ."

He let out a wheezy cough. Pushed his glasses up to wipe at his eyes. Took in a deep, shaky breath.

"It's her birthday and she can't take being alone anymore. So she's going to . . . she . . ."

Noah coughed again and broke down in tears, sobbing like a little boy.

25

PARKER

Parker waited until after lunch. She figured it would look more suspicious if she left earlier in the day. Plus, eating lunch meant she could stretch her food supplies a little further. She'd pocketed a few extra rolls at breakfast. Two pieces of green fruit on the way out the door. A handful of vegetables at lunch. A kitchen knife.

She'd emptied out one of the pillows from the guest house to make a sack. Using Logan's backpack would draw too much attention. This way she was stepping outside to . . . look at dinosaurs or gather berries or whatever people did here.

She tried to walk casually down the path to the main gate. The Egyptian woman stood outside, and Parker's heart thudded a little faster. If the woman decided to stop her, or chase her, there wasn't any doubt how things would go. Parker was long legged, but she could count the number of times she'd run in the past five years on one hand.

But the woman barely gave her a glance. An ever-so-faint movement of her head Parker thought was polite acknowledgment. And then she went back to staring or watching or whatever her job description was.

Parker tried to keep her pace slow and easy as she walked along the paths through the various vegetable plots and fields. No sign of anyone.

A few casual steps put her in the rows of corn, and the next few put her out of sight of the Egyptian woman.

Time to pick up the pace.

The corn grew in straight rows, and she had to stop twice to get her bearings. She'd looked from the top of the wall, figured out how she could get her bearings off the spacesuit scarecrow and Roanoke itself. And once she was far enough along, it should be clear which way to go. She just needed to find—

There. The dull, sun-faded red of the spacesuit, a few yards ahead. She slowed again, pushed between two corn stalks, and—

"Good afternoon."

Diedrich stood there. Admiring the scarecrow. His hands behind his back. At ease again. He didn't turn his head to look at her, but she was absolutely in his field of vision.

Okay, she'd run into someone. She'd planned for this. She knew there were people working the fields, and there was a chance she—

"May I ask where it is you are running to?"

Something heavy dropped in her gut, dragging everything down. She tried to keep her face calm. Neutral. "Hi. Are you . . . working on the scarecrow?"

"I am not."

"Oh." She stretched. Let the sack slide casually off her shoulder. Let it hang at her side to show she absolutely wasn't trying to hide it.

He turned his head. Smiled at her like a grandfather. "Would it shame you to know how many people run away in their first week or two here?"

"Run away?" she echoed, stalling.

He laughed. A small, precise sound. "You are not in trouble. Unlike some here, I will not try to stop you if you truly wish to leave."

Parker debated trying to stall again, but lying wasn't one of her strengths. She felt pretty sure Diedrich knew that too. "I'm not running away. I'm running to."

He raised an eyebrow. Looked over his shoulder. "For most newcomers I would say there is nothing here you could know to run to.

But you and your friends, you are not most newcomers, are you?"

"I guess we're not."

He nodded in agreement. "Very well then. Where are you running *to*?"

The thought of running off into the woods flitted through her mind. She wondered how fast Diedrich was. He had the lean body of a worker or an athlete, but he had to be pushing sixty. Definitely older than Noah. If he tried to grab her, she should be able to dodge him. And outrun him. But the simple plan collapsed as quickly as it formed in her mind, her personality defaulting to the facts. "I'm going to the Ice Castle."

Diedrich's face froze. "Why?"

"I need to talk to the Castaway."

He blinked twice. Three times. "The Castaway? But they . . . no, of course." He shook his head.

"What?"

Diedrich pushed his heels together. "Will you walk with me? Brunhilda needs to go back to her pen."

"Brunhilda?"

He gestured back the way she'd come. "The dinosaur. She gets temperamental later in the day."

A handful of thoughts flitted through Parker's head. Did she need to run? Would they come after her? Everyone kept saying they were free to go wherever they wanted, but also kept trying to limit where they went.

He sensed her hesitation. "I am trying to stop you, ja. For your own safety."

"I've got it on good authority the Castaway's peaceful. And helpful."

"They were. But the Castaway is most likely dead."

"What?"

He nodded.

Parker's plan crumbled in her head. Questions bounced in to fill the void. "How?"

"No one knows. No one has seen them in centuries. And they no longer live in the Ice Castle."

"You're sure?"

Another agreeable nod. "The Empress calls it home now, and has for hundreds of years. You would not receive a friendly welcome there. Assuming you survived the journey."

"The Empress?"

"Ja. Shall we walk?"

She glanced at the red scarecrow. Calculated the direction to the tower. "How do I know you're not lying to keep me from running off?"

Diedrich considered this. "I could probably come up with a better lie. One not involving aliens."

She snickered. Couldn't help herself. And then she sighed and fell in next to him as he walked back the way she'd come.

"If I may, why were you so determined to see the Castaway?"

"Well, first off . . . alien."

"Of course."

"Secondly, information."

"About . . . ?"

They stepped out of the rows of corn and she waved her hand at the fields, the distant cliffs, the wooden walls of Roanoke. "This place. The vanishing sun. All of it."

"Ahhhh."

The dinosaur stood at the far edge of the field, tail to them, munching on what looked like a tree branch. As they approached, Diedrich slid the length of bamboo from his belt and gestured Parker deeper into the field, circling around the rhino-sized creature. "She startles easy, so always get into her field of vision before you get too close. You don't want her swinging her head around to see what's touching her." He whistled to the big dinosaur and the big creature made a low, warbling noise that reminded Parker of whale songs.

She studied the sky while he patted and prodded the dinosaur. She hadn't looked at it as much as she should've. She'd been a wreck the night they arrived, then a night indoors, and last night when she saw the sun go away . . . well, there could've been three moons in the sky and she probably wouldn't've registered it.

Diedrich tugged at the dinosaur's long nose horn, tapped her legs with his bamboo stick, and slowly got her turned away from the fields. He gave her a firm pat with his hand, then tapped her big bony frill with his bamboo stick. It made a deep, annoyed squawk. He waved his bamboo stick up at the sky. "May I ask what you're looking for?"

"The Moon. Its orientation will give me an idea where we are. At least enough to narrow down north or south of the equator."

Diedrich chuckled.

"Something funny?"

"Forgive me. With all you know through your professor, I forget there are things you do not know. Like with the Castaway." He waved the baton up at the rim of the cliffs. "There is no Moon."

"What do you mean?"

"There is no Moon. Not yet. We are so far back in time, it has not formed yet."

"That's not possible."

"It is very possible."

"If the Moon hasn't formed yet, we're four and a half billion years in the past. Earth doesn't have any life at all. I don't think it even has an atmosphere. We wouldn't be able to breathe."

"And yet . . ."

"It's not possible."

He took in a deep, dramatic breath through his nose, letting it puff his chest out.

Parker sighed. Closed her eyes. "I hate this place."

The dinosaur shuffled its feet. Bleated again. Diedrich rubbed her neck behind the big armored frill. "Brunhilda doesn't like to stand still out in the open too long. I need to get her back to her home."

"Yeah, sure."

He slapped the dinosaur's shoulder and barked out a command in German. The dinosaur lumbered forward. He glanced back at Parker. "You're welcome to come along."

Parker thought of her wasted day. Adjusted her plans. Slung her pillowcase sack over her shoulder. Took a few quick steps through the field.

"She won't hurt you," he called back to Parker. "Not on purpose. But sometimes her belly swings a bit when she walks. And it is a big belly." He reached down and patted the pale skin of the dinosaur's underside.

Parker felt a smile tug her lips. "I'll keep an eye out."

He glanced at her as she caught up. "There was a man here . . . ten years ago? Hamdun. A Moorish navigator from Portugal. Early fifteen hundreds. He used to stare up at the sky, too."

"Yeah?"

"Ja. He didn't like it, either. Said it was all wrong."

"Where's he now?"

Diedrich gestured across the field with his bamboo stick, toward the cypress grove. "In the cemetery. Third row."

"Oh." She took a few steps. "Was it a dinosaur or . . ."

"The Klaa. Hamdun slipped out one night a few months after he got here. He wanted to see the sky without any lamps or torches spoiling his night vision. A Neanderthal stabbed him in the throat while he looked up. Right over there." He pointed back toward a swath of beans, or maybe peas.

"Why did they kill him?"

"Because he was outside at night."

"No, I meant . . . did they fight or did they have some sort of grudge against him?"

Diedrich shook his head. "They killed him because he was there."

"Is that . . . common?"

"Death?"

"Death by Neanderthal."

"It isn't a rare thing."

Brunhilda let out a tuba-honk and came to a sudden halt. She twisted her head side to side, like a dog trying to shake off water. Diedrich waited for her to stop and gave her a few big, wide scratches behind her frill. She honked again and lumbered forward.

Parker looked at the gray-haired man. "So what's your story? Were you working with rhinos or elephants and one day you were here?"

"No, nothing like that." His face shifted, and she saw it settle into some well-worn lines. "My crew and I turned a corner, the street dropped out from under us, and suddenly we were a few yards into a lake."

"Crew?"

"Oberfeldwebel Diedrich Rommel. I commanded a Panzer. In France. 1941."

"Oh."

He gave Brunhilda a few gentle slaps on her armored neck-plate. She shifted her path to the left. Diedrich went with it. Parker let the distance grow between them.

They reached the end of Roanoke's long wall and she saw a simple fence up ahead, tucked away behind the town. Bamboo tied into thick bundles like logs, propped up on crosspieces. The fence marked off a small field, and Parker saw another horned dinosaur lazily munching away near the middle of it.

Dak Ho leaned against the fence, right by a wide opening. A hole big enough to drive a truck through. Or a dinosaur.

"So," she said. "A German tank commander. In the '40s."

"Yes."

"You're a Nazi."

His face could've been carved from wood, all the lines a deep grain. "Not for a long time now. But back then . . . ja."

"But not now?"

"No, not now. Not anymore."

"You'll forgive me for being skeptical."

"Most everyone is."

"Why the change?"

He gave the styracosaurus another whack with his bamboo swagger stick, guiding her toward the gate. "It is one thing to dream of the future, another to see it. To hear about it from people born fifty years, a hundred years, five hundred years after you. Imagine learning you are the villain people warn children about for almost six centuries."

"I guess that could be a slap in the face for some people."

"It was. It took a while to believe, but . . . it was." Diedrich leaned against Brunhilda's huge shoulder as they walked, giving her a few firm pats with the palm of his hand. The styracosaurus altered course a little more, heading for the bamboo gate. He straightened up and slowed his pace. Parker slowed too, and used it as a chance to put another foot or two between them.

He gave the dinosaur one last swat on the rump and she lumbered into the pen. Dak Ho dragged one of the thick bamboo bundles across the opening in the fence. It thumped into place on the far side, and he looped a rough rope around it to hold it in place.

Parker looked at the two dinosaurs, warbling at each other like a pair of gigantic songbirds. "Can that actually hold them?"

"The fence?" Diedrich shook his head. "Not at all. They stay inside because we give them no reason to leave. They could push through it with no effort if they wanted to. They have a few times. It's why I like them. They're like living Panzers."

He turned and led them back toward the gate.

"So you're the . . . the famous guy. The tank-strategist guy."

"I am not. You are thinking of Erwin Rommel. We were not related. He held a much higher rank. And much more respect, as my crew often reminded me. They called me 'the little Rommel' sometimes. A good-natured joke."

"Yeah, that's what the Nazis are always remembered for. Their good-natured humor."

The old farmer gave a weak laugh. "Do you know what the true sign of a Nazi is?"

"Well, it's tiki torches and red hats in my time, but you probably mean swastikas, right?"

He shook his head. "For the Nazi—for all the fascists—everything bad is someone else's fault. It must be, because the fascists are all unified in their nationalism. It cannot be them, because the fault of one must be the fault of all. So they must always blame someone else for any problems they encounter in their lives. Especially the ones they create themselves."

"But not you?"

"Oh, ja, me as well. I was a good Nazi who took no responsibility for the things that were wrong in my life. It was all the fault of the Jews, the Romani, the Negroes, the British, the Americans . . ." He waved his hands absently. "I hated them all, just like I'd been told to. I can, at the very least, say I only killed other soldiers in the war. Never civilians."

The story felt a little polished to Parker. Rehearsed. Not like a speech, but like someone who's given the same lecture too many times and knew just when to pause for a breath. Just how to get the best reaction out of their audience.

"My crew were just boys. Foolish boys who loved their country, feasted on propaganda, and signed up for a war they did not understand. And then they ended up here, in a world they did not understand. Like all good fascists, we had to blame someone. So we turned on each other. My driver died in the first ten minutes. The rest of the crew barely lasted a week."

Parker stared at him. "You all killed each other?"

"No, no. We landed here on the outer edge of the lake. A swampland. Our Panzer immediately sank into the muck. Our driver, Johann, stayed at his post, sure he could get it out. He drowned when the turret went under and water poured in. So at first, we blamed him for everything. After all, a competent driver would've somehow gotten our twenty-five-tonne Panzer out of six feet of water and soft mud."

"And the rest?"

"A raptor killed Karl that night, though we didn't know what it was at the time. Just some monster. The Klaa killed Ruprecht and Max a few days later while they hunted for food. Horst and I made it a week, and then he tried to slip past a stegosaurus to get some berries. It flicked its tail and impaled him on two spikes. Two days later, I stumbled across a group from Roanoke." He waved his hand up at the wall. "And for a time everything was their fault. For not finding us sooner. For letting my crew die. But months turned to years and I had to admit it was my fault. It was my responsibility, as their commander, and I had failed them. Only me. No one else."

"How long did that take? To figure out you were the bad guy?"

"Longer than it should have. Long enough several people here still have misgivings about me."

"So this friendly talk is about getting me on your side?"

"No, no. Only me being honest and up-front about my past. What you do with that knowledge is up to you."

They were back at the gates. The Japanese woman, Shino, had replaced the Egyptian woman, standing there in the shade of a propped-up bamboo panel. She bowed her head to Diedrich. Made a slight dip of her chin to Parker.

Parker realized she'd stepped closer to Diedrich as they walked through the gate. She let her next two steps carry her back away from him. Then she stopped, held out her hand, looked at the shadow beneath it. "How long until the sun goes . . . away?"

"Less than an hour now."

"How can you tell?"

He shrugged. "You feel it. The body grows used to it, the same way you can train yourself to wake up at the same time every day. It will come to you."

She nodded. Bit off her next words. Rolled them around in her mouth for a few moments. "Thank you. For stopping me from running off to the Ice Castle."

"Of course."

"And thanks for the . . . the talk."

"Thank you. For listening." Diedrich reached up and touched the brim of his straw hat, gave her a bow that now seemed a little too military for her comfort, and walked away up the central dirt path.

Parker looked around, found the ladder that led up to the walkway at the top of the wall. When she got to the top she saw Warwick in his tattered cowboy-police uniform over at the far corner, on top of the guardhouse. She gave him a small wave. He waved back and she walked over to him.

"Heard yeh were up here this morning looking for something," he said.

"The Moon."

He gave her a sad little smile. "No Moon here in the valley, love."

"I know. Now."

"Sorry yeh wasted your time."

"Even if someone told me, I would've checked for myself."

"Lot of people are that way at first. This place is a real handful, y'know?"

She held up a hand to block the sun and examined the bright blue sky. Not a sign of stars anywhere. Of course not. It was broad daylight. Halfway through the day, going off the sun.

"What're yeh looking for now?"

"I want to look at the stars. If I can see the night sky, I can get a better sense of exactly where and when we are."

"Yeh couldn't tell the other night?"

"I was a little overwhelmed."

"Was yehr first time nightfall, yes?"

"Yes."

Warwick smiled broadly. He had white teeth, almost as white as Josh's, and she found herself wondering about dental care in the valley. Maybe fast healing and the lack of sugar made a lot of it unnecessary. "Astronomer, yeah?"

"Yeah."

"Don't think there's ever been an astronomer here before. We had a navigator a few years back."

"I heard." Parker double-checked the cliff edges for the Moon. Just in case. Nothing.

"Klaa got him."

"Heard that too."

"Word of advice? Don't get too wrapped up in tryin' to find a way out. Sent a lot of folks off their kadoova. Or to the cemetery. Or both."

"Yeah?"

He nodded sagely. "So many people thought they found a way out. Secret tunnels. Underground rivers. One fella thought the obelisks had magic gateways in them. Years back a woman tried to make a hot air balloon to get over the cliffs. I'd guess . . . maybe one outta four who end up here get stuck on it."

"That many?"

Another sage nod from Warwick.

"You?"

He shrugged. Shook his head. "Not anymore."

He didn't say anything else, so Parker walked past him and along the next length of wall. Her stomach grumbled. A small warning of future complaints if she didn't put something in it soon. Wouldn't be the first time she'd skipped dinner to get in as much observation time as possible.

She heard the distant song of the styracosaurus. Styracosauri? Sauruses? If she walked a little further, she'd probably be able to look down and see them in their pen. But she wanted to be out front when the sun went away, with the village and its random lights behind her.

The memory of the Portuguese navigator sneaking out to look at the stars danced in her mind again. Standing somewhere down there. Looking up at the stars. Getting a knife in his throat.

The more she heard about the Neanderthals, the more it sounded like Noah'd vastly misunderstood his relationship with them.

One of the styracosaurs let out another long, low note and she wondered how the animals here dealt with the sudden day-to-night shift. Could they sense it coming? How would a rooster act here? Would it still let out a few morning cock-a-doodle-doos or would it just give up that part of its nature?

Parker headed back toward Warwick as the sun dimmed. She didn't look at it. Common sense, not staring at the sun. Plus she didn't want to risk her brain freezing up again.

Instead she dug in her back pocket, pulling out the four pages of notebook paper she'd originally torn free to take notes while talking with the Castaway. She unfolded them, thought again how rare paper seemed here. Hopefully it would be enough for one night of notes.

The valley got darker. Down below she saw a few lanterns light up. Turned her eyes away. She wanted to get used to the dark fast. The sudden change was probably rough on night vision.

She reached Warwick. His gaze stayed out at the trees past the fields. She set her hands on the top of the wall and closed her eyes. The warmth on the top of her head, her shoulders, the back of her hands slowly faded. Through her eyelids she watched the last of the daylight dim and vanish.

Parker opened her eyes and looked up at the stars.

No sign of Polaris or Ursa Minor, just like that first night while she'd been stunned from her now-healed head injury. Which made sense. Polaris was a relatively young star. It wouldn't even form for another thirty million years or so. She'd probably be dealing with a lot of that. Stars she knew that hadn't formed yet, others that had died by her time.

Observation now. Theories later. That looked like Arcturus over there, which meant *that* was Boötes, and Virgo above it. And, okay, yes, there was Ursa Major down near the tops of the cliffs. And a little beyond . . .

"What the fuck?"

Boötes. Virgo. Ursa Major. She turned, tilted her head and found Orion and Gemini. Big, easy constellations. No mistaking them, even if she wasn't used to seeing them at this angle.

Warwick half turned his head to her. "Somethin' wrong?"

She checked the stars again. There was Canis Major and Minor. Cancer. Centaurus. She heard the paper crumple, realized she'd made a fist. "This is . . . I hate this place. I fucking *hate* this place. Nothing here makes any sense."

"What's the problem, then?"

Parker couldn't take her eyes off the stars, turning as she pointed out the constellations. "Boötes. Ursa Major. Orion. Centaurus."

"Yeah?"

"This is a modern sky. We're not a hundred million years in the past. We're in the present. The twenty-first century."

26

NOAH

He'd lost track of time.

He didn't know how long he'd cried for. Choking, coughing bawls like he hadn't done since . . . well, since he'd been a little kid. Since Dad had been killed. He'd wandered around the cave, spiraling in guilt and shame and despair, and his thoughts and memories had whipped it all up into a maelstrom. And at some point, after . . . an hour? Two? . . . His breathing had finally slowed and the hurricane in his chest collapsed back in on itself, leaving him feeling so goddamn hollow.

He'd failed her.

The smell pushed its way into his nose. Smoke. Hot stones. And under it a flat scent he could taste on his tongue.

Someone was cooking mushrooms in the cave.

Noah looked around. He'd been staring at the walls, at the old bed areas, at so many things for the past however long it'd been but he hadn't really seen any of it. Now he registered the dark mouth of the cave and the warm flickering light and the quiet, whispered conversation.

Someone had gathered firewood. Pyr. She'd slipped away and Sam had stayed with him. Giving him space but keeping an eye on him.

Now they both sat a few yards away on either side of the little fire pit. As far away as anyone could in this little cave that'd seemed so much bigger when he was young. Sam turned to look at him and Noah could see the uncertainty and pity in the grad student's gaze.

"How are you?" Sam asked quietly.

"I . . . I'm . . ."

He considered how he felt and came to the decision he couldn't feel anything. The hour or so of sobbing had drained everything out of him. If he had anything left, his mind had hidden it away to deal with later.

"I'm how you'd expect," he said.

Pyr pointed at a washed-clean rock just outside the fire, and a few soft chunks on it. "There's food. Mushroom. Some bread. Water."

He stared past the fibrous lump and into the flames. "I'm not hungry."

"You haven't eaten in six hours."

"Maybe later."

Noah settled down with them, close to the little fire. He looked at the rocks. At the bricks. He remembered finding those bricks thirty-five years ago, just scattered half buried in the jungle, and carting them home with . . .

With Beau.

To surprise Dad.

Sam cleared his throat. Gestured at Pyr. "We could go hang out on the ledge or something, if you still need a minute . . ."

"No." He shook his head. "No, I'm okay."

"Are you sure?"

"No."

Across the fire pit, Pyr's mouth flexed into a brief smile. "Admitting the damage is the first step toward fixing the damage."

No one said anything. She pulled another small branch from the pile between her and Sam. Fed it into the fire. The light gleamed off her fingers, her arm, the socket around her eye.

Sam had a knife of dark metal and sliced pieces off his chunk of fire-roasted mushroom. He looked around the cave, taking it all in. Someone looking at a museum exhibit. Or maybe more like one of those behind-the-scenes displays of movie props and costumes, showing how your favorite stories had come to life.

Noah looked around too, finally taking a good look at the cave. At the rest of the cave. The flickering firelight made so many shadows, and the thick cobwebs changed a few shapes here and there, but he still recognized most of it. The hash marks on the wall that had been the family's calendar until they found Ross in the swamp. The piles of crumbled wood and bamboo that had been chairs and tables and cots. The piles of dusty rags and fragments that had been clothes and sleeping bags and packs.

He leaned toward one shred of rumpled fabric, brushed or swept up against the wall. A faint puff of air cleaned some dust off it. Enough for him to see a faded pattern.

"What is it?" asked Pyr.

He turned away from the remnant. "It's one of my old T-shirts. Masters of the Universe."

Her lips pulled into another smile. So did Sam's. "One of your four shirts."

"Yep."

Sam nodded, then shoved another slice of mushroom into his mouth to block whatever comment or question clearly tried to force its way out. He chewed. Swallowed it down.

So much time had passed here. Decades. Centuries.

"I'm sorry," Noah said to the flames closest to Pyr's knee.

Sam stopped chewing the mushroom.

Noah kept his eyes on the fire. "I should've listened to you. The valley's changed. It isn't . . . it's not the place I thought it was. The place I grew up."

On the edge of his vision, past her knee, he saw Pyr nod slowly. "It's understandable."

"I . . . I've spent my whole life focused on the valley. On the valley I remembered. I never thought of it as something that could change and grow." He closed his eyes, watched the soft afterimage of the flames on the inside of his eyelids. "All the interviews and the books. My own obsession with getting back here. Reliving it again and again kind of . . . froze it. In my head. I mean, it took me years to even consider I might be remembering some of it wrong. But even then, I figured it'd be like I left it. The valley would still be here. And so would . . ."

The name caught in his throat like a pill. Jammed in place. Needing a cough to knock it loose.

"It's okay," said Sam. "You don't have to talk about it if you don't want to."

Noah shook his head. "It's okay."

"It's not. You've spent years planning this. To find out she'd—that she—I can't imagine how much pain you're in."

His voice dropped a little bit at the end. Enough so that Noah looked up from the fire. Sam almost sounded . . . ashamed?

"Are *you* okay?"

Now it was Sam's turn to study the little fire pit. "Just feeling kind of petty. I'm not—it's not a big deal." He shifted on his stone seat.

A trio of shrieks echoed from outside the cave. Not close, but not too far, either. Noah could picture the area the call probably came from in his head. All the old acoustics came back fast.

Sam looked toward the pillars at the mouth of the cave. "What was that?"

"Raptors," said Noah and Pyr at the same time.

"Two of them," she added. She looked at Noah. He nodded in agreement.

Another pair of eagle-like shrieks. Sam craned his neck, wanting to look but also picking up on their calm. "Are we safe up here?"

"Yep." Noah waved a hand toward the pillars. "They might see the light from the fire, but it's not enough for them to react to. Even if they did, the staircase is too steep for the little ones and too shallow for the big ones. They might get halfway up at best." He closed his eyes again. "I remember one time one of the little microraptors, the four-winged ones, flew in here. It was like having a bird in your house. Beau and

Ross and I spent fifteen or twenty minutes waving towels and shirts at it, trying to get it back outside before it got too comfortable."

He'd said her name. Said her name without thinking. Without a reaction. Was that good or bad?

Pyr picked up a longer branch. Snapped it across her knee. "Even though you wanted to keep it as a pet."

Noah blinked. "How'd you know that?"

"The Timekeeper." She broke another branch. "It tells stories about you and your family."

He digested the idea. Tried to look at it in this new context he'd been given. That he was finally admitting. "Why doesn't he know what happened to her?"

Pyr fed the pieces of wood into the fire. Just reached in with her synthetic arm and set them down in the center of the blaze. "What do you know about it? The time it came from?"

"He's from the future. He's an all-purpose android. Butler, nanny, teacher, house cleaner, gardener. He says he's not a real artificial intelligence, but I never believed it."

"Ever wonder why it's not an AI?"

"I was ten."

Her face formed that one-sided smile again. "We fought two wars against AI. One in the twenty-fifth century—the one I fought in—and then another one in the twenty-sixth. That's Thate's. The Timekeeper came between them. But people were still worried about AI, so it's specifically designed and limited to not be self-aware or networked. And it's got gigs of code to keep it from hurting people or letting them be hurt."

Noah thought back over discussions he'd had with Ross. "So you fought a war against the machines and when it ended you built more machines?"

"One thing you can always be sure of with humans. Tell us we can't have something, we'll want it ten times more."

"True that," said Sam.

"Over the years, people've told Ross what happened to your sister.

Sometimes deliberately, sometimes it overheard them talking. Whenever it happens, the data jams up its algorithms because it let her walk off and—"

The void yawned wide in Noah's gut. The hollowness. How had she done it? So many ways to die in the valley. Or to be killed. Did she walk up to a dinosaur? Or eat a lot of poisoned berries? Or maybe just slit her, no, she wouldn't've done, oh god, he was spiraling again.

His arm felt heavy. Pyr had stopped talking. Set her dark blue hand on his forearm.

"Sorry," she said. "The Timekeeper did one of the hard-coded things it's absolutely not supposed to do. It let someone die. So it has sys failures, gets stuck in loops, basically gets more and more useless until we have it wipe its memory far enough back to erase the data."

Noah considered it. Thought how protective Ross had seemed when he was younger. Remembered the android overreacting to scrapes and cuts. His, but also Beau's. And one time that gash in Dad's calf.

Pyr reached for another arm-thick branch. Cracked it across her knee again. "You should also know, your sister . . . your whole family's been an inspiration for so many people."

"How so?"

She settled back on her stone seat. "When people get here, they're scared. They don't understand what's going on or where they are. And once they do understand, they get scared again. Even with Roanoke, with dozens of other people around, all they can think of is, how are they going to survive here? How long can they hope to last? There's not many of us, but it's a big enough community we have a suicide rate.

"So we tell them stories about the first family that ended up here, and the dad who kept his two kids alive and happy and healthy for over a year. Then how those two kids survived for a year all on their own when they lost him. And then how the daughter made it another two years all alone." She fed one of the branch pieces into the fire.

Noah felt something in the empty pit of his insides. A fresh swell of guilt, rising up out of the nothingness. "But she had Ross."

"You may not have picked up on this as a child, but it was built to be a poor conversationalist. It's a design choice to reassure people it's just an unthinking machine. After a while with no one else, I'd guess being with it is probably worse than being alone."

"I could see that," said Sam. Then he glanced at Noah and regret spread across his face.

"My point is, these stories end up being a lifeline for people. Or a challenge for some. This family, these kids, this teenage girl. If they made it so long with so little, surely *you* can make it that long. You can last as long as their dad did. You can hold out as long as *she* did. It lets them know it's possible to survive here, no matter how bad it seems at times. It's why everyone knows your name. We've all heard dozens of stories about you and your family." She waved a hand around the cave. "That's why this place is pretty much a shrine. A lot of people come out here to look at all this and think about what it must've been like for them. For you."

Noah looked around at the ruins of his old home. "But you don't tell them the end of the story," he said. "You don't tell them how . . . you don't say what happened to her."

"No, we don't. We try to hide it, truth told. I'd guess half the people in Roanoke now don't know what happened to her. They just accept she was here four centuries ago and she's gone now."

Noah stared into the fire. Thought about it. Nodded once.

"But they have to—four hundred years isn't that long," said Sam. "People have to know what happened."

Pyr looked at him. "Four hundred years before your time is . . . the founding of the United States?"

"It's closer to two hundred fifty years ago. From then."

"Good enough. Can you tell me how any of your first rulers died? Washington? Jeffersonian? Frankling?"

"That's not how you—what do you mean?"

"How did they die? Were they killed? Did they die in accidents? From disease? Old age?"

"I don't—history's not my field of study."

"But it was less time, and you have texts and videos. Here there's nothing but word of mouth."

"And Ross."

"Who doesn't know." She reached into the fire and set another piece of wood on top of the blackened branches.

Sam took a deep drink of water from one of the bottles. Wiped his mouth on his shoulder. "It makes sense everyone reacted so poorly when we arrived. We weren't just mocking the dead, so to speak, we were insulting the legend."

"Exactly." She focused on Noah again, and he couldn't help looking at her bright blue eye. "I know what you've learned here is hard. But try to remember that dozens and dozens of people are alive because of your sister. She inspired them. Convinced them *they* could stay alive."

She punctuated the last word by slicing off a piece of mushroom and popping it into her mouth.

He closed his eyes. "Thank you."

"It's just the truth." He heard her chew some more. "You should eat something. The mushroom won't keep until morning."

"I know. I remember." He opened his eyes. "Y'know, it never hit me until now . . . this is why I hate mushrooms."

Sam coughed, shook his head, swallowed. "What?"

"Yep. I can't stand them. I hate the taste, the smell, the texture, everything. Because I ate them at least five or six times a week for two years."

Sam laughed.

"Any other big secrets we should know about the living legend?" Pyr asked.

Noah considered it. Felt another little swell of guilt and failure. "I've seen," he told them, "every T-Rex skull in every museum on Earth."

They both waited for him to continue. He tried to organize his thoughts, then decided to just talk.

"In our time," he said with a nod to Pyr, "there are twenty-six of them. Real ones, not casts or reproductions. Some of them are reconstructed from partial remains. Some aren't on public display. Plus I saw a few that were in private collections most folks don't know about."

"How'd you find out about them?"

Noah shrugged "Fame has its privileges. I was Dino Boy. Lots of people wanted to impress me for . . . reasons."

Sam coughed again. A more polite one this time. "Are we talking—is this a—a sex thing?"

"No. I don't think so, anyway. I think some people just like knowing they impressed the popular kid. Even if that kid's just a teenager famous for living in a trauma-induced fantasy world."

"Dino Boy?" echoed Pyr.

"Please don't ask me to explain it."

"Sore subject," Sam told her. "This wasn't in any of the books. Sorry. Looking at the skulls."

"I don't think most people realized I was doing it. 'Low-level celebrity goes to the museum' isn't much of a headline, especially pre-internet. And it took years. I was thirteen when I started, almost twenty when I saw the last one."

Pyr poked at the fire with a stick, then pushed the whole stick in. "What were you looking for?"

Noah watched the stick burn. "I kept hoping I'd see a skull—or at least a jawbone—with oversized incisors."

Sam's breath came out as a whistle. "Fang."

"Yep. Even then, I knew the odds were ridiculous. There are so few surviving T-Rex skeletons, and even fewer skulls. But once the idea hit me I looked at all of them. Every time I wasn't in some hospital with a doctor trying to help me with all the unresolved issues from my 'abduction.' I'd be in a ward for four or five months and then they'd let me loose and I'd go find my next museum."

"Why?"

"Why what?"

"Why were you trying to find Fang? Or his skull?"

The stick crumbled in the flames and he thought of all the skulls, the little breath of hope each one started with. "Because if Fang got out of the valley, if he made it home, maybe it wasn't just dumb luck I got out. Maybe there was an actual exit anyone could use. One she could've found and used and ended up . . . somewhere."

The guilt swelled out of the void in his gut. So much guilt. So much he'd been wrong about. So much failure. Noah stood up. Walked to the pillars. Took a few deep breaths of the valley's cool night air.

Someone moved behind him, deliberately scuffing their shoes on the cave floor. Shoes, not plastic feet. "You okay?" Sam asked.

"I just . . . I need a minute."

"Sure."

Sam retreated. The fire crackled again. Noah set his hands on the pillars, on their familiar smoothness. The shape of them felt off, and he realized his hands were higher up than they'd been all those years before.

How many times had Beau stood here? Alone. Staring out at the valley. Had she made an empty grave for him, like they had for Dad? Had she gone after Scarnose and the others? Charged into their camp with Dad's knife and wooden club?

Had they killed her?

He took a few more deep breaths, tasted life and smoke and the mushroom forest in the air.

He turned back to them. Cleared his throat. "Anyway . . . I never saw Fang. Because there's no way out of here. Nothing gets out."

Pyr pointed at him. "You got out."

"I did. By dumb, random luck. A million to one fluke. Seeing all those tyrannosaurus skulls convinced me I had to figure out how to come back here. Because she was supposed to get out one day, and I was going to have to come get her."

"And you did it," said Sam. "You figured out how to track the wormhole and travel back and forth through it."

A lifetime's worth of orbital charts and calculations and computer simulations all spun through his mind. "Remember that bit from the books? How the Castaway answered all our questions differently?

Telling my sister she'd get out. Telling my dad it wasn't safe to leave."

Sam nodded, but his confusion was clear even with the fire backlighting him. "And how it helped you realize the orbital aspect of the wormhole."

"Right. And it convinced me I'd rescue Beau. I was so focused on those, I never considered what the Castaway told *me*. Not until just . . ." He waved his hand around the cave.

Sam took in a quick little breath. "'No, Billy Gather. Someday you will call this place home.'"

He walked over to the little fire pit. "That's not what they said."

"It's not?"

"I was young and it was out of context. Even knowing they could see through time." He crouched and let himself drop onto the floor. Felt the impact shudder up his back. Felt the heat of the fire on his eyes. "They didn't say *no*. They said *Noah*."

Sam sucked in a deep breath.

"They knew because they could see me here. Now. They knew I'd come back and what I'd be calling myself. They knew all the things I'd get wrong. And they knew I was going to get all of us stuck here for the rest of our lives."

27

BILLY

Billy followed Dad across the open plain of white rocks. They weren't supposed to move out in the open because it didn't leave them anywhere to hide from Fang, but Dad didn't want to spend the time to go around. He told Billy to move slow so they didn't attract too much attention.

Then they were in the forest again. Running. Dodging between trees. Jumping over logs. They passed through the clearing with the marble obelisk. Billy looked at all its scribbly runes as they ran by and felt its deep hum prickle the surface of his skin. Then they were back in the forest and the hum faded behind them.

They reached the edge of the Saurus Swamp, where the big duck-billed dinosaurs ate weeds and ferns. One of them honked at them as they ran by, turning its head to follow them as they ran along the muddy shore. The ground squished under their feet. For a moment Dad stumbled, one boot stuck in the soft ground, but he pulled it free and gave Billy a little shove to keep him moving, too.

And then they were past the swamp and at the entrance to the Ice Castle. They still called it that even though it wasn't actually made of ice. Beau had told Billy sometimes crystals grew sort of like plants, and it left him wondering if the Castle had grown somewhere and ended up falling into the valley like they had. Or had the Castaway grown it here to remind them of their home, the same way Billy and Beau and Dad had tried to make their cave into a home?

Running up the not-ice entrance ramp was a lot like running up a playground slide. Billy's sneakers didn't slip too much, but Dad's boots did. One of his feet slid out from under him as they headed toward the top, and then it slipped again when he reached the front door. Billy had started thinking of the entrance as a front door ever since they discovered the Castaway lived in the Castle.

Dad had called the inside walls of the Castle "biomorphic architecture" on their second or third visit. He moved a little slower through the hallways, even though Billy could tell he wanted to keep running. The Castaway had explained that the Castle would always bring visitors to the big room as long as they gave it time to make a path. People who moved too fast could get lost, and it might take the Castaway several years to find them.

Billy had laughed at the joke, but Dad and Beau hadn't.

They passed side hallways and alcoves, went around sharp turns and curves, and finally found the big octagonal—a word Dad had taught him—octagonal chamber Beau called the throne room.

The Castaway stood at the center of the big room. Even when the alien wasn't doing anything, Billy always felt like he was interrupting them. They were one of those people who always seemed like they were in the middle of something. Probably because they sounded distracted a lot of the time.

At the moment, they didn't look any taller than Dad. They were shaped like a purple person with four—no, five arms, although the arms were a little long and didn't look like they had hands. Four horns grew out of their head, but Billy watched two of the horns moved and he realized they were short, stubby tentacles. Instead of legs, the Castaway had two straight columns going down toward the floor. Billy followed them down and saw they ended a few inches above the not-ice platform. The alien floated in the air, like a cartoon character who'd forgotten to fall when they ran off a cliff.

The Castaway turned to look at them as Billy and Dad walked into the room. They had a simple face, like one of the dummies stores put clothes on. Dad marched closer and the face found some more details. A nose. Cheekbones. A groove where the mouth would be.

"I did not intend to give you information that would prove harmful to you and your offspring," said the Castaway.

Dad stopped. Clenched his fists. "So you know why we're here?"

The Castaway's head turned to the left, but their face slid across the purple skull to stay pointed at Dad. "Salutations, James Gather, Billy Gather. It is, as always, a pleasure to make your acquaintance."

"Did you know about the berries?"

"I am unclear which berries you refer to."

Dad's fists shook. Billy had only seen him mad like this once or twice before. "The blue ones. The berries that grow on the shrubs with the long leaves. You told us they were safe to eat."

The Castaway spread two of their arms wide, and three-fingered hands sprouted at the ends of them. "My apologies. I have not yet had that conversation with you."

"When we came in here you said—"

"I did not intend to give you information that would prove harmful to you and your offspring."

"Yes. That."

"My apologies. Your query about the nature of the berries was unclear."

"We asked if they were poisonous."

"They are not."

"But they made Beau sick," Billy chimed in. "Really sick."

The Castaway looked down at him, crossed two of their arms across their chest and the limbs melted into the torso, leaving them with three. "Another simplification of the events and relationships, but again, accurate enough."

Billy recognized another drifting comment from the Castaway and tried again. "Beau ate the berries and they made her sick."

The alien focused on Billy. "Certainly they did. The berries are not safe for human consumption."

"Then why did you just tell us they were safe?" growled Dad.

"I will be asked if the berries are poisonous. They have no effect on stegosaurus biochemistry."

Dad took in a breath and counted to ten. Billy didn't hear him count, but Dad had explained it to him once. It was how he made himself calm down when things went bad at work. He also did it at least once every time they talked to the Castaway.

"Beau," Dad said, "isn't a stegosaurus."

The Castaway pulled the third arm into their back, and the tentacle-horns shrank down to tiny lumps on their head. They stared past Billy and Dad, toward the far wall. "Did you think she was, James Gather?"

"No!"

The Castaway's bright purple chin went up and down, stretching out into a long spike as it did. The tip of the spike curved down and melted into their chest. "I believe I now understand where the confusion occurred."

"Do you?"

"I believe so."

"Then help us. Is there a cure?"

"Yes."

Billy smiled and the dark worry in his chest went away. He knew the Castaway would help them. The alien looked strange—and talked strange—but they were a good person.

Dad didn't look as angry, but he still didn't look happy.

Nobody spoke.

"Well?"

The Castaway straightened up, and suddenly it had four arms again. "Salutations, James Gather. How may I help you today?"

"Is there a cure?"

"A cure for what?"

"The berries!"

Another slow nod from the Castaway. "Yes."

Another long pause.

"What is it?" asked Dad.

"There is an herbaceous plant that grows in the region you have allowed Billy to name Saurus Swamp, on the shore farthest from this structure. Its leaves resemble this."

The Castaway held out their hand. The wrist narrowed into a stem and the fingers divided and flattened into leaves with pointy edges. The arm stretched out, putting the display close enough for Billy and Dad to get a good look. The leaves grew in a clover pattern, and thin veins branched out across each one.

"Cooooool," Billy whispered.

"Steeping these leaves in boiling water will create a simple analgesic which will also counteract the strongest symptoms of the berries."

Dad nodded and the leaf-hand retreated, melting back into normal fingers. "This'll cure her?"

"If she is given the mixture within the next eight hours, fifteen minutes there will be no lasting effects. She will be fully conscious tomorrow when your wrist chronometer indicates four sixteen post meridian, at which point she will humorously inquire if she may . . ." The Castaway's simple face turned up toward the vaulted ceiling, like they were trying to read something they couldn't quite see. " . . . stay home from school tomorrow and order pizza. It will take her an additional twenty-three hours, forty-two minutes to regain full functionality."

"I . . . thank you." Dad's shoulders dropped a bit.

"Thanks are not necessary, James Gather. I regret whatever discomfort this has caused you and your family, especially Beau Gather. Please convey my apologies to her. I did not intend to give you information that would prove harmful to you and your offspring." The Castaway let their arms drop to their sides. The limbs blended into their body and they became a column of purple jello topped by the lumpy head.

"I know you didn't. It's partly our fault. My fault. I should know by now not to immediately take things you say at face value."

"That is a correct assessment of the facts."

Billy barked out a laugh. Dad looked down at him with annoyance, but it quickly turned to a smile. "Whose side are you on?"

Billy tried to hide his own smile. Failed. "I'm sorry. It was funny."

Dad laughed. Put his arm around Billy's shoulders and hugged him. "Come on. Let's go find that plant and get your sister back on her feet."

"Okay." Billy waved at the bright purple column. "Bye, Castaway."

"Goodbye, Billy Gather."

"Thanks again," said Dad.

The gelatinous pillar tightened itself back into the shape of a human. "It has been good to see you again, James Gather. You have been absent from this place for too long."

"Sorry?"

"My apologies. Your absence has not yet occurred."

Dad laughed again. Took a step toward the door. "Well, what is it they say? You can't miss me until I'm gone."

"Yes," said the Castaway, "this is true."

28

JOSH

Josh wondered if he should've waited until later in the day to bounce his idea off Parker. After lunch tended to be prime sales time, but he'd been excited. And, okay, yes, maybe wanted to see Monique again, so getting them all together at her office seemed like a good idea.

"By the way," he added, casually glossing over Parker's reaction, "I like the new fit. Roanoke looks good on you."

"Don't change the subject," Parker said. She gave one wrist a twist as she spoke, letting the cuff settle.

"I'm not. Just making an observation. I could probably use a change of clothes, too." He mime-sniffed his shoulder.

It did look good on her. On the spectrum from ren faire to *Moulin Rouge*, it was closer to the latter, like a peasant shirt someone had dressed up with a few buttons, cuffs, and a wing collar. Not tailored, but not—

"You want to give her meth?" Parker gestured at Olivia, still limp on the bed beneath her rough linen sheet.

"No." Josh put up a hand. High enough to be calming and reassuring, but not so high to seem dismissive or condescending. Body language mattered a lot in these talks. "Stop thinking of this like we're in a crack house. We're talking about specific, carefully engineered, lab-manufactured pharmaceuticals."

"They manufacture meth in labs, too."

"Not remotely the same thing. Seriously." He nodded his head at Olivia, and at Monique standing near the bed. "We were talking yesterday about our limited options when it comes to treating her condition, and it occurred to me I might have something helpful."

He held up the baggie. Three small bright orange pills. They almost looked like children's aspirin. A design decision he'd been part of. More appealing visually and also made certain parties second-guess them.

"The main ingredient of this is called JT-108415. Created by a biochemist in the Midwest, never went anywhere. It's an ADA activator and also blocks certain adenosine receptors in the brain, sort of a double-punch. We also added some minoxidil for a little more kick, a microdose of psilocybin, and a smidge of octyl acetate for flavor."

"Psilocybin?"

"Just a microdose."

"Also, isn't minoxidil a hair loss drug?"

"Topically, yes, but taken internally it's a vasodilator."

Monique's eyes went wide. "And this is . . . for enjoyment?"

"Well, this one was designed with, well . . . students in mind." He glanced at Parker and shrugged. "It makes you more alert, increases blood flow to the brain, stimulates creativity. A five- or six-hour boost once it kicks in. It was a fairly popular product, especially when midterms and finals rolled around. They originally wanted to call it Einstein's Dream, but I pointed out ED has some other connotations we probably didn't want people associating with our product. Then I suggested Hawking's Dream, which is HD. A much better sell overall."

"You know who Stephen Hawking was?"

"I'm not an idiot. They mention him in *The Avengers.*"

A few memories danced in Josh's head, reminding him of some *Stranger Things* fans who'd nicknamed the drug *Hawkins*'s Dream when exceptionally vivid nightmares turned out to be a less-than-rare side effect. But he knew that wouldn't help convince Parker, and sometimes good marketing meant not mentioning drawbacks unless someone specifically asked about them. Besides, it was more brain activity. Which was their goal here.

Parker held out her hand for the baggie. She held it up to the little window. Another standard part of the transaction. Television had taught people to look at the product. Feel it. Weigh it on their fingertips. Like they could somehow tell quality by weight, see flaws in the chemical bonds by the shape of a tablet.

"His proposal does have some merit," said Monique, and his heart bounced a little bit to have her supporting him. "There is not much else I can do for your friend. I have tried to keep her clean, nourished, and hydrated, but this is a losing battle. I am only keeping the inevitable at arm's length, not reversing course. If these compounds give us even a slight chance, it is more than she has now."

Parker looked down at the comatose woman again. "And if it kills her?"

Monique sighed. Her fingers fiddled with the pleats of her dress. "Then she will die sooner rather than later."

Parker focused on Olivia, then back at Josh. "You just happened to have these on you? While out guiding a school trip."

He brought his hand back up, slightly higher this time. "Not like that at all," he assured her. "They were lost in my coat. Monique will back me up on this. I wasn't even sure if I had anything. It took me a couple hours to go through it."

He couldn't read Parker's face at all. She handed the baggie back to him. "It took you a couple hours?"

Josh took a beat. Legality was always a tricky part of the discourse. Especially with someone like Parker, who'd already made up her mind about some things. He decided to go cards on the table with her.

"It probably won't surprise you someone in my line of work occasionally finds himself under scrutiny from law enforcement officers. The gendarmes, so to speak." He gave Monique a quick wink and her little smile almost knocked him right out of his pitch. Holy crap. He hadn't fallen for someone this fast since high school. And now he was taking too long to start talking again.

"Anyway, a trick I learned early on was to have an escape hatch in each pocket. Pull a few stitches out of the side of the pocket and you've got a little opening just big enough to slide a few items through. Practice with it a few times and you can do it as you're turning the pocket inside out. The items go through, drop into the lining of the coat, and you've got empty pockets to show the authorities. Get good at it, you can hold onto your keys or AirPods while you push stuff through, and now your pockets aren't *suspiciously* empty."

Josh pulled out the pockets on each side to demonstrate, holding the packet under his pinkie and ring finger as he did. He wiggled a free finger in the little gaps in the stitching. Parker almost looked impressed. Monique definitely did.

"The downside," he continued, "is now whatever you pushed through is lost somewhere in the lining of your coat. Most of the time I didn't bother digging it back out when it was just a few bucks worth of product. So I knew there were a half dozen, maybe even ten things down in there. I figured I'd take a look and see if I had anything potentially helpful. Probably would've gone faster if I ripped the lining out, but I really like this coat."

"So this was all random samples you had on you?"

"Essentially."

"But you're sure what this one is?"

"It's my job. They're generic pills, naturally, but I know the shapes and colors and a few of them even have distinctive scents. Usually just something they drop in for aesthetic purposes, y'know, a drop of peppermint oil or something like that. It can make a real difference in the overall experience."

"That didn't answer my question."

"Orange pills. Orange scented. Round. Fifty-milligram size. These are HD. No question."

And there it was. Parker's neck and jaw loosened. He'd closed the deal. Her eyes turned back to Olivia's unconscious form. "How many are you going to give her? All of them?"

Josh handed the baggie to Monique and shook his head. "Three might be pushing it. One's the usual dose, but we want this to have some kick, and I know a few people—bigger guys—who'd take two now and then."

Monique eyed the pills. "I don't believe she can be made to swallow these as is. Will the compounds still work in solution?"

"They should. Most people wash them down with some Coke or an energy drink."

"One moment, please," she said, stepping out into the hall.

Parker looked at Olivia. At him. Back at Olivia.

"So," he said. "Trying to blend in a little more?"

"What?"

He tugged at his own collar.

She shook her head. "My clothes were pretty ripe. I could take what they offered me or wash mine and sit naked in the guest house until they dried."

"You could probably walk around in them. They'd dry pretty fast in the sun."

"Too much dirt and dust. They'd be filthy again before they dried."

"So only a shirt? Did they have pants or—"

"We don't know each other well enough for this conversation to go any further, Josh."

He nodded and closed his mouth.

Monique returned with a small mortar and pestle. A few quick twists of her wrist turned the pills to powder, which she tapped out into a cup of water. She swirled the mixture with a thin stick as she stepped close to the bed. Josh and Parker both moved forward to help, but she shushed them away. She set her hand at the base of Olivia's neck, lifted slightly, and tilted the cup against the comatose woman's lips. "À votre santé."

29

SAM

They stopped to get their bearings at the border between the grove of gigantic mushrooms and the rainforest with trip-hazard roots. Pyr continued getting Noah caught up on a few centuries of geography changes in the valley. Since last night, he'd been a lot more open to the idea someone might know more than him. Sam continued to zone out most of it. He'd been zoning out a lot since last night.

Morning in the cave and this first leg of their hike back to Roanoke had made Sam realize how much he'd been seeing the valley as a temporary place he'd eventually leave. Sure, Noah had messed up his calculations a bit, but all of them working together, they'd figure it out. Find the flaws. Get them home.

But last night had driven home the permanence of it. They weren't getting out. Ever. The Castaway had warned Noah he'd call this place home. They just hadn't mentioned all the other people who'd be along for the ride.

And just like that, the valley had lost a lot of its childhood appeal.

Noah pointed off into the rainforest with a pink-red finger. He'd taken a lot of sun on the hike yesterday, and the burn had manifested overnight. "So the obelisks are all still more or less in the same place, but now some of them are in different . . . areas? Zones?"

"Yes. According to Ross, when the valley changes, it's like the ground shifts under them. Everything else may move around, but they seem to stay in the same position relative to each other."

"Are you sure?"

"As sure as someone can be of anything here. Qiang's lived through three big changes, and he compares notes with Ross a lot."

Sam stared at the ground. At the almost perfect line where the mushroom forest pressed up against the trees with their spidery roots. Wedged up against each other by flukes of nature and cosmic-level physics.

What an idiot he'd been. Going on a bullshit, glorified field trip just so he didn't have to be in the apartment with Gabe. In *his own* apartment! He'd run away again and now . . . Well, it looked like he'd have plenty of time to regret this one.

One of the black-feathered microraptors perched on a looping vine and hissed at him as he walked past. He stopped to stare at it and it hissed again. Not even here a week and already used to seeing the little four-winged dinosaurs everywhere, like sparrows or finches in a garden.

What was it going to be like at the one-month mark? At the end of his first year? He wondered if little Billy Gather would've remembered this place as fondly if he'd spent a decade here? Or if he hadn't had his dad and sister constantly trying to keep him entertained. The thrill of the valley had worn off pretty quick for Beau Gather. She'd had Ross, and she'd still only lasted two years.

The guilt worm twisted in his gut.

The shafts of light around them vanished, a big shadow rushed toward them across the twisting roots, and the little crow-dinosaur leaped away, sailing off between the trees. Sam looked up through the branches and caught a glimpse of one of the big pteranodons soaring above them, its leathery wings wide and pink in the sunlight. A third one flew by. They were low, barely above the trees, and he caught quick glimpses of clawed wings and splayed legs.

"Should we be worried about them?" he asked.

Noah shook his head. "They couldn't actually pick you up. Probably just headbutt you if they did anything. Sort of a flying tackle. But they'd need a lot of open space for it."

"Didn't one of them grab you once?"

"When I was ten. I'm a little bigger now."

Pyr glanced up as one last pteranodon skimmed above them. "One of those grabbed you and you got away? How have I never heard that story?"

"Well, it was a . . . yep. I think it happened a week before we found Ross. Dad and Beau were right there. They pelted it with rocks and it dropped me pretty quick." He reached up and tapped his shoulder. "Dad accidentally hit me with one. Beau told me he tried to knock me out so I'd stop fighting it. One less mouth to feed."

Pyr snort-laughed.

Another detail of the story popped into Sam's mind. "You sprained your ankle when it dropped you."

"Yep. Lucky it hadn't gotten any higher or I probably would've broken something."

How long would someone last here with a broken leg, Sam wondered. So many things seemed a lot more important to know now. The valley let you heal faster, but what about a really bad break? You could probably still bleed out here. And you'd need to avoid predators, but still gather food somehow.

How had the Gathers survived here? How had Billy and Beau survived here? Alone?

Noah and Pyr had started walking again. He followed behind, watching every root that tried to trip him. Aware of how many ways there were to die in the valley.

An hour and a half of walking—punctuated by the occasional, unavoidable stumble—brought them back to the edge of the wasteland plains. Sam only had half a bottle of water left, and he remembered what crossing it the first time had been like. The sun wasn't brutally hot, but it was intense. Noah's nose, cheeks, and ears were proof of it.

A thought crossed his mind, and he shielded his eyes to look higher into the sky. "No clouds." Mostly an observation, but partly a question.

"Barely ever," said Pyr. "Wisps at best."

Sam looked at Noah. "But it rains sometimes."

"Sometimes." Noah turned his own gaze at Pyr. "Every three or four weeks?"

She nodded. "Still, yes. Last time was thirteen days ago."

Sam noticed she looked out across the wasteland as she spoke. Checking for dinosaurs, probably. Had she done that on the way out to the cave? He'd been so wrapped up in the excitement of being out in the valley he probably hadn't noticed a lot of things.

They walked along the border of the wastelands until they found the path again, and Pyr led them back out into the bright sunlight.

Sam wasn't sure if the sun was more intense or if it was his general weariness, but the plains of low scrub seemed like much more of a slog than they had yesterday. A bead of salty sweat slipped down his forehead and into the corner of his eye. He squinted it away. The half-bottle of water crossed his mind, and he reminded himself they'd barely been in the wasteland for twenty minutes.

The path meandered back and forth, past small mounds of red stone and low spiky bushes. It led them from the shade of one twisting tree to the next, giving them brief moments of relief from the high-noon sun. He needed a hat. If he hadn't been an idiot, he would've packed one of the half dozen baseball caps floating around his apartment. But he'd been too busy running away to pack anything useful.

He let his eyes drop to his feet, following the path while sparing himself the sun. Something scraped at his arm. A spine from a cactus, one of the only spots of bright green out here. He'd drifted to the side as he walked. He glanced at his arm. A thin scratch with a few small droplets of blood.

They walked beneath another tree and back out into the sun. The uneven trail made Sam's legs ache, but at least now he'd ache evenly on both sides. It crossed his mind he could use his shirt to make a loose headwrap. Cool his scalp and maybe give his eyes a bit of shade.

Noah stopped abruptly and Sam bumped into the professor's back. The hot scents of body odor and back sweat forced themselves up into his nose, sharp enough to make him wince, and he wondered if he smelled this bad. He took a step back, started to apologize, and froze as a dozen thoughts fought to be first in his mind.

A gigantic hawk, or maybe an eagle, stood off the path maybe thirty feet ahead of them. The twisting tree and a taller cactus had blocked it from sight until they were almost right on top of it. And even then a new thought fought into his mind, telling him despite the brown and gold feathers and the harsh yellow eyes the creature was a dinosaur, a raptor of some kind, and it was at least the size of a horse. *Had to be* the size of a horse.

Because the kid was riding it like a horse.

The bare-chested, heavyset kid—no, a small man—had skin that could've been brown naturally or from a life in the sun. A thick ledge of a brow shaded his dark eyes and the top of a broad, turned-up nose. He glared at them, but something about his expression made Sam think the caveman hadn't expected to run into them, either. A beard stretched down to his pecs and a wild mane of black-brown hair was decorated with a few strings and . . . sticks? Bones? Animal teeth?

The Neanderthal wore a string of random yellow-white teeth around his neck. Jewelry? Trophies? More strings of bones and teeth decorated his biceps and wrists. Below the waist he was wrapped in swaths of leathery hides and pelts, like the crude skirt of some B-movie barbarian.

The raptor opened its mouth and took a step forward. The man jabbed it in the side with his heels and yanked on a thick cord, halting it. The thing he sat on looked like the design halfway point between a blanket and a saddle. A few bundles hung from it, and a heavy piece of wood. A little too shaped to be a club, but not quite a wooden axe.

Pyr had one arm out blocking Noah. The reason for his sudden stop and their collision. Her other arm—the dark, biomechanical arm—pointed straight at the Neanderthal. Or maybe the dinosaur. Her fingers spread wide, displaying her palm to them.

The hairy man shifted on his almost-saddle and the raptor sidestepped. It moved a few feet out onto the path, but never looked away. Its yellow eyes settled on Sam, the little nostrils huffed in some air, and the irises tightened. He remembered the scratch on his arm, the little drops of blood, and his heart kicked beneath his ribs.

The dinosaur took a few steps forward. It had one gigantic claw on each foot. Just like in the movies. Big, curving scimitar claws.

Pyr shouted something, a sound or maybe a word, and threw her arm forward. Her palm moved a few inches toward the dinosaur. Her fingers flexed.

The rider kicked his heels into the raptor's sides again. It shrieked this time, the sound of a three-ton falcon hunting for squirrels or rabbits. Sam could feel the air coming from its lungs even from a dozen yards away.

Pyr yelled her word again.

The Neanderthal brought the spear up to his shoulder.

Noah stood up a little taller. Took in a deep breath. Let out a string of coarse syllables that sounded like a grizzly bear trying to speak Arabic.

"Shut up," hissed Pyr.

The Neanderthal's eyes went wide. The spear wavered. His hips shifted on the almost-saddle.

Then his face hardened again. He straightened up, pulled back with the spear, Pyr's arm dipped down—

Lightning strobed and the ground near the raptor splashed up in a cloud of dirt and dust like a cannonball had struck. The dinosaur screamed again and took four quick, stumbling steps back. The spear came down as the Neanderthal tried to regain control, yanking hard on the reins. The raptor steadied. The rider glared at them.

Pyr trembled, but she kept her arm straight out.

The rider glared at her. Glanced down at the basketball-sized crater in the ground. Back at all of them. Sam could see the hate in the man's eyes and the calculating look on his face.

Pyr barked out the word one more time. Raised her arm ever so slightly. Sam was pretty sure it pointed straight at the Neanderthal now.

The Neanderthal seemed pretty sure of it, too.

A bead of sweat slid down Sam's back. Pyr's shoulders glistened with it. Noah took in another breath, but this time she bumped his stomach with her free elbow. He let the air out slowly. Quietly.

The Neanderthal spat out some syllables. Yanked the reins hard to the side. The raptor's big claws kicked twice at the dirt path, then it turned around and crashed back through the spiny brush. It moved with big, loping steps. The rider turned his head to glare back at them once.

Noah let the rest of the air out of his lungs in a big sigh.

Pyr followed the retreating dinosaur and rider with her hand, the palm pointed at them. When they were about two hundred feet away, she let both arms drop to her sides. She let out a long sigh and swayed. Her shoulders slumped and she bent over, resting her hands against her knees as her head hung low. She took a few deep, heaving breaths.

Sam's heart still fought to break free of his ribs. His breath stumbled again and again. "What the—what the hell was that?"

"Built-in biochemical blaster." She wiggled her synthetic fingers without looking up. "Last ditch weapon. Standard millex for most soldiers who get replacements."

Noah looked over at the little crater. "You couldn't've used it sooner?"

"It runs off my own energy reserves. Blood sugar converted to energy. One shot feels like sprinting a few klicks. Two, I'm useless. Three would knock me out cold for a couple hours."

Sam watched the raptor blur into the distant wasteland. Toward the lake and the sparkling tower of crystal. He took a deep breath. Felt his heart slow down. "I mean the—what the hell was *that*?"

Pyr took another deep breath. "That was Breaker. Probably just on a patrol."

"Breaker?"

"His real name's closer to B'Kar. Top Klaa male. Closest thing they have to a military commander."

Noah stared after the Neanderthal. "They ride dinosaurs?"

"Only the big raptors." She straightened up, took another deep breath, and swung her pack off her shoulder. "We have to get going. Now."

Sam looked away from the distant speck and turned to Noah. "What'd you say to him?"

"I think I told him we're friends, we live here, and he shouldn't hunt us."

"You think?"

"My pronunciation might be a little rusty. There haven't been a lot of opportunities to speak Neanderthal back in the twenty-first century."

"You confused him," said Pyr. Her breathing was still heavy, but didn't seem as desperate. She'd found a chunk of bread in her pack and pulled it apart with her teeth. "Humans aren't supposed to know more than three or four words of their language."

"Ahhh."

Sam looked back and forth between them. "Why does that sound bad?"

"Can the two of you not walk and talk at the same time?" Pyr snapped her fingers. "Move. Now."

They headed down the path. Pyr kept checking after the raptor, making sure the Neanderthal hadn't guided it back toward them. Her feet dragged a bit and her fingers danced on the handle of her big knife.

"So confusing them is bad," Sam asked again.

Noah glanced back at him. "They react poorly when they get confused. It means something they don't understand or didn't expect is happening. Something different."

"Which usually means they attack," Pyr said over her shoulder.

"It means they fall back on fight or flight," Noah corrected. Then he glanced at the ground. "Sorry. At least, that's how they used to react back in my day."

"It still is. And if we've got numbers they'll normally back off. But when they're mounted, they know they've got a serious advantage. So they take confusion even worse."

"Sorry. Again."

"You didn't know. And your pronunciation wasn't bad for a thirty-year break."

The path curved around a dense patch of bushes with leaves like brown broken glass. Sam looked over the wasteland, toward the center. "If they're that much of a . . . if they're that dangerous, why didn't you just shoot it with your—your blaster-arm?"

"I'd only be able to shoot one of them. Breaker or the raptor. After an attack they definitely would've fought back, and I'd probably be too exhausted to even aim for a third shot."

"So we would've been fighting it. Or him."

"Probably him. You'd have better odds fighting Breaker, but I'm not sure the blaster would do more than stun the raptor. The warning shot was our best move, make him think the odds were much more even than he thought."

Noah nodded slowly. "You've done this sort of standoff before."

"A few times, yes." She turned around, walking backward so they could face each other for a few moments. "It'll take him an hour to get back to their territory, another hour to decide to take it to the Empress, and then . . . well, she was going to find out about you sometime."

"The Empress?"

"Yes," said Pyr. "She rules the Klaa. The whole valley, truthfully."

"The valley? With what? Is the Neanderthal population that much bigger than Roanoke?"

Pyr sighed. "Noah, the Klaa outnumber us almost ten to one. There are hundreds of them here in the valley."

"What?"

She turned back around and a pair of cactus spikes scraped ineffectively on her biomechanical wrist. The arm came up and pointed across the wasteland. "They live on the far side of the valley. About as far from Roanoke as they can be. It's just by luck, not any sort of diplomacy."

Sam followed her finger, looking at the hazy, distant cliffs of the far side. "How are there so many?"

"There just are."

Noah still seemed to be processing. "And the Empress is their . . . latest matriarch?"

"More or less. A figurative mother more than an actual one."

"Empress seems like an odd title," said Sam. "Who decided to call her that?"

"She did."

Noah stopped walking. "What?"

Pyr looked over her shoulder and nodded. "She speaks English."

"Well? Or just a few words?"

"Keep moving."

Sam coughed out a laugh. "Kind of odd if her . . . if she only knows ten or twelve words and one of them's 'Empress.'"

"She speaks English as well as you and me," Pyr told them. "And German. French. Swahili. Mandarin and Yue Chinese. At least as many languages as Ross."

Noah looked out across the valley, and Sam could see the doubt and confusion on the man's face. "And she's a Neanderthal?"

"We're not sure what she is. But they all obey her. And to be honest . . . so do we, for the most part. The valley trembles beneath her feet."

"That's oddly . . . poetic?"

"No, it's not. The ground actually shakes when she's out walking around."

Sam looked past Pyr and saw the far tree line, close enough he could make out the barren, black trunks. He wondered if they'd be safer there. He couldn't imagine someone riding a horse full tilt through the woods, and had to imagine riding a dinosaur wouldn't be much easier.

He looked back at the path in time to stop himself from drifting into one of the bulbous little cacti. "I thought Qiang ran the town?"

"More or less. But we're an occupied territory. We're technically free to do what we want, but in reality the enemy's all around us."

Noah let out a huff of air, either from the pace or his own frustration. "Is it really that bad?"

"We are . . . second class citizens, I believe is the phrase you'd use. They take what they want. Do what they want. Breaker probably would've killed us just now if I hadn't driven him off. We're just another strange thing that needs to be deleted. Disposed of. You're lucky you found Roanoke before they found you."

"Yep," Noah said, "so lucky only two of my students died and a third's in a coma."

She shrugged without looking back. "I saw them stone someone to death once. We've found bodies. People who landed too deep in the valley, and the Klaa wounded them and left them for the dinos. Some of the bodies get strung up."

"Jesus," muttered Sam.

"The scarecrow out on the edge of the corn field? It's more for them than anything else. In their eyes it's a body hanging on a tree."

"Something they—something familiar? To keep them calm rather than to scare them?"

"More or less."

Noah cleared his throat. "I wish you'd told us all this sooner."

"You scrambled a lot of our usual procedures. Most people are overwhelmed by surviving their first few dinosaur attacks and finding out they're trapped at the dawn of time. We give them a week or two to adjust and then explain our xenophobic Neanderthal overlords."

"How've you lasted this long? I mean, if they outnumber you ten to one, why haven't they wiped you out?"

"We pay a tribute of food and goods. Every two months. They want that to continue, so they usually leave us alone. Except when they don't."

"How long's this been going on?"

"A few hundred years."

Sam took a longer step. Got himself a little closer to her. "And this, the Empress, she keeps them under control?"

She glanced at him. Looked back after the long-vanished raptor. Forward at the approaching trees. "I think the Empress wouldn't mind killing us, either. But she likes having power over all of us more. So she lets us live over here on our side of the valley. As long as nothing changes . . . she's got no reason to eliminate us."

"Nothing changing," said Noah. "Like a new human who speaks Neanderthal?"

Pyr pointed at the forest line ahead of them, the charred trees like so many black wooden needles. "If we keep this pace, we should be able to reach Roanoke in a little over two hours."

As they headed for the trees, Sam took another look back the way Breaker had vanished.

Being out in the valley had lost a lot of its appeal.

30

PARKER

Parker was waiting at the gate when Sam, Pyr, and a very sunburned Noah returned an hour before the daylight vanished. She'd tried to do a bit of small talk first, but then Noah explained what his sister had done, and Parker heard the hollowness in his voice and gave him a long hug. She wasn't really a hugger, but he needed it. Pyr had slipped away while Noah and Sam filled Parker in on valley politics with the Empress and her Neanderthals. The talk carried them to the main hall, where Josh joined them. By the time Ross arrived to stand next to Noah they'd moved on to Josh drugging Olivia. And then, when things had calmed down and the men had all stopped talking to shove food in their mouths, Parker threw her grenade on the table. All of them froze, even the android, Ross.

Sam recovered first. "How can we—what do you mean, we're not in the past?"

She pointed up at the ceiling. "I stayed up most of last night studying the stars. It's a modern sky. And since the sky doesn't move here, I'm betting it always has been."

"It can't be," said Noah, although his words didn't have the conviction they had for the past few days.

"It is."

Josh raised his hand. "How do you know?"

"The constellations," Parker explained. "They're all up there, just not where we're used to seeing them from North America. If we were a hundred million years in the past most of them would be so distorted they wouldn't even be recognizable."

"Because the stars all move, right?"

"Right. But they're all moving in their own directions at their own speeds. Two thousand years ago Polaris wasn't the North Star. If we were millions of years in the past everything would be different. A lot of stars we know wouldn't even exist yet."

"Like Polaris," said Noah. "Which isn't there at all."

Parker gave a quick shake of her head. The collar of her new shirt scratched at the back of her neck. "It's not there because we're at the equator and it's springtime. Ursa Minor's just peeking over the top of the cliffs. Polaris is probably just below it, out of sight."

"You're sure?"

"Absolutely."

"But, I mean . . ." Sam waved at the door. At Ross. Took a few quick breaths. "Dinosaurs. Android. I've just spent the past two days with a future—with a woman who's got a Winter Soldier arm with a blaster built into it."

"White Wolf arm," Josh said as he tore off a piece of bread.

"What?"

He gestured with the bread crust. "When he's the Winter Soldier his arm's silver with the red star. When it's dark he's the White Wolf."

"Dude, please."

Parker cleared her throat. "I'm not saying there isn't some level of time travel going on."

Sam frowned. "So everything traveled through time except us?"

"I mean, we could still be locally in the past. Present-adjacent. It might be the 1950s or sixties—"

"Great."

"—or maybe even as far back as the 1800s. Or a hundred years in the future. Without actual star charts and tools it's hard to be precise. But it's definitely not one hundred million BCE out there. That's our sky."

Her stomach rumbled. She didn't want to eat anything until she'd gotten her point across. Didn't want to look distracted. The smell of hot bread was getting hard to resist, though.

"If it's our—a modern sky," said Sam, his breath picking up again, "then where's the Moon?"

"I don't know. But it's a modern, present-day sky."

Noah bit into something that looked like a green apple a little bigger than a golf ball. "I'm not sure about this."

"We can go outside and look up," said Parker. "It's all right there."

He held out the hand with the apple. "No, sorry. I mean, I'm not sure the valley's always been in the present."

"Why not?"

"Well, because . . . it wasn't."

She fought the urge to roll her eyes.

"I stared up at the stars all the time as a kid. I would've noticed the constellations."

"Would you, though?" Josh waved his bread at the ceiling for emphasis. "In all fairness, you were just a little kid. How many would you've known?"

Sam nodded. "Didn't you and—you and your sister, sorry, make up a lot of your own constellations? Because you didn't recognize anything."

"You can say her name. It's okay."

Sam nodded and looked at the floor.

"And we . . . we did make up a lot of our own constellations."

"Did you travel south of the equator when you were little?" asked Parker.

Noah raised an eyebrow and wrinkled his bright red forehead.

"You were a little kid from the northern hemisphere. You probably knew a couple of the basic constellations, right? The Big Dipper. Orion. You'd never seen the sky from anywhere else, so it all would've looked completely different to you. And to your sister. Maybe your dad. And if you'd been making up your own constellations, sectioning off the sky in your own way, you probably wouldn't've recognized it when you studied it later as an adult."

"Maybe."

"Especially if you were absolutely convinced you weren't looking at a modern sky back then. And that's before we even add in the lack of Moon."

She recognized Noah's expression, knew the way his mind was spinning. The professor learning from the student. She'd put that look on his face twice over the past few years.

He bit off the last of his apple, dropped the little core on his plate. "I suppose," he said, "if everything's traveling through time to get here, then *here* could be anywhere."

"Anywhen," Josh pointed out. He held up two fingers. "Question."

"Yep?"

"If we haven't traveled through time, why is everyone here so convinced they have?"

"Dinosaurs," said Sam.

"And Neanderthals," added Parker. "It's a natural assumption."

"I think . . ." Josh twiddled his hands in front of his chest. "It's natural if you're the only one here. No offense, Noah. But once you've got all these people, all from different places and times, wouldn't it cross someone's mind they could be . . . anywhen?"

Ross tapped his walking stick on the floor. "I beg your pardon, Josh, but I believe this would be my fault."

They all looked at the android. "I'm sorry, what?"

"I'm the Timekeeper. For the past four hundred years, people have depended on me to keep track of the passage of time here in the valley. If there's a fault in their understanding, it's because of me."

Noah sat up. "No. It's because of me."

"No, it's because of *me*," Josh insisted, thumping his fist on the table.

A quick laugh burst out of Sam's mouth. Parker let her eyes roll this time, but the stupid joke did relax her a bit. A little of the accumulated tension slid away from the table.

Josh settled back in his chair, looking satisfied.

Noah plucked another miniature apple from the tray. "When Beau and my Dad and I got here, it was a place with dinosaurs and cavemen. So we assumed we'd traveled millions of years back in time. And when we found Ross, that's what we told him. And then he told the people after us, and the people after them, and so on. It's our mistake getting passed along for four hundred years."

Parker nodded. "But it's coming from the voice of authority, the Timekeeper, so even if people have some other ideas, nobody really questions it."

"I'm sorry, again, for the mistake."

"It wasn't your mistake, Ross."

"You're kind to say so, Noah."

Parker put her hands together. Not a clap, but enough to make some noise. "So that's *when* we are. And I think it also tells us something about *where* we are."

"Near the equator."

"Not exactly." She went over everything in her head again, making sure there wasn't another way to say it that might make her sound less concussed. "If nothing's moving in the sky, it means *we're* not moving. We're at a fixed point in Earth's orbit. Heliostationary."

"You think we're inside the wormhole," Noah said.

"Maybe."

His lips twisted into a doubtful expression. "But by its nature a wormhole puts us somewhere else."

"We are somewhere else."

"If we were somewhere else, why are we seeing our constellations?"

Sam stopped tapping. "What if it's not a wormhole? What if it's a black hole? If we were past the event horizon, that could—it would explain why time runs differently here. And why the sky doesn't seem to move."

"Time dilation," said Josh proudly.

Noah shook his head. "No. That's backward. If we're at the event horizon we'd look frozen to outside observers. The rest of the universe wouldn't look frozen to us."

"Unless we're beyond the horizon," said Sam. "In which case everything we know might be wrong."

"Okay, again, just speaking as a guy who watches some sci-fi in his spare time," Josh said, "Doesn't going into a black hole stretch you into spaghetti or something?"

Parker pointed at him and nodded.

"Unless," Sam said, "it's a supermassive black hole. Lesser tidal force, no spaghettification."

Josh's fingers went back up. "How does a supermassive black hole have less force than a regular one?

"I can explain it," Parker told him, "but it's a lot of math."

"Never mind, then. I'm good."

"Regardless," said Noah, "I think we can rule out a supermassive black hole in our solar system that nobody's ever noticed hitting Earth once a year."

Sam's mouth formed a quick smirk. "But we're cool with a wormhole hitting Earth every year and nobody noticing?"

Parker cleared her throat. "Even if we accepted we're somehow beyond the event horizon and time's frozen, why does the sky change from day to night?"

"Maybe it's—it could be changing normally, but we're perceiving it at an accelerated rate."

"Wouldn't the days and nights be faster too, then?" asked Josh. "Like, a day would only be an hour or something like that, wouldn't it?"

Noah plucked another apple from the tray. "We'll make a scientist out of you yet."

"Thanks, but I couldn't take the cut in pay."

"Ouch."

Sam put his hands up. "Okay, I renounce my theory. It's not a black hole."

Josh shook the last drops out of his cup. "What about this? What if we're frozen in time, but we're also bouncing back and forth through time?"

Parker blinked. Noah turned his head. "I'm sorry, what?"

"You know how vinyl records can get a skip in them? They start repeating because the needle drops back to the last groove. Like a loop." While he spoke, Josh traced a circle in the air a few times with his finger, making an exaggerated twitch every time his fingertip reached the top.

"Okay," she said.

"Maybe that's what's happening here. We're frozen at noon, then the valley skips ahead to some point in the night where we can't see the Moon, and we're frozen there until it skips back to high noon and starts the loop again."

Noah finished off his apple. He had a pile of little cores on the plate in front of him, like someone picking all the meat off hot wings. "That's . . . an interesting idea. I remember my dad saying something similar once."

Parker tried to picture a model of it. "How would it work, though? What would be causing the skip?"

"What would be causing us to be frozen in time?" asked Sam.

"Are we back at black holes again?"

"Maybe. If we're past the event horizon but inside the photon sphere . . ."

"I don't like it."

"Neither do I," said Noah.

Josh put his hands up. "I'm just the idea guy. You're the ones who figure things out."

"But what if—if the sky's a photon sphere, and we're below it, that could be why it looks so wild to us."

Now Noah shook his head. "If we're inside the photon sphere we wouldn't be able to see anything. Gravity would pull all the photons to the ground."

"Which wouldn't be here," Parker pointed out, "because we'd all be crushed flat."

"Okay, then, here's another idea." Josh swallowed another mouthful of bread. "We keep talking about how things work in the valley."

"Right."

"What's outside the valley? Wouldn't that give us some information, maybe?"

"They never . . ." Sam looked at Noah. "You never found out what was beyond the valley, right? Nobody knows what's beyond the cliffs."

"Normally I'd say no, but it turns out I'm not the expert I thought I was. Ross?"

"Yes, Noah?"

"Has anyone made it out of the valley?"

"You did."

A few smirks and chuckles skipped around the table. One of them was Noah's. "No, I meant . . . has anyone climbed out of the valley? Have they made it up the cliffs to get a look around?"

"Not to my knowledge, Noah."

"Has anyone made it higher than Beau did? Maybe gotten a better look at what's beyond here?"

"Again, not to my knowledge."

Noah looked back at them and shrugged.

"Probably just as well," said Parker. "If it was a photon sphere up there, we'd look out and see the backs of our own heads."

Josh's eyebrows went up. "Really?"

"Yeah."

"That's amazing."

She nodded and yawned. "Science can be very cool."

"How many people have tried to climb the cliffs?" asked Sam. "Just out of curiosity."

"Eighty-six that I'm aware of in the 434 years since Miss Beau made her attempt, although it's possible there have been more I didn't observe. Nine of these attempts were Neanderthals. Eleven involved groups of people, totaling thirty-seven individual climbers."

Parker felt her brow furrow. "And none of them got higher than his sister?"

"That's correct, Parker."

Noah set his forearms against the table. "Something wrong?"

"Well, no offense, but isn't it a little weird that out of so many attempts, the best one was your sister?"

"Somebody's got to be the person who went the highest. Why not Beau?"

"Did she do any rock climbing before? You know, before you ended up here?"

"No." Noah shrugged. "She was lighter. Stronger. Had youthful energy. I don't think it's that weird."

"It feels weird to me."

"Why?"

"It just does. I mean, almost a hundred people try it and the person who made it furthest is the one whose name we happen to know. That doesn't seem like a weird coincidence?"

"I know sixty-six of their names, Parker. I can list them chronologically or alphabetically."

"Thanks, but no."

The android gave a shaky nod and nobody spoke for a moment. Parker took the moment to finally appease her rumbling stomach and shove two forkfuls of scrambled egg in her mouth. She swallowed it down and used a piece of bread to wipe the rest of it from her tongue.

Josh stepped next to her and plopped another spoonful of egg onto a piece of bread, folding it in to make a little bite-sized bread bowl. He cleared his throat. "Minor segue, speaking of feeling weird. Despite all the bonding we've done, it's a little odd to me, having a bunch of roommates. I haven't lived that way since college, no offense to anyone. So I moved into another house."

He popped his little bowl of egg into his mouth.

Parker's brain took a moment to shift gears and catch up. "You what?"

He swallowed. "Moved out. Didn't want anyone worried when we were done eating and we all went different directions."

"I wouldn't've been worried," said Sam.

"How are you . . . how did you get a house?"

Josh shrugged. "I asked."

Ross twitched to life. "If I may, Noah."

"Yes?"

"There are currently eleven unoccupied residences here in Roanoke. As newcomers, you're all welcome to claim any of them."

Parker thought of being up on the wall and hearing the quiet of the town. Being alone in a silent house felt . . . wrong? Unearned?

Sam seemed put off by it, too. "You claim a house? How does that work?"

"It's common for Roanoke to have more houses than residents," Ross explained. "When newcomers begin to feel comfortable here, they're given the offer to move from the guest house and choose a house of their own."

Josh nodded. "See? Everyone does it. It only seemed weird because I'm the first person you heard about doing it. Oh!" His face lit up and his shoulders straightened. He pointed two fingers at the android. "Ross, how many people have climbed *just as high* as Noah's sister?"

"Forty-one, Josh."

Parker felt a little thrill run through her. "That," she said, "is very interesting."

Noah leaned forward on his wooden chair. "Almost half the people who've ever tried to climb the cliffs all stopped at the same point?"

"That's correct, Noah."

He looked at Parker. "Yep, you're right. That's weird."

31

BILLY

Billy stood between Beau and Ross and stared up at the cliffs around their cave. He wasn't sure what she was looking at. They'd headed out to gather some of the big potato-things they'd found growing on the other side of Dickwood Forest, and probably some mushrooms, too. Because they always had mushrooms.

Then Beau had looked back over her shoulder, and looked up, and kept looking. Billy thought she'd seen one of the big pterodactyl-dinosaurs, which had given him a quick, scary memory of being carried up into the air, but he didn't see one up there above the cave. He didn't see anything. No big dinosaurs or little dinosaurs or cool statues or jets. The cliffs over their cave were just lots and lots of rock.

But Beau kept staring up, holding one hand over her eyes to block the sun.

Billy looked around the Boneyard. Counted up random skulls and ribs and leg bones and backbones. Looked up at Charlie the not-quite-Siamese cat, sunning himself halfway up the big stone staircase. Charlie sat up, yawned, and started cleaning his butthole.

He looked at Ross, and the shiny-white robot looked back down at him. Ever since Billy learned Ross was solar-powered, he always figured the robot was happier out in the sun. He was pretty sure the big blue eyes looked happier.

"I bet I could do it," Beau said.

"Do what?"

She waved a hand up at the cliff. "Climb it. Make it to the top."

Billy snorted. "You couldn't last time."

"Shut up." She gave him a gentle whack on the head. Really gentle. She'd been treating him like a baby ever since Dad had . . . since Dad saved them from Fang.

"Last time I just did it," she said. "I didn't rest up ahead of time or take anything with me. I bet I could do it if I planned it out a little more."

"Bet you can't."

"Whose side are you on, twerp?"

"Ross's."

"Thank you, Master Billy."

"Both of you shut up." But she smiled a bit when she said it. She took a step back and looked up again. Billy watched her eyes and thought she was trying to figure out if there was a spot where the cliffs weren't as high.

Billy remembered the last time Beau'd tried to climb the cliff. Wondering if she'd make it to the top and what she'd see. Wondering if one of the pterodactyls would see her hanging to the cliff like a bug. Dad trying to be calm, doing his counting to ten thing again and again.

"Maybe . . ."

She glanced down. "What?"

He squirmed a little. "Nothing. D'you want to go get potatoes or what?"

She ruffled his hair. "Yeah. Let's go."

But she didn't move. She just stood there and stared up at the cliff like she was daydreaming about stuff. She put up both hands together to shade her eyes and looked back and forth across the top edge of the valley.

Billy kicked at something on the ground. A big tooth, the size of his thumb. He'd tried collecting dinosaur teeth for a while, but there were sooooo many of them in the Boneyard. His collection got big fast. Then it was too big. And then one day three weeks ago dinosaur teeth stopped being cool and he'd spent an afternoon chucking them off the ledge in front of their cave, trying to get one all the way to Dickwood Forest.

This tooth might be one of the ones from his collection. It looked kind of familiar, but it also looked like a tooth. He tried to figure out if one of his teeth could've landed here.

Beau was still looking up at the cliffs.

Billy sighed. Loudly. Deliberately. "C'mon, Ross. Let's go find some food." He walked off toward the giant mushrooms, knowing Ross would follow him.

"Of course, Master Billy. Will you be comfortable alone, Miss Beau?"

"What? Yeah, sure."

Billy stepped one-two-three over a trio of big ribs and kicked at another tooth. Beau and Ross were still talking. She'd been a lot less fun lately. Things had been fun, sure, but she was being more serious. Less like a sister, more like a grown-up.

"Pilla?"

Zock was at the edge of Dickwood Forest. He always stood and moved like a kid on the playground in the middle of getting bullied, always ready to curl up in a ball. He had on his furry skirt and a rough string around his neck with a big tooth on it that Billy hadn't seen before.

Billy hadn't seen Zock in a while. Not since before . . . well, it'd been at least two months. He'd seen Andre the Giant once, and the cavegirl they'd been calling Juliet maybe three times. And he'd seen *her* at least twice. Scarnose. Lurking in the distance like a storybook witch in the forest.

"Hey, Zock." He waved and Zock waved awkwardly back, adding a Neanderthal word that meant something like "hello" or maybe "I'm over here." Billy said it too. Zock always grinned when Billy used caveman words, and he was never sure if his caveboy friend was delighted or laughing at him.

"Hey," called out Beau. "Be careful."

"It's just Zock."

Zock waved again, and gestured Billy closer. He looked sad. Billy wondered if Beau would let Zock spend the night in the cave sometime. It was probably warmer and dryer than the Pakka camp, and it'd be nice to have someone else in the cave. It'd felt too big since Dad had . . .

Billy took a few more steps, jumped over a big skull, and in midair he saw the movement behind Zock, the figure stepping out from behind one of the big mushroom stalks. *Her.* Scarnose.

His feet hit the ground and Billy froze for a moment. Tried not to be scared—tried *so* hard—as she came out of the forest. One step. Two steps. Like a cat hunting a mouse or Fang hunting Dad or no no no . . .

Billy backed up and something hit the back of his legs. The dinosaur skull. He tried to step over it without looking away from Scarnose and the heels of his sneakers caught on the skull's holes and ridges and then he was stumbling and someone grabbed his wrist to stop him from falling and no no NO IT WAS HER.

Scarnose glared at him with her one bloodshot eye and spat out a few Neanderthal words he didn't recognize. Her other hand grabbed his neck and dragged him back to his feet. She squeezed his throat, sank her long fingernails into his skin. He yelped and kicked and tried to throw punches and—

Beau slammed into Scarnose. The hands holding Billy vanished and he fell backward over the skull, his feet up in the air. His head smacked into the sand but he shook off the dizziness and kicked his legs up and off the skull. Beau was screaming and his heart was pounding and he couldn't lose her too he couldn't be alone here he had to help.

He got to his feet and froze again.

Beau was on top of Scarnose. Her knees had the cavewoman pinned and she was punching her again and again. Billy didn't think his sister was hurt but she kept screaming. Not even words, just a sound like she was angry or in pain.

Scarnose had one arm free and she thrashed and flailed, knocking away a lot of Beau's punches but not all of them. Her nose and lip were bleeding, and her bloodshot eye was squinting. She snarled and kicked at the ground, heaving her hips, trying to throw Beau off of her.

Zock stood a few feet past them, crouching even lower. And there was Andre. And the boy Beau had named Romeo. Andre and Romeo hooted and yelled, but they stayed far back, still in the mushroom forest. It was like they were all watching a playground fight. Lots of shouting, but nobody joined in.

Beau finally stopped screaming, but not punching. She hit Scarnose again and again, but the punches were slower and not as wild. Billy knew this stage of playground fights, too. Trying to figure out if it was over or not.

Scarnose twisted and thrashed and reached under Beau, and for a moment Billy thought the cavewoman had tried to punch his sister in the nuts, or maybe grab her there with those long fingernails. But then the hand came back and he saw something shiny and Beau screamed again. She threw herself off Scarnose and the cavewoman lunged after her, swinging her arm wide.

Billy saw the knife.

Beau moved back, holding her arm tight against her belly. There was a lot of blood. Billy wasn't sure if it was coming from her arm or her stomach.

Scarnose yelled a few cave words, lunged forward with her stone knife, and Ross batted her arm aside.

The robot put himself between Beau and Scarnose. The cavewoman lunged forward again and again, but if this had been a playground fight Ross was the teacher. He put a hand up and walked forward. "Please stop," he said, raising his voice. "I can't allow this activity to continue."

Scarnose tried to push past his hand, but she didn't try too hard. None of the Pakka liked Ross. They weren't scared of him (well, *she* definitely wasn't scared of him) but they didn't like him. Billy wasn't sure if it was the robot's voice, his big eyes, or his skinny head. Whatever it was, Scarnose made two wild attempts to get past Ross, then a kind of lazy for-show one, and then she backed away. As she did, she said a lot of cave words Billy didn't know, but they sounded like swears the way she said them. Zock and Andre and Romeo had crept back into the mushroom forest, too, and Billy was sad that his friend hadn't checked to see if he was okay or even said goodbye.

Ross took another few steps forward and Scarnose kept backing away. For a moment Billy thought she was going to try to run around the robot to get to Beau, to keep fighting. But she went back into the forest and stabbed at one of the big mushroom stalks again and again, cutting and slashing and yelling the whole time she did. After a minute of that she pointed her knife at Beau, but then Ross took another step and Scarnose turned and ran into the forest.

Billy ran to Beau. She still had her arm pressed over her stomach. She'd heal fast. She had to. Everything healed fast in the valley.

Ross reached her at the same time. Beau held out her arm to the robot and Billy could see the blood on her shirt and, okay, it was her arm. Just her arm bleeding. A long cut, definitely more than a scratch, almost from her elbow to her wrist. He knew it was bad for germs and infection, but he also knew it was better than her guts being cut open.

"This is deep," said Ross. "It'll require cleaning and bandaging. We should return home."

"We don't have any bandages," she said.

"I can use one of Mr. Gather's shirts, or a—"

"No!" Billy said, louder than he meant to. "You can't cut up Dad's shirts."

Beau turned her head, her eyes met his, and Billy instantly knew he had done something wrong. There was no mistaking that look. She took two quick steps and grabbed his arm.

"What were you *thinking*?"

"What'd I do?"

She looked angry again, like she was trying not to yell at him, but not trying that hard. "You can't do stupid stuff like that, Billy! Not anymore."

"But what did I do?"

"I told you to be careful and you ran right at them. You ran away from me and Ross and you ran right to the Pakka."

"I didn't *run*."

"You sure as fuck didn't stay *away* from them."

Billy gasped, Beau hadn't sworn in months. She'd been trying to be good. Trying to be a grown-up. But now her eyes were angry and her brow was wrinkled and her turned-up nose was flaring with every breath.

"I keep telling you not to trust them. Zock might be your friend, but the rest of them just want to hurt you. Hurt *us*."

"I didn't know they were there! I just saw Zock."

"I . . ." Her anger went away all at once and she wrapped her good arm around him. Pulled him tight. "You've got to be more careful, okay? Responsible. Think before you do stuff."

"Sorry," he said into her armpit.

"It's just the two of us now. Dad . . . Dad can't bail us out anymore if we do something dumb. So you've got to be careful, okay? Because I'm not as good at saving your butt as he is. Was."

The word made him shudder. And it shook other thoughts loose. Earlier thoughts that he hadn't really put all the way together. "Okay. But then you can't do stupid stuff, either."

"What do you mean?"

"You can't climb the cliff! What will me and Ross do if you . . . if something . . ."

And it all washed over him. Beau falling. Plummeting down the side of the cliff. So high up he'd only see a little shape of her. The way the bad guys died in Disney movies, but Beau wasn't the bad guy.

He tried to say something else and realized he was gulping air. Getting ready to bawl like a baby. He tried to stop it and made little hiccup sounds.

She squeezed him even tighter. "Hey. *Hey*. You're right. You're right, that was stupid. I shouldn't climb it. I won't do it."

"You promise?"

"Yeah."

"A *real* promise?"

"A real promise. Ross can be my witness. Ross?"

"Yes, Miss Beau?"

"I promise Billy and you that I'm not going to try to climb the cliffs. Never again. Cross my heart and hope to . . . cross my heart again."

"Thank you."

"Thanks," said Billy.

"Is that a good enough promise?"

"Yep."

She wrapped her other arm around him, the bloody arm, and squeezed tight.

"Please be careful, Miss Beau."

"It's okay." She gave Billy one last squeeze and let him go. Even gave him a little playful shove.

"Loser."

"Jerk."

"You probably couldn't've made it to the top anyway."

"I could've, twerp, but now I can't because I promised."

"Are we still going to get potatoes?"

She looked into Dickwood Forest. "Probably not tonight. The Pakka might still be hanging around."

Billy sighed. "So we're having mushroom again."

"Sorry."

"It's okay. Does your arm hurt?"

She looked down at the cut. Pressed the sides with her other hand. "It's not as bad as it looks. Don't worry. You're not getting rid of me that easy."

32

NOAH

The doctor, Monique, kept staring at Noah with accusing eyes. At first he'd thought she still doubted his identity, but Ross had introduced him and surely everyone in Roanoke trusted Ross. While she explained Olivia's present state, he tried to remember if he'd said something that could've been seen as dismissive of her ability as a doctor. Then again, he'd been so obsessed with locating Beau it was possible he'd said something that *was* dismissive of her ability.

And then, as she applied a damp cloth to the patient's lips, Noah realized the woman's glare was because he hadn't come to check on Olivia before this morning's visit. Five days his student had been comatose and he hadn't even asked about her. Hell, he'd taken off and left her here. Abandoning her, just like Parker had accused him of doing to them.

So he deserved the glare.

He took in a breath. Glanced over at Ross standing by the little room's doorway. Looked Monique in the eye. "You've clearly been doing everything you can. We're lucky you're here. She's lucky."

"Oui. Ahhhh, you see?"

One of Olivia's eyelids trembled. It stopped, then both eyes moved in sync. Rapid eye movement. Dreaming. It continued for a few seconds and then her eyes went still beneath their lids.

Noah tried to remember what little he knew about comas. "This is good, right?"

"Oui. She has been completely unresponsive this past week. Now, thanks to Joshua's compounds, her pulse is stronger, her breathing is deeper and I am getting small reactions. Observe."

Monique reached down and squeezed the skin of Olivia's forearm. Not a pinch, but close to it. The fingers at the end of the arm shifted. A tiny movement, but definitely movement.

Monique lifted her arm and pulled aside the simple curtain above the bed. The room brightened notably. Olivia's eyes twitched again, and for a moment her eyelids tightened enough to make faint wrinkles on her face. Monique let the curtain drop back into place.

"She still does not wake, but I believe she is much closer to being asleep now. Not so much comatose."

"This seems good. Do you think . . . is there a chance she could wake up?"

Monique shook her head, and her dangling curls swished back and forth across her shoulders. "I cannot say, especially when we consider the source of her condition. Up until now I could not even say if this had been a true coma or if the glass obelisk had caused irreparable brain damage. She may wake up in an hour, tomorrow, or in a few days. But I feel more confident that she may wake up."

Noah glanced down at Olivia. One of her eyes twitched again. Still dreaming.

He cleared his throat. "I have to be honest. When Parker and Josh told me you'd given her drugs, I was worried. But . . . I was wrong. You all knew what you were doing."

"We did not. We made what we felt was the best choice at the time. Even so, I thank you for your faith in us. It is . . ."

She closed her mouth. Looked down at Olivia.

"Yes?"

Monique straightened her shoulders. Looked him in the eye. "Forgive me for being so forthright, but it is good to hear you speak more like the Billy Gather I have heard stories of, and not like the man who first appeared at our gates."

Noah looked at Ross. Back at her. "I'm sorry. I wasn't . . . I wasn't in a good place then."

Monique bowed her head politely and made a low sound, not even a whisper.

Then her head turned quickly, and Noah realized she hadn't made the sound.

Olivia's lips moved. Brushed each other. Another sound, barely more than breath.

"Is she—"

Monique silenced him with a finger. She lifted her hair, set her ear close to the other woman's mouth. Another faint noise. And another. Two more, close together, but the last one faded into a soft exhale.

Monique straightened up. Looked at Ross. "Could you hear her?"

"It was at the edge of my range of hearing, but I believe so, Madame Cadieux."

"Did you hear the first two words?"

"Yes."

Noah looked back and forth between them. "Well?"

"Mx. Olivia said six words. Skull. Self. Place. Own. Discomfort. She lost strength with the last word, but I believe it was 'bee.'"

"Bee?" echoed Noah.

Monique nodded. "That is what I heard as well."

He ran the words through his mind again. "I don't know what any of that means."

"It may not mean anything. Random words as she talks in her sleep. But it means she is closer to waking up. This is a good sign."

Noah looked at Olivia. The young woman had gone still. Low, shallow breaths. But something about her face looked more alive than it had.

"Thank you. Again."

Monique bowed her head. "I will let you know if she regains consciousness, of course."

Ross's head bowed with a faint squeak of plastic and metal. "Thank you for your time, Madame Cadieux."

Noah showed himself out. Ross followed, his walking stick thumping on the floorboards. He paused at the door to lift his hood over his head. After a few hundred years, even an android feared sun damage, apparently.

Parker, Sam, and Josh waited for them outside by the obelisk. Three Roanokers walked past them, all headed for the gate. Two men and a woman. Each of them carried a big sack of grain or an overfull basket. The woman, dressed in a long, patch-covered jacket, gave them a long stare as she walked past.

"How is she?" asked Sam.

"Better," said Noah. "She spoke."

Sam's brows went up. Josh smiled triumphantly. "I knew it would work. Well, suspected. Hoped."

Parker looked at the door, as if expecting Olivia to step out dramatically. "What did she say?"

"Just random words. Talking in her sleep nonsense. But she's talking."

Sam sighed in relief. "Does she—does the doctor have any idea when she's going to wake up?"

Noah shook his head and shrugged. "Hopefully soon."

"So we're still waiting."

"Still waiting. Sorry."

They all stood there for a moment.

"There's something else we should probably talk about," Noah said, remembering the long-coated woman's accusing look.

Parker laughed. "There's *so* many things we need to talk about."

"True enough. This is one more thing Ross and I talked about over breakfast. We're getting close to . . . you know that old saying? House guests and fish?"

"They're throwing us out?" Fear climbed across Josh's face.

Noah shook his head. "We're not being thrown out. We're being asked to, well, give back. This is sort of a commune. They've been giving us time to get adjusted, but it's getting to the point where we need to start thinking about chipping in."

"Chipping in?" echoed Parker. She turned to look after the trio lugging supplies toward the gate.

Ross shifted his fingers on his walking stick. "It's customary for individuals to contribute to Roanoke's daily requirements," the android explained. "Guard duty. Food production and preparation. Repairs."

Sam coughed out a little laugh. "Oh no. Socialism at the dawn of time."

"It's not the dawn of time." Parker's face had an expression Noah knew too well. She was ready to argue. "Do we have any say in this?"

Noah looked at Ross. Back to her. "Again, they're not going to throw us out. But we are eating our fair share of food right now. And claiming houses." He glanced at Josh.

"Nobody told me the houses came with strings attached."

"The only attached strings are in the thatch bundles," said Ross. He extended a skeletal finger and pointed at the rooftop across the street.

"That's not what I meant."

"I'm aware, Josh. It was my attempt to inject some humor into what's clearly a difficult discussion for some of you."

"We need to figure out what's going on with the sky," said Parker. "And the cliffs. And where we are. Has it occurred to anybody that 'everyone chipping in' is probably the reason nobody ever learns anything about this place."

"No point learning anything if you can't survive," Josh replied.

"Right, but shouldn't the ultimate goal here be getting out of this place? Not just getting to tomorrow or next week."

"We can't get out if we don't make it to next week," Noah said. "We learned that quick when I was a kid."

"This isn't like when you were a kid. There's a support system now. You figured this out, at least on the other side. You can do it from here, too. But we're not figuring anything out if we're all busy . . . watering corn or something. We need to have priorities."

Another beat of silence. The trio, empty-handed now, half-jogged up the path toward them. Past them again. Noah felt a distant tremor. Something big—lots of big things—on the move. Maybe Diedrich taking his dinosaurs out to the field.

Sam felt it too, and looked off toward the gates, where more people carried bundles and baskets. "What's going on?"

"It's a tribute day," explained Ross. "The Klaa collect their bimonthly tithe of food and goods from Roanoke."

The mention of tribute danced through Noah's head. Pyr had said something about it on the walk back from the cave. He'd glazed over it at the time.

"That's why you grow so much food," said Sam.

"That's correct, Sam."

Noah looked at the people at the gate. Back up toward the storehouse. Wondered how much tribute Roanoke handed over.

"I used to stay with my aunt in Boston when I was a kid," said Sam. "She had a community garden plot. I liked working it with her. Plus it'd—I'd get to work with dinosaurs."

Josh tapped his chin slowly. Thoughtfully. Nodded toward the doctor's house. "I could probably help Monique. I don't know a lot about chemistry, but I could share what I know about interactions and . . ."

Sam shook his head. "Oh, just ask her out, for Christ's sake."

"No," said Parker. She shook her wrists to adjust the sleeves of her shirt. Glared at the cuffs. "I'm not doing this. I'm not giving up."

"No one's asking you to give up," said Noah.

"Yes, you are. Listen to yourselves. You're all agreeing we're stuck here. You've just accepted we're never getting out and moving on with our new lives here."

He tried to come up with a counterpoint and couldn't.

She turned her attention to Ross. "You're the Timekeeper, right? That's your job here?"

"That's correct, Parker."

"Well then maybe I can be the . . . the star-keeper or something. I can be the person whose job it is to watch the sky."

Noah bit back a sigh. "Parker . . ."

"I'm not going to give up who I am to . . . to bake bread and scramble dinosaur eggs for the community. For two communities." She waved a hand toward the gate and took three hard steps away and back. Almost stomps. Hard enough Noah felt them through the ground. The vibrations tickled the soles of his feet.

Josh looked around. "What *is* that?"

The trio appeared again. Coming out of the storehouse. Then another man joined them. And another woman. All carrying sacks and bundles. They marched past the obelisk, heading for the gate.

Now there were voices, too. Shouts. The low drone of the didgeridoo echoed across the little village.

Noah turned to the android. "Ross, what's going on?"

"It's the warning tone. Something is approaching Roanoke."

"Something?" Josh asked. "Like a dinosaur?"

Noah took a few steps, then realized he was jogging toward the gate. Then running. He heard the others behind him.

He could hear the rumble now. Like a line of big trucks were driving by outside the walls. He'd been out in Los Angeles years ago for a conference and felt the same thing. One of the other attendees laughed when he mentioned it, told him he'd survived his first California earthquake.

The valley trembles beneath her feet, Pyr had said.

Someone sprinted out from the side path ahead of them. A man with sawdust-flecked hair tied back in a bouncing ponytail. He ran past the guardhouse, also heading for the gate.

Noah caught a quick glimpse of maybe twenty baskets and sacks piled up outside and then blue-skinned Thate dropped the bar across the closed gate. The Vietnam vet, Emerson, stood by one of the open closet doors of the guardhouse, handing out weapons. Wooden bows and quivers of arrows. More spears. Ponytail guy already had a quiver slung over his shoulder. A woman climbed the ladder up to the walkway.

Emerson glanced at them. "Any of you know how to use a bow?"

Noah looked at the weapons. "I know the basics."

Emerson shoved a longbow and quiver into his hands. "Anyone else?"

"It's been a few years," Josh began, "but I could probably—"

A bundle of weapons slapped into his chest. "Go. Get up there. You two?"

Noah looked back over his shoulder, saw Parker shake her head. Sam opened his mouth to say something, but Emerson was pushing spears at them. Pyr waited behind them. Their eyes met and she silently directed him up the ladder.

Noah went up.

At least a dozen people already manned the walls. Shino. Warwick. The two farmers, Diedrich and Dak Ho. A handful of other people he vaguely recognized. They stashed their spears and bows down by their feet. Out of sight, but easy to grab. Most of them stared out toward the forest.

Many of them looked nervous.

"Go!" Warwick waved him down the walkway. "Spread out down the wall. Try to space yehself evenly."

He glanced over his shoulder, saw Josh coming up over the top of the ladder. Parker a few rungs below him. Down at the guardhouse, Monique slung a quiver over her shoulder.

Noah headed down the wall. Heard more people get called-out instructions. He passed a few people, found himself standing alone on the walkway, decided he'd found his place. A few people had stashed their bows with one arrow free of the quiver, so he did the same.

The tremors reached up through the wall. Tapped his toes and heels and calves. The rumble hung in the air, still more felt than heard. Big trucks. Low-flying planes. Charging dinosaurs.

It would take a lot of arrows to stop a dinosaur stampede.

The Egyptian woman, Neith, stood at the wall's far corner. Her hand shielded her eyes as she looked out over the distant trees. Tiny shapes leaped into the air. Microraptors fleeing, deciding the open sky was safer than staying below the canopy. A pair of arrows hung from her belt, almost hidden in the pleats and lines of her skirt. A shorter, thicker-looking bow balanced on one of her feet.

Josh took a place next to him. Sam and Parker filled in the rest of the way to the corner. Pyr squeezed in on his other side, and he shuffled down the wall to accommodate her. Everyone shifted, found space, looked out at the forest.

Parker looked at the Egyptian woman. Over at Pyr. "What do I do with this?" She held up her spear.

"Set it where it's out of sight, but you can grab it quickly," Qiang told her. He walked behind them, like a general inspecting his troops. Noah noticed he'd pushed the knife on his belt around to be hidden at the small of his back.

"Yes, but what do I *do* with it?"

"If you need to do anything, you won't need to ask." Qiang settled in between Pyr and Noah.

"What's going on?" Noah asked him.

Qiang traded looks with Pyr. "She usually doesn't come to collect tribute. She's probably here to see you."

"She? You mean . . ."

Pyr nodded. "The Empress."

Another tremor shook the walls.

33

JOSH

Josh wasn't sure why he said he could use a bow and arrow. Partly a bit of peer pressure when Noah had said he could. Partly because all the CW shows and *Hawkeye* had made it look easy. Of course, the whole point of Clint and Kate was they'd been training for years, so, yeah, sure it looked easy for them.

That and they were just actors playing a part.

And now here he was, up on the big wall with a quiver and bow at his feet, looking out over the cornfields and the bean fields and the . . . the whatever-those-green-things-were fields.

The ground shook like a bridge at rush hour. A low, deep vibration he could feel in his bones. It pulsed up in waves, the ultimate concert bass. It rattled the bamboo under his feet.

Noah and Qiang and Pyr were talking about the "Empress" and none of it sounded good. They'd talked a little bit last night about the Neanderthals and the balance of power, but political stuff always bored Josh. Especially while they were all safely inside the walls.

Now he wished he'd paid a little more attention.

A couple people had pulled arrows out to have them ready, so he fumbled one out of the quiver and set it near the longbow's grip. Was this a longbow? Longbows needed a lot of strength to pull the string, didn't they? Not like the high-tech ones with the wheels, like Clint used. More like Kate Bishop's.

He really had to stop thinking about *Hawkeye.* It wasn't going to help. They hadn't even given him any trick arrows. Or if they did, they hadn't told him which ones they were.

More of the black raptor-birds flew up out of the trees. Like every horror movie, where the birds take off before the big disaster. Or ahead of the monster.

The little murmurs and quiet conversations along the walkway had stopped. He looked down the line, saw Monique far down the wall. She looked a little nervous, even from here.

He looked back at the trees in time to see the dinosaur stride out into the field.

Noah had told them about the Neanderthal riding the dinosaur but holy shit it still made Josh's brain freeze up for a minute. Big, feathered raptor the size of a horse. Muscly caveman riding it. A crude saddle without stirrups. The rider held reins in one hand, a long spear in the other.

Another rider came out of the trees a few yards away. They both urged their mounts forward. They half-vanished in the fields, like swimmers in a deep pool, only appearing here and there. The raptors knocked down stalks and crushed plants under big clawed feet. Josh didn't think the riders were being deliberately destructive, but it didn't look like they were making any real effort not to be. One of them glanced up at the red astronaut scarecrow as it went by and jabbed the spacesuit with his spear.

Then something else moved in the shadows of the distant trees.

Because of the distance, Josh's first thought was "cat," even with the bulldog stance and heavy shoulders. There'd been a big old unfixed tomcat who'd hung around his apartment, and the tan-and-brown spotted one pacing out of the trees reminded him of that grumpy boy. He could see its muscles rippling, the way it swung its head side to side, even a thick ruff of fur around its neck and shoulders. Not a full mane, but longer and thicker than the rest of its fur.

Then it stepped fully out of the trees and two things hit Josh at the same time. The first was the sheer size of it. His brain used the nearby cornstalks and the astronaut scarecrow as a size reference. It had to be close to four feet tall at the shoulder, and maybe twice that long. Not a cat, but a friggin' monstrous leopard-tiger thing with two huge teeth that hung down past its lower jaw.

Then there was the saber-toothed tiger's rider. The woman.

The Empress.

In the corner of his eye, he saw Sam's jaw drop. "Holy fuck."

Big white hair, teased out and making a bigger mane than the tiger had. The pale furs she wore let her blend into the big cat. From this angle and distance, Josh couldn't tell exactly where she ended and the tiger began. And then the taller crops blocked any clear view of her.

The first Neanderthals made it into the clearing around Roanoke just as a second set came out of the trees. Honor guards? Four of them all around their Empress as she rode the sabertooth forward. And then a small crowd on foot after them. Maybe fifteen or twenty of them. They moved up to collect the sacks and baskets piled in front of the gate and retreated with their armloads of tribute.

Josh suddenly realized how low the walls around the village were. They were bigger than anything else, but they still only stood fifteen, maybe sixteen feet tall. He wondered how high the raptors could jump. High enough to reach the top of the wall, maybe, although Noah had insisted a couple times the movies got a lot of stuff wrong.

One of the Neanderthals looked up at him. At them? He could see simple beads in her hair and a few leather ties. Her glare drifted from one person to the next. He'd been in a few business negotiations where things had gone bad and seen eyes like that. The woman on the dinosaur's back was thinking about how she'd kill some people.

And then the big tiger stepped clear of the fields. It rolled its head side to side. Yawned to show off those massive, curved fangs. Yawned again, but this time a grumbly roar shook the air. It blended with the tremors running through the ground and up the walls, like some high-tech sonic weapon designed to make people shit their pants.

The woman looked up at them lazily as the saber-toothed tiger took a few more paces forward. Utterly confident. Knowing without any doubt she was in complete control of everything here. Of every life here.

Josh had seen that look once or twice in his career too.

The Empress looked like some weird fantasy painting by Boris Vallejo or Frank Frazetta come to life. The sort of barbarian fantasy woman you'd see on the cover of an old fantasy novel or an '80s album cover or maybe the side of a van. The billowing mane of white hair. Tight brown skin striped with white paint or chalk. Muscled arms and shoulders and legs and abs. What she wore looked less like clothing and more like furs and hides that'd been tied in place across her body. Small horns or maybe large teeth surrounded her head, but Josh couldn't tell if they were a crown or some kind of decorations woven into her thick cloud of hair.

She looked up at them, casually noting the line of villagers at the top of the wall. A small chin and narrow cheeks gave her a wedge-shaped face, accented by a half dozen vertical white stripes of paint. Small, upturned nose. White brows over wide, super-pale eyes. She didn't look like a Neanderthal, but she didn't really look . . . well, human, either. Something he couldn't put a finger on. Uncanny valley stuff. He had absolutely no idea how old she was. She could've been a mature-looking twenty-five or an in-great-shape fifty.

The saber-toothed tiger let out another roar. The Empress twisted her hand deeper into its short mane. The big cat made a bone-rattling noise somewhere between a growl and a purr, then went quiet.

"I'm told there are newcomers in my valley. That they can speak the language of the Klaa."

Josh felt his eyes bug. He'd expected halting caveman grunts or a gruff accent or . . . something. But the Empress's words could've come from any demanding executive or lawyer. The faint hint of an accent almost sounded . . . European? It reminded him of an old acquaintance, an arrogant chemist who'd used a fake accent for so long the man forgot how to speak normally.

Qiang stepped forward. "There are newcomers. They are our people."

"Everyone here is mine. My subjects."

"Yes. My apologies."

"Show them to me."

She never raised her voice. Utter confidence and authority.

Qiang took a half step back on the bamboo walkway. He and Noah traded a look, and then Noah turned to look at Josh, gave a little nod, and they both turned to look at Parker and Sam.

Noah stepped forward, right up against the top of the wall. Josh did the same, shuffling over his bow and as close to the upright logs as he could without tipping himself over. The Neanderthals below raised spears. One of the raptors let out a trill that grew into a shriek.

"There are more. I've been told seven appeared here a week ago."

"One of them is sick and cannot move." Qiang gestured behind him, at the village. A slow movement, the kind you made around people with itchy trigger fingers. "Two more died as they crossed the valley on their way here."

The Empress stared at him for a moment.

Her heels moved against the tiger's flanks and it turned, pacing along the wall. She looked up at them, studying each face before the big cat carried her in front of the next one. She locked eyes with Josh for a moment, studied him, dismissed him, and moved on to Sam. Her hips swayed on the tiger's back as it walked, and Josh had to admit it would've been kind of sexy if the woman and the animal didn't both have so much cold-blooded murder in their eyes.

The Empress got to the end of the wall and the tiger turned again, carrying her back to Qiang and Noah. "You attacked B'Kar. One of my people. You know the law."

Qiang shook his head. "My people defended themselves."

"You know the law."

She barked out three coarse syllables and one of the Neanderthals threw its spear at the wall. Threw felt like such a slow word. Josh only saw a blur, an afterimage of movement, and it took two more heartbeats before he realized the spear had gone toward the section of wall where Monique had been standing. He leaned back, saw her sprawled on the bamboo walkway, one arm hanging over the edge, and Josh's already-pounding heart tripped and stumbled in his chest.

Her fingers moved. Her arm came back up. She rolled away from the edge, turned her head to look at the person standing near her.

Thate stood with one arm stretched out. He'd shoved Monique aside. Saved her. The blue man's other arm wrapped tight around his body, holding the bloody spear in place. Even from here, Josh could see the bright red blood. A sign of high oxygen.

Thate set his other hand on the spear, straightened his arms, pulled the shaft out of his side. More blood ran down his thigh. He held the spear out over the wall. Let it drop down below. Squeezed his arm over his wounds.

The spear-throwing Neanderthal scowled. One of the others pulled back its own arm, ready to throw, but Qiang yelled a rough sound and they paused. "Blood has been spilled. Blood for blood. We know the law."

The Empress smirked up at him. "You know the law."

She spoke a few quick words to the Neanderthals, and they grudgingly lowered their spears.

Her eyes came back up. She looked Josh in the eyes, and then her gaze jumped to Sam. "Which of you speaks our language?"

Josh glanced over at Noah. The professor looked . . . confused? Stunned? Like all of his happy memories had crashed headfirst into the actual violence of this place. Like when Kyle got eaten by the dinosaur.

Qiang set his hand on Noah's shoulder. It woke Noah out of his trance, but he still looked uncertain. His eyes never left the Empress. "It's me," he said. But something about those two words sounded a little off to Josh. Like Noah was answering a different question that just happened to have the same answer.

Noah spoke a few Neanderthal words, and then a few more. Down below, the Empress and her minions scowled up at him. Noah spoke maybe another two sentences, going off the rhythm of the sounds, then stopped to stare back at the Empress.

Now everyone looked a little confused.

"What the hell is going on?" whispered Sam.

The white-haired woman studied Noah's face. His clothes. "How do you know our language?"

"I learned it as a boy."

"Who are you?"

"Who are *you*?"

A low murmur ran along the wall. Josh felt the tension climb a few notches. Saw Neanderthals shift their grips on their weapons.

"I am your Empress. This is my valley."

Noah straightened up a little. "The valley doesn't belong to anyone."

"It belongs to me!" The saber-toothed tiger picked up on her tension, her aggression, and let out another long, dangerous purr. "It has always been mine. I have been here since the beginning. I have watched it grow."

Qiang took a quick breath. Josh glanced at him. Saw the face of a man who knew a situation was spiraling out of control, who desperately wanted to calm things down, but also had absolutely no idea how to do it.

"I was here at the beginning," said Noah. "I knew the valley when it was small. When there was no lake. When the Castaway lived in the Castle. And I don't remember there being an Empress. Just me and my dad. And my sister."

She took in a breath, and Josh saw her nostrils flare as she let it out. Her expression showed absolute confidence and control again. The brief flare of anger and uncertainty was gone. She stared up at Noah. "Who are you?"

"My name's Noah Barnes. When I was here as a boy, with my family, I was called Billy Gather."

The Empress almost hid her flinch. "Billy Gather died hundreds of years ago."

"I didn't."

"You lie."

"Nope."

She locked eyes with him. Josh could see the coldness in her gaze, but also . . . worry? He was good with people—maybe even with cave people—and the vibe coming off the Empress was she'd been . . . caught? Worried she'd been found out?

"You are not him."

Noah didn't say anything.

"You are not him," she repeated.

"He is," said Qiang. "He knows the valley. Ross—the mechanical man—knows him."

"You are lying to your Empress. Billy Gather is dead."

"I'm not. I went away. I came back."

The Empress kicked her heels and the big cat wheeled around in a full circle. "Nothing comes here without my permission. Nothing happens here without my consent." She pointed up at Qiang. "You know the law."

She yanked on the sabertooth's mane. It let out a roar and paced back through the fields toward the forest. The Neanderthals took another moment, glaring at the villagers, and then their raptor mounts turned around and stomped after the Empress.

For a moment Josh waited for someone to grab their bow. For an arrow to appear in a Neanderthal back. For half a dozen of them to sprout from the dinosaur's feathered hide. But then he figured out what these people probably already knew. They didn't have enough arrows to stop them all. He imagined one of the raptors suddenly without a rider, leaping up onto the wall, right into the guards.

The last of the dinosaurs vanished into the woods and Josh looked down the line of people along the wall. Lots of nervous, on-edge faces. Monique checking Thate's pierced side. Emerson glaring out at the woods, after the Neanderthals and the Empress.

Qiang had his eyes closed. "You shouldn't've angered her."

The stunned expression had found its way back to Noah's face, his brief confidence gone. He stared after the Empress, then glanced at Qiang. "I answered her questions."

"You didn't give the answers she wanted."

"I gave her the truth."

"The only truth that matters is the one she wants!" Qiang snapped.

Pyr picked up her quiver. "She would've known if he lied to her."

"Yep," said Noah. "I think she would've."

He slipped past Qiang and Pyr, past half a dozen other villagers, and swung himself down onto the ladder. Sam and Parker headed after him, giving Josh quick looks of concern. Pyr followed close behind them.

Josh fell in line. While he waited for his turn on the ladder, he looked for Monique again. Still patching up Thate, wrapping his wounded stomach with rough linen bandages. Josh wondered if the blue man had some kind of pain resistance or accelerated healing or something.

Monique met his eyes as his turn on the ladder came. She sent a nervous smile at him. He tried not to make too much of it.

Noah had passed the guardhouse but didn't seem to be heading anywhere. Walking because he needed to walk, to not be standing still. Parker, Sam, and Pyr all hung a few yards back, watching him. Ross had followed too, and Noah looked like he was muttering at the robot.

Josh caught up to them in time for Noah to turn on Pyr. "Why did you lie to me?"

"Lie? About what?"

"Don't . . ." He paced back and forth a few more times, displaying *big tweaker energy*, as one of Josh's coworkers called it. "I can still do it. She's alive. She's still here and she's alive."

Josh saw the looks on everyone else's face. Parker. Sam. Pyr. Awe, dread, some despair. Faces for when the deal has somehow, inexplicably gone south again. He blurted out the question even as the answer stumbled into his mind. "Who's alive?"

Noah looked at him. "The Empress. She's my sister. She's Beau."

34

SAM

Sam saw it coming, but it still left him dizzy. "What?"

Noah looked at Sam as if he'd missed the most obvious thing on Earth. "I mean, who else could she be?" He turned his attention to Ross. "Why didn't you tell me?"

"I didn't know, Noah."

"How could you not—they must've wiped your memory of this, too."

"Nobody wiped his memory," said Pyr. "Not of this, anyway."

Sam nodded in agreement. "She doesn't look anything like Beau."

Noah's brow knotted up. "How would you know?"

"I've seen at least three dozen pictures of her. There's almost as many of her in the books as there are of you."

"And you didn't recognize me."

"You're thirty years older. And you've got a beard now!"

"She's older, too. Ross, you remember what Beau looked like, right?"

For a moment Sam swore the android was considering how to phrase a response. "There are a few physical similarities between Ms. Beau and the Empress, Noah, but their behavior is markedly different."

"I remember her eyes. Those are her eyes."

"They were twenty feet away," said Josh.

"The shape of her face. Her nose. Her size. Her voice. She speaks English!"

"Lots of people here speak English," Pyr said.

Parker stepped next to Sam. A wall of two against their professor's beliefs. "Noah, if that was Beau she'd have to be over four hundred years old now."

"Four hundred and fifty-one," said Ross.

"Thanks. It can't be her."

"It can. It is."

"But how?"

"It might have something to do with the regenerative nature of the valley. People live longer, healthier lives here."

"That's debatable," murmured Pyr.

Noah pushed past her comment. "Plus, the valley exists outside of time. It could explain any number of—"

"It doesn't exist outside of time," said Parker. "It exists now. Here in the present. All the evidence—"

"No!" Noah's hand slashed through the air, cutting her off. "It's her. The slower time flow could explain it."

"Time doesn't flow any differently here."

"It does. Trust me, I understand the valley better than—"

"Oh for Christ's sake NO YOU DON'T!"

Sam hadn't meant to yell. He hadn't meant to say anything. But now the shout was bouncing between the wooden buildings and they were all looking at him and the words were pouring out too fast to stop them.

"You keep—you don't know this place at all. You don't know anything about it or how it works. Everyone here knows more about it than you. *Everyone.* You knew some idealized version of it your dad and sister fed you because you were ten and they didn't want you to snap. And you're so fucking desperate to hang on to—to have your life mean something, you're ignoring the facts staring you in the face. You're like some goddamn fanboy whining because something doesn't line up with your memories of a movie you saw when you were eight."

Noah took in a breath. "My sister is still ali—"

"Your sister's DEAD, Noah. She died years ago! Centuries ago!"

Parker flinched. So did Josh. And Pyr. Even Ross shuddered at the shouted words.

Noah pointed at the gate, the fields, the forest with a shaking finger. "Then who is that?"

Sam sighed. His anger was spent, an energy drink explosively spraying its contents for a few seconds and now it was flat. He felt like a dick, but he knew it had to be said. "I've got no idea. She could be absolutely anyone. From any point in history. But I'm sure she's not Beau Gather."

"A good scientist should always be open to new possibilities."

"Well, then I guess you're not a good scientist."

Noah's mouth flapped open and shut, but no sound came out. For an awful moment Sam thought the professor would start crying again, like he had in the cave. "She knew me. You all saw it."

"She knew you stood up to her," Josh said. "That's what got her attention."

Noah shook his head. "No. No, it's her. It has to be."

Sam tried to think of another angle, another line of reasoning, and then Monique spared him by calling at them to clear the road. She had one of Thate's arms around her neck, and blood covered the blue man's side. Thate moved with a stagger but seemed to be doing pretty well for a guy bleeding out of an eight-inch gouge.

Pyr set a hand on Thate's shoulder as he hobbled past. "How bad is it?"

He turned, even though Monique tried to keep guiding him toward her little office. "Had worse."

"It looks awful," said Sam, thankful for the interruption.

The blue man managed a weak smile. "This isn't even the first time they've impaled me with a spear."

"You will be fine," said Monique. "Halfway healed already. I don't know why I will waste my good thread on you."

"You need help?" asked Pyr.

"It would be appreciated."

She stepped in and replaced Monique, pulling Thate up a little taller as she looped his arm across her own shoulders, and they hobbled away.

Noah stared at the gate. At the walkway along the top of the wall.

Sam's mind slid back to lines of reasoning. Ways they could reach Noah. "Ross?"

"Yes, Sam?"

"How long has the Empress been in the valley?"

"The exact date of her arrival is unknown. Her first known appearance was three hundred nineteen years ago."

Noah was paying attention again. "So she's over three hundred years old?"

"Again, I can't say. I did not see her in person until two hundred seventy-three years ago. Her appearance hasn't changed much during this time frame, so it's possible she's significantly older."

"Who's the oldest—" Parker stopped, started her question again. "Who's the longest-lived person in the valley that you know of?"

"Diedrich Rommel is currently the oldest human resident of the valley at sixty-three. Juliette Ford, the previous village elder, was one hundred and seventeen at her death."

"So people *do* live longer here."

"Longer is a relative term, but there have been several notable lifespans during my time here."

Noah nodded. "See?"

Qiang and Emerson approached, and Sam got the immediate vibe the elder was trying to walk away from a conversation and the old soldier wouldn't let him. "You know we should do it," insisted Emerson.

"It's too big a risk."

"No, it's not. Neith can do it."

"That's not what I mean and you know it." He saw Sam watching, listening, and gave a polite acknowledgment. Turned his head to each of the others in turn as they passed by. "We're done, Emerson."

"It needs to happen!"

They walked up the path, deeper into Roanoke.

Parker watched them go. "What do you think that's about?"

"I'm guessing something else caveman-related," said Josh. "Maybe some defense budget thing."

Noah stared back at the wall, out at the valley. "Has the Empress always ruled the Klaa?"

The android set both hands on his walking stick and lowered his head slightly, shading his eyes with his hood. "Again, I can't say. My understanding is the Klaa tribe deferred to the Empress from her first appearance. It's been discussed over the years how unusual this is, given their inherent xenophobia."

Sam frowned. "Were the first tribe, the Pakka, assimilated into the Klaa or . . . y'know, killed off?"

"I'm afraid I don't know."

"I'd guess assimilated," said Parker. "At least the women. Need all you can get to grow the tribe."

Sam ran some quick numbers in his head. "Do they reproduce faster than humans? Cro-Magnons, I guess?"

"Wouldn't matter," Josh said.

"Why?"

He shrugged. "Nothing gets pregnant in the valley. Monique told me about it the other day."

Sam's brows furrowed. "They can't carry them to term?"

"As I understood it, nobody ever gets pregnant. Human or dinosaurs. Nothing has kids."

"Nothing?"

Josh shook his head. "That's why there's no little Roanokers. The only time you get kids in the valley is if they get wormholed here or whatever." He dipped his head to Noah. "She's never even heard of a human baby being born here. Or a dinosaur baby."

"Seriously?" asked Parker.

"Yeah. They still lay eggs, like a bird would, but no little dino-babies."

She looked back at the gate. Up at the walls. "So if nothing has babies, where are all the Neanderthals coming from? There's ten times more of them here than us, right?"

Another shrug from Josh. "They're just getting wormholed like everything else."

"Let's not call it that."

"He's right, though," said Sam. "I mean, if things can't breed in the valley, it's the only way anything increases here, population-wise. The wormhole scoops up Neanderthals now and then. Or dinosaurs. Us. The occasional android butler."

One of Ross's joints squeaked. "To the best of my knowledge, Sam, I'm still unique in the valley's history."

Parker shook her head. "No. No, that still doesn't make sense."

Sam juggled a half dozen topics in his head and bit back a snort. "Which part?"

Josh's hand went back up. "I've got an idea."

"Sure," said Parker. "I'll take anything."

Josh let his hand stretch out, swinging to take in the valley. "We were talking last night about what's past the cliffs, right?"

"Yeah?"

"Well, what if we're in Neanderthal time? Sixty thousand years ago or whatever. So the Klaa are the majority because they wander in here and then they can't get out, like us."

Parker shook her head. "No. Star positions don't lie. Furthest we're back is maaaaybe 1800."

Noah cleared his throat. "Neanderthals are matriarchal. If they recognized Beau as an elder presence in the valley, they might've accepted her. And then maybe she could've made a challenge for leadership. She would've been taller than most of them. And smarter."

Sam bit back a groan. Parker's shoulders tensed. Josh didn't even try to hide his eye roll.

A shout from up the road saved them from saying anything else.

"M'sieur Gather! Joshua! Quickly—your friend is awake!"

35

PARKER

Olivia looked up at her from the bed. Her gaze flitted to Noah, Sam, and Josh, kept lingering on Monique. Parker wasn't sure because they kept moving around so fast, but it looked like one of Olivia's eyes was dilated more than the other one.

"Self," Olivia said. "Region individual identity existence being."

Across the bed by Monique, Josh's eyes went wide. "Wow."

Monique nodded. "She has been like this since she awoke. She seems aware, but does not seem to be able to speak."

Sam stood at the foot of the bed with Noah. "Is it brain damage? From the shock? Like a stroke or something."

"I cannot say. I heard her from the other room while I was suturing Theta's wound."

Olivia glared at Sam. One eye definitely open more than the other, Parker noted. "Wrecked state self processor peer invalid." She spoke at a normal pace, but with clumsy, flat words. It sounded like she didn't know which ones to emphasize.

"So it's some sort of aphasia?" Noah asked.

"Perhaps. It is too early to say. This may be some disorientation after waking."

Parker crouched low, trying to get herself close to eye level. Olivia's head flopped over on the pillow to look at her. Parker saw the usual glare of resentment there, which she took as a good sign. "Don't talk," she said. "Do you know who I am?"

Olivia took in a breath. Pressed her lips together. A few muffled sounds came from her throat. Then her head jerked up and down.

"Good."

"That might not mean anything," Sam pointed out. "If she's suffered brain damage, she may think she's saying no. Or maybe she thinks you're Noah."

Olivia turned her head. Rolled her eyes at Sam. Then looked at Noah and spat out, "Total self second person others identify."

Josh's lips flexed. "She sounds kind of . . . computery. No offense, Ross."

"Thank you for your concern, Josh," came a voice from the hall.

Parker reached out her arm and pointed at Monique. "Olivia? Do you know who she is?"

Olivia turned. Looked. Shook her head side to side.

Monique smiled at her. "I am your doctor. I have been looking after you while you slept."

"Can you look at Sam?"

She did.

Parker kept pointing at Monique. "Can you look at Parker?"

Olivia looked her in the eyes. The glare of resentment softened a bit. Almost looked appreciative.

Parker looked at the others. "She seems pretty aware to me."

"Unconscious state self extent duration calendar."

"Hey," said Sam, "that sort of made sense."

Parker perked up. "Are you asking how long you've been asleep?"

Olivia's eyes lit up. She bit down on another handful of words, catching them in her mouth and smothering them behind her lips. Her head went up and down.

Parker looked at Noah. Noah looked at Monique, back at Olivia. "It's been almost a week. Five days."

Her eyes went wide. She looked at Parker with desperation in her eyes, and Parker nodded in confirmation. "Whereabouts mystery location group clue area."

Noah crossed his arms and stared at Olivia. "Is it just me, or does anyone else feel like there's a pattern to what she's saying?"

Josh cleared his throat. "I think she's asking where we are."

Parker shook her head. "No. I mean, yeah, that's what she's asking, but Noah's right. There's a . . . a rhythm? Something about the words." She sifted through them in her head, trying to remember the nonsense sentences Olivia had blurted out over the past few minutes.

Sam had his eyes closed. Brow furrowed. He turned his head slightly toward the hall. "Ross?"

"Yes, Sam?"

"Have you been able to hear Olivia talking?"

"I have."

Olivia raised her head, tried to look through everyone crowded into the little room.

Sam's fingers danced back and forth against his thumb. "Is she always saying six words at a time?"

"Yes. Since she first showed signs of consciousness earlier this morning."

Sam opened his eyes and smiled.

Parker straightened up. She looked past Sam's shoulder, saw the hooded android out in the hallway. "Is she also saying all the words in alphabetical order? Or reverse-alphabetical?"

"That's correct, Parker."

Olivia gave up trying to see into the hall and let her head flop back on the pillow. "Whereabouts mystery location group clue area."

Sam pointed a finger. "Same words."

Monique nodded. "A good sign. She may have no actual damage, merely some confusion."

Parker crouched down next to the bed again. "We're still in the valley. Noah's weird dinosaur valley."

Olivia's gaze flitted around the room of bamboo and rough planks, paused on the bedsheets covering her, on Monique, and then back to Parker's face.

"Yeah, we . . . we've found some friends. It turns out Noah and his family weren't the only people who got pulled into this place."

"Substructure region negative mobile location group."

"This is the doctor's office. Clinic?" She looked at Monique. "Apothecary?"

"I am comfortable with either."

Olivia's head thrashed side to side. "Substructure region negative mobile location group."

"I'm not sure that's what she's asking about," said Noah.

"Ummm, question, sorry." Josh had two fingers up again. "How much should we be telling her? Y'know, what she's missed?"

Olivia's eyes went wide. She looked from one face to the next. She twisted her head to look out into the hall. "State pending partner location former being."

Parker didn't need to put too many of those words together to figure out what Olivia had asked. She looked up at Sam. At Noah.

"We probably shouldn't strain her . . ." Sam stopped, looked Olivia in the eyes. "We probably shouldn't overwhelm you with things right now."

"It is probably for the best," said Monique. "Right now what she needs most is some peace and quiet to organize her thoughts."

"State pending partner location former being."

"I'm sorry, Olivia," said Noah. "Logan's dead."

Parker glared at him. So did Sam. Monique put a hand to her mouth.

Noah ignored them. "He died in the same . . . the same accident that put you in a coma. He died, but he saved your life."

Olivia's head thrashed again and she rolled toward Parker, twisting up the sheets. Parker caught her. Tried to keep her on the bed. Olivia fought like a tired little kid, moving her arms back and forth more than actually doing anything with them. She sagged against Parker, then flopped back onto the bed.

It randomly occurred to Parker it was the most physical contact she'd had with Olivia in, well, years.

Monique clapped her hands. Three firm taps of her fingers against the other palm. "Everyone out. All of you. Go. You have seen her, she has seen you, she needs to rest." She shooed them out of the room as if she was waving away flies.

Noah left. Ross moved in the hall, following him out of the apothecary. Sam lingered for a moment, traded looks with Parker, and stepped out.

"You as well," Monique said to Josh. "You have been most helpful, and you have my thanks, but for now . . ." She flicked at the air in front of him, pointed toward the door.

Parker beat him out to the hallway. She hadn't even reached the front door when she heard Sam's raised voice.

"What's your—what the fuck is wrong with you?"

Sam stood outside Monique's flowerbed. Noah and Ross stood a few yards past the obelisk, clearly already off to do something more important. Probably involving Noah's sister.

Noah looked at Parker. Over at Josh. "She needed to know."

"Did she need to know right now?" snapped Sam. "She's been in a coma for a week and ten minutes after she wakes up you tell her her boyfriend's dead?"

Parker stepped closer. "It was an asshole thing to do."

Noah sighed. "I know it seems like it, but I'm willing to bet I've gone through more trauma counseling than all of you put together. Trust me."

Sam shook his head. "I don't have—I'm running real low on trust."

"As soon as the idea was in her head, as soon as she realized he wasn't there, we had to tell her. If we didn't, she'd spend every bit of energy trying to find him. She wouldn't rest, she'd just be worried nonstop until she got answers. It's human nature. This way she can get over it, move on, and start healing."

"Like you have?"

Parker glanced at Sam. He sounded tired again. Then she realized they'd formed a loose line across from Noah and the android, like two groups of old-timey gunfighters squaring off.

"I'm sorry," Noah said. "I know you don't believe me. But it's Beau."

Parker tried to break the silence that followed. "Noah . . ."

He held up a hand. "I don't know how she could've lived this long. How she—how the whole valley ended up like this. But everything we've heard and seen tells me that woman we saw out there is Beau."

Sam sighed. "It's not."

"It's her, Sam. She's alive and I'm going to get her home. Just like the Castaway said."

"You can't even get us home."

They stared at each other for a few more moments. Then Noah walked away. Ross bowed his head politely to Parker and the others, adjusted his skeletal fingers on his walking stick, and followed Noah down the dirt-and-weed path.

Something sank in Parker's gut as they walked away.

Josh stuck his hands in his pockets. Prodded the dirt with the toe of his shoe. "So," he said, "why do you think your friend's talking backward?"

"What?"

"I figured everybody'd want to avoid all the emotional stuff that just went down. It's what I'd do. So I thought I'd get us back on science-talk."

Sam shook his head. "We're not—you know we're astronomers, right? Not neurologists."

"I'm not even sure we're astronomers anymore," said Parker. "I think our boss may have just fired us."

Josh gestured back at the doctor's house. "You want to know what I think's going on with her? Olivia?"

"Sure. But walk while you do."

"Where to?"

Parker waved at the path. "Show me where the empty houses are. The ones up for grabs."

"Moving out after all?"

"Maybe. Just walk."

Josh gave a last hopeful look back at the apothecary's door and led them deeper into Roanoke. Parker still didn't know half the village. Most of it she'd only seen while walking the walls, where every building was thatch roofs and the occasional wooden planks.

"So, you know how sometimes a person might have a bad experience with pharmaceuticals and it'll take them a little time to readjust back to normal once the chemicals wear off?"

Parker let out a sigh. "For someone who's not a drug dealer, it's amazing how often talking with you circles back to drugs."

"Designer pharmaceuticals."

"I had a roommate junior year who went through something like that," Sam said. "He didn't deal well with magic mushrooms. Spent most of the night talking about fingers coming out of the walls and floor, trying to hide in his bed. He was over it by morning, but it was so vivid he still spent a lot of the next day stumbling around, watching everything, not sure if the fingers were going to come back or not."

Josh pointed two fingers at Sam. "Exactly. Your friend's mind had to recalibrate. Sort everything out, get it all back where it's supposed to be."

Parker thought about her little shared office back at the university. In a near-constant state of chaos as grad students moved in and out. "Like rearranging a bookshelf. You've got to pull a lot of it off to organize things by a new method."

"Oh, good analogy. Yeah, I think when Olivia got zapped, it basically dumped her bookshelf out on the floor. Her brain's got everything back up on the shelves, so it's all there, but she still needs to put them all in the right order. So right now she's got this sort of Tourette's thing going on."

A dinosaur screeched up above them as they walked through Roanoke's more or less central intersection. One of the big pterodactyls, or maybe something else. Parker shaded her eyes and watched it do a slow circle. Wondered how high up it was. Wondered if the dinosaurs flew higher than halfway up the cliffs?

"The other possibility," she said, "is she got brain damage from a massive electrical shock and this is how she talks now."

Sam kicked at a tuft of grass. "Yeah. That's more likely, isn't it?"

Josh stopped walking and turned to them with a shrug. "Is it? She got struck by lightning that came out of a mysterious crystal obelisk in the valley at the dawn of time."

"We're not at the dawn of time," said Parker, tugging at the collar of her shirt with a finger. Something about the cut made it feel tight. Constricting.

"My point still stands. This whole place is really weird and I don't think we should be taking anything for granted here. Even cosmic lightning strikes to the brain. What do you think?"

"I think it's not a very scientific way to approach things, but you might be right."

"No, I mean this." Josh looked at Parker, gestured up at the building. "What do you think? Pretty much everything back here's empty. I took the one over there."

Parker looked at the building. Another cottagey house that looked like a small barn. Stone chimney. A small platform had been built over the thatch roof, something between a watchtower and a rooftop deck.

"Ross said a guy lived here years ago and built the platform so he could look at the stars. A navigator from the fifteen hundreds."

"Fifteenth century." Parker shook her wrists and let the cuffs settle again. Pictured putting a table up there, mapping out the sky at night. It was an astronomer's fantasy resort house. The kind of house a grad student could only dream of owning.

It didn't feel like a dream.

36

SAM

Sam stood on the wall and stared up at one particular star.

It was a little odd seeing it like this, but he was 99 percent sure it was Miaplacidus. He could fit the width of two fingers between the star and the top edge of the cliffs behind Roanoke. Almost four degrees. A lot of folks used the trick for sunsets. Sam had been thirteen when he figured out it would work for star movement, too. You just couldn't look away. It was a lot easier to lose track of a random star than a sunset.

Miaplacidus had been four degrees above the cliff top for a while now. Since he started looking, he'd counted off three hundred seconds, five whole minutes, and then lost interest. It didn't move. Nothing up there moved. Nothing had moved since their first night here. Well, since he'd first started actively looking. The exact same sky, all night, from the moment the sun vanished until it reappeared again.

After almost two decades of studying the night sky his brain struggled with seeing it frozen like a photograph.

A low rumble echoed out of the forest and across the fields. He let his gaze drop. Stared across at the forest. Something big moved among the trees, a ripple in the dark shadows.

"Burn," said a voice off to his left. The Japanese woman, Shino. She held a spear loosely upright in one hand, like a walking stick carried for show more than need.

"Sorry?"

She pointed out toward the forest. "Burn. One of the allosauruses. He has red on his face. Like a sunburn."

"You can see that? At night?"

She tapped her ear. "Burn's growl is smooth. Gnash's rattles, like an old woman breathing."

"Okay."

"If you hear Gnash, stay alert. Every few months she tests the walls, and she's tall enough to reach us up here." She tilted her head toward the ground below. "Jump if you have to. Better a broken leg than end up between her teeth."

He looked down at the ground below.

"You have a spear?"

He nodded at the wooden shaft behind him, leaning up against the walkway's railing. He'd been told if he wanted to hang out on the wall, it could serve as a rotation on warden duty.

Their free ride as newcomers was definitely coming to an end.

Shino gave him an approving nod, making her topknot sway. "Keep it close." She turned and moved off toward the far corner of the walkway.

As far as Sam could tell, there were two full-time wardens up here on the walkway at night, plus two or three regular citizens doing their mandatory duty for the village. At the moment that was Shino, Warwick, '70s hippie Marissa, and a scruffy man named John.

And him.

He looked back up at Miaplacidus. Found it easily. It hadn't moved.

The creak and rattle of bamboo pulled his attention. A figure came down the walkway toward him. Parker. Back in the clothes she'd had on when they arrived. Also carrying a spear, although she had it across her shoulders, her wrists hooked over it. "Thought I saw you over here. You taking measurements, too?"

He shook his head. "Couldn't sleep. Wanted to do something familiar. But the sky's just—it's too odd."

"Yeah, I get that." She leaned her head back to look up at the sky. She'd redone her braid, rope-tight again.

They both stared up at the unmoving stars.

"You got rid of your new shirt?"

"Yeah. I don't . . . it wasn't my style. Just needed something while I washed these."

He nodded without looking at her.

"I don't know what I'm going to do when these clothes wear out."

"You can patch them. And they've got more clothes."

"Yeah. I guess so." She let the spear swing down and leaned it next to his.

"Are we—do you think we're stuck here? Forever?"

She sighed. "Noah spent thirty years figuring out how to get back here, and he had a lot more resources than we do. I don't know if we can solve it from this side. Especially without his help."

"Assuming there's even a solution."

"There's got to be something. He had enough of it right to predict where and when he needed to be to get us here."

"Could've been sheer luck."

"Fuck, I hope not. I'm not going to be able to deal with a lifetime of Josh's sci-fi nonsense."

"He's not that bad."

"I can't put up with it. I'm like Carl Sagan that way."

"That and the modesty."

"Hah."

"Plus, he put up with some of it. His son was a writer on one of the old *Star Trek* shows."

"Lies."

"Pretty sure."

She waved him away.

Sam decided what the hell and felt his breath quicken. "I avoid conflict. Run away from it. From everything."

"Could've fooled me, the way you ripped into Noah."

"Yeah. That was—it takes a lot, y'know?"

She gave him a little nod. "I get it."

"I've been—I *was* seeing someone for the past year. Long enough we got a place together. First time I've ever lived with someone."

"Really?"

"Well, I mean, romantically. Got close a couple times but it never felt like the right move until Gabe."

He tried not to blurt the rest out, to find the right words with the right weight, and Parker beat him to it again.

"He dumped you."

Sam stumbled. Relived it was out there, depressed it sounded so . . . basic. "Yeah. He'd been cheating on me. Like, full-on dating someone else. He was going to move out as soon as he found a place, but it was taking too long, so he just told me."

"That sucks."

"Yeah. And I—I ran away. Again. Even though it was technically my apartment. I didn't want to be there with him. Didn't want to watch him packing up his stuff. I remembered that email Noah sent around. Bodies needed. Found out there was—I had two hours before the bus left." He sighed. "Thirty-one and I still deal with breakups like I'm in high school."

"That's why you didn't pack anything useful."

"I don't have anything useful. I hate camping."

"I thought you wanted to live here."

"Yeah. In the well-furnished cave with the loving family and the robot butler. Not in a tent five miles from the closest toilet. And now I . . ."

"Yeah?"

"Now I just want to go home."

A throat cleared.

The scruffy man. John. Looked and dressed like a background character from *The Witcher*, or maybe *House of the Dragon*. From what Sam had picked up, John turned trees into planks, a job that sounded incredibly labor-intensive without power tools.

It'd also made him incredibly thick and muscled. Enough so that Sam needed to tighten up for him to move by on the wall's bamboo walkway. Even then, their bellies brushed as John shuffled past.

"First time on watch, hey?"

"Yeah." Sam noticed the man didn't seem to register Parker. Old-school misogyny? Only talking to the closest person?

"Helps to move around. Change locations. Keeps you awake and you don't get bored looking at the same thing for half the night." He pointed back down the wall. The direction he'd come from.

"Ahhh. Got it. Thanks."

John gave him another nod of acknowledgment. Then turned his head and awkwardly nodded at Parker. "M'lady."

"Ummm . . . yeah. Thanks."

They picked up their spears and walked along the wall.

"M'lady?" she whispered.

"I think he might be from medieval times or something."

They'd reached the far corner when they stopped. Sam could see someone else—Marissa, maybe—over on the next section of wall past the corner. Parker leaned her spear against the railing again, and he set his next to it.

She squinted out at the dark trees. "Do you even know what we're keeping watch for?"

"The Klaa, mostly, I think. Maybe the occasional rogue dinosaur or woolly mammoth." He shrugged.

"I'm sorry."

"What for?"

Parker leaned against the top of the wall, still looking out at the valley. "For thinking you had some ulterior motive for being here."

"Well, I mean, I did."

"Yeah, but I immediately went to 'sinister ulterior motive.' To be honest, I had *you* pegged as the drug dealer on the run."

"Really?"

"Maybe. You definitely weren't here to shape young minds."

"Hah."

Parker tilted her head back, her gaze going from the forest to the sky. "Are you sure it's not his sister?"

The thought had been dancing in the back of Sam's mind for hours. "I mean she—it's not *impossible.* I know a few people who look completely—you'd never guess *that* kid became *that* adult. But it's always, like, a five-year-old and then a thirty-year-old. There are photos of Beau from when she was fifteen, from just two weeks before they vanished."

"And it's not her? It's been four hundred years. Maybe she broke her jaw and it healed weird or something."

Sam pictured the Empress again. Remembered the old photos of Beau Gather. Softball uniform there. Fluorescent tank top here. Big smile. Big '80s hair in several of them. Between the sunlight and the camera exposure, her blond hair looked near-white in a few. Broad shoulders. The cheekbones didn't look right but Beau did have a bit of an upturned nose . . .

"I don't know. Maybe? My gut says no. He's been so—he's been wrong about a lot of stuff."

"He's been right about a lot, too."

"Not enough."

Parker huffed in some air and Sam braced himself. Then she let it back out. "You're right. I just . . . it's his own sister."

"It'd be a good—it'd be nice if she is."

"I know I get . . . I got super defensive around Noah. About Noah."

"I hadn't noticed."

"For a long time I just sort of checked off a box for a lot of people. Smart Asian girl all through high school. Angry Asian girl for most of freshman and sophomore year. And then I got really wrapped up in trying to *not* be what everyone else wanted me to be. After I got into Monrovia's grad program I just kind of . . . cut loose for a few weeks. Almost a full-time party girl. To the point I almost blew it all right there, three months into grad school. And Noah just went to bat for me and saved my ass. No questions asked. Not even some lecture about wasted potential or my . . . what? What are you looking at?"

"You were a *party girl*? You? Parker Sangthong?"

She made a noise somewhere between a snort and a sigh. "I mean I didn't dye my hair fluorescent colors or anything, but that summer and the first few months of grad school, yeah. Drank a lot. Danced a lot. Had a wild one night . . ."

Parker stopped talking. Tightened up. A jumble of thoughts fell through Sam's consciousness, like a domino display falling in dozens of directions and then out of his mouth. "You slept with Noah?"

Even in the dark, he could see the horror on her face. "What? Oh, god no. How could you even think that?"

"Because you immediately stopped talking about your one-night stand, which means it was either entirely awful or you think I might know him."

Parker said nothing.

"Would I know him?"

She turned to stare out at the tree line.

Sam's brain leaped ahead on its own, going through faces and names from Monrovia's astronomy department. He thought back on those first hours with Logan and Kyle, tried to remember if he'd sensed any sort of emotions between either of them and Parker. Or if she'd displayed any particularly strong emotions after they'd—

"You and *Olivia*?!"

"It's stupid."

"It's not stupid. It explains a lot."

"No, it doesn't."

"Are you still—do you still have a thing for her?"

"Jesus, no. Seriously, no. I didn't have a thing for her then. I was drunk and horny and she was there and just as horny and a lot more drunk. Fuck, she was so drunk she didn't even remember me. Which is all for the best, I know, department-wise, but it's just . . . it's so goddamn annoying to not even *register* with someone. Someone looking right at you."

"And then to be stuck working with her."

"Yeah. And she can be kind of a bitch sometimes."

Sam decided to focus on the stars and not say anything.

"I don't want to be stuck here," she said.

"I don't think anyone does."

"I don't want someone else deciding who I get to be."

"We'll figure it out. You, me, Noah. Maybe Olivia. Maybe Josh."

"Not Josh."

"Us then."

She picked up one of the spears. Let it bounce back and forth from hand to hand. Stared out at the dark forest. "I knew the thing about Sagan's son. Nick. He wrote for *Star Trek: Voyager*."

"Yeah."

"I wanted you to feel good."

"Thanks."

The spear went back and forth and then she wrapped her fingers solidly around it. "And I'm sorry you got dumped in such a shitty way."

"Thanks. Again." He picked up his own spear.

"It sucks being stuck around someone who doesn't like you anymore."

"Yes, it does. And you know what the ironic part is?"

She shrugged.

"He left me for a paleontologist."

Parker's face stayed blank for a moment, and then her lips started to twist. She tried to rein in her laugh and failed miserably. It burst out, followed quickly by, "I'm sorry."

"It's okay. Trying to be funny."

She leaned her head back, still smiling. And the smile faded. She held up her free hand, extended one finger. Studied the spaces between objects. She pointed at a constellation hanging low over the cliffs. "Do you see Gemini?"

Sam tilted his head. Found the twins. "Yes."

"Castor's leg. Mebsuta. Tejat. Geminorum. And then . . . ?"

He turned his eyes off to the side. Seeing faint things by looking at them from a different angle. And there it was. He tapped his fingers against the knuckles holding the spear. "Is that . . . Jupiter?"

"That's what I thought the other night, but it's too dim."

He tried to run a celestial model in his head, to remember what else might pass close to Gemini and Orion. "Mars, maybe?"

"Maybe. But whatever it is . . . it's moving."

"What? Are you sure?"

"Yeah." She squinted at her outstretched hand again. "I think almost a full degree in the past two nights."

"So it's Mars."

"Yes."

Sam looked up at the curiously dim planet. "And if it's moving, it means we're not frozen in time."

She slowly shook her head. "No, we're not."

"So what the hell is going on here?"

"What's going on is this place is driving me mad."

37

BILLY

Beau shushed him and waved him back against the tree. Billy turned around and did the same to Ross. The robot took two sidesteps and vanished behind one of the big trunks.

Beau crept forward to the next tree and Billy snuck up behind her. They peered around the tree and watched Hornygirl lumber off through the woods. The giant triceratops headed away toward Saurus Swamp and the watering hole, pausing once to rub her shoulder on a rock as big as her.

It had been Billy's idea to name her Hornygirl. Beau and Dad had tried to talk him out of it, but he'd made a strong case, explaining that she was a girl because she laid eggs and she was horny because she had the three big horns. They'd both laughed—Beau'd laughed so hard she'd cried—but they finally agreed to the name.

They waited until she vanished into the woods. Hornygirl was pretty easygoing most of the time. You could walk around and not worry about her charging or stomping. But the whole reason they'd come out here was because it wasn't most of the time.

Beau took a few more cautious steps. Stretched up tall. Glanced back at Billy. Smiled. "No mushrooms tonight, twerp."

"Really?"

Billy and Ross joined her at the hole. It was about the size of a small pool, one of the ones you set up in the summer and took down in the winter. One of the kids in his grade had one, but Billy couldn't remember who. Maybe a girl? It'd been a long time since he'd thought about school. The hole had rough sides and a stomped-flat bottom. There were some sticks and grass in it, but Billy was never sure if Hornygirl put those in herself or if they just fell in after she was done.

Every six or seven weeks Hornygirl dug a new dirt-nest and dropped a few eggs in it. Usually two, sometimes three. Beau said they'd never hatch because there wasn't a Mister Hornygirl. Again, though, she'd smirked when she said it so Billy wasn't sure if she was making a joke or not.

But each egg was three or four days of food. Scrambled, fluffy, not-mushrooms food. Okay, they usually mixed in some mushrooms near the end. But it meant a week of not looking as hard for sort-of potatoes or kind-of apples. And the Castaway had assured them the eggs were healthy and loaded with nutrition. Granted, it had taken a whole afternoon of Billy and Beau questioning their alien friend to be sure these specific eggs from this specific dinosaur would be healthy and nutritious for them, the two humans in the valley.

So gathering Hornygirl's eggs had become a regular thing. Ross kept track of the days, and when the right time rolled around they'd spend a day or two following her until she dug a new nest. Like she did this morning.

Beau stepped down into the hole and brushed some dirt away. Billy saw brown, brown, and then bright green. Hornygirl's eggs were celery green with grass-green spots. Billy thought she buried them because they'd be too easy to spot otherwise. There were a lot of little dinosaurs and other animals that'd eat anything they found.

Beau used her hand to dig away some more dirt, then carefully lifted out the first egg. She handed it to Billy. "Careful."

"I've got it," he said, taking the egg with both hands.

"I'm not sharing if you drop it."

"I'm not going to drop it! It happened one time!"

"Quiet. Inside voices."

"Sorry."

The egg was about the size and shape of a big loaf of bread and felt a bit like a playground ball that needed just a little more air. Dinosaur eggs weren't hard. They were all kind of springy, like the shells were made out of rubber.

Beau carefully dug out another egg and handed it up to Ross. Then she looked at Billy. "I think there's one more."

"Really?"

"Yeah." She crouched back down and started digging again.

The not-sound hit Billy in the gut. Actually hit him. He felt it all over his skin, even though he could barely hear it. His arms and legs got tight.

Beau froze down in the nest. She looked scared. She knew the not-sound, too.

Billy raised his head. Looked to his left and saw trees and forest and the path Hornygirl had gone down. Looked to his right . . .

No no no no no *no* . . .

Fang pushed through the trees. Maybe forty feet away. Another low, rumbly noise came out of his throat and shook everything.

Billy took a step back. His foot slipped on the edge of the nest. He didn't fall but dirt and rocks slid down the side of the big hole. He was right next to it and he could barely hear it.

Fang heard it.

The tyrannosaurus's big head swung around to stare at Billy. Such big, yellow-white eyes. Fang took another step forward. Another step right toward Billy.

So many things collided in Billy's head. Don't run. If you run Fang will chase you. Don't make noise. Don't get caught in the open. Try not to be scared or breathe too hard. He can smell fear. He has a good sense of smell.

He'd killed Dad. Fang had *eaten* Dad. And now he was another big, heavy step closer to Billy.

Another sound. A wobbly sound, and more dirt falling. His hands were empty. He'd dropped the rubbery egg and it'd rolled down into the nest.

Beau moved fast and Billy almost screamed, sure Fang had grabbed her, bitten her in half, gobbled her up. But she'd just moved her arms. Thrown something. Billy heard a wet smacking sound.

Fang's head swung away from Billy. Followed the movement. His little nostrils opened wide. He turned. Took a step that way. And another.

Something clamped down on Billy's shoulder. Ross. The robot stepped past him, one foot in the nest, and grabbed Beau's arm. Then he backed up, dragging them both with him.

They went back two steps. Three. Four. Something big loomed in the corner of Billy's eye and he almost screamed again but it was just a tree. Just the big tree they'd hidden behind before.

Fang sniffed the ground on the far side of the nest. Billy saw a puddle of something gooey, like snot, shining there. Egg. Beau had thrown her egg.

Fang's eye rolled in its socket, pointing back at them. They all froze in mid-step. The pale yellow eye stared at them for three beats of Billy's heart—he could feel each of them in his throat—and then it swung forward again.

Ross moved them back another step. They were past the tree now. If Fang charged, they could hide behind a tree.

Dad had tried to hide behind a tree. Fang had knocked it down. Just set his car-sized head against the tree trunk and pushed it aside. The tree went down and then Dad wasn't hidden and then . . .

No no no no no . . .

Fang took another deep sniff of broken egg. Billy could smell him. Could he smell them?

Ross tugged them back again and Billy and Beau both stumbled back as something snapped under one of their feet. He wasn't sure who stepped on it. Just a little branch. But dry enough to snap.

Fang came at them.

Ross dragged them away, almost running backward into the trees. Fang stumbled just for a second, his huge foot sinking into the soft ground of the nest, and then he was past it, each one of his heavy, lumbering strides more than ten of theirs. He opened his jaws so wide all Billy could see was teeth and tongue and the deep red hole of the dinosaur's throat, and then the roar hit them, shook their bones, and Ross yanked them back, putting them further away from Fang, putting himself closer to the teeth.

And then Hornygirl slammed into Fang's leg. Her big spiky horns hit him right in the meaty part, above his knee. He let out another rumbly roar and turned around.

Ross dragged them away from the dinosaur fight. Beau kept up, Billy stumbled a bit. Beau pointed and Ross led them between trees, deeper into the forest.

Billy looked back, saw Hornygirl and Fang stomping and snorting on either side of her nest.

"This way," said Beau. She'd twisted free of Ross's grip and taken the lead, zigzagging through more trees.

Billy managed to get his own arm free and straighten himself out and now he could run easier. He knew they had a good head start now. It'd be tough for Fang to catch up with them.

But they kept running, just in case.

More trees, more zigzagging, and Beau finally waved them to a stop. Even then she got them inside a bunch of trees that had grown into a big circle, the trunks just a few feet apart, like a big cage made of wood. They'd hidden in this spot a few times before.

Beau crouched, looked at him. "Are you okay?"

Billy nodded. "Yep."

She checked him over anyway. Hugged him. "Ross?"

"Yes, Miss Beau?"

"Are you okay?"

"I've used up a bit more power than usual, but I don't detect any structural damage."

"Good." She turned her attention back to Billy. Looked at his hands. Her face got serious fast. "Where's your egg?"

The look in her eyes made Billy cautious. "I . . . I dropped it."

"You *what*?!"

"I didn't mean to!"

"I told you to be careful!"

"I got scared! Fang came out of the woods and I thought of . . . I thought he was going to—"

"Ross, you kept yours, right?"

"I'm afraid not, Miss Beau. When Fang arrived, keeping you and Master Billy safe became my priority."

Beau's mouth twisted up and Billy knew this expression. Beau started pacing back and forth in the circle of trees, making fists and opening them, starting to make words and then not talking. She didn't look at him and Ross. Wouldn't look at them. Billy saw the little sparkle under her eye and realized his sister was trying not to cry.

"Maybe we could go back," he said. "Hornygirl probably scared off Fang and we can—"

Beau screamed. A long, angry scream. She aimed it up at the treetops and a couple of the little four-winged dinosaurs scattered out of the branches.

Billy flinched back.

Beau punched one of the trees. Hard. Just slammed her knuckles into the trunk and screamed again.

Billy looked around. "Inside voices," he started to say, but he hadn't even finished the first word when she let out another shriek and punched the tree again and again and again.

Ross stepped forward and set a hand on her shoulder. "Please, Miss Beau. You're going to hurt yourself."

She spun around and swung at Ross and screamed in his face when she missed. And then she stood there, breathing heavy like she did when she ran all the way from the watering hole to the cave. Her eyes were still sparkly, but she hadn't cried yet.

She looked down at him and Billy thought she looked surprised. Like she'd forgotten he was there. She looked up at Ross. Back at Billy. She swallowed, and for a minute he was worried she was going to puke.

Instead she crouched, then dropped to her knees. Pulled him into a tight hug. "I'm sorry," she whispered. "I'm sorry. I didn't . . . I didn't mean to scare you."

"I wasn't scared."

"Twerp."

"Jerk."

She hugged him even tighter and started to cry.

"It's okay," he told her. "We can have mushrooms again. I . . . I don't mind."

His sister laughed into his shoulder. But she didn't stop crying.

38

NOAH

Noah was outside the wall, talking with Ross, when the Neanderthal came out of the woods.

Noah'd been talking with Ross a lot, trying to learn everything he could about the Empress. When and how she'd first appeared. When they'd realized she lived in the Ice Castle now instead of the Castaway. How she'd taken control of the Klaa and the valley, bringing everything under her heel.

And then, as they passed through the main gate, the gold-feathered raptor and its rider strode out past the tree line. Noah saw them as the resonant sound of the didgeridoo pulsed out across the fields. Recognized all the teeth decorating the rider's arms and throat.

Breaker.

"We must retreat behind the wall," Ross told him. The robot turned and his walking stick thumped against the ground. Noah took a few backward steps, not wanting to take his eyes off the Neanderthal, not wanting to miss if anyone else had come with him.

As the thought slid through his mind, another rider stomped out of the woods, and a third. They stopped on either side of Breaker, holding back a few feet. They stood at the edge of the forest, their raptors scratching at the dirt.

Noah waited. Hoped to see the saber-toothed tiger. But nothing else came from the woods.

The didgeridoo sounded again.

"Noah." Ross touched his arm, and he realized he'd stopped moving to watch the trees. "We must go. Now."

A few more backward steps. He glanced back once, a quick look to make sure he wouldn't trip over anything, and then focused on the Neanderthals again. Still standing there. Waiting. Watching.

He locked eyes with Breaker. The Neanderthal stared at him. Remembering him from the other day with Pyr and Sam? Staring at him because he was outside the walls?

Because he'd been *told* to watch for him, maybe?

He turned and found the gate. Saw Ross already inside, his hood knocked down around his shoulders. Emerson waved him through.

Noah took one last look over his shoulder and someone grabbed his wrist, yanking him into Roanoke. The door swung closed. The bar dropped.

A few people were already running toward the ladders. He followed. Reached the walkway and looked across the field.

Breaker and the other two Klaa still stood by the trees. Definitely waiting. Noah couldn't be as sure, but he thought Breaker looked along the wall and stopped to stare at him again.

Pyr appeared by his elbow. "You okay?"

"Is he staring at us?"

"It's the brow ridge. Shadows their eyes, makes it look like they're always looking at you."

"It's not that."

Breaker jabbed his heels into his raptor's side. The dinosaur twisted back and he yanked hard on the reins. The raptor clawed at the ground and took a few slow steps forward.

The other two hung back by the trees as their boss moved toward the wall. Noah couldn't remember ever seeing a raptor move this slow as a child. It felt like the Neanderthal knew about the stashed spears and bows and was daring the humans to try something. His own weapon hung loose in his hand, but Noah remembered how fast it had moved out in the badlands.

"What the hell is going on?"

"Proclamation," murmured Pyr. "Every couple of months the Empress sends us a message. Usually a new list of tribute items. Food. Supplies."

Noah made a small gesture toward Breaker. "And he delivers it?"

"If it's simple enough he'll just tell us. Sometimes it's a written list from her."

"Written?"

"I told you, she speaks at least a dozen languages. Can write them, too. When Qiang became the elder, she started writing in Chinese."

Noah had a moment to wonder where Beau might've learned Chinese and then Breaker had passed the fields. He shook the reins. The dinosaur shrieked once and stopped a dozen yards from the gate. Its big talons scratched at the path.

Breaker pulled something from the mess of rawhide strings and furs around his waist. A short, pale rod, or maybe part of a branch. Held it out toward Roanoke. His eyes slid across the people gathered along the top of the wall. Glared at Noah again.

The Neanderthal barked out a few quick words. Noah caught *want* and *stranger* but not the rest. Too out of practice. He got the scorn though. And the underlying threat. Those came back quick.

Breaker opened his hand and let the rod drop. It bounced off the raptor's neck, and the way it moved told Noah it was light. Maybe hollow. It hit the ground silently. Breaker didn't look at it as he turned away. So much confidence and disdain in his movements.

A quick jab with his heels and the raptor broke into a jog, long strides carrying it back to the tree line. Breaker never slowed. The dinosaur dashed between the two flanking Neanderthals and plunged into the forest. The other two turned and followed.

Noah looked down at the white rod. A message from the Empress. Waiting below.

Emerson had opened the gate and stepped outside by the time Noah got back to ground level. He held the rod. A piece of birch bark, maybe, with a thin string of leather looped around it.

Noah cleared his throat. "Is that . . ."

Emerson walked past him and handed the scroll off to Qiang. The elder unrolled the rough paper. His face hardened. He glanced at Noah and let the scroll pull itself back into a cylinder. "Would you walk with me, please?"

They went out the gate and turned left, walking along the wall. Noah glanced out at the forest, the cornfields, the red spacesuit scarecrow. "Is it safe to be out here?"

"I'd say we're safe for the next day or so. From the Klaa, at least." He tapped the scroll against his palm. "Pyr says you think the Empress is your sister."

"I do."

Qiang handed Noah the scroll.

The bark had been beaten and pressed until it almost felt like heavy construction paper. Noah couldn't guess how time-consuming it'd been. He pulled it open and it resisted, curling back at the corners.

Your Empress
Demands the presence of the man
who claims to be Billy Gather
In her castle
Tomorrow by midday

The handwriting was exquisite. Bordering on calligraphy. The lines were dark and firm, like fine brushwork. He tried to remember what Beau's handwriting looked like but mostly he pictured big, round teenage girl letters.

He'd looked over the five lines of text at least half a dozen times before Qiang made a polite noise in the back of his throat. "One thing about the Empress is she's consistent. If she wants to see you tomorrow, she won't do anything that might stop that from happening. Neither will the Klaa. They don't want to upset her."

"Until tomorrow."

"Yes."

Noah relaxed his fingers and the bark-paper rolled back into a cylinder. "Why tomorrow?"

"I think you'd call it a power play. She wants to make us wait. She wants you to come to her. She enjoys having her orders followed, even when they're pointless orders."

They reached the corner of the wall, went around it. Another field, this one rows and rows of simple stakes holding up thin bean plants, or maybe peas. The people of Roanoke ate a lot better than he had as a kid. Then again, he wasn't sure how much of it went to the Klaa.

"To the best of my knowledge, she's never asked to see anyone in the Castle before."

Noah's heart jumped. "Never?"

"She's demanded to see newcomers, like she did the other day. But we're rarely invited into their territory. And never into the Castle. As far as I know. Ross might remember someone."

"This is good then. She recognizes me. She wants to meet."

Qiang made the polite noise again. Not a sigh. Not a clearing of the throat. A good, professor-y sound, and it struck Noah that Qiang gave off the same vibes as his dean back at Monrovia University.

He guessed where the conversation was going. "It's her."

"How can you know?"

"I mean . . . I can see her. It's obvious to anyone who knew her."

"Ross knew her. He's never once suggested the Empress could be your sister."

"I know it's her."

"Forgive me, Noah, but you also 'knew' we were all wrong about the valley and you were the only one who was correct."

"That was different."

"Was it?"

Noah tried to think of a simple answer. A quick response. One with more behind it than the solid confidence in his gut. But he knew the first three or four things that came to his mind could all be individually dismissed as coincidences or reaching, and then Qiang spoke again.

"I've been here for forty years. I barely remember my family back in China, or even the friends I arrived here with. My whole life's been in the valley. And the Empress has been here for all of it."

They took another step and the ground shifted beneath their feet. Earthy farmland to stone. Hundreds and hundreds of smooth, round stones, like a beach in Maine, clicking and shifting beneath their feet. Two more swaths of space and time butting up against each other.

Qiang noticed him looking at the stones. "It appeared about twenty-five years ago. All those and a few hundred thousand liters of seawater. One of the loudest things I've ever heard. And we still can't get anything to grow out here. Too much salt." He gestured past the stones to a barren swath of ground that looked like gray sand dotted with a few scraggly patches of grass.

"My sister . . ."

Qiang made the dean sound again. "You know, everyone here knows your name. Everyone here owes their lives to you and your family, one way or another. Beau more than any of you. Surviving here over four years, with only Ross for the last two."

"She's still—"

A quick gesture from Qiang silenced him. The man really had all the professor tricks down. "The Empress, on the other hand, is a brutal dictator. I've seen her kill as many of her own people as ours. With her own hands. I couldn't even guess how many people were doomed just by arriving on the wrong side of the valley. Confused about where they were and how they got here, and then brutally killed for 'violating' Klaa territory. A few times, out in the forest, I've heard screams and wondered . . ."

He sighed. Shook his head. Made a point of not meeting Noah's eyes as they turned another corner.

"For a few years now, Emerson and Neith have pushed to kill her."

"What?!"

A calming hand from Qiang. "We've always said no. The risk is too great. If the Empress dies, the Klaa will turn to B'Kar."

"But he's a man."

"And until they determine a new matriarch, who will they turn to? The right hand of the Empress. He's been her lieutenant for the past decade, and he's as bad as her."

"They're people. Just like us."

"Yes, people. Like us. People do ridiculous, horrible things all the time, Noah. You know this. Especially when they're scared and their leader tells them to. And this place . . . this place scares the Klaa just as much as it scares all of us. They don't understand it, but they know it's unnatural."

"Thank you. For not letting them kill her."

"The Empress is vicious. Hateful. Selfish. In every way the opposite of what we've been told Beau Gather was like."

"It is. The opposite of what she's like."

Qiang shook his head. "No, Noah. This is who's asking to meet you. There's half a chance the Klaa will kill you as soon as you walk into their territory. An excellent chance she'll kill you herself the moment you say something that annoys her."

"She won't."

"I'd like to think that, but I must be honest. From my point of view, I'm letting you walk into the lion's den. Every encounter I've ever had with her, every story I've ever heard, going back centuries, tells me the most likely outcome is we'll never see you again."

"I appreciate your concern."

"Oh, it's not about you, Noah. I'm looking out for my people. My friends. The truth is, your return's brought a lot of life and energy back here. But by the same token, it would crush many of them to find out Billy Gather returned here only to be killed by the Empress."

"She's not going to kill me."

"I wish I shared your confidence."

A waft of something awful and familiar struck him in the face. Big herbivore waste. Hard to forget that smell. They had to be getting close to whatever corral the farmers kept their styracosaurs in.

"What about this," he said. "You're absolutely certain I'm wrong?"

"I probably wouldn't say 'absolutely' but . . . yes. I'm certain."

"Have you considered what it means if I'm right?"

Qiang finally met his eyes.

"You're right. I don't know what's happened here over the past four hundred years. I don't know how things shifted. How the Neanderthals became so aggressive. How she came to rule them. How she became so . . . terrible. But if I remind her of who she was, who *we* were, think about what it could mean for the valley."

"Go on."

"There could be peace. My sister isn't a bad person. Not at heart."

Qiang sighed. "Noah, I'm afraid you're missing the point. Even if the Empress was Beau at one point, I don't believe there's anything of your sister left in her."

39

JOSH

Josh found them all one by one around dinnertime and asked them to come to Monique's cottage. He told them Olivia had improved, but didn't want to say much more than that. Easier for them to see it.

He'd been playing word games with Olivia for a lot of the day. Trying to see how she responded. How she *could* respond. It made him feel like a World War II codebreaker. Or maybe Amy Adams in *Arrival.* Normally a little too hard sci-fi for his taste, but now it paid off.

Olivia seemed happy for the company, but still looked a little worried and confused. She'd be talking with him—trying to talk with him—and then it was like she suddenly remembered where they were. She'd look all around the room like she expected the walls to close in on her, or monsters to crawl out of the ceiling. The kind of behavior a small dose of alprazolam could do wonders for, if he'd had any. Instead, he'd talk to her some more, calm her down, and she'd start babbling out more random words.

And then, a few hours after lunch, they had her big breakthrough. They'd worked on it for another hour before he'd called Monique to join them, and maybe an hour later he'd gone to collect everyone. And now they were all here in the largeish room inside her front door with the chairs and couch, what he'd first considered the waiting room, but Monique had since referred to as her parlor.

Olivia sat on the couch, wrapped in an old quilt. Monique sat next to her, ready to end things if she felt it got to be too much. Sam and Parker sat in some of the other chairs. Noah stood by the door with his android. Apparently he was heading out again tomorrow so the album cover Empress could kill him.

Josh pressed his hands together, realized he was starting to make a presentation, forced himself to put his arms at his side. He looked at Olivia. "Do you still feel up to this?"

"Yes truth positive correct confirmed accurate."

Everyone straightened up. Sam smiled. "Hey, she's making sense. Are you feeling better?"

"Self recovery problem partial improvement difficulty."

"Still doing the backward-alphabetical thing," Noah observed.

"And still six words." Parker frowned.

Josh shook his head, held up his hands. Presentation after all. "No, no, no. Sorry. I see where it looks that way. I should've explained a little more up-front."

They all looked at him. Waited. Even the android.

"So, I've been talking to her all day, and it's pretty clear Olivia can understand us, she's just having trouble responding. Or saying anything. Her brain's this big jumble and she can't find the right words or get them in the right order."

Parker nodded. "That's what we'd already figured."

"Right. And she and I worked on it all morning and couldn't find a way around it. Too many random words, essentially in random order, it's too many . . ." He waved his hands, encouraging them to finish it for him. To get them involved.

"Too many variables," said Noah.

"Right."

Sam shook his head. "It's not random though. It's alphabetical. Backward."

"But it's random as far as you'd normally put the words together," Josh explained. "It doesn't have, y'know, grammar or emphasis or sentence structure or any of those sort of things."

"Okay."

Parker gestured at Olivia. "So how did she answer you before?"

Josh smiled. "Because I asked her a question that needed less words to answer."

Parker's brows went up. Sam's jaw went down. Olivia looked relieved. Even Noah looked impressed. And Monique beamed at Josh in a way that made his whole chest feel light and swirly and he had to stay focused here.

"It took some trial and error, but we figured out that if she gets a question she can give a one-word answer to, her brain will dump out six words that are all close to the word she wants. It's still trying to do the six-word backward-alphabetical thing, but this gives her a bit of a workaround."

Now Sam looked doubtful. "But I just asked her how she felt. That's a one-word answer and it was random words again."

"Ahhh, that's the catch." Josh looked at Olivia. Gave her a reassuring nod. "You know how someone can ask you what seems like a simple question but it's really not?"

They all nodded.

"That's what happened. You can ask a simple question, but if she has more to say on it or thinks it's not that simple, her brain does this. I've been talking to her all day. Monique's spoken with her, too."

"I have," agreed the doctor.

Noah looked past him, focused on Olivia. She stared back at him. "Do you understand what he's been saying?"

"Veracious truth positive faultless correct accurate." Her smile was a little crooked, but unmistakable.

"Do you think you could . . ." Noah stopped. Reconsidered. "Are you able to answer questions if we can word them correctly?"

Her head swayed side to side. "Yes positive faultless correct confirmed absolutely."

"It's a lot of the same words," Sam said.

Parker leaned forward. "There's only so many different ways to say yes."

Noah glanced at them. "Could Olivia speak any other languages?"

"Wrong no negative invalid incorrect false."

Monique laughed. "And there is your answer."

Parker raised a finger, got Olivia's attention. "Do you remember what happened to you? To you and . . . Logan?"

Olivia sighed. Bobbed her head up and down. "Unconsciousness self resulting overload monument cerebrum."

"Okay, this might be difficult."

"It takes a couple of tries," Josh explained. "Everyone just needs to be patient."

Noah looked at Josh. "Did she tell you anything? You said you were talking for a few hours."

"Yeah, but a lot of it was word salad while she got used to talking again. Once we hit solid yes and no answers, I figured you'd all want to know."

Sam tapped his fingers. Looked over at Josh. "Olivia . . . did anyone tell you about the obelisk?"

"Wrong negative mistaken incorrect false erroneous."

Noah glanced at him. "Why'd you ask that?"

"Just . . . she said 'monument' when Parker asked about what happened. Which I'm pretty sure is supposed to be the obelisk."

"Yep, probably."

Sam's fingertips bounced off each other. "I just—it seems odd that she knows that."

"Why?"

"I don't think we mentioned it yesterday. You just said there was an accident. Why doesn't she think she fell down a hole or got hit by a rock or something?"

"Self plunge one negative descent aperture."

"The obelisk was the last thing she saw," Josh pointed out. "Is it that weird she'd think it had something to do with it."

Sam stopped tapping his fingers. "Okay, odd idea. I'm—what if we're looking at this totally wrong? Backward, even?"

Olivia looked up at him. So did Parker. "How so?"

"Well, we keep looking at this in terms of what the obelisk did to her, but do we have any idea what the obelisks actually are?"

Now they all looked at Noah. He shrugged. "We always assumed they were random artifacts from the future that ended up here."

Josh felt his brow scrunch up. "Why the future?"

"Force fields. Lightning blasts. Plastic. They're not from the past."

"They're plastic?"

"One of them is," said Sam. "Or maybe high-end resin."

"The resin obelisk is now in the region of the valley considered as Klaa territory."

Noah looked at the android. "Now meaning they've claimed that territory or has the obelisk shifted as the valley's expanded?"

"I believe both of these are correct, Noah."

"If they're random artifacts," asked Parker, "why do they all look the same? They're identical, just made from different materials, right?"

Josh shrugged. "I mean, soda cans all pretty much look the same. So do wine bottles. Maybe they're a future art exhibit or something."

Sam raised an eyebrow. "An art exhibit booby-trapped to electrocute people?"

"I mean, only one of them. And there's some weird art out there."

"I never considered it back then," Noah admitted. "Knowing what I do now, I'd guess maybe they all landed here closer together and got spread out over time."

"Ross?"

"Yes, Parker?"

"Do you know what the obelisks are?"

"I'm afraid I don't. The obelisks are from a time beyond my own."

"Do you understand the language on them?"

"I'm afraid I don't."

"Who here at Roanoke is from the farthest in the future?"

Monique ended the sudden silence that followed. "That would be Thate."

"Not Ross?"

Ross's head went side to side with a squeak of old metal and plastic. "Theta Sigma-Seven arrived in the valley from twenty-three years in what would have been my own future. "

"And he doesn't know what they are either?"

"I'm afraid he doesn't. Or if he does, he's never shared that information."

Sam nodded. "So nobody in the valley knows when they're from or what they are."

"Wrong no negative invalid incorrect false."

They all looked at Olivia.

Noah took another step forward. "Are you saying someone . . . do *you* know what the obelisks are?"

Olivia breathed in, then covered her mouth with her hand to muffle the string of words spinning out of her throat. Her head bobbed up and down, side to side, and up and down again.

"Was that an overcomplicated *maybe*?"

Parker raised a finger again. "Olivia, can we try something new?"

Olivia settled back against the couch. "Possible perhaps optional maybe depending could."

"Do you know what the obelisk did to you?"

"Yes truth positive correct confirmed accurate."

Josh felt a little jolt. "Hey. She's getting some inflection on her words now."

Parker slid off her chair and moved a little closer. "Okay . . . I'm going to ask you what the obelisk did, but before I do I want you to think about it. Try to distill it down into one word. Just one. Okay?"

Olivia put a hand over her mouth, but the muffled noises sounded positive.

"What did the obelisk do to you?"

"Surge superfluity overload glut flood excess."

Sam sighed. "Well, we already knew that. Too much electricity to the brain."

"Now I know what superfluity means," Josh said.

Olivia's bare foot slapped the floor. "No mistaken invalid incorrect false erroneous."

Parker straightened up. "What?"

"What's she saying?" Sam shifted in his chair, facing Olivia. "Are you saying . . . I don't know what you're saying."

"Terminal overload negative couple charge cerebrum."

"I still don't know what she's saying."

Josh picked at the words. "I think . . . I think she's saying it wasn't electricity."

"Or it wasn't an overload?"

Olivia stamped her foot three times. A crooked smile spread across her face, but it had an edge to it. Something . . . desperate?

Parker looked the other woman in the eyes again. "Okay, same thing. I'm going to ask what it zapped you with. One word. Focus on one word."

Olivia took in a long, slow breath.

"What did the obelisk zap you with?"

"Instruction input information figures facts data."

The room went quiet.

"Holy fuck," said Sam.

"Is this . . . can this be correct?" asked Monique.

"Veracious truth positive faultless correct confirmed."

"It pumped *information* into her brain?" Sam was out of his chair.

Josh tried to make sense of it. "So Logan was killed by . . . too much information?"

"So they aren't an art exhibit," said Noah, "they're more like a . . . a library?"

She stomped her foot and rolled her eyes. "Substructure propulsion others negative mobile location."

Josh shook his head. "I'm lost again."

"Didn't she say something like this yesterday? Ross?" Noah turned to look at the android.

"Yesterday Mx. Olivia said the words 'substructure region negative mobile location group' in that order."

"Mobile location," echoed Parker.

"Still lost," Josh said.

Sam tapped his fingers. "Maybe the way places move around the valley?"

Monique adjusted her dress on the couch and patted Olivia's hand. "If her words have been alphabetized, it is possible these two words were not meant to be used together."

"She also said propulsion," Noah pointed out. "Propulsion and moving."

Josh ran the words through his head. "She said negative both times, right? Maybe she's saying things weren't moving."

"So she's talking about the sky?"

"The sky's moving," said Parker. "It's just not moving . . . right."

"The Castle then," said Monique. "It is the one fixed point in the valley, never moving from the center."

Olivia stamped both feet this time. "Substructure region propulsion negative mobile location."

"I think . . ." Josh said, "I think she's trying to correct us."

Olivia flopped back on the couch. Monique pressed the back of her hand against the other woman's forehead. Pressed her fingers on the inside of her wrist. "She is very tired."

Noah looked at Josh and frowned. "Correct us about what?"

Josh shrugged. Played the words back in his mind, tried to rearrange them like a puzzle clue. Sam's fingers tapped wildly against each other. Parker's eyes were closed.

Sam held a hand up. Tipped a finger back and forth like a conductor. "Mobile propulsion region. Negative location. Substructure?"

Noah's frown deepened. "Substructure of what?"

Sam looked at Monique. "Are there caves, or maybe tunnels somewhere in the valley? Under the valley."

Inspiration flared in Josh's mind. "I've got it. Didn't you say there's a riverboat here?"

Noah nodded. So did Sam and Monique. "Yep. An Egyptian riverboat. From the '50s or '60s I think. 1960s."

Josh spread his hands wide. "A mobile location with propulsion."

"And it doesn't move."

Olivia rolled her eyes. She swung her foot at the floor, but settling back on the couch left it too high to make contact. Her gaze settled on Josh and he was pretty sure the look in her eyes meant she thought he was an idiot.

Parker shot up straight. "Oh my god." She stumbled back like she'd been hit. Bounced against her chair, fumbled past it, grabbed the back. "Oh my *god*."

"What's wrong?" asked Noah.

"Negative region." Parker looked at Noah. At Josh. Her eyes had the same oddly panicked, frantic look he'd seen in Olivia's throughout the day. The look of someone suddenly seeing way too much. "She's trying to tell us this isn't a valley."

Olivia sighed with relief.

"Mobile location with propulsion. We're on a *spaceship*."

40

PARKER

So much of it fell into place in Parker's mind. Too much for it to be wrong. The skeptic in her scoffed at the idea as ludicrous, but the scientist saw so many puzzle pieces line up.

Noah's face had gone completely blank. He looked like she felt. The robot had more of an expression, and it didn't even have a nose or mouth. Parker could see Sam still processing things. Confusion covered Monique's face. Olivia looked relieved. Satisfied.

"So the wormhole," Josh said, "dumped us on a spaceship?"

"There's no wormhole," said Parker. "No time rift. There never was. We're not a million years in the past. It's just this gigantic ship, sitting in space."

Sam finished processing. Shook his head. "That isn't—it's not possible."

"It makes sense." Parker waved a hand at the ceiling, past the walls of the cottage, taking in the whole valley. "Everything makes sense if this is an artificial environment. The fact nobody can climb up the cliffs. The way day and night happen. It's sitting at a heliostationary point close to Earth's orbit, so it explains what we're seeing in the night sky. It's just showing us the solar system from a fixed point, maybe through a big filtered viewscreen or something. It even—"

"Why would there be," Sam tried to calm his breathing. Failed. "Why would someone park a giant—we're talking about a *massive* spaceship in Earth's orbit. A starship at least three times bigger than Manhattan that's been parked here for centuries, maybe millennia, and nobody's ever noticed it? Even while it's randomly beaming up people and animals whenever Earth gets close."

"And fields and obelisks and things," added Josh.

"It would've been spotted decades ago. *Centuries* ago."

"It's not parked here."

Noah looked like he'd thrown up. Like he'd felt that hunched-over-the-toilet humiliation, but ultimately knew it had all been for the best. He stared back at Parker for a moment, then turned his attention to Sam.

"It *crashed* here. We're on the Castaway's ship."

Olivia's hands muffled the six words she tried to say, but her toes danced excitedly on the floor.

"They told us their ship was destroyed and I, my family and I, we assumed they meant there was nothing left and they'd been . . . I don't know, ejected into the valley. I think they tried to tell us and we didn't understand."

Josh coughed. Raised two diplomatic fingers. "I'm not a physicist or anything, but . . ."

"Yes?"

"Well, if the ship's just a wreck, shouldn't it be, what would you call it . . . drifting in space? I don't know the technical term for it."

"Drifting," said Parker.

"Right. Like, if it moved an inch it'd move forever, right? Momentum and inertia and stuff. So why isn't it?"

She nodded. "Oh yeah. There're a hundred reasons something can't sit in space like this. Especially in a solar system. But if we're talking about an advanced alien spaceship twenty miles across . . . I mean, it's probably got a great parking brake."

"Better question." Sam turned his attention to Olivia. "How do *you* know it's a spaceship?"

Olivia returned the stare. "Obelisk needle monument input data column."

"Hey, she actually said 'obelisk.'" Josh beamed proudly at Monique.

Another thought rose up in Parker's mind, slipping out through her lips before she even had time to fully register it. "The obelisks aren't from the future. They're part of the ship."

The skin around Sam's eyes scrunched up tight. His finger tapping hit a manic rate. When he didn't say anything, she continued.

"They're constants here in the valley, yes? Everything else moves around them? They're always in the same place, relative to each other, with the Castle at the center of the valley."

Sam's shoulders dropped. "Where the Castaway lived."

Monique cleared her throat. "Forgive me. If what you're saying is true, that we are on a starship and the obelisks and Castle are all part of it, why would they all be composed from such a variety of materials?"

Josh shrugged. "Cars are made from all sorts of materials."

"Automobiles?"

"Yeah. They're made of fiberglass, regular glass, steel, aluminum, copper wiring, silicon chips, rubber tires. I mean, if you think of a wagon, a horse-drawn buggy, they're made of wood and iron and cloth cushions and rope, right?"

"Oui."

"They might not even be different materials." Noah's face still looked a little . . . queasy? But he had his thinking face on. His scientist face. Parker hadn't seen it since they arrived here in the valley, and the sight of it soothed her mind. "It stands to reason the Castaway's ship would be multidimensional, like they were. So it's the shadow puppets thing all over again. But now they look like the same shape, we're just perceiving them as different material."

Sam closed his eyes. Tapped his fingers. "How is that like shadow puppets?"

"Think of it like . . . like how a shadow can appear soft or sharp depending on where the wall and the light are. The object casting the shadow doesn't change, but we perceive different textures."

Parker nodded. "Or even numbers. How you get two or three shadows off a fixture with multiple bulbs. Here we're seeing a bunch of things that look like different material, but they've all got the same dimensions and the same symbols."

"Symbols nobody can read," Sam said, "because it's not—because it's an alien language."

Parker nodded again.

Sam's breathing slowed down. "Holy fuck. We're on a spaceship."

Olivia scooted her ass down the couch and stamped her foot on the floor. "Total negative propulsion partial location incomplete."

Josh glanced at them. "You're getting corrected again, I think."

Sam rethought his words. "So we're not on a spaceship?"

"We're on a crashed spaceship," said Noah. "The wreck of a spaceship?"

Parker looked at Olivia. Crouched in front of her again. "One word. Just give us one word."

Olivia closed her eyes. Took a breath. "Support subassembly rescue part component beacon."

"Okay." Sam's fingers started tapping against each other again. "Okay, to me, subassembly, part, and component says we're not on the ship. Not on the complete ship, anyway."

"So it did break up when it crashed," Parker said, "just like you thought."

Noah nodded in agreement.

Olivia's bare foot hit the floor again. "Subassembly small separate safe location beacon."

His lips twisted. "Beacon again."

"And subassembly," said Sam. "She keeps using that."

Josh held up two fingers. "But it's probably not the actual word she meant."

"Unless it is. She's starting to get individual words here and there, I think."

"So one of these might be the exact word," Parker mused, "and others might be sort-of-close words?"

"Sub . . . division?" Sam suggested. "It'd go with component and part. And separate."

"Subsystem?"

"Substructure?"

"Sub-Mariner?"

"Not helping," said Parker.

Josh shrugged. "Sorry. Trying to cut the tension a bit, keep the ideas flowing."

Sam's fingertips bounced against each other. "Beacon might mean a signal? GPS? Or the interstellar equivalent."

"Galactic positioning system."

Parker chuckled. "Small separate safe location. With a GPS system." As she repeated the last word, the answer crashed into her mind. She saw Noah's face brighten.

"An escape pod," he said.

She felt her chin bounce up and down. "A lifeboat."

"The Castaway did eject from their ship."

Olivia smiled and tapped her feet rapid-fire on the floor.

Monique's brows came together. "So there is also another starship?"

"Not exactly. I think . . ." She looked at Noah and he nodded. "We think this *is* the other ship. The Castaway's ship was destroyed but they used this smaller ship to get away and stay alive until they could be rescued."

"This *smaller* ship?" echoed Monique.

"Yeah."

"Which contains the entire valley?"

Josh shifted his feet, leaned slightly toward Monique. "She's got a point. If all of this is in the lifeboat, it'd have to be enormous. Which means the original ship would've been . . . what, the size of North America?"

Noah shook his head. "We'd only perceive the parts extending into our three-dimensional space. From our point of view, it could be almost any size it needs to be. Most of it would be in another dimension."

Sam tapped his fingers again. "So things are—they get pulled into the lifeboat as it passes Earth, and it stores them all fourth dimensionally. Just sticks us in different times within itself." He glanced at Noah. "The same way we'd shove things in a random drawer just to get them off the counter."

Parker realized she was pacing. Stopped by the couch. Felt the thrill of more pieces falling together. "So we've got a super-advanced multi-dimensional lifeboat. And what do lifeboats do?"

"Keep you out of the water," said Josh.

Monique pressed her hands together. "Keep people alive."

"And that's what the valley does," said Parker, touching her unscarred forehead. "It keeps you healthy. People heal faster here. Don't get sick."

"Don't get pregnant," added Josh.

"Why would the lifeboat keep things from being with child?" Monique asked.

"I mean, pregnancy is a health issue," said Parker. "It puts a strain on your body. It can kill you. Maybe the lifeboat's just trying to proactively avoid complications."

Monique frowned. "Why, then, do the dinosaurs still lay eggs?"

"They're not fertilized, though, right?" Josh moved his hands in the air, miming an egg shape. "Just yolks, right? No little dinosaurs."

"Because dinosaurs are birds," Sam said. "Or they're related, the ancestors of birds. They can't be, can't get pregnant, but they still lay the eggs. Like chickens when there's no rooster around." His fingers stopped apart, spread wide. "Nothing ever gets hurt when it arrives here. Everyone lands safely in the lifeboat."

"It's trying to duplicate our environment." Noah stared past Olivia at the fireplace. "Oxygen levels. The day-night cycle. It's part of what made us all think this was Earth, but we had it backward. The lifeboat created an earthlike environment for everything here."

Sam looked up. "So what happens to the sun?"

"Sun star solar question problem mass."

Noah shook his head. "I'd guess it's . . . I don't know, filtering out the sun for half the time here because that's the environment everything in the lifeboat is used to."

"How would it filter out the sun?" asked Sam. "And only the sun? It's not as if, not like they're closing the blinds. All the stars are still up there."

Noah shrugged. "Highly advanced sixth-dimensional alien technology."

Josh straightened up. "And any significantly advanced technology would be indistinguishable from magic."

"Yup. Bye-bye sun. Thank you, Arthur C. Clarke."

Parker got another little mental jolt. "The stars."

"What about them?"

"They're the stars six months from now. We're still at September twenty-second, our orbital position, but we're facing the sky for mid-March. It's just normally we can't see it because the sun's there."

Noah's scientist face deepened. "But if something takes the sun out of our view, now we're seeing across the solar system."

She nodded. "And two astronomical units isn't that much, relatively speaking. Almost everything would look the same, once we knew how to look at it."

"Except the planets."

"And the Moon."

Sam's fingertips bounced off each other again. "Okay then. Elephant in the room question. Doesn't all this—isn't it even more odd the Castaway was trapped here? Why didn't their people come looking for them? Are we saying super-advanced multidimensional aliens built a lifeboat and forgot to put a radio in it?"

Parker dipped her head at Olivia. "She's said beacon a couple of times now."

"Right. But they—the Castaway was here in the valley for at least a century or two, by the sound of it. So if they—if this is their lifeboat . . . why?"

Parker's mental gears, which had been churning along wonderfully and picking up steam, came to a crashing halt.

Monique raised a hand, copying Josh. "The Castaway, from the stories I have heard, was much like Ross or Thate. Like us, but different in many ways, yes? Ross says they could see through time?"

Sam nodded. "Yes. They could—they saw things before they happened. Or long after, sometimes."

"Would such a being view the passage of time as we do? Perhaps for the Castaway waiting for centuries was a mere inconvenience?"

The gears in Parker's head started to move again. "That's a good point."

Noah gasped. "That's it."

Parker knew the tone. Everything had just fallen into place for him, too. She met his eyes, saw the gleam of excitement and understanding. "What?"

"It's why nobody's seen the Castaway in hundreds of years. They *were* rescued, and they left the lifeboat for Beau. That's how she's still alive."

41

BILLY

For his twelfth birthday, Billy announced he wanted to have pizza and McDonald's cheeseburgers for breakfast. And then maybe ice cream for breakfast dessert. Then he'd play Atari until lunch, which should be spaghetti and meatballs. Then they could go see all the *Star Wars* movies—the Castaway and Zock could come, too—come home to play with Charlie the cat while they got another pizza delivered, and finish the day opening presents. Which should all be *Star Wars* figures. Mostly the ones he needed, but he'd also be okay with lots of stormtroopers or Jawas.

"That sounds like quite a plan, twerp," Beau said.

"All sorts of things end up here," said Billy as Ross handed him a wooden plate of mushrooms and scrambled eggs. "Maybe we'll find a movie theater tomorrow. And a toy store. And a pizza place."

"One that delivers."

"It's my birthday. I don't want to waste time going to get the pizza."

Beau smirked. She didn't laugh much anymore. Billy'd come up with his outrageous list of birthday requests hoping to get at least a smile out of her, so the smirk made him feel pretty good.

Ross slid eggs onto another plate and handed it to Beau. "Thank you."

"Of course, Miss Beau."

"But what do you really want to do tomorrow?" she asked Billy.

He shrugged. "All that stuff."

"What do you want that we could actually do?"

He sighed. "We could go visit the Castaway. Ask them to tell us stories about other planets or something."

"Okay."

"Maybe go look at the big Egyptian statue with the dog's head."

"You've seen it at least fifty times."

"It's my birthday, jerk. It's cool. I want to go look at it."

"Fiiiiiine."

"We could try to make pizza. For real."

Beau looked at Ross.

"I could make another attempt," said the robot, "but without new ingredients I'm afraid the results will be the same."

She looked back at Billy. "You sure you want to go through that again?"

He nodded.

"Okay, then. Anything else?"

He thought about it. Last birthday before he became a teenager. Last birthday as a little kid. His first birthday without Dad. His third birthday in the valley, although the first one had just been a few weeks after they ended up here. Fourth without Mom.

"What do you want to do for *your* birthday?"

She swallowed a mouthful of scrambled eggs. "What?"

"I don't know what else I want to do for mine. Let's start planning yours."

She smiled. "Mine's not for two months, dork."

"We can start planning it now."

"We're planning yours now."

"I'm being grown-up and thinking of other people first."

Her fork clattered on her plate. "Oh crap!"

"What?!?"

"You're sick!" She reached out and pressed a hand against his forehead. "No fever, but you've definitely got some kind of brain infection. Maybe like the *Star Trek* worms!"

"Shut up."

"Maybe they crawled in your ear while you were asleep and took over your brain!"

"Shut *up*!"

"Ross, did you see a worm crawl in Billy's ear last night?"

"Unfortunately, Miss Beau, I was in sleep mode, but my sensors detected no foreign—"

"Maybe the Castaway can make a really skinny finger and reach in there after it. Hopefully there's only one."

"I'm going to train Charlie to poop in your sleeping bag." Billy looked over at his own bed, where the cat was asleep in a ball.

She smiled at him over a forkful of breakfast. "He won't. He likes me better."

"Does not."

"Does."

"You stupid fuckbutt."

She choked on a piece of mushroom. "What?"

"I said you're a stupid fuckbutt." Sometimes when he was off getting water or gathering potatoes, he practiced making new swears and seeing how they sounded. He'd been saving that one for a while now.

"Jesus," she said. "Sometimes it's like you're still nine."

"Well, I'm not. I'm going to be twelve tomorrow and I can say whatever I want and call you whatever I want. Fuckbutt, fuckbutt, fuckbutt."

"You done?"

"Maybe."

"Eat your eggs before they get cold."

He didn't want to do what she said, but she was right. Cold triceratops eggs were the worst. Like trying to eat a spoonful of soft margarine.

"You should be in school right now," she said. "Screwing up your math homework and making friends and complaining about having to read *Romeo and Juliet* for English class."

He nodded. "So it's a good thing we're here."

"No. It's not."

He shrugged and shoveled some more food into his mouth.

Beau pushed eggs around her plate. "So you don't want to do anything else for your birthday?"

"No."

"You sure?"

"Yeah. You don't want to do anything for *your* birthday?"

"We'll worry about it when we get there."

Billy speared a chunk of mushroom on his fork. Considered eating it while a few other thoughts rolled around in his head. "Dad's birthday is five months after yours."

Beau put her fork down again. "I know."

"Mom's is three months after his. Two months before mine."

"Yeah." She took a slow breath, and Billy wondered if she was counting to ten. She looked past him. "Do you have a birthday, Ross?"

"I don't, but thank you for asking, Miss Beau."

Billy scooted around on his rock. "Do you have a turned-on day?"

"My program was initialized on 19 April, 2576, Master Billy, but my systems weren't fully activated until 16 May of that year."

"That can be your birthday from now on, if you like."

"That would be nice, thank you."

"Sorry we missed it this year."

"That's quite all right, Master Billy."

Ross didn't say anything else. Beau went back to eating breakfast. Billy ate a little more and thought a little more.

He cleared his throat. Kept his eyes on his plate. "In seventeen days it'll be a year since Dad died."

Beau stopped eating.

"We're going to die here too, aren't we?"

"No!" She almost dropped her plate. For a second Billy thought she was going to yell at him again, but she crouched in front of him. "We're not."

"But we're never getting out. So we're going to die here."

"We *are* going to get out," she told him. "We just haven't figured out how yet."

"But—"

"That's what we're going to do for my birthday, okay? We're going to look for a way out. There's got to be something."

"The Castaway doesn't think so."

"Well, the Castaway doesn't know everything."

"I mean, they kinda do."

She handed her plate to Ross. Then took Billy's plate and handed it off, too.

"I wasn't done eating."

"You need a hug." She wrapped her arms around him.

"No I don't."

"Too late."

"Loser."

"Dweeb."

"Fuckbutt."

She hugged him harder. "Language."

He hugged her back.

"We're going to get out of here. You and me. You're not going to die. I'm not going to die."

"Promise?"

"I promise to make your life miserable until we're both old and gray, you little jerk."

42

NOAH

Noah swore he could feel his pulse run down his arms as they walked through the forest. He could almost hear it in his ears. He took a deep breath and tried, not for the first time since waking up that morning, to calm himself.

The trees could've been redwoods. He'd always meant to see the California redwoods. He'd gone to half a dozen different conferences out there over the years. Things just never lined up. It looked like that forest he'd seen in books and web clips and other people's travel photos. He wondered if this broad swath of trees had originally been in California or somewhere else. Some *when* else, maybe.

Another deep, calming breath. This one didn't sync up with his pulse and came out as a shuddering *whoosh*. First-date jitters meets first-day-of-classes anxiety.

Emerson looked back at him. "You okay?"

"Fine. Sorry."

Pyr let a few steps carry her closer. "We can slow down."

"I'm fine. Really. Just a little . . . y'know . . ."

"Nervous?"

"No."

Emerson faced front again. "Scared?"

"I was going to go with anxious."

"Whatever. Should be scared."

After all these years, he was going to see her again. Face-to-face. Not twenty yards apart. Not with dozens of other people around. Her and him. Talking. Together.

Pyr and Emerson had come with him as escorts. Noah'd wanted to come alone, but Qiang had convinced him the Klaa would see being by himself as a sign of weakness. And Pyr had suggested he might want help finding the way there. He'd tried to tell her he wouldn't need help finding the giant crystal tower at the center of the valley, but ultimately decided it wasn't worth the argument.

The trees ended and Emerson led them across a field of black rocks. It looked familiar, and it took Noah a moment to realize why. He stopped to check out three large stones, each with an X the size of his hand scratched in them. Centuries of dust filled the rough lines. "We made these," he explained. "Beau and I. This is where the glass obelisk used to be. Reminders not to touch it."

Pyr smiled. Emerson looked bored. "You needed to be reminded of that?"

"We were kids."

He turned away again. "We should keep moving."

A new forest sprang up on the other side of the lava field. This one felt more like the woods in New England. A good mix of trees. A few random shoots coming up through the thick mulch of the forest floor. Like the forest behind his home growing up, before they'd ended up here. Half a dozen childhood memories zipped through his mind.

Beau. Beau was up ahead. Finally.

Emerson's pace slowed for a moment while he scanned the forest. Noah's pace brought him next to the man and Emerson held an arm out to keep him from going further. A few heartbeats later and they headed forward through the forest.

Noah took another breath. Tried to distract himself. "My uncle—my mom's older brother—he was in Vietnam."

Emerson gave him a quick glance. "He make it back?"

"No."

"Sorry. Lot of guys didn't make it back."

"I never knew him."

"Sorry for your mom, then."

"She died when I was little."

"And then you ended up here. Twice." Emerson made a coughing sound that might've been a laugh. "No offense, buddy, but your family's got shit luck."

"Well . . . maybe that changes today."

"Hope so. Otherwise . . ." He glanced at Noah, at Pyr, and let the sentence die on his tongue.

"I know you want to kill her."

Emerson shook his head. "Don't want to kill anyone, man. But sometimes people need to die. Greater good, American way, all that."

"Not this time."

Emerson shrugged and grunted. Quickened his pace until he'd moved a few steps ahead again. Noah looked over at Pyr and saw a somewhat pitying expression on her face.

"It's going to be okay. She's going to remember me."

"We'll find out soon enough."

They walked in silence through the trees. Made a detour around a hungry dimetrodon tearing apart a velociraptor, its broad, spined fin swaying side to side with each jerk of its head. Walked some more until Noah saw brightness up ahead. The tree line. The edge of another area of terrain.

As they continued forward, Emerson's hand slid up toward his waist. He had one of Pyr's iron daggers hidden there. His fingers brushed the hem of his camouflage vest.

Noah looked around. Realized Pyr had moved close to him again. "Problem?"

"Just being safe." She had one of the daggers under her hooded wifebeater-tunic, but wasn't reaching for it.

"Why?"

Emerson gestured forward with his free hand. "Walking out of the trees, into the sunlight, it's going to take our eyes a moment to adjust. If they wanted a surprise attack, it's the best time."

"They're not going to attack us. She invited me here."

"No reason not to be cautious." Pyr stepped past Emerson and out into the sunlight.

Noah moved closer. "The Neanderthals don't like her because of her synthetic parts."

"Nope."

"So why let her go first?"

"Because the change in light don't affect her eyes. Not the plastic one, anyway."

"Clear," she called back into the trees.

They walked forward and Noah blinked as the full sun beat down on them. Pyr and Emerson settled in on either side of him, Emerson moving a few steps forward. Noah shaded his eyes with his hand and looked out across the grassland.

A full savanna spread out in front of them. At least a mile and a half of yellow-green grass. Every fifty or sixty feet a narrow-limbed tree spread itself toward the sky like a fountain of wood and leaves.

And past it all . . .

The Ice Castle towered above everything. A good four hundred feet over the tallest tree. Part iceberg, part architecture, part alien artifact. The legacy of the Castaway. Abandoned here to catch unfortunates throughout history.

It jarred his mind, seeing it at the far end of the savanna. Like running into someone from work in another city.

Noah's heart did something in his chest, and he heard another breath shudder out of his nose.

Emerson looked back and forth across the savanna. "You see anything?"

"No." Pyr shook her head.

"Gives me the creeps, being this close to the place."

Maybe a football field away, off to their left, a dinosaur stretched its neck up out of the grass. It had armored fins down its back and an array of long, straight spikes on its swaying tail. Noah chuckled, felt himself relax.

Pyr followed his eye line. "It's a stegosaurus. They're herbivores. Harmless."

"I know. First dinosaur I ever saw here."

He started across the grassland. Pyr fell in with him almost immediately. Emerson took a few quick steps to catch up.

The grass whisked against his knees as they walked. No paths here. Not even beaten-down grass. Was this area relatively new to the valley, or just rarely used? Did it matter?

The nervousness worked across his shoulders, into his chest, down his arms. Why was he nervous? This was it. A mile to go before their reunion.

Another stegosaurus lumbered through the grass, moving closer than the first one. Its head never rose, but Noah heard it sniff and snort as it moved along. If it noticed them, it didn't care.

A distant eagle shriek echoed across the savanna. Emerson tensed up. He scanned the broad grasslands. Watching. Waiting for a dinosaur to leap out from behind one of the skinny trees.

Noah stepped past him. "We need to keep moving."

"This could still be a trap," muttered the old soldier.

"It's not a trap. And even if it was, why would they go through all this just to get me?"

"Because you mouthed off to the Empress."

Fifteen minutes of walking through the tall grass and Noah could see the sloping ramp leading up into the Castle and the dark shadow of the entrance. It sent another shiver through his chest. Not long now.

They'd gone maybe another fifty yards when a series of tuba-like honks drew his attention off to the right. Maybe a quarter mile away, a massive rust-orange boulder marked the line where the savanna became a swamp, and past those shallows he saw the sparkle and shimmer of open water. The lake.

A group of bluish-gray dinosaurs waded in the swamp, pulling up clumps of reeds and what looked like oversized lily pads. The duck-billed hadrosaurs. The water looked like it hit them around the middle of the leg, grazing the underside of their bellies. Maybe waist-deep for him.

One of them honked again, reached up to grab a mouthful of leaves from a tree, and showed off the long red crest on the back of its head. Not hadrosaurs, Noah realized. Not the ones he remembered, anyway. Something else that had changed in the valley.

A dozen more steps and the lines of the boulder shifted. The real shape of it became clear. The memory hidden under centuries of rust. He gasped.

Emerson tensed again. "What?"

"It's the riverboat. The Egyptian riverboat from when I was a kid."

Rusted holes pitted the whole surface of the hull. It looked like most of the railing had crumbled away. Or maybe been broken off.

"Ross's mentioned it in some of his old stories." Pyr tilted her head slightly and the sunlight gleamed on the synthetic sections of her face. "I don't think anyone's seen it this close in decades."

"Nobody who lived, anyway," muttered Emerson.

"It used to be a lot closer to the Castle," Noah said. "Maybe a hundred feet between them. And that's my little-kid memory of it."

The dinosaurs in the swamp honked again, like an adult talking in an old *Peanuts* cartoon.

They continued across the savanna. Now Noah could see the figures around the base of the ramp. One of them on a raptor.

Another two minutes of striding through the grass and they passed the last tree. Every facet of the ice tower looked the same, each gleam sparking another memory. Noah felt another thrill run down into his fingertips. Nothing between him and Beau now but a few Neanderthals. "Maybe you should let me take the lead."

Pyr glanced at him. "Why?"

"They're expecting me, but from what you're saying this is all new to them, too. Less of a surprise if I'm out front."

"Guy's got a point," Emerson said grudgingly.

"It's going to be fine."

They continued forward.

The mounted Neanderthal was a woman with red-brown hair in a massive tangle of dreadlocks. She held a spear in both hands across her body, resting against the back of the raptor's neck. Two more stood at the base of the ramp, each of them holding one of the crude axe-clubs. Another crouched a few yards away, like a hunter watching prey through the grass.

Noah led them toward the ramp. When they were a few yards away, one of the Klaa held out his weapon. Pointed with it. Said a few words.

Noah recognized the simple numbers and the hard emphasis. Without taking his eyes off the fur-draped man, he turned his head to Pyr. "Not you," he repeated. "Only me."

Another grunt from Emerson.

"I'm pretty sure it wasn't a threat. I think they're just saying what she told them to say."

Pyr eyed the guards. Flexed her biomechanical fingers. "Are you absolutely sure about this?"

"Yep." He considered saying something more, but his mind skipped ahead. Pictured the reunion.

Noah walked to the ramp. The two Neanderthals shuffled their feet, moving ever so slightly out of his way. They both smelled of leather and sweat and wood bark. He saw one of them tighten its grip on the long shaft of the axe-club and realized they were probably as nervous as Pyr and Emerson were.

The ramp was still glossy and spotless. He recognized a few different patterns in the not-ice. That starburst of facets. The long trio of ridges over there.

Halfway up he raised his eyes to the entrance. Would she be there, waiting for him? Maybe welcoming him? The scales gone from her eyes and her own memories present again.

She wasn't there. The entrance to the Castle loomed, the mouth of a yawning giant. Noah felt the cool air from inside rolling out and tumbling down the ramp.

He reached the top and looked back. Emerson still had one hand near his waist, trading stares with the Neanderthals. Pyr stared past them, up at Noah.

He gave her a little nod of his head and went inside.

The feeling of peace settled over him. Soft light, cool air, and that ultraclean scent. Thirty years back in the present—back on *Earth*—and he'd never smelled anything quite like it. Maybe little whiffs of alien air being manufactured by the lifeboat.

The hallways seemed smaller, and a minute later he chuckled. Nothing had changed, he'd just gotten taller. And a little wider. After so many things being different in the valley, the sameness of the Ice Castle caught him off guard.

He let the tunnels guide him deeper inside. So much of the Castle was a mystery. More so now that he knew what it really was. Beau could be anywhere in the massive structure. But his feet only knew one room to take him to.

It took him four, maybe five minutes to reach the Castaway's chamber. His mind grabbed at the familiar sights. Across the room, the dais where he'd first seen the bright purple alien. Over there, the alcove where he'd slept the time he'd come here searching for Charlie the cat.

But reality settled in fast. Someone new had moved in and put the furniture in different places, their own decorations on the walls. They'd all but buried the familiar, only the largest details still visible. Just like at the cave.

In this case, the decorations were pelts and hides. Furs he couldn't identify. The bedsheet-sized piece of raw leather stretched across the floor reminded him of the blue-gray dinosaurs outside in the swamp. A collection of rocks held down the edges of the leather rug. A few shiny chunks of quartz. A small slab of volcanic glass, cleaned and polished by hundreds, maybe thousands of touches. One piece that looked like a fist-sized ruby.

At least two of the rocks were actually skulls. Maybe a third. One of them had overly large eye sockets, tiny nostrils, and a peaked crest across the top of its cranium. The other one . . .

The other one looked human. Not Neanderthal, but plain old *Homo sapiens*. The third one was probably human, too. So were all the skulls piled up—displayed—in the sleeping alcove.

He looked away. Looked up at the thing on the dais that definitely wasn't a shape-changing purple alien. The one thing he knew on sight. He'd recognized it as soon as he'd walked into the room and forced himself not to look at it until now.

The tyrannosaurus skull stood in the middle of the dais. The bony snout and eye sockets pointed up at the ceiling. The huge jaw hung loose, sitting flat on the glassy floor. More furs and hides filled the space where the tongue had been, almost spilling out over the knife-sized teeth.

Noah walked slowly around the dais, studying the throne. The front four, maybe six teeth had been knocked out of the jawbone, giving the person seated there somewhere to put their legs. The remaining ones were glossy, polished by decades of use, of hands caressing them.

The teeth on the upper jaw were what held his attention, though. One on each side. Unnaturally large. Almost double the size of the others. If the other teeth were knives, these two were swords.

Or fangs.

He remembered those big teeth closing on his father.

Something scraped behind him.

His breath caught as he whirled around and his heartbeat went from bouncing to hammering.

Beau stood by one of the entrances to the room. Her wrist moved in slow circles, and the obsidian knife in her hand scratched short lines in the archway. She stared at him. Noah saw curiosity in her gaze. Some dismissal.

She broke their stare and walked across the chamber. A few strides carried her past him, and for a moment they were side by side and he almost laughed. Years of threatening it as a kid, but he was finally bigger than her. At least six inches taller. Maybe eight.

If she registered the size difference, she didn't show it. Her bare feet carried her onto the dais. She turned, lowered herself onto the tyrannosaurus skull throne, leaned forward to rest her arms on her knees.

A huge wave of relief crashed over him. The sudden lightness of achievement. A massive, years-long task finally complete.

He'd done it.

"Hi, Beau."

She stared at him some more. Pursed her lips even as her jaw shifted back and forth. She had different face paint on now. Black rings around her eyes, so wide they touched on the bridge of her nose and almost made a broad stripe across her face.

She still held the knife. Let the point swing side to side. In the light, it clearly wasn't obsidian. Too bright. Too translucent. It looked like sky-blue glass.

Noah looked at the tanned, painted face, the mane of white hair, tried to pull his teenage sister out of it. He'd always imagined Beau would get older and look like their mother, but her jawline had turned out more like their father's. Her pixie nose was still there, and he tried to add those last bits of baby fat back to her cheeks, mentally rounding out her face.

Still no reaction. She looked him up and down. Examined him. Tapped the flat of the crystal knife against the side of her bare knee.

"It's me. Billy."

The knife came up. Pointed at him. "You lie."

"No, it's me."

"You lie to your Empress."

"It's me. I know it's been a long time—a really long time—but it's me." He turned his head left and right. "The beard's probably a little weird, too, right?"

The knife slowly tipped down. "Billy is dead. He died centuries ago."

Noah shook his head. "No. I went down to the watering hole to fill the gourds and I . . . slipped. Ended up in the right place at the right time. The valley sent me home."

Beau's eyebrows went up. "That isn't possible."

"It is. I went home. Back to Earth." He gestured at himself. At his adult body. "It was dumb luck. I spent years trying to find out how I could get back here. Back for you. And I finally did it."

"No."

"Yep."

"Nothing enters my valley without my permission."

"Seriously, it's—"

"What color were Billy's shoes?"

"What?"

The tip of the knife came up. "What color were his shoes?"

His mind derailed, went blank for a moment, and then the answer came back. "Black. They'd been Batman sneakers but the logo was just ironed on. They came off a week before the . . . the raft trip. I left them on my desk at—"

"What color was his backpack?"

"Dark blue. The bottom and straps were black. It had a little silver plastic anchor on the top loop. Mom gave it to me on our first rafting trip, so I wouldn't fall out of the boat. Said it was an old sailor thing."

"What killed Billy's father?"

He stared at her. Tried to imagine her blue eyes getting that pale. Her dirty blond hair going white. His sister had always hated long hair. One of their mother's favorite stories had been about how she'd given little Beau pigtails once, and Beau'd hacked them off with a pair of scissors.

"You know what killed him." Noah pointed above her, at the massive skull throne. "He did. Fang."

She tilted her head this way and that. Studying him the same way he'd studied her, mentally subtracting years. He put a hand up and covered his beard, opening his eyes a little wider as he did.

Her lips dropped open. "The eyes of the boy in the face of the man," she whispered. "It is you." Amazement softened her harsh tones into a low hiss. Made her voice sound more like . . .

Like . . .

The warm thrill left Noah. No more tingling. No more hammering heart.

The woman's face hardened again. She smiled at him. A cat's smile. "Little Billy Gather. Not dead after all."

"No, I'm not. And you're not Beau, are you?"

"I am not. Your sister died by her own hand so many years ago, finally wiping the valley clean of your family's stain. Or so we all thought."

Everything rushed out of him again. The void that had hollowed him out as he'd read Beau's last journal entry opened wide. The emptiness tried to take all his strength again, to drag him down, and only one thing let him hang on.

"Who are you?"

She settled back into the throne. One hand stroked the oversized teeth set into the massive jaw. "Another lost soul trapped in the valley, much like you were. Trapped here for so very long.

"Perhaps three years after your sister killed herself, I wandered in the forest not far from here. Well, not far then. So many things have moved. A velociraptor attacked me. A small thing, not much bigger than a wolf, but it caught me unprepared. It knocked me down. Slashed open my abdomen. Gutted me. Severed the muscles in my forearm while I tried to hold it off. I caught its neck. Strangled it. But the damage was done. A wound so severe even the magic of the valley couldn't help me.

"I crawled through the forest and ended up here. I only wanted to hide from predators so I could die in peace. But the Castaway found me collapsed inside their doorstep and they took pity on me, in the way children sometimes take pity on wounded animals." Her face lit up, and she leaned forward on her throne. "You nursed an animal back to health here, didn't you Billy? The tan-and-black cat?"

He nodded cautiously. "Charlie. How do you know about him?"

"This is my valley. I know everything that has happened here."

They stared at each other for a few heartbeats. The woman's face was so eerily timeless he couldn't figure out how to picture her younger. But familiarity lurked just beneath her features.

She sat forward and tapped the crystal knife against her knee again. "The Castaway repaired my wounds and more. They were so far beyond you and me, they didn't understand some of what they perceived as damage was only the natural limitations of my body and mind. They fed intelligence and knowledge into me the way a field medic might default to giving an injured soldier a fluid drip."

She leaned back. Gestured at the flawless skin of her six-pack stomach with her smooth, golden arm. Vamping like a model. Or an angry ex showing off what he'd missed out on.

"And so I was reborn. My arm and stomach and face repaired. My power increased. My vision of how things should be, my destiny as the Empress, all written into the very fabric of the valley."

Noah's mind spun, trying to get past decades of expectations, trying to make sense of what he was hearing. He latched onto one thing, the inconsistent thing. "You said the raptor slashed up your stomach and arm. So why did the Castaway have to repair your . . ."

A flash flood of memories swelled and filled the void in his heart with icy childhood terror.

The Empress saw his expression and smiled, baring her teeth like a cat that had played with its food long enough. She pointed the dagger at him again. "There's the boy I knew. There you are, Billy."

He struggled to catch his breath. Fought not to be overwhelmed by fear. The phantom smell of urine tickled his nose, and he got enough air to gasp out her name.

"Scarnose."

43

JOSH

Shino led them through the cypress trees. Sam brought up the rear easily enough, but Olivia and Josh were having trouble keeping the pace. They slowed again and kept getting closer to him, further from her.

"Hey," Josh called out.

Shino turned. Saw Olivia and Josh lagging behind. She nodded. Let her spear tip rest against the ground while she waited for them to catch up. Josh wished she looked a little more alert, but told himself she'd probably done this before.

He hadn't wanted to go on this little trip, but Olivia really wanted to and she still seemed more comfortable talking with him than Sam or any of the random Roanoke folks. And the wardens had sworn up and down things were at their safest for a week or two after tribute was collected. At least from the killer Neanderthals. There were still the killer dinosaurs.

So Josh was finally back outside the wall, walking alongside Olivia, his free arm ready for her to grab if she wanted it, or to grab her if she stumbled. The uneven ground gave her a bit of trouble, but overall she seemed to be doing okay. She'd only taken his help once, but she'd also slowed down a few times rather than accepting it.

She glanced up at Sam as he took a few quick steps and got alongside them. "You doing okay?"

"Yes positive okay good fine." She gave him a lopsided smile with some smirk in it. She'd woken up this morning with a slightly more casual vocabulary and the ability to speak in five-word sentences. Everyone saw it as a good sign, and it had improved her mood a bit.

"I think we're almost there."

Olivia took a deep breath. Lifted her head a little higher. Gestured for them to keep going.

"Are you sure you're up for this?" asked Josh. "We don't have to do it today. I mean, this is only like your third day awake and moving around."

"Yes perhaps no maybe depending."

He chuckled.

Sam smiled and repeated her gesture, directing them toward Shino. "Let's go, then."

Up ahead, Shino turned and continued through the large grove of trees.

They'd been issued weapons. Told to carry the spears with the point down so they looked like walking sticks. Apparently a pretty standard thing for going outside with the killer dinosaurs and killer Neanderthals and all that. Sam also had a knife Pyr had given him for their trip out to Noah's cave. Josh wondered how much of it was just security theater. Would any of it matter if Gnash or Burn showed up?

A wide field of tall grass stretched beyond the trees, surrounding the graveyard. No baby people or animals allowed, but plants seemed to grow well here. Of course they would. It was one big controlled environment.

Josh looked up at the sky. Was it a big dome? A force field? Some kind of projection? Did it reach beyond the clifftops?

Hell, were there even cliffs? Maybe that was why nothing could go past a certain height. Maybe the top third of the valley was just a big hologram.

The graveyard looked like something out of an old western, just a lot bigger. He guessed it might have close to a hundred graves in it. As they got closer to the wood-rail fence, he doubled his estimate.

Shino looked around. Nodded. "Take your time," she told them.

She took a few more steps past the graveyard entrance, her posture and attitude making it clear she'd keep watch.

Olivia stopped to stare at the little arch of twisted branches. The rough fence of stacked stones and wood beams. The field of so many markers and cairns. She turned and for a moment Josh thought she was going to start walking back toward Roanoke. But she just stopped to stare across the wide expanse. She took a deep breath. "Serene relax peace easy calm."

Across the field, a low, rounded boulder wobbled side to side and took a few heavy steps. Josh's heart rate shot up. Epinephrine spike.

The turtle-like dinosaur let out a bored whoof and chomped down on a new bush closer to the far tree line. It dragged the whole thing out of the ground, slowly grinding the branches up in its beak.

They all stared for a moment while it devoured the bush. Josh relaxed, glanced back at Sam. "That's the one you saw, right? The clone?"

Sam peered at the distant dinosaur. "It's the same kind, yeah. Ankylosaurus. But I don't think it's the exact one we saw. Pyr said there were other ones in the valley."

"Other clones?"

"I think just regular dinosaurs?"

"Okay."

"Yeah, this one looks like its armor is a little different. Bulkier."

"Like Gamera."

Sam chuckled.

The dinosaur sneezed or coughed or spat out a few clumps of dirt that had clung to the bush's roots. It shook its head, shifted its massive weight to the side, and grabbed another beakful of shrub. This time it broke the branch off.

A random memory drifted up through Josh's thoughts. "When I was a kid, I had a turtle in a big terrarium. Took up the whole top of my dresser. It had plants and a little pond and a log."

"Yeah?"

"Yeah. I always wondered if he thought he was really outside or if he just knew something was off about all of it."

Olivia drifted past them into the graveyard. Josh stepped after her, staying a few feet behind, giving her space. She made it to the first row of graves. Paused. Looked back at Josh, then Sam. Sam pointed off to the corner, walking toward it as he did. She fell in next to him.

Blue-skinned Thate had told them where they'd put the marker. Apparently symbolic graves weren't that uncommon here. It only took a few minutes to find the small pile of stones. Behind the pile stood a wooden plank with some black paint that spelled out LOGAN. Whoever put it up apparently hadn't known his last name, but they'd left room for additions. Very considerate.

Olivia stared at the sign. At the pile of rocks. She swayed on her feet for a moment, taking a few deep breaths. "Strategized pending partner former excursion."

Josh and Sam traded a look. He juggled the words, parsed meanings, remembered earlier conversations he'd overheard. Sam figured it out first. "You were going to break up with him on the trip. Or right after it."

"Yes positive correct confirmed accurate." Her mouth and nose made a sound. The start of awkward laughter. Or maybe tears. Or both.

Josh gently touched her arm. "This isn't your fault. Seriously. This didn't happen because of you. Because of anything you did or were going to do. It was a . . . a freak accident."

Sam took in a quick breath as if to speak, and seemed to think better of it. Josh was pretty sure the shorter man was carrying some guilt about Logan, too. He'd been talking nonstop about how he'd read all those books and then let his colleagues get fried on the electro-obelisk-thing. Plenty of guilt to go around. Plenty of time to sort it all out.

Josh let his gaze drift past the grave marker and realized there was another new one behind it. Almost identical, but this one said KYLE. Again, space for a last name. He wondered how often symbolic markers ended up here in the graveyard. Percentage-wise, how many people died in the valley and left a body behind?

Olivia knelt, leaned back, dropped onto her ass in front of the grave. She stared at the wooden plank. At all the other mounds of stone and their faded signs. She made her laughing-crying sound again. Put a hand over her mouth.

Sam went to move closer, but Josh held out a hand. "Just give her a sec."

"She—"

"She just needs a minute to get it all out."

He leaned in, lowered his voice. "Now you're a grief counselor?"

Josh let his own voice drop. "Believe it or not, a lot of my clientele are trying to deal with something. We had a few products that created a state of . . . call it extreme emotional release."

"Why?"

"Sometimes people just, y'know, need a good cry."

"And they pay for that?"

"Cheaper than therapy. I mean, if we're comparing one dose to an individual session. Long-term, you can still make an argument for—"

Sam quieted him with a wave.

Olivia let out a few more laugh-sobs. "Self occurrence negative effect desire. Outcome negative individual effect consequence." Josh saw her watery eyes and lopsided smirk and the deep breaths that made her nose quiver.

Sam took a small step forward. Crouched. She glanced at him, looked away, wiped her face with her arm.

"It's okay. You can take all the time you want. We're not in a rush."

"On your guard!" Shino's words echoed across the graveyard.

Josh spun and his heart rate spiked again. Found her halfway between the graveyard's entrance and the fence's far corner. Closer to the distant tree line. Farther from Roanoke.

The ankylosaurus had turned around. It backed away, holding its club-like tail high, swinging it back and forth in slow, heavy arcs. It made short chuffing sounds, like angry snorts, that carried across the field.

Shino took a few steps back toward the entrance. Lifted her spear. Didn't turn it around, point up, but gave herself space to do it.

Josh only saw the two Klaa at first, because their mounts were head-on and the raptors' coarse, golden feathers semi-blended with the terrain. In the few seconds it took his mind to register the two riders, they'd crossed half the distance between the tree line and the graveyard. Not running, but a heavy jog. One of the raptors let out an ear-splitting screech.

One of the riders wore a ton of teeth-jewelry. The one Sam had told them about. Breaker.

Apparently Shino recognized him, too. Even from a few yards away, Josh could see her grip tightening on the spear. She stood her ground.

"We should get closer to her," said Sam.

"The *dinosaurs* are getting closer to her," Josh pointed out, feeling like a jackass as soon as the words came out.

"Whatever spoken guide correct agreement."

"The Klaa—they—the Neanderthals don't like being outnumbered. She's alone." Sam's breath was speeding up, catching in his throat.

Josh's fingers twitched on his own spear.

"Come on." Sam headed off through the cemetery.

Josh stared at the approaching raptors. Felt all his self-preservation instincts kicking in. Knowing the deal had just gone south. Impending violence. A desperate urge to try to talk his way out or slip away.

He took a breath. Mentally rattled off half a dozen compounds that'd be fantastic to have right now and how they'd calm his heart and his breathing and help him think clearer.

He looked at Olivia. "You up for this?"

"Yes yeah definitely confirmed absolutely."

Josh tried to speed-walk through the cemetery. Tried to keep his spear up so it wouldn't get caught on one of the grave markers. Tried to keep it low enough so it didn't look like he was carrying a spear. Olivia kept up, only stumbling once and catching herself quickly.

The Klaa slowed a few yards away from Shino and Sam. Breaker grunted something and the two riders separated, guiding their mounts ten-fifteen-twenty feet apart. Shino still stood between them and the entrance to the cemetery. Sam stood just behind her with his spearhead down in the grass, like a wizard standing with his staff.

The other Neanderthal had black hair and the same tied-on furs and hides they all wore. One of the rough wooden weapons hung by her thigh. She held a spear of her own up at her shoulder, ready to stab down.

Josh slowed a bit as he made it to the twisted-branch exit. Didn't want to look too anxious. Too threatening. His spear clattered on the arch as he walked out and stood between Shino and Sam.

Breaker's raptor let out a quick huff of air.

"Both hands on your spears," she told them. "Look at them, but don't look them in the eyes."

"What's going on? I thought they stayed away after tribute."

Shino gave a quick shake of her head. "They normally do." She spoke one loud word, directing the sound at Breaker. He responded with rough, barking syllables, shaking his axe-club at her. Josh wondered if they actually understood each other, or if it was all about tone and body language.

Breaker dug his heels into the side of his mount and the raptor took a few loping steps, shifting further away from the other rider. Shino tracked him, pivoting slowly at her waist. Her hands slid wider on her spear. The Neanderthal grinned. Shouted a few more coarse, short words.

The other rider shifted her legs and her own dinosaur moved beneath her. The raptor let out a quick, hissing squawk, like an angry crow.

Something moved next to him and his heart bounced in his chest. He locked eyes with Olivia for a second. The four of them standing there in a knot now. Three of them with long sticks. Hopefully a bit more of a presence to Neanderthal eyes.

Shino shouted at Breaker. He shouted back, and his raptor added a shriek Josh felt in his teeth. The other Neanderthal's raptor snapped its jaws in the air, thrusting its head toward Sam as its feet clawed at the dirt and rocks. Still a good ten feet away, nowhere near him, but the lunge made Sam stumble back.

Something shot through the air and cracked into the Klaa woman's forehead. She tipped back on her almost-saddle, yanking on the reins, and Josh saw a flash of red above her eye. The raptor reared around, roaring and hissing, circling back away from them. The woman straightened up and blood covered one side of her face. Her eyes didn't look focused. Stunned, maybe mildly concussed.

Breaker's raptor lunged, kicking up dirt and dust. The dinosaur thundered past Shino, and Breaker lashed out with his foot as she spun her spear around. The kick caught her in the shoulder, knocked her back, sent her crashing into the wooden fence rails. She bounced off, stumbled, faceplanted. The Neanderthal kicked his raptor, turned it around again. He snarled gleefully at Sam. No, past Sam, at . . .

Josh risked a glance over his shoulder and saw Olivia picking up a rock about the size of a tennis ball. *Another* rock, he realized. She looked uncertain, and Josh wasn't sure if she was confused by the situation, the fact that she'd just thrown a rock at someone, or the fact that she'd scored a solid hit.

Sam took two steps and threw his spear as hard as he could. Wildly off target, but strength made up for skill and gave it some speed. It missed Breaker and his raptor. By a lot. But it got his attention.

Made him pick a new target.

Breaker did something with his feet and the gold-brown raptor shuffled around and let out another sharp-edged growl. It lunged, cut the distance between them in half as Breaker raised his heavy axe-club. Sam stepped to the side and Josh realized he'd just made himself a better target for the weapon.

He let go of his spear and took three quick steps. Reached Sam maybe two seconds before Breaker. Tackled him. Had a brief moment of panic when he realized how goddamned solid Sam was. Short but heavy with muscle. Momentum won out, though, and they both went down as Breaker's club swung through the air.

Josh felt the hit. Felt the pain surge up and overwhelm everything in his head. For a second he couldn't see, couldn't hear, couldn't feel anything. Just blackness and pain and more pain and then . . .

Then he was on the ground. Next to Sam. Sam was okay. He'd saved him. He'd been brave. Maybe it'd impress Monique?

Sam looked horrified, though. Not happy at all about being saved. Talk about being . . .

Being . . .

What was the word?

His head still hurt. Hurt so much. He needed . . . he needed headache pills.

The blond woman standing behind Sam looked scared too. What was her name? Why couldn't he remember her . . .

He tried to roll over. Get back to his feet. His arm twitched on the ground. His foot kicked. Had he tried to move his foot?

Why couldn't he . . .

Why was everything dim?

Was it night already?

. . . was the sun going out?

44

NOAH

The Empress leaned forward on her throne. The glass dagger wove back and forth between her fingers, like a pen spun absently during an exam. "Yes. That was your name for me, wasn't it?" Her wicked, catlike smile never wavered. "Trying to hide how scared you were with silly titles."

Noah'd always remembered her face with its Freddy Krueger scars and the gaping hole where half her nose had been torn away. Hell, he couldn't remember ever seeing her without sweat grime on her face or leaves in her tangled hair. He'd never considered what she would've looked like under all that.

But once he pushed away all those childhood impressions, he could see her sitting there. The shape of her eyes and chin. The broad shoulders. Her widow's peak hairline was virtually the same. Hell, her hair was longer, bigger, but still whitest at the temples, shot through with gray and dark brown everywhere else. Enough familiarity to spark his old memories without being enough for him to actually recognize her under the face paint.

Until now.

"You're the Empress," he said.

"I am."

"How?"

"Because the valley is mine."

Noah bit his lip. The initial rush of fear had washed through him, and now he felt . . . well, definitely not calm, but rational. Slightly braver. No more confusion about who he was dealing with. He wasn't a little boy anymore. She wasn't a monster. Just a woman.

A very muscular woman with a long knife in her hand.

"I meant, how did you become the ruler? How'd you go from bossing around four members of the Pakka to . . . ?" He gazed around the throne room.

"The Pakka were weak. Little more than children. I kept them alive here, but even among my people, they were limited in their aspirations."

"And then you found the Klaa?"

"Then I brought the Klaa here. I wanted fighters. Warriors. And the valley gave them to me. Because I am the Empress."

"Because you're the Empress," he echoed.

The amusement vanished from her face. The blade stopped spinning to point at him again. "Do not mock me, little Billy."

Qiang's warnings danced in his head, her stabbing him if she got annoyed. Noah felt a little nervous chill between his shoulders and realized the power dynamic between them hadn't changed much after all.

They stared at each other for a few more moments and the dagger resumed its slow, irregular orbit around her fingers.

"I came here, to the Castle, because I thought you were Beau. Why did you . . . summon me?"

Her grip loosened on the knife. "You truly are the arrogant little boy from all those centuries ago. Not dead. Returned to the world outside and then brought back to my valley."

None of it was questions, but he answered anyway. "Yep."

"How did you return?"

Noah shrugged. "About twenty years of math."

She was on her feet, her arm stretching out, and the glass dagger was a blur. It was already back at her side by the time he felt the pain in his face. *Under* his face. She'd scraped his cheekbone under his eye and the bridge of his nose so hard the bone ached. But how could her blade hit bone without—

The sting of pain burned across his face. The first drop of blood touched his tongue. Then the stream hit his lips and the line of pain caught fire. His nose was red and wet. His cheek was coated with it.

She settled back on her throne. "I warned you not to mock me. Now you can be Scarnose."

"*Christ!*" He felt the stinging flap of his cheek. A thin, deep slash, like a gigantic paper cut. Hot blood ran across his mouth, down his chin. The childhood fear surged up with it, danced on the underside of his brain.

But the fear came with old assurances. How many times had the thought rang in his head over the past decades—*if I was in the valley, this would barely slow me down. It wouldn't even leave a scar.*

Noah tried to ignore the stinging pain, spread his fingers wide and held his cheek and nose together. Blood still slid down his neck, soaked into his shirt. "I wasn't mocking you. That's how I got back here. Years of research and calculations to find the exact spot, right where and when I needed to be on Earth to get back here."

All the old hatred simmered in her eyes. How had he ever thought she was Beau? The knife spun once on her palm and then the blade pointed at him. "Explain."

He wondered how much information the Castaway had given her. Should he try to explain planetary rotation and orbital mechanics? Simplify or use specifics? "What do you know about the valley itself?"

"Everything. It is mine."

He bit back a sigh. "Do you know this place isn't really a valley?"

She said nothing.

He took it as a sign to continue. Also a sign she didn't know what he was talking about, so he racked his brain for a metaphor. "Okay, you know how a log floats in the water, and then you can use the log to cross a lake or a river or—"

"I understand the concept of a starship. The Castaway put a great deal of knowledge in my mind." She leaned back in her throne. "The valley is a secondary vessel he used to flee the destruction of his interdimensional craft, in the way mindless animals flee a forest fire."

Noah nodded and the cut across his cheek and nose flexed, burning sharp enough to make his eyes water. A reminder not to underestimate her. "The lifeboat stays at a certain fixed point, and that point is in Earth's orbit. Once a year their paths intersect. But the nature of the Castaway's ship means that intersection can also reach through history."

Her eyebrow twitched.

"But wherever and whenever it ends up, things at the intersection point end up here. Inside the lifeboat. In the valley. It's like . . . like a bug in the water that gets trapped on that log. The log doesn't mean to grab it. It's just random chance."

"No. Nothing comes here unless I will it. I control everything. The lifeboat is mine. The valley is mine. The ground itself shakes in fear of my power."

He shook his head and set off another surge of pain. "I'm sorry, Empress, but that's how . . ."

A blink of light over her shoulder caught his eye. One of the random sparkles that ran through the walls of the Ice Castle. He'd never considered there could be meaning behind them.

"Why?"

Her grin vanished. Her brow furrowed as she studied him. Still a Neanderthal at heart.

"The Castaway. When they left, why did they give you control of all of this?"

Her eyes opened wide. The grin returned. She took in a breath, tilted her head back, and laughed up into the tyrannosaurus skull. "Still a silly little boy. Still so much you don't know or understand. I am the Empress. I do not wait for things to be given to me. I take them."

"What's that supposed to mean?"

"Mind your tone, little Billy. The valley heals many things, which means I can cut you deep for days on end without fear of you dying on me." She pointed the glass dagger at him again. "I had one man last for almost four weeks."

The nervous fear nestled in his lungs again. He felt his pulse throb in the wound across his face, and a few more drops of blood fell from his cheek to his chest "I . . . I'm sorry. Please . . . what happened when the Castaway left?"

"The Castaway did not leave. I killed them."

The air in the chamber felt cold on his skin. "That's not possible."

"I am the Empress. All things are possible for me."

"How?"

She leaned back in the throne, vamping again. "It took time. Decades. Only part of them was ever *here*, after all. But all it takes to kill something is knowing where to put the knife. I only had to watch. And wait. And stab the right part."

"You . . ." His mind raced back and forth between the horror of it and the sheer nonsense. "You killed a multidimensional alien? With a *knife*?"

The dagger of blue glass spun between her fingers again. "A knife made from their own home. I watched them die. And then I claimed their power as my own."

He watched the blade. Looked at the walls behind her. The vaulted ceiling. The floor, splattered with a few small puddles of his blood. Another drop fell as he stared.

What color had the Castaway's blood been?

She'd killed his friend.

"Why am I here?"

The dagger stopped spinning. The blade away from him this time. Her icy eyes burned. "I sent for you. And you obeyed."

He felt like a cowboy facing down a gunslinger at high noon. "No. How did I get *here*? How did little Billy Gather come back to the valley with his friends if the Empress decides what enters?"

Just for an instant he saw something else in her eyes, something else he remembered from childhood. Whenever Dad had to confront the Pakka about something. Dad who'd been a giant in their eyes.

She was nervous. Angry, but nervous too. Maybe even scared.

But only for an instant.

The blade pointed at the floor. "Kneel before me. Kneel in your own blood."

"Why?"

"Because your Empress told you to. Because you annoy me, little Billy-now-Noah. You are not part of my vision of the valley. You do not belong here."

He debated kneeling. Doing what she wanted. Would it make things go better or worse?

She tapped the dagger against her knee. Stood up on the dais in front of the throne, putting her head above his. The blade whipped out again, slashing up. So fast. Slicing the other cheek from the corner of his mouth to the corner of his eye. *Just* missing his eye.

He screamed and staggered back, grabbed at his face, pressed the cut together. Another razor-cut into the meat. More of his blood hit the floor. Had she missed the bone this time or had he just missed it in all the pain? Holy *fuck*, so much pain.

So much for facing down the gunslinger.

"Go back to your little village, man-boy. Go back and take this message with you. This is what the Empress demands of the people of Roanoke.

"Tell them you are a liar. You are not Billy Gather, but you have reminded me of the past and so your very existence in the valley is an insult. You are to be executed. You and ten others from their village. Penance for insulting the Empress with your lies. Your bodies are to be hung in the forest by their fields."

He took in a breath. Bit his tongue. Stared at her through the fingers holding his face together.

"Because I am a generous Empress, I will give the people of Roanoke one day to do this. Tomorrow I shall come to view the bodies. And to bury my dagger in each one to be sure they are dead.

"When I come, I shall bring the full might of the Klaa. And if I do not find your body strung up, and the fresh bodies of ten others of your kind, then I will give B'Kar free rein to do what he has wanted to do for so many years. The Klaa will kill everything within the walls of that little village. Every one of you. We wipe your stain from the valley, and this time I will make sure of it."

She met his eyes. Pointed the dagger at his eyes. The tip of the blade blurred in his vision. "Do you understand what you have been told?"

He nodded clumsily, his hands holding his bloody face together.

"Then run away, little Billy. Run away from me, like you always do. The next time I lay eyes on you, one way or another, you will finally be dead."

45

PARKER

Parker stood in the main hall and listened to Qiang try to explain why Josh was dead. She knew *why* he was dead. She'd seen his . . . she'd seen the body. The head. She was just trying to find a bigger understanding past that.

The lamps and the simple chandelier had been lit, banishing the shadows up to the ceiling and the far corners. At least half of Roanoke had gathered to hear the news of the Empress's identity, her threat, and Breaker attacking the group at the graveyard. A lot of them had heard the news already. It was a small village.

"We think Breaker was looking to hurt someone," Qiang explained. "Between your encounter out in the valley and the Empress's attitude toward you, well . . ."

"Breaker's a pretty solid name for him," said Warwick.

Parker watched the crowd. She didn't know every name, but at this point she recognized all the faces. Some of them were angry. Some of them were scared. All whispering in pairs and trios.

Qiang sat at the head with Noah next to him. Some of the wardens—Warwick, Emerson, and Neith—gathered on the other side of the table. Marissa had tried to give her seat to Ross as they all wandered in, but the android had politely refused, preferring to lean on its walking stick near the head of the table.

Parker stood with Sam and Olivia, somewhat behind Noah. Sam had dragged one of the wooden chairs away from the table for Olivia, and now he and Parker stood on either side of her. Olivia hadn't said a word since they'd come back from the cemetery. Sam hadn't said much, either. Parker was pretty sure his little-kid enthusiasm for the valley had been shattered.

Noah wasn't any better. The clotted gashes across his face made him look like he'd stepped out of a war movie. Or maybe a slasher. But it was more than that. He wouldn't meet her eyes. He barely met anybody's eyes. Just sat slumped back in his chair.

"Again," Qiang said, "I'm so very sorry for you. Death is frequent here, but that doesn't make it any easier."

Parker searched the crowd again for Josh. Felt another sharp twinge. In her gut it still felt like Josh would wander into the meeting any moment now. Probably with food in his hands and a stupid sci-fi reference to make.

She looked at Monique, a few seats away. The doctor hadn't said much since arriving, except to announce she'd set and splinted Shino's arm. Her eyes had the watery look of someone who hadn't quite figured out if she wanted to cry or not.

Parker wished she hadn't always been so dismissive of Josh. It didn't seem to bother him much, but it gnawed at her now. What was the last thing she'd said to him? He'd been around enough she hadn't really thought about it. When did she become the mean girl again?

Qiang cleared his throat. "I also think we need to remember Joshua Redd's death as we discuss the Empress's threat."

The whispers in the room surged into murmurs. Parker could guess what was coming next. She just didn't know who it would come from.

"We should kill her." Sam didn't look at anyone as he spoke. Just stared into the space above the big table. "The Empress. Breaker. All of them."

"Hell yeah," said Emerson. "Seconded. We should've offed her years ago."

A mutter of agreement fumbled its way through the main hall.

Qiang sighed. "We can't kill her."

"We can and we should," said the old soldier.

"We have no idea how the Klaa will react."

"Losing their leader will break their chain of command!"

Diedrich rapped his knuckles on the table. "Ja. But which way will it break?"

"What do you mean?"

"Fight or flight," Diedrich said. "Their most common reactions, ja? So without the Empress, do they run away and scatter across the valley? Or do they fall in behind Breaker and try to kill us all anyway?"

"That's the big question, ain't it?" Warwick sat with his fingers laced before him on the table. "Damned if we do, damned if we don't."

Neith clapped twice. She spoke several sentences, looking at each of them as she did. She pointed at herself, then crossed her arms.

Ross took a shuffling step forward. "Neith has heard us use the Empress's name several times and hopes we are in agreement to kill her. She believes it is the simplest solution and the right thing to do."

Emerson looked over at the woman. Gave her a thumbs-up. She sent a sharp, military nod back at him.

Sam made one of his quick breath sounds. Parker glanced at him. He was studying the crowd too, with the distinct air of a student desperate to be called on so he could contribute to the discussion.

Qiang turned his attention to Warwick. "Is there any chance we can hold her off?"

"Not bloody likely." He shook his head. "The walls are fine for basic defense, keeping things from sneaking into town, but they won't stop anything really big that directly attacks us. The Klaa could goad a big dino right through the front gate. Hell, probably right through the wall in a few places."

"And if what Noah says is true," added Pyr, "if she's bringing most of them, they could surround us and attack from all sides. We'd have to defend from every direction."

"Or they could wait us out," said one of the other villagers. Parker recognized the bulky man from the top of the wall the other night, but she'd forgotten his name.

Warwick nodded. "Yeah, we'd do lousy in a siege. Especially an extended one."

Qiang's gaze stretched down the length of the table, and Parker followed it to Marissa. The wavy-haired woman shook her head. "We just did the tribute. There's not much food in the storehouse. The next big harvest is, what, six weeks away?"

Dak Ho nodded.

She shrugged. "So if they pinned us in here, and we all went on a diet, we'd make it . . . a week? Maybe ten days?"

A low murmur went around the room. Qiang raised a hand. Waited for quiet. Parker'd never realized how much politics was like teaching an undergraduate class.

"I know it feels like we don't have any options," he told the group, "but we need to be very clear what we're talking about. If we decide to attack the Empress, there will be no going back. It will be war, and we cannot win a war against the Klaa."

"*If* they fight back once she's dead," said Emerson. "They might not."

"That's a big *if*," said a woman wearing something that might've been a Victorian overcoat ten or twelve repairs ago.

Qiang nodded in agreement. "And that's why we don't want to make any quick decisions."

"It's an easy decision," said Emerson. "We can kill her or they're going to keep killing us."

"Yeah," Sam said, raising his voice just a bit.

"Or we could kill her and they'll *still* kill all of us," said Pyr.

Diedrich rapped his knuckles on the table again. Waited for quiet. "The unpleasant option we have all carefully not discussed is that the Empress does not want to kill us. She wants to kill him."

He pointed at Noah.

"To be exact, she wants *us* to kill him."

Noah finally raised his head. He stared at Diedrich. Met a few other gazes. People shifted in their chairs or shuffled their feet.

"Jerk jackass excrement cranium bastard," muttered Olivia.

"Just what I was thinking," Parker whispered.

Diedrich glanced in their direction, and Parker wondered how good the old German's hearing was. "I merely say what has no doubt been on several minds."

"She also wants ten of us dead," Emerson pointed out. "That's what's been on my mind."

"Ten's still better than all of us," said the overcoat woman.

"Depends if you're one of the ten," said Parker, a little louder than she intended.

A low mumble crept through the main hall. More feet shuffled. People gave each other uneasy glances.

"How would we even pick the other ten people?" asked Marissa. "Who'd want to do that?"

"That's almost a quarter of the village," added the bulky man.

"We could start with them," Overcoat said, waving her hand in Parker's direction. "This is all their fault anyway."

Pyr snapped her fingers, and the sound echoed in the big room. "We're not going to kill Billy Gather."

Qiang set his hands flat on the table. "We're not killing anyone. That's not an option. We should be looking to avoid death, not add to it. Are we all agreed?"

"Agreed," said Pyr. Warwick nodded. So did Emerson and Monique. A wave of affirmatives rolled through the room. Parker realized she and Sam had chimed in, too, and Olivia had added a string of positive words. A few people stared at Overcoat. She let her head hang low and muttered something like an apology.

Diedrich nodded. "In my experience, it is best to publicly stomp out the unsavory ideas early on rather than let them fester and gather strength."

Strength sent another thought spinning through Parker's mind.

Something that had been nagging at her, but she hadn't been able to put a finger on it. A few thoughts bounced in her head and she leaned a little closer to the table as they gelled. Used her teaching assistant voice. "Question."

The room's attention settled on her. Had she interrupted someone? Qiang, maybe?

"I'm wondering . . . why does the Empress need a Neanderthal army? Why does she have it?"

Emerson snorted out a laugh. "For killing us."

"But . . . why? If she controls the lifeboat systems like Noah says, she's more or less God here. She can move things around the valley. Maybe even move them through time. So why does she need a few hundred guys with spears and clubs? Why doesn't she just level this place with a California-sized earthquake?"

Another uneasy murmur tiptoed through the main hall. Their working theory about the valley had gotten around even before the meeting. Most everyone seemed to accept it, even if a few folks had needed it explained in detail. Parker could see this new spin on it didn't sit well with a lot of them.

Warwick frowned at her. "What's yehr point?"

She looked around the table. "I mean, if she wanted everyone dead, it seems like she's had hundreds of chances to pull a few tons of rock out of a mountain and drop it on Roanoke. Or a few million gallons of the Pacific Ocean. Hell, if she's bringing the dinosaurs here, why doesn't she drop a dozen raptors inside the walls?"

Marissa shuddered. "Don't give her any ideas."

"She does, however, have a point," said Diedrich. "If the Empress has control of the—the *lifeboat*, a standing army feels a bit . . . redundant?"

"Exactly." Parker nodded.

"You all realize what we're saying, right?" Emerson thumped the table with his hand. "She's got more power here than we thought she did. She could kill us all at any minute."

Noah cleared his throat. Met Parker's eyes. "Maybe she doesn't do anything that drastic because at the end of the day, she's still a Neanderthal. She thinks differently. Sees the world differently. Maybe it doesn't occur to her to use the power that way. Or she brought the Klaa here before she realized the full extent of what she can do."

Emerson smacked the table again. "Look, we all know the person who needs to get killed, so let's stop pussyfooting around it."

"Calm down, Em," said Pyr.

Someone pushed one of the heavy chairs away from the table, and Parker looked to who was getting up. Qiang and Warwick shared an uneasy look. So did Emerson and Neith. Diedrich stared across the table at Noah.

Another faint sound rolled across the floor.

"The valley trembles beneath her feet," murmured Sam.

Marissa let out a breath. "Guess we don't need to wait for Thate to get back from his scouting trip."

Emerson nodded. "She's on the move."

Pyr shook her head. "Not at night. She's probably just been out with Breaker, getting them all whipped up."

"How long until daylight?"

"Seven hours, fifty-one minutes, Qiang-Shizhang."

"How long for them to get across the valley?"

Parker guessed he already knew the answer. It felt like more undergrad class stuff. A professor guiding his students to a big answer by walking them through some smaller ones.

Warwick looked at the table. "Depending on which way they come, five, maybe six hours. They don't have enough raptors for everyone, so they'll have to go slow for the folks on foot. She'll want them all to show up at once. Big display of force."

Qiang nodded once. Looked past Warwick. Parker followed his gaze. Ended up at Neith.

"You're absolutely sure you could do it?"

Ross translated. Emerson grinned. Parker felt a little chill in her arms as Neith responded in her rolling language.

"Neith says she can make the shot."

"Good," murmured Sam.

Another low rumble. Not even enough to make the lamp flames flicker, but everyone noticed it. Most of their faces looked nervous or uncertain. A few looked . . . determined.

"Wrong violent scared protection desperate."

"Yeah, I agree," said Parker.

"Why are there tremors when she walks in the valley?"

Parker looked around, realized the question had come from Noah. He was still slumped in the chair, but his voice had a bit of its strength back. Almost like he was confronting a class with a problem.

"It's a show of power," said Warwick. "For years it seemed like some primordial thing, that she'd tapped into the magic of the valley."

Noah nodded. "Except it's not magic."

"Right. So yeh say."

"So back to the question. Why? These quakes are minor, like someone dropped something heavy in another room."

"You feel they should be more intense?" asked Diedrich.

"I think they seem . . . wrong. Like Parker said about the Neanderthal army. What's the point of them? From what you've all been saying, she's used them in the past to let you know she's coming, but she doesn't do anything once she gets here."

"PsyOps," said Emerson. "Trying to keep us nervous, wear down our morale."

"No offense," said Parker, "but morale's never seemed super high here to me."

"Means it's working."

Noah sat up a little. "I know a lot of you . . . you have a lot more experience with this than me, but in my own experience Neanderthals aren't big on seeing other viewpoints. Psychological warfare isn't really their thing."

A few people exchanged glances and murmured to each other. Parker could tell they didn't see the point of all this. Neither did she, honestly, but it was another question. Another anomaly.

"Very well," said Qiang, raising his voice. "We've narrowed our options. Now we have a decision to make. Do we want to wait until we hear what Thate has to tell us?"

"We know what he's going to tell us," said Emerson. "We can all feel her."

A few mutters of agreement from the crowd.

Qiang nodded. "Very well. Do we try to kill the Empress, knowing all the risks it involves? Or do we ignore her demands and attempt to hold off the Klaa when they come? This won't be binding until we get everyone else's vote. Everyone has to have a say in this."

The random shuffling and murmuring in the room settled down.

"A show of hands. Should we try to kill the Empress?"

Sam's hand shot up. So did Olivia's. And Emerson's. Neith's. Warwick's. Parker gazed around the room, watching hand after hand go up. Monique slowly raised her hand. Pyr did a moment later.

Robot Ross didn't move its hands from its walking stick. She wondered if it was some Asimov's three laws thing. Or maybe it just didn't get a vote.

Parker thought about Josh making funny comments and coming clean about his job back . . . back on Earth. Thought about the unanswered questions about this place that would probably never be answered. Thought about Sam's numb eyes when he told her Josh was dead.

She watched Noah's hand go up.

She still didn't raise her hand. No one gave her an accusing stare or frowned at her. The ayes still overwhelmingly had it. She could only see five other people with their hands down. Six counting Qiang, but she was pretty sure he was trying to stay impartial.

Qiang looked at all the raised hands. Nodded. "I'll speak with those who aren't here. If Thate has anything new for us, you'll all know."

He stepped back, away from the table. Other discussions broke out about the strength of the walls. The strength of the gate. How many spears and arrows they had. Emerson, Neith, and Warwick were having an intense discussion while Ross acted as a translator.

Sam gave Parker a numb look and walked away. He worked his way around the table and through the crowd toward the wardens.

Noah pushed himself out of his chair. Turned to face her and Olivia. "It's a good question," he said. "About why she needs all the Neanderthals."

"It just doesn't make sense why there's so many of them. In so many ways."

He nodded in agreement. "Like the tremors. Things she does for no reason."

"Or for a reason we don't understand yet."

"And probably won't."

Olivia stood up. "Tired return rest leave headache." She gestured at the door.

"Do you want help getting back?" asked Parker.

"Unnecessary self no negative adequate."

"Okay, then."

"Be careful, Olivia," added Noah.

She bowed her head awkwardly and headed through the crowd. Pyr was speaking to Monique. Qiang had moved to stand near Neith and Ross.

Noah let out a deep sigh. His we-didn't-get-the-funding sigh. The one that meant he had a lot of things to rethink. "I never really knew anything about this place at all."

"You knew more than any of us."

He shook his head. "Bad science. I ignored the evidence. When I found facts I agreed with, it was the truth. When I got facts I disagreed with, it was everyone else who didn't understand."

"You still had the data, you just weren't looking at it the right way."

"Thanks. Nice of you to see it like that."

They watched the crowd split, regroup, shift. Overheard fragments of conversations and plans and strategies. Olivia made it to the door. Sam talked actively with the wardens. Another faint tremble ran through the floorboards. Everyone was quiet for a moment, and then the discussions resumed with even more intensity.

Parker looked down at her hand. Back at Noah. "Do you think this is the right thing to do?"

He shrugged. Reached up and touched the scabby lines across his nose and cheeks. "I think it's the best of a bunch of really shitty options."

"Not really the answer I was hoping for."

"Sometimes we don't get the answer we wanted. We just get the answer there is."

46

BILLY

Billy crouched behind the tree and let Fang stomp off. The tyrannosaurus hadn't seen him. Or smelled him. Or maybe he'd smelled something better. They'd crossed paths in the woods, and like Beau kept telling him, he just had to stay calm. Fang could smell fear-sweat, too.

It was tough to stay calm. This was the seventh or eighth time he'd seen Fang since the big dinosaur had killed Dad, but the first time he hadn't peed himself. Good thing he'd managed to not be as scared and hold it this time. Fang could definitely smell pee.

The tyrannosaurus took a few more thundering steps, turned to glare back in Billy's general direction, and then headed off toward the swamp. Billy counted to one hundred before Fang vanished into the trees. He kept counting to three hundred, just to be sure the big dinosaur didn't circle back around.

Beau was going to be furious when she found out Billy had gone this far into the jungle without her permission. He knew she'd find out sooner or later. He'd sworn Ross to secrecy when he left, even though he knew the robot didn't understand secrets.

But Charlie hadn't come back to the cave for three days now. Not since the rhamphorhynchus had shoved its way between the stone pillars two days ago and tried to claim their cave as its own, and Beau had fought it off with her homemade axe. Billy couldn't stand to lose another member of the family. Even a scruffy jerk cat who still hissed at him sometimes. If Charlie hadn't come back, it meant he was probably lost, or stuck, and he needed Billy's help. These were the only acceptable reasons for the cat's absence.

Beau had tried to play grown-up, to tell him Charlie was only a couple steps above being a feral, and he was probably off doing cat things. She'd also shot down Billy's simple and clever plan to find the cat. Mostly because it meant a trip deep into the valley, and she'd had them stick pretty close to home since . . . well, for the past year.

Which is why he was alone in the jungle, heading deep into the valley, counting to a hundred one more time to be safe.

Billy came to the big field and walked around the edge, keeping close to the trees. He banged his palms twice on the hull of the riverboat (listening to things scurry around inside), banged them again on one of the big propellers, and then broke into a run around the base of the Ice Castle. A minute later he was up the ramp-bridge and in the cool tunnels.

He walked through the hallways, turning slowly as he did. The Castaway's home always amazed him. The little lights that ran through the walls. The way the tunnels never went in the same direction as they did last time, but always ended up leading to the same place.

And then he was in the big chamber with the raised platform. The Castaway stood there, like always. At the moment, they looked like a bright purple tree. A thick, three-legged trunk going up ten feet and then splitting into dozens of thinner branches. Or maybe they were arms.

Billy never knew how to start conversations with the alien, so he just stood there for a minute, watching the Castaway's tall branches sway slowly back and forth.

The purple tree slowly melted, shrinking back into itself. It became a grape-jelly column, then compressed into the rough shape of a person. If a person had four arms and a horse's head.

"Salutations, Billy Gather. I have looked forward to your visit for some time now."

"Hello, Castaway."

"I observe that you are here alone."

"Yep." He thought about explaining why, but decided against it. They'd visited the Castaway a few times since Dad had . . . since it'd been just him and Beau, and the alien seemed to accept that Beau was the grown-up now. And grown-ups, Billy knew, tended to stick together. "I was wondering if I could ask for your help with something?"

"You are always welcome to ask. How may I assist you?"

"You know everything that's happening in the valley, right?"

The Castaway's elongated purple head bowed low, touching their chest and dissolving into it. The back end stretched up and formed something closer to a human head, with almost-eyes and a sort-of-nose more or less in the right place. "I have seen the individual feline you have named Charlie several times, and will see him several more."

Billy smiled and straightened up. "You have?"

"Certainly." A long moment stretched out between them. The Castaway used it to twist their arms together on either side of their body, creating two long tentacles coming off their shoulders.

"Are you answering things I haven't asked yet?"

A ripple ran through the tentacles. "Quite possibly."

Billy sighed. He liked the Castaway a lot, and it was cool having an alien as a friend, but he also understood why they frustrated Beau and Dad a lot. Well . . . Beau.

Something caught in his lungs, and made a little hiccup in his breath.

"Are you unwell, Billy Gather?"

"I . . ." He could feel a surge of tears swirling behind his eyes, waiting for a chance to escape. He wanted to talk to his friend, to talk to someone who wasn't Beau or Ross, but he knew if he opened his mouth he'd start bawling. He bit down hard and shook his head.

The Castaway folded over, rolled forward on their crystal platform, and pulled itself back into the rough shape of a person. They were kneeling now, their head at the same height as Billy's. They reached out a hand—a completely normal, purple hand—and set it gently on his shoulder. He felt the little static-electricity crackle the Castaway's touch always had. A few tears squeezed out and ran down his face.

"You are in emotional distress over the possible loss of your feline companion so close to the anniversary of your father's terminus, while still recovering from the loss of your mother. This amplifies both their absence and your own loneliness."

Billy nodded hard three times.

The Castaway leaned their head a little closer. "Believe me when I tell you there is a point when this distress has faded, and you remember both your father and mother with more joy than sadness. The point is distant, but you are strong, Billy Gather, and you will reach it." They squeezed his shoulder. Let their hand slide down his arm. Held his hand, and sent another electric tingle through his fingers.

Billy's chest relaxed. The storm behind his eyes calmed. He reached up with his free hand and wiped his cheeks. "Thanks."

"Certainly." The Castaway leaned forward and pressed their head against his with a faint crackle of static. Then they flowed back, like a wave rolling back into the ocean, and stood up straight. Their legs melted together into a single column and an extra arm sprouted out of their chest. "How may I assist you?"

"Have you seen Charlie? He freaked out when a rhamphorhynchus tried to get into the cave the other day and I haven't been able to find him."

The Castaway's head swelled until it was the size and shape of a playground ball. "I have seen the individual feline you have named Charlie several times, and will see him several more."

"But have you seen him recently?"

The alien spread all three of their six-fingered hands. "My perception of the fourth dimension is unlike yours, Billy Gather. The most recent time I have seen Charlie was when you brought him here to make introductions."

"That was ages ago."

"And yet, in my perception, that is the most recent time I have seen him."

Billy sighed. A wasted trip. All this walking and no closer to finding Charlie. "Beau said you wouldn't be much use."

"My apologies."

"It's okay. I know you try to help when you can."

"This is the purpose."

A wave of lights rained down inside the walls like a fireworks show. Billy watched them wink out one by one. "What's that?"

The Castaway tilted their head upward. "Your sister is likely worried about you, Billy Gather. The valley has reached the night cycle."

"Oh no! Already?"

"Yes."

"I don't suppose . . . could you walk home with me? She'd be a lot less angry."

His alien friend sucked their left arm all the way into their shoulder, then rolled the middle one across their chest to take its spot. "I cannot leave this place."

"Right. Sorry."

"If you wish, you may remain here for the night cycle and replenish your biochemical reserves."

It took Billy a moment to figure out that one, and then he yawned. "I am kind of tired."

The Castaway gestured across the chamber, their fingers braiding together as they did. There was a little alcove on the other side of the room, with what looked like a bed made out of the same not-ice as the rest of the Castle. When he touched it, it flexed under his fingers, almost like an air mattress.

He hopped up onto the bed and smiled at his friend. "Thanks, Castaway."

"I shall make the replenishment efficient for you." The Castaway's three-fingered hand came up.

But Billy didn't sleep.

He waited and waited, because he remembered falling asleep almost instantly when the Castaway spread their fingers. A sleep so deep and restful he didn't even realize time had passed when his very relieved—and then very angry—sister woke him up the next morning.

Then he realized he couldn't remember that unless it had already happened. He was just reliving the past in a dream. And, in the strange way of dreams, he'd shifted his point of view, standing outside of his memories, watching them happen.

The Castaway lowered their hand and nodded at him agreeably. "In your dreams, you perceive the fourth dimension in a manner much closer to my own."

Shifting point of view and spinning off the rails, too. Although it did sound like something the Castaway would've said.

"You now believe this to be a fictitious memory created by your replenishing mind. This is incorrect. I have repositioned your consciousness to this point in space-time so I may impart certain facts to you."

He found his voice. "Wait, what?"

The Castaway's legs dissolved into a purple wave that carried them back up onto the crystal dais. "In the morning I will promise you that we will see each other again soon. This is the event to which I will be referring."

Noah looked down at his child-hands. His skinny chest. His feet in their battered black Batman sneakers. Looked back up at his old friend.

"But you . . . you're dead."

They nodded. Half a dozen arms blossomed from each of their shoulders like a Hindu god, each one gesturing or pointing in a different direction. "From your perspective, my existence has ceased through the actions of the individual you currently refer to as the Empress. This imparting of facts is occurring at a point before that event."

Another little piece of his heart sank in his chest. "So you . . . you know she's going to kill you. You knew all along."

"Certainly. Since the moment she first appeared in the valley. Yes, I shall still preserve her life. This is the purpose." The Castaway folded half their arms behind their back, half across their chest, and all of them melted into their torso.

"But why? If you knew what she was going to do to you—to everyone—why didn't you just let her die?"

The alien's round head rippled and split down the middle. The two halves sagged down and merged with the purple shoulders. The ripples continued down their body even as their neck stretched up to become a tall column. "Preservation of life is the purpose."

"But you'd still be alive. Now."

"I *am* alive now."

"No, I mean now . . ." He balled his little eleven-year-old hands into fists. "I forgot how annoying these conversations could get."

"My apologies, Noah Barnes."

"She's killed so many people."

"Yes."

He looked up at the purple figure and saw his own distorted face reflected in the smooth column of their neck. "If preservation of life is so important, why didn't you save Beau?"

"Beau Gather is no longer in the valley."

"I know."

"It is important," said the Castaway, "that you understand the nature of this place."

Noah waited for a moment. "Are you talking to me?"

"Yes."

"We figured it out. The valley's your spaceship, right? Or a lifeboat."

"This is a correct interpretation of the facts, Noah Barnes."

He got off the crystal bed and wobbled. It'd been a long time since he'd balanced a body this light on legs this short. "Can I ask a question?"

"Certainly."

"How do you crash a multidimensional spaceship?"

The Castaway pulled themselves into an egg the size of a desk chair, then expanded back out to become a seven-foot humanoid with a squared-off, oddly Frankenstein-like head. "I was unexpectedly subjected to a forceful disagreement in this location."

"A forceful disagreement?" It sparked a random memory. "One time

Dad made this joke. Said you'd told him you were attacked by giant space squids."

"A simplification, but accurate enough. There are those who do not wish to propagate life, but to use it only to further their own considerable existences. We oppose their acts of consumption across numerous planes of existence. They, in turn, resist our opposition. Sometimes in a proactive manner."

Noah rolled the words around in his head. "You're at war."

"Another simplification of the events and relationships, but again, accurate enough. You have already provided an answer for this question, Noah Barnes."

His mind briefly chased after the last sentence, trying to determine if it was a future or past response. But then another thought wormed its way in. "This . . . disagreement. Did you lose?"

The Castaway's head swayed side to side, like a snake hypnotizing a mouse. "The disagreement is ongoing."

Noah looked at his friend. "Then why didn't anyone ever come to rescue you?"

"I cannot leave this place."

"Right. But the rest of your . . . your people. What happened to them? Why did they leave you here to die?"

The Castaway's legs merged and spread out like a wide skirt, pooling around them. "It is important that you understand the nature of this place."

His little-boy hands balled into fists. "I do understand it. It's your lifeboat. What do you . . . what are you trying to tell me?"

The alien responded with a series of grunts and barking syllables. Neanderthal. They were speaking Neanderthal to him now. Or maybe to someone else, two or three hundred years ago. Maybe to the Empress? So goddamn roundabout and frustrating.

Except . . .

The Castaway always told him and his family the truth. It had taken Noah years to realize it, but almost every answer the Castaway gave made perfect sense. Like Parker'd said, he had all the data, he was just looking at it the wrong way. Making the wrong assumptions.

He'd made so many wrong assumptions about the valley.

"Okay. Okay, fine, let's break this down. This place. The valley. The valley is your lifeboat."

The Castaway let their arms drift down and melt back into their body, becoming little more than a pillar of purple gel.

"It's keeping you alive and safe until your people come to rescue you." He recognized his tone, what Parker called his working-through-problems voice. He also realized how silly it sounded coming from his eleven-year-old mouth. "But they never came and you were stuck here."

"I cannot leave this place."

"Right. So the lifeboat's trapped in Earth's orbit, and once a year they overlap and things get pulled in here. Into the valley. That's why you told my dad it wasn't safe to leave, because right at that moment we weren't anywhere near Earth. And over time the lifeboat's accumulated . . ."

His voice trailed off. He'd missed something. He could feel it tickling the edge of his consciousness. Something else he'd been looking at the wrong way. He tried to force it for a moment, the way he'd tried to force so much of his understanding of the valley, and then he stopped.

Averted vision. You don't see a faint star by looking right at it. You look off to the side. You look at it from a different angle.

Noah looked up at his friend. "When you say you can't leave, you don't mean you're *unable* to leave. You're saying there's a reason you *shouldn't* leave."

A ripple ran through the Castaway's purple form.

"So you shouldn't leave the valley. Your lifeboat. Because the lifeboat . . . is in enemy territory? No, because they'd've found it already, right? And it's been centuries, so it's probably not an issue of supplies or power or anything like that."

In the corner of his eye, a lone sparkle of light darted through the wall and slowly faded away. Understanding hit him in the chest, dragging down his heart, pulling at his throat. A wave of sadness shook his little body.

"You can't leave, because once somebody gets rescued from a lifeboat . . . you don't need the lifeboat anymore."

The Castaway's bulbous head stretched up on a slender neck that coiled back on itself.

"We always thought you were trapped here like us. But you couldn't leave because if you left, the lifeboat would . . . shut down. The *valley* would shut down."

The Castaway bowed its head. "This is a correct interpretation of the facts, Noah Barnes."

"So you just . . . stayed here? You gave up ever being rescued, going back to your own kind, to keep all of us—to keep everything in the valley alive."

"This is the purpose. To preserve life."

He stared at the alien as their form creased, flowed, and rolled into a new form. Mostly human, but with long arms that brushed the floor. The shape didn't have eyes, just the barest hint of features, but he still felt their approving gaze, like a student who knows they leveled up by answering a difficult question in front of the class.

Another thought stumbled through his mind, ruining the moment. "But you're . . . you're gone. In the future, where I am, physically, you're not there. You're dead. If you're not in the lifeboat anymore, why is the valley still here?"

"You have already provided an answer for this question, Noah Barnes."

"I did?"

The Castaway gave a single, serene nod.

He replayed his thoughts. Briefly wondered if he hadn't actually provided the answer yet and this was another future-fragment. Looked around the huge chamber. It was good to see it like this again, not like . . .

"It's her, isn't it? The Empress. She was here in the Castle, so before you died you shifted everything to her. That's why the lifeboat responds to her."

"This is a correct interpretation of the facts, Noah Barnes."

"So now she's keeping . . ." All the discussions and thoughts from last night rushed through his mind. Qiang. Emerson and Neith. Sam. Parker. "If we kill her, the lifeboat shuts down. If she dies, everything in the valley dies."

The Castaway crossed their long arms, the limbs shrinking and flattening and vanishing back into the alien's torso. Their head stretched out into a horizontal tube, almost like a hammerhead shark. "I have imparted the facts you require, Noah Barnes. You understand the nature of this place. I shall now return your consciousness to its appropriate location in space-time." A ribbon-like arm grew from halfway down their torso, and the end split into a flat hand that gestured back at the crystal bed.

Noah walked back to the alcove. "Thank you. For everything. You . . . you're a good friend."

"Certainly. As a token of our long acquaintance and the fondness I have for your existence, I shall repair the epidermal damage inflicted upon you."

He shook his head. "No, not like that. I mean, you took care of us, but you also . . . you were just good to us." He waved his hand around the Castaway's chamber. "This day, this . . . point in space-time. It's always been important to me. When you kneeled down and talked to me, I felt safe. I believed everything was going to be okay. For the first time since Dad was killed."

A little tremble ran through the Castaway. "Thank you. That is good to know. I will do that when this moment arrives."

He almost laughed. "And talking with you's always interesting."

The Castaway's hand came up. Their fingers spread. "Goodbye, Noah Barnes. It has been pleasing to once again converse with this future incarnation of you."

"You too, Casta—wait, what?"

Someone shook Noah awake.

47

SAM

Noah launched off the bed and Sam jumped back, colliding with Ross. "Oh, Jesus, thank God."

Noah blinked, his eyes opening wider as he looked around the little room of the guest house. He'd sat up so fast all the blood had rushed from his face, leaving him sickly pale. "What . . . ? Where . . . ?"

"Are you okay? I couldn't—we've been trying to wake you up. I thought you'd gone into a coma or something. I was about to send Ross to get the doctor."

"I would've suggested you go and I remain, Sam, as you can move much faster than I can."

Noah stood up and staggered, like he wasn't used to his legs. Or he was drunk. Sam watched the man sway and wobble. "Seriously, are you okay? I was shaking you and pretty much yelling in your . . ."

Sam felt his breath quicken. His thoughts collide.

"Where did—what happened to your face?"

Noah reached up and ran his fingertips over his cheeks. Just a minute ago Sam had been trying not to look too closely at those cheeks, to be honest. The slashes had crusted into thick, rough lines, and the skin around them had bruised up. Almost a third of Noah's face had been a sickly red and purple. If someone had asked Sam, he'd've guessed one eye would only be able to squint at best.

It was all gone. The clotted blood. The cuts. The bruising. Even the peeling sunburn.

"I'm fine. I was . . ." Noah's voice trailed off and he looked around, his eyes settling on his boots. He balanced, tugged one of them onto his foot, then dropped the foot fast. "I was with the Castaway."

More thoughts collided in Sam's head. "You had a dream?"

Noah tugged on the other boot, bent down to yank at the laces. "I was with them. In the past."

"Are you—what are you talking about?"

"The Castaway pulled my consciousness back in time to talk. And then they healed my face." He waved a hand at his face.

"I'm pleased to hear that, Noah," said Ross.

Sam tried to get his breathing under control. "You sure it wasn't just—this is what the lifeboat does, right? It heals you."

"Not like this. Not this fast." He grabbed his shirt from the chair.

A tremor shook the room. They'd been going on since Sam woke up a few hours ago. This one lasted for maybe ten seconds. The Empress was getting closer. Or angrier, maybe? He wasn't sure how to judge them.

He looked at Noah again. "So you actually time traveled? For real?"

"Yep. I was in my own body. My twelve-year-old body. Have they gone to kill the Empress yet?"

"They . . . I don't know. I don't think so."

Noah headed out the door, buttoning his shirt as he went. "Where's Qiang? And Warwick?"

Sam and the android followed him into the hall. "At the front gate. They were, anyway, twenty minutes ago. I came looking for you."

"It's been seventeen minutes since you entered the room, Sam."

"Maybe closer to half an hour?"

Noah pushed open the front door and led them out to the street. Sam realized the man was shaking with nervous energy, like he'd guzzled all the coffee he could drink and then some. He speed-walked down the dirt path toward the gate.

Another rumble shook the valley. Sam heard this one as much as he felt it. It reminded him of crossing a bridge as cars drove by. Not enough to knock anything over, but no way to miss it. Dust drifted down from the beams of several buildings, forming a hazy cloud in the street.

Noah turned the corner and started to run with manic speed. Desperate. Maybe scared. "What's going on?" Sam called out, but Noah'd already passed the obelisk. Sam threw each leg forward and tried to keep up.

Qiang and Thate stood in the far intersection. Noah waved the men down as the vibrations in the ground hit a new level. Not cars driving across a bridge, Sam realized. Big trucks. The level of vibration that makes you wonder, just for a moment, if you could make it to the closest side if the bridge started to collapse. Sam could feel them even through his heavy stride.

"We can't kill her," Noah called out.

"What?" said Qiang

"The Empress. We can't kill her. We just need to stop her."

"That's the plan." Thate gestured back to the main gate. It looked to Sam like most of the town was up on the wall with bows and spears. A few of them down on the ground were moving heavy beams into place, reinforcing the walls around the big doors.

"No," said Noah, "We have to stop all of this. No fighting. No ambush. We can't risk a battle. "

"That's a lovely idea," Qiang said. "But it's a little late. The Klaa are on the march. Almost all of them."

The ground rumbled again, as if to emphasize his words.

"If we kill her, the lifeboat shuts down."

"What?"

"The lifeboat only existed here, in this dimension, to support the Castaway," explained Noah. "When the Empress killed them, it latched on to her. The Castaway transferred, I don't know, command codes to her or something right before they died. Something to keep everything active. The key thing is, now the lifeboat recognizes the Empress as the person it's supposed to keep alive. That's why she's lived so long. But if she dies . . ."

"Then the lifeboat goes away," said Sam. "It'll—it powers down or folds itself back up."

Noah waved his hand, taking in all of the valley. "And everything in here is left with no life support at best. In deep space at worst."

Qiang and Thate traded a glance. The elder focused on Noah again. "This seems like a big leap."

"It's not."

"How can you be so sure?"

"He talked to the Castaway," said Sam. "Sort of—in a dream."

Qiang's eyebrows twitched.

Noah put up a hand. "I know it sounds ridiculous—"

"Yes, it does," Qiang agreed.

"—but they helped me understand what's going on here."

"Look at his face," said Sam. "All his cuts. They're all healed."

Qiang, suddenly looking a lot less certain, turned to the gate. "Emerson and Neith left an hour ago."

"What?"

"It's what we decided last night. The people who weren't at the meeting agreed, too."

"Emerson knows the jungle," said Thate. "He's going to set some booby traps to slow their advance. Then Neith eliminates her."

Noah blinked. "Just like that?"

"She's an amazing shot with a bow. I've seen her hit a target the size of my fist from three hundred meters when she had time to set her shot."

"You have to stop them. Call them back."

Qiang shook his head. "It's not possible."

"The horn thing," said Sam. "You could sound a warning."

"We don't have a 'come back' tone," Thate said. "If they heard it right now, they'd assume some of the Klaa got here early."

"So they might stop and come back to help."

"Maybe. Knowing Emerson and Neith, they'll both probably be hung up on completing their mission."

Sam took a few quick breaths. "So we need to go after them."

Qiang shook his head. "They're an hour ahead of you."

Noah headed for the gate. "But they're going to stop to set up an ambush somewhere, right? We could still catch them before the Klaa gets there."

Another tremor ran up through Sam's legs as he followed Noah. It took some effort to keep his balance. Not a lot, but he felt his calves and thighs flex to make it happen.

At the gate, Pyr helped the woodcutter guy, John, brace a rough beam up against the big door's frame. Parker and Olivia were doing something near the weapons locker. Sam got a little closer and realized they were stuffing arrows into quivers.

Noah glanced at Thate. "Do we know where they're setting the ambush?"

"No. But we know the Klaa are coming around the lake side of the Ice Castle, and I know the best points between here and there to set an ambush. We'll find them."

"We need to find them fast."

Parker locked eyes with Sam. Walked over, with Olivia a few steps behind her. "What's going on?"

Sam tapped his fingers. Took a few quick breaths. "Short version, the lifeboat's keyed to the Empress and if we kill her it shuts down."

Parker's brows went up. "Shuts down as in . . ."

"Support life heat extinguish collapse."

"Yep," said Noah. He turned to Qiang. "We'll need the doctor. Monique. In case something goes wrong."

"We'll need her here."

"If this goes wrong, it won't matter if she's here." He looked at Sam and Olivia and Parker. "You should all—"

"You think I'm not going to be part of saving the valley?" A tingle ran through Sam as he said it. Not excitement. More like the relief of putting down something heavy.

Of not running away.

Noah locked eyes with him and took another few steps toward the gate. "It's going to be dangerous."

"From what you're saying, everywhere's going to be dangerous. And somebody's got to keep Breaker off you while you talk to the Empress."

"I can help with that," said Pyr.

Olivia shook her head. "Too slow self hinder drag."

"It's okay," said Noah. "They can use you here in case I'm wrong. Again."

Another tremor hit. Sam had to shift his feet this time. Halfway through the shaking, a breeze blew in through the open gate. No, not a breeze, Sam realized. Wind.

"It'd be nice if you were wrong again," said Thate.

"I can get you there faster," said a voice from above.

Sam looked up and saw Diedrich on the bamboo walkway along the wall. Crouched low. Listening.

"Brunhilda can run at thirty kilometers an hour. Forty on even ground. And she can carry four people while she does it."

Sam glanced at Noah. Could see him considering it. "Really?"

"I will need perhaps twenty minutes to get her out of her pen and get her harness on, but—"

"We don't have the time. Try to catch up to us." Noah was through the big gate now. Sam followed. So did Pyr. Thate took a few jogging steps, got himself alongside Noah, and pointed them toward the edge of the cypress grove.

Then someone came up alongside Sam. Parker. "You think this is going to work?"

"I have no idea. I hope so."

Noah glanced back at them. "It's going to work."

Sam had gotten back to not-quite-running speed again. "How can you be sure?"

Noah gave them a wry smile. "Because the Castaway was always right. And I'm Billy Gather. And this is my home."

48

PARKER

As everyone ran through the jungle, Parker tried her best to keep up. She'd spent almost all her time here inside the walls of Roanoke, trying to track the stars and create astronomical models. Now everyone else skipped across roots and wove between bushes and she already had a ton of scratches on her arms.

And she'd never been a runner. Being on campus meant obligatory exercise. Walking everywhere. Maybe the occasional jog. She was too organized to ever have to run anywhere, and right now her legs and arms, heart and lungs were all reminding her of that.

Thate had taken the lead, his magnificent thighs and shoulders moving in time as he bounded between the trees. Monique was right behind him. The friggin' eighteenth-century French woman in a dress was moving through the forest faster than her. Pyr and Sam brought up the rear, keeping them safe from surprise attacks. Which might've sounded ridiculous before a goddamn caveman smashed Josh's head in with a club.

Noah kept pace with her. Well, a little ahead of her. Partly urging her on, partly . . . reluctance. She recognized this, too. He'd had to go to a few faculty parties, some with random state reps or actors or comic book artists who'd all been alumni. Things he understood he had to do, but still didn't want to.

Like trying to talk the Empress into turning her army around and going home.

Parker had an ugly idea. She hoped it wasn't right. That Noah's thoughts hadn't gone this way, but . . . the idea checked too many boxes on her mental hypothesis.

She took a few quick strides, managed to not trip over a root that looped up off the ground. Got herself close to him. "How are you going to convince the Empress?"

Noah glanced at her.

"What are you going to say to make her go back?" The idea crossed her mind again. "What are you going to do?"

Noah looked at the ground. Ahead at Thate. Anywhere but her face. Picked up his pace. "I've got a few ideas. We'll see what happens when we find them. Play it by ear."

Parker's stomach churned. She took a few more quick steps and managed not to slip on a patch of soft earth. Tried to look him in the eyes while he tried to avoid her gaze.

They covered another dozen yards.

"You're going to let her kill you."

He still didn't look at her. "If I have to."

"Why?"

"Because everyone's right and this is kind of my fault, even if it's all been simmering for a while. Maybe since I was here the first time. The Klaa want blood. We can't let it happen, and our best bet to stop it is giving her the thing she wants."

"You. Dead."

"If she gets to kill me herself or watch it happen in front of her, maybe she'll turn back and . . . everyone'll be safe."

He tried to speed up his slow jog, but she managed to keep pace. "You know there's a good chance she'll keep marching to Roanoke out of spite. Or stubbornness."

"Maybe. I'm hoping I can reason with her before she . . . before things go too far. That she'll be willing to listen."

Parker skipped over another arching root, "I've got to be honest. She doesn't strike me as a great listener."

"I'm out of ideas, Parker! This is all I've got."

"Then let's take ten minutes and come up with something else."

"We don't have ten minutes."

"You don't know that."

Noah stopped dead in his tracks. Stepped over and slapped his hand against the trunk of a tree. "Feel this."

"Why?"

Sam and Pyr caught up to them. "What's wrong?"

"Parker, please," begged Noah. "We don't have time."

She set her hand against the trunk, her palm flat against the dry, husk-like bark. And she felt it.

Running through the forest had hidden the vibration in the ground. Pressing her hand against the tree was like completing a circuit. The tremors came up through her boots, through the tree, and met in her palm. They'd been erratic back at Roanoke, but now the shaking was so steady it almost felt . . . mechanical. It reminded her of riding the telescope platform when the observatory turned to a new heading. A constant, deep vibration, enough to rattle pens off desks and the occasional coffee cup left by a first-timer, and the animal awareness that moving too fast might be hazardous.

"The tremors aren't stopping anymore," said Noah, "just surging."

Sam looked around. "So she's close?"

Pyr shook her head. "No. I don't think she's ever made quakes this intense before."

Parker looked at Noah. "Is this because of you? Because she hates you?"

Noah shook his head. "She's not shaking the valley. Not on purpose."

"I thought she had control of the lifeboat," said Sam.

"No, it's like . . . Remember when they put that automatic lighting system in Jaeger Hall, back on campus?"

Parker flipped it over in her mind. "The ones that shut off after a couple of minutes if they don't detect any movement in the room."

"Right. This is . . . It's why the Castaway never left the Ice Castle." Noah gestured at the ground. "It's why the valley shakes when she walks outside. It's not some big show of power, it's the lifeboat shutting down its systems because it's not registering her in the Castle. The valley's collapsing, and it's going to keep collapsing unless she gets back inside."

Sam shook his head. "But that doesn't—why would she do it then? Why risk it?"

"Because she doesn't know." Noah's nervous energy started to flag, turning into plain desperation. It showed on his face. "The lifeboat's linked to her, but she doesn't understand any of it. She's not actually in control. It's like how little kids used to visit the cockpit of an airplane. They get to sit in the captain's chair, maybe flip a few switches, but they weren't really flying the plane. Everything she's done here has just been luck and raw instinct."

Another tremor pushed up through Parker's boots. "Are you sure?"

"All the different people back at Roanoke. The Empress doesn't have any control over who or what ends up in the valley. That's why we're here. She gets Neanderthals if she happens to be thinking of it at the right time, but otherwise . . . it's all just running on automatic. And right now it's automatically shutting down because she's left the Castle."

He waved them to start moving again. He did, and didn't look to see if they kept up. Parker and Sam traded glances and started after him.

"So she's never gone outside before? She's been in there for hundreds of years."

"Maybe," said Pyr. "She makes appearances, but before this week I'd only seen her four or five times."

"Until she decided—she's spent all night out rallying the Klaa." Sam huffed out some air as he hopped over a thick root. "And all morning preparing to march."

"Maybe she knows exactly how long she can stay outside of the Castle," Parker called out. "She might have this all down to . . . well, a science."

Noah glanced back at them. "I don't think so. The valley's coming apart at the seams. You can feel it in the air. The ozone's buzzing, like before a thunderstorm hits."

She'd felt that too. Hadn't thought about it. The tree canopy hid the sky, so she'd been assuming it was going to rain.

The rhythm of the tremors changed. It felt . . . chaotic? It sounded like thunder getting closer, overlapping and rumbling. A pulse, like an erratic heartbeat or a subwoofer. She looked at him a few yards ahead and saw the worry on his face.

Thate had stopped too, turning to show off his phenomenal abs and magnificent—*no*, focus—trying to stop the Empress and save the valley. Thate's arm was up, pointing at the forest around them. "Up against the trees," he called out over the rumble. "Get behind them. Now!"

Monique moved quickly. Parker and Noah a little slower. Pyr wrapped an arm around Sam's shoulders and lifted, swinging him toward one of the trees as the first dinosaur came charging by.

It was one of the ones with a tiny head and Godzilla-plates on its back, galloping through the forest on all fours. A stegosaurus. Its tail swung back and forth and holy crap those spikes probably would've left bigger holes than a shotgun.

It ran past, staggering into one of the tree trunks with all the grace and subtlety of a car crash. The tree shuddered under the impact, and on the other side of it Sam's eyes were huge. Anything between the dino and the tree would've been pulped.

Which is also when Parker realized it wasn't alone.

Two-three-five more stegosaurs charged through the woods, each one crashing against the trees like a drunk running through a crowd. A big, splayed foot came down hard near Parker, and a tree root snapped under it. She saw a glimpse of blue as Thate leaped up, grabbing a low branch and pulling himself up out of the way. A tail slammed into the tree sheltering Sam and Pyr, embedding itself in the hardwood and then ripping free just as fast, spraying splinters and bark everywhere. The sound of cracking wood almost drowned out the hammering of massive footsteps. The tree groaned and swayed. The dinosaur barely noticed.

The last one's head swung to look at Parker as it lumbered past, and she could see the panic in its little, dark eyes. Almost feel the question in its mind as they locked eyes.

Why aren't you running?

She stayed pressed up against the tree for what felt like another minute. Then she heard someone clap. Noah, stepping away from the shelter of his tree.

Thate's legs dangled down, and he dropped from his branch. "Everyone okay?"

Monique shook out her long skirt. "Oui."

Pyr released Sam's shoulders and they stepped away from their half-shattered tree. "I think we're fine."

Parker stepped out from behind her tree. "Yeah. Yeah, all good here."

Noah nodded once. "We have to keep moving."

Monique looked after the dinosaurs. "They're stampeding."

"Probably scared by the tremors."

"And maybe the Klaa army bearing down on us," said Thate. But he turned and launched back into his effortless jog as he said it.

Pyr gestured after the stegosaurs. "We've seen this a few times before. They're going to run in circles around the valley until they drop from exhaustion."

Sam glanced back. "Why?"

"Because they've got nowhere else to go."

"Please." Noah gestured after Thate, now several yards away from them. "We have to keep moving. Our best chance of stopping this is just giving her what she wants."

They all fell back into the fast jog. The stegosaurs had made a rough path through the trees for them. Sam puffed out air as he stomped along. Pyr slowed, guarding their rear again. Parker watched the ground, quick stepping over broken roots and dangling vines. Avoiding rocks. Watching out for the occasional deep footprint or hole in the ground. She kept her eyes low, giving up a little speed to keep herself from sprawling.

Through the trees. Into a grassland, past the remains of a wooden shack that could've been from almost any country, any century. Then back into the woods.

She could tell Noah wanted to go faster. Was frustrated by their pace. They'd been on the move for . . . half an hour? Maybe forty minutes? Not counting five minutes hiding from the dinosaur stampede. She had no idea how far they'd gone.

The trees fell away into a loose clearing. One that looked like it was a natural part of the forest, not a random area patched in between the trees. A few yards away, on the side of the clearing, sat a squat boulder.

No, not a boulder. A massive stone head with empty eyes, a wide nose, and some kind of elaborate headband. There was a guy in the astronomy department who had a tattoo on his arm like this and goddammit Parker was letting herself get distracted by minutia instead of focusing on Noah or the valley and then Monique tripped over a root and slammed to the ground.

The French woman had scrambled to her feet by the time Parker and the others reached her. Dry grass and earth stuck to her curly hair and outfit. She brushed furiously at herself. "I'm fine. Let us keep moving."

Noah looked her up and down, leaned to get going again, and stopped. He crouched low. Reached for Monique's foot. She went to step back and her leg jerked out in front of her.

A loop of thick cord wrapped around her ankle. The thin, raw rope blended in with the dry grass and dusty soil. Noah wiggled it loose and slid it off Monique's boot.

Thate had reached the far side of the clearing, doubled back, and he was crouched down too. "There's a trip line over here."

Sam gestured at Monique's feet. "Looks like she got caught in a snare."

"A snare?" echoed Parker.

"I was a Boy Scout."

Noah looked around. "Who set these? Emerson and Neith or the Klaa?"

Pyr shook her head. "The Klaa aren't trappers."

The rumbling ground spiked for a moment, a sharp tremor, and then settled back to its earlier levels. Maybe a little higher? Parker tried to gauge the vibrations coming through her feet. She locked eyes with Noah, saw the worry in his face.

She looked at Thate as he came closer. "I thought the ambush was supposed to be further than this."

"It was. That's what we discussed. There's another clearing about two klicks from here they'd planned to use." He waved a hand at the snare. "That's Emerson's work, though."

Sam looked around. "Why would they move the ambush closer?"

"Because they didn't have time." Pyr looked at the trees. "The Klaa are closer or moving faster. Or both."

"That's not good," said Parker.

Noah gazed at the edge of the clearing. "If this is the ambush, where are they?"

"Taking up position? Maybe *in* position, trying to figure out what we're doing here?" Thate raised a hand in the air, waved it slowly side to side. "Somewhere high enough to give them a clear view of the target area."

Parker looked around. Saw so many trees, including some maybe half a mile away that looked like redwoods. A tall column of orange-red stone that looked like it should be part of a Utah landscape. The cliffs beyond all of them.

Sam raised both hands over his head, waving them back and forth like someone trying to flag down a car. He turned slowly, keeping his head raised. If anyone saw him, they made no sign.

Noah pointed across the clearing. "We should keep going. If we reach the Empress before she gets here, none of this matters."

Thate swung his head side to side. "If they set up here, it means something's changed. They may be on a different route. We shouldn't just run off into the woods."

"I'm not saying we should run into the woods."

Parker felt the tremors shift again. Not so much an increase but a change from the steady vibration. The ground pulsed and pumped, enough to feel. Near her shoe a clump of grass trembled. She looked up, saw Monique staring at the ground, too. Pyr watched the forest.

Noah felt it too. "The stampede?"

Even as he said it, Parker knew what they were feeling. She looked across the clearing, saw movement getting closer through the trees. Tried to swallow down her fear.

The first raptor lunged out of the trees and let out a shriek that made Parker's skull throb. Its rider wrapped her hands around the reins, but let the dinosaur take a few more quick steps into the clearing. Then a second raptor came out of the woods, its clawed feet pounding on the ground. And a third. A fourth. A dozen of them, all with riders. All holding spears or clubs. Another raptor screeched, then another, and then they were all cracking the air with their shrieks.

Thate reached back over his hips and pulled the two knives sheathed across the small of his back. Pyr stepped forward and held out her biomechanical arm. Parker realized she didn't have a spear or a bow or even a knife. Bare hands against cavemen and dinosaurs.

Another raptor stomped out of the trees and headed for them in a few big strides. Breaker. A shiny new pair of teeth stood out on his trophy necklace. Dental-spokesman white.

Another pair of mounted raptors came out on either side of him. Parker saw more and more of them coming into the clearing, surrounding them. Twenty now? Thirty? One of them leaped up onto the stone head, its big claws scraping for balance.

"No," shouted Noah. He ran forward, putting himself between the two sides. "No fighting. We can't risk it."

The raptors shrieked and hissed. They looked at the ground, too. The tremors were more obvious when you tried to stand still.

More figures came out of the woods. Dozens of the Klaa on foot. Moving slower, but so many of them. All shorter than Parker, but thicker and muscular. Most of them had heavy clubs. A few had long spears. They filled in behind the raptors.

She took a step back. Bumped into Sam. They traded a quick look and she tried to think of something reassuring to say.

Breaker kicked a heel into his dinosaur's side and yanked on its reins. The raptor hissed and sidestepped, bringing its body around even as it kept its eyes on the little group. Parker was pretty sure it was staring at Noah.

The saber-toothed tiger loped forward, each massive paw coming down silently. Its huge skull swung back and forth, looking at the raptors on either side as if it was daring them to make a sound. It marched past the Neanderthals, past Breaker, and carried its passenger out into the sun. The huge cat stopped maybe fifteen feet from Noah.

The Empress had the same smile as her tiger. Mean. Hungry.

"Little Billy Gather," she said. "You're supposed to be dead by now."

49

NOAH

Noah took a cautious step forward. Not too close. Although at this range, there wasn't much doubt the sabertooth could pounce and have him before he did anything. Those two big fangs were almost as long as his forearm. He could smell it from a few yards away. Cat breath, meat, and blood.

He tried to focus past it. Past the huge jaws and monstrous teeth and the shaking ground and just look at her. The Empress. He took in a deep breath. Tried to calm himself. Almost felt confused when it worked.

He looked her in the eye. Even mounted on the big cat, she wasn't much taller than him. Everyone saw her from a distance, thought of her and the cat as larger than they were. One more thing in the valley that wasn't what it seemed.

Although the sabertooth could still probably kill him with little to no effort.

Another deep rumble came from the ground. This one made him shift his feet. It was followed by a harsh gust of wind that set off a flurry of hisses and thrashing tails among the raptors. Neanderthals jerked on reins and kicked at flanks. Even the sabertooth stomped back and forth, pacing in front of Noah.

The Empress leaned forward and rested her arms on the back of the tiger's scruffy head, calming it. If she registered the quakes and the wind, it didn't show in her eyes. "Why have the people of your village defied me? Why haven't they gutted you and hung your body up for me to see?"

"I was going to let them," he admitted. The truth. He'd considered it the whole way back to Roanoke and all through the late-night discussion.

"Have you come to beg for mercy?"

"Would it work?"

"No." She slid the blue crystal knife from her belt. The multidimensional dagger.

"I understand. Not mercy for me, then. For everyone else."

One of her pale eyebrows went up.

"I'm the one you want. Kill me, but please end this now. Just . . . just go home."

"This is all my home. All of the valley is mine." A deep, grinding echo punctuated her words. Or maybe violently disagreed with them.

"Let's go back to the Ice Castle. You can kill me there."

"You do not make demands of me, little Billy."

"Not a demand. A last request."

She straightened up on the sabertooth's back. Studied his face. Spun the crystal dagger in her hand. "Why?"

"Because . . . it's where I want to die."

"Liar!" The dagger stopped, the tip pointing at him. "What trick are you playing? Why do you run to sacrifice yourself?"

He took another breath. Pictured Parker and Sam behind him. Olivia back at Roanoke with Ross and Qiang and the others.

Breaker called a few coarse syllables to the Empress. Noah recognized *hunt* and *kill* and the often-used word that stood for anything *different*. She snapped two back at him, suddenly the old matriarch again. *Silence* and *still*.

She never looked away from Noah. He couldn't tell if she was intrigued or amused. Maybe she just wanted to kill him herself.

Noah dared another step closer and wobbled as the valley convulsed again. Trees shook. A few of the raptors squealed. Some of them stomped. Even the Klaa looked disturbed by the intensity of it.

He tensed so many muscles, trying not to lose his balance, not to fall, not to move too quickly. Less than ten feet between him and the sabertooth's jaws now. It stretched its head forward and he saw the big nostrils flare.

"When we spoke in the Castle," Noah said, "you told me you knew the truth of the valley. That it's the Castaway's lifeboat. That you killed them and took their place."

Suspicion flickered across her face. "Yes."

As she spoke a thundercrack echoed across the valley, followed by distant rumbling. Noah followed the sound, glanced behind him. A section of the high cliffs slid free of the valley wall, breaking into rubble as it plunged down.

"It cuts both ways, though," Noah said. "You gained all their . . . their power. But you also have their limitations."

"The Empress has no limitations."

"You do. We're all seeing it right now."

Her dagger came up to point at him again. "Explain."

He tried to organize his thoughts and the arrow slammed into the Empress's skull, pushing her other ear down to her shoulder. She tumbled off the saber-toothed tiger, and the big cat took the movement as a signal to turn. It paced around, and by the time it realized it was free its eyes faced almost completely away from Noah, inadvertently saving his life.

B'Kar let out a savage roar and followed it up by bellowing *Attack*. He kicked his raptor in the ribs and the dinosaur launched itself forward with a shriek. The Neanderthal raised his axe-club and guided his mount at Noah.

A blast of white light hit Breaker's raptor in the side of the head, and with the shifting ground it stumbled and fell, throwing its rider. Breaker rolled, came up with his axe-club over his head. The dinosaur glared at him and he roared at it. The raptor threw itself upright and hissed back.

Pyr swayed for a moment, then lifted her blaster-arm again.

The rest of the Klaa surged forward. Some moved too close to the saber-toothed tiger and it let out a monstrous yowl that drove back

Neanderthals and dinosaurs alike. It padded back toward the forest, clearly not looking for a fight but also clearly not against the idea. Everything in its path scattered. The ground shook and more of the raptors shrieked. One of them charged forward and stumbled, a pale snare around two of its toes. The dinosaur didn't trip, but it slowed and twisted, and another raptor plowed into it, driven by its rider.

Thate lunged forward and Breaker caught one of the blue man's long knives on the shaft of his axe. He twisted away from the other one, spun around, swung the axe-club at Thate's exposed side. Thate stepped back, dodged, lashed out again.

Pyr grabbed Noah. She had her arm out in front of her, biomechanical fingers spread wide. She tried to pull him back. Somewhere behind him Parker yelled. Sam bellowed something. Monique talked loud and fast, almost shouting.

Noah barely registered any of it. He only saw the crumpled figure of the Empress sprawled in the grass, one of her eyes staring across the clearing, the other half-closed. Blood streamed down her face, bright against the chalk-white hair. One of her arms flopped over her head. From this far away, he couldn't tell if she was breathing.

He shook off Pyr's grasp and dashed forward. A Neanderthal charged him and he bellowed *Stop* at it, loud enough to be heard over the growls of dinosaurs and the dull roar of the valley. The man froze, confused, and Pyr punched him in the throat.

Stillness rippled across the assembled forces of the Klaa as Noah's shout echoed across the clearing. Their advance halted, looks of confusion and shock on their faces, and Thate took the moment to kick Breaker's legs out from under him.

"Stop!" Noah shouted again, this time for the English-speakers. "Everyone stop trying to kill each other for five minutes." He took a step, pointed at the Empress's body. Racked his brain for the Pakka words he'd known as a kid. He'd written them all down once. Numbered them.

He jabbed his finger down at the Empress again. *Family*, He shouted. *Not fight. We help family.*

He gazed across the clearing. Still so many looks of confusion. But a few of relief. Two or three yanked on their reins and stopped the advance of their raptors. Enough weapons went down that the Klaa looked back and forth among themselves.

Noah dropped to his knees and felt the surging, thrashing ground against his shins. A full earthquake now. No more timid vibrations.

He lifted her wrist. Pushed the furs and leather strings away until he had space to set his fingers against her skin. Tried not to think about all the blood pooling up in her ear and covering her cheekbones.

A pulse. Fast, but definitely there. A little erratic, but that might be from him trying to do something delicate with his own heart racing.

He crouched and put his ear close to her bloody lips. He couldn't hear breathing, but he felt it. A wisp of air tickled his inner ear. And then again.

Someone pushed him aside. A mass of curly hair filled his vision. He brought his fists up and Monique shoved him again, setting her large leather case next to the body. "Out of the way."

He knee-walked to the side and the doctor crouched over the Empress. Gently probed the bloody wound in her head. Noah realized he couldn't see the arrow. Had it snapped off when she fell? Neith's bow couldn't be strong enough for it to go *through* the Empress's head, could it? Not at this range.

He looked up. An uneasy truce seemed to have settled over the clearing. Definitely more uneasy in some quarters than others. B'Kar glared at Thate, his axe-club held in one hand. Thate returned the glare, both of his knives ready. Some of the Klaa looked ready to charge, others looked around the shaking valley with worried expressions.

We help, he called out again. What was the other word? The one they'd all called her back in the day? They'd thought it was her name and then the Pakka had used it for Beau a few times. *We help mother!*

Another ripple of confusion. A few more relieved faces. Parker stepped a little closer. "What are you telling them?"

"I think that we're all family and we're trying to help her. Make sure nobody gets too aggressive." Noah focused on the Empress again. "How is she?"

Monique waved him away. Dabbed at the wound with a bit of linen. Gently touched the white hairline with her other hand.

"Well?"

The clearing lurched and she almost fell over. "These aren't the best conditions—"

"Is she going to live?"

"I do not know!" She set another piece of linen gently over the wound. "The arrow has broken off in the skull. I see tissue damage where it tore through her flesh. I believe a fracture to the skull itself at the point of impact. Blood loss. Probably concussion and neck trauma. So much depends on if the arrowhead is lodged in the bone or actually penetrated her skull."

"How can we tell? What can we do?"

She shook her head. "The fact that the bone is fractured is a bad sign. Neanderthal skulls are very solid, but if the arrow has broken it, it most likely has entered her brain."

"But that . . . that's not a death sentence, right?"

"Possibly not. With a great deal of rest and care she may recover. I have seen the valley heal many injuries I believed to be fatal."

"I don't think we can count on the valley to help her. Not right now, anyway." He straightened up, stared past the Klaa and above the tree line. "I'm not sure how far it is to the Castle from here. We'll need to make a stretcher, or maybe—"

Monique put a hand up, gently pushing back. "No."

"We need to get her to the Castle."

"She cannot be moved. Her condition is far too fragile."

The valley groaned again, and Noah's panic rose with the sound. "We *have* to."

Monique shook her head. "She would not survive the trip. She might not even survive being moved to a stretcher."

The Empress and the ground around her went dim as the sky

flickered above them. Not so much dim as . . . stark. Like the whole clearing had been bleached of color, like a film that also released a black-and-white version. By the time he looked up, the blue sky had reasserted itself. The wind picked up and grit peppered his face.

He straightened his legs and pointed at the sky. "What happened? Did you see?"

Pyr stared up. "The sky . . . shut off for a second."

Parker nodded in agreement. "It just went black."

"They're not liking it," Sam added, gesturing at the Klaa.

Noah crouched next to Monique. "How long to make her safe to move?"

"I could not say. A few hours at the very least."

He looked up at the sky again. "We don't have that much time."

50

PARKER

Parker felt an odd sense of relief they'd figured out the valley was on a spaceship. Without that knowledge, seeing the whole sky flicker on and off like someone playing with a light switch would've snapped her brain. As it was, every instinct she had screamed she'd just seen something impossible.

The Klaa didn't like it either. She didn't know if the Empress and Breaker ruled out of fear or tradition or family loyalty, but whatever it was, it wasn't enough. Not for people whose brains were wired against change.

Some of the Klaa on foot broke and ran, cutting across the open space and taking off through the trees. A few of the mounted ones too. The one perched on the stone head gave her raptor a quick snap of the reins and they dashed off into the forest.

Parker saw all of this as good since the six of them were basically facing down about two hundred angry Neanderthals. Well, four of them were, since Noah and Monique were trying to figure out if there was anything they could do for someone who'd been hit in the head with a high-speed arrow. And really only Pyr and Thate had weapons, but Thate was tied up in his standoff with Breaker, and Pyr had already used one shot from her bio-cannon thing. So Parker and Sam were left trying to look tough and determined against most of the Klaa. Granted, Sam had his new knife tucked in his belt, but he'd forgotten to draw it. Parker worried if she mentioned it and he pulled it out now, it would look bad.

Most of the Klaa looked uncertain, but a few dozen of them were seriously pissed off. Angry something was happening to their valley. Angry a lot of their tribe-mates were dragging their feet.

Angry at the people crouched around their leader.

Something crashed through the trees behind them and more raptors shrieked. Another charging dinosaur. It took Parker a moment to recognize Brunhilda as the styracosaurus thundered across the clearing, head angled to point her horn straight ahead, her massive feet pounding the ground. And right behind her armored frill, Diedrich the farmer. He reached down and tapped the dinosaur between her eyes with his bamboo swagger stick and she lumbered to a halt a few yards from Parker.

"I thought you may still need assistance," shouted the farmer over the rumbling. "My apologies for the delay. The earthquakes have her skittish."

"Just hold on," Parker called to him. "We might have a truce here."

He pointed his stick at the Empress. "Is she dead?"

"No," shouted Noah from over by the Empress's body. "She's alive but we can't move her." He turned back to the Klaa and shouted a few more coarse syllables.

Parker ran over to them. Saw the mess of bloody linen. The worried look on Monique's face. "Oh shit."

"Shit," echoed Sam from behind her.

Noah looked up at them. "I've told them she's hurt and we're trying to help her."

Parker couldn't stop staring at all the blood. "Is it the truth?"

"Oui," said Monique without looking up. "But her condition is extremely delicate. There is a good chance she will not survive."

"Okay." Parker tried to clear her mind. "Okay, can we build a stretcher or—"

"No," snapped Monique. "She cannot be moved."

Sam tapped his fingers furiously. "What if we also made, like, a neck brace? Something to immobilize her for the move."

Noah gestured at the Empress's wounds. "We'd have to immobilize her head, too. Completely."

Parker tried to picture it all in her mind. "This sounds like more than half an hour of work."

"It is irrelevant," said Monique, "because she cannot be moved. Not even slightly. It could kill her here and now."

Another thunderclap rumbled across the valley as a massive section of cliff crumbled away, dropping boulders the size of houses. It reminded Parker of videos showing casinos or apartment complexes being demolished. Or the World Trade Center collapsing.

"What if . . ." She tried to get an idea to gel in her mind. "Is there some way we could bring the Castle to her?"

Monique glanced up for that. "What?"

"Like, if we could bring part of it closer?" asked Sam. He raised his bouncing fingers. "Enough that it can sense her again?"

Noah reached down and pushed away some furs to reveal the crude, empty sheath the Empress wore on her hip. "She's been carrying part of the Castle around with her. Her dagger. She dropped it when the arrow hit her."

Parker looked around them, trying to spot the crystal blade. People and dinosaurs shifted on their feet. The shadows leaped and jumped as the sky flickered. The grass shifted in the wind and there it was! About ten feet away, right by Brunhilda's front leg, almost under the bulky dinosaur's belly.

"Got it," Parker yelled. She crouched, scooped up the dagger, and stretched her arm back, holding it out to Noah. He took it. Set it on the Empress. Put it in her hand.

Nothing happened.

Sam stopped tapping his fingers and clenched them into fists. "Maybe a more specific part? A bigger piece? Something in the Castaway's chamber?"

Noah shook his head. "I'd have no idea what."

Parker looked up at the distant cliffs. Watched a piece of rock the size of a space shuttle tumble-roll down the valley wall. "This place has adjustable dimensions, right? If the distances between things grow, is there a way to make them shrink?"

"Probably," said Noah after a moment. "Again, though—no idea how. It's not like the Castle has a big lifeboat control room in it."

"Are you sure?"

The sky fritzed again. For the space of a heartbeat it was night, and the stars stretched above her. Then daytime. And then darkness *and* the sun. The airless view from satellite pictures and Moon landings. And then the blue sky returned.

Noah saw it too. "We don't have time to search a six-hundred-foot tower for a room that might not ex—"

A sharp tremor shook the clearing and knocked them all to the ground. A few of the raptors went down, too, crushing their riders as they thrashed back to their feet. Even Brunhilda swayed on her squat legs, letting out a whale-like moan. The wind picked up and Parker couldn't shake the feeling the air wasn't moving as much as being sucked away. A tree trembled and tipped over in slow motion, soil and grass spraying out around its roots. The sounds of other trees falling echoed through the forest around them. A few of the Klaa shouted words that sounded like warnings. Or maybe swears.

Breaker got halfway to his feet and hurled himself back. Thate leaped after him but the Neanderthal rolled, ducked, lashed out with his axe-club, and quick-stepped back. Ten feet between them, and then fifteen, and then Breaker was closer to the rest of the Klaa than to the blue man. He shouted to them. Pointed his weapon at the group gathered near the fallen Empress.

"Not looking good," Pyr called out.

An idea danced in Parker's mind, a last puzzle piece she spun to figure out how and where it fit. The valley and the Castaway and the Empress in the Ice Castle and—

"We have to move her," shouted Noah, interrupting her train of thought. His voice barely carried over the sounds of wind and cracking stone and shifting earth.

Monique put a hand out and yelled back. "You'll kill her."

"You don't know that."

"I know if you kill her there is no saving this place!"

This place.

It was right there. Something about the Castaway. Something Noah and Sam had both said. Something else they'd all misunderstood.

A pair of trees crashed to the ground on the far side of the clearing. Brunhilda let out another mournful wail and stomped her feet.

"If we don't risk it everything dies." Noah leaned closer to the Empress's body. Reached for her arm. "I'm sorry."

The idea slammed home and Parker held out a hand. "Wait."

"What?"

"The Castaway never left the Ice Castle."

"They couldn't." He tried to wave Sam over to get the Empress's other arm.

"So when they told you that someday you'd call *this place* home . . . you were in the Castle too."

It all slammed together for Noah, too. She saw it in his eyes. "Oh my god."

In that same moment Parker realized the tremors shaking the valley floor had picked up again. She'd thought it was Diedrich and Brunhilda, or maybe everything had kicked up another order of magnitude again. A deep cracking sound came from the forest. Tree trunks breaking. The heavy sound of impacts.

A few yards away, Thate raised a hand, pointing with one of his long knives. "We've got a stampede."

51

SAM

Some of the Klaa dashed across the clearing, heading toward Sam and the group. Their faces looked scared more than aggressive. A few more glanced back through the trees. Then the screaming began and they all scattered. Tried to scatter.

A group of triceratops charged out of the woods, flattening a few smaller trees as they plowed into the clearing. Two styracosauruses, like Brunhilda, ran with them. They thundered along almost shoulder to shoulder, trampling everything in their way. A trio of Klaa warriors vanished beneath the elephant-like feet. One raptor shrieked a challenge and was battered aside, sending its Neanderthal rider soaring through the air. They went down in the stampede, lost between the massive creatures.

Two of the Klaa ran past Sam and a triceratops charged after them. He took a few frantic steps, tried to get out of its way, and realized the whole group of dinosaurs was coming right at them, a wall of horns and muscle. They were aimed just past Brunhilda, at Noah, Monique, and the Empress. Not straight at them, but the trio would be crushed in just a few—

Pyr stepped in front of Sam and everything went hot neon white as her arm-blaster hit one of the styracosaurs right above its eye. A second blast struck its bony, horn-covered frill. It let out a keening moan, the sound of a sad whale, and veered away to crash against one of the other dinosaurs, knocking them both off course and away from the group.

Pyr dropped to her knees. Took a deep, ragged breath. Her head wobbled and her organic eye looked glazed. Sam reached to steady her, but before he could she slumped back against him, so much dead weight. He lowered her to the ground near the Empress.

So many dinosaurs. Wouldn't be surprising if most of the creatures in the valley were reacting to the imminent collapse in one way or another. The air was filled with panic and fear. Five or six of the larger ones with the feather-crested heads stampeded out of the trees, leaning forward like they were falling into their run. A trio of ankylosauruses thundered behind them, like living tanks. A dozen smaller dinosaurs raced through the chaos.

And all of them aimed across the clearing.

Noah stood up and shouted more Neanderthal words, waving his arms. Some of the random Klaa tribe members changed course. Ran toward them. Some were plowed down or battered aside by the dinosaurs. A dog-sized raptor leaped up and rode a Neanderthal's shoulders, slashing at him until he dropped and it raced away. A lone triceratops made a big arcing charge that forced Thate to lunge out of the way, crashing face-first into the ground to avoid being gored or trampled.

A dark-haired woman dressed in loose furs that smelled of meat and blood squeezed in next to Sam, pushing him into a man who reeked of nervous sweat. Fifteen, maybe twenty of the Klaa formed a tight wall around their Empress and Pyr and Sam and Monique and Noah. They brandished spears and clubs and stone daggers and Sam remembered he had his iron knife. They formed a wedge, braced for the stampede, and then Brunhilda's bulk filled Sam's view.

Diedrich guided the styracosaur forward and she became a living wall between all of them and the stampede. Thate came speed-crawling under the big dinosaur's belly, dragging himself on his arms. "We have to get to cover."

"How?" said Parker. She gestured at the Empress and Pyr.

"I can carry them."

"No, you cannot," said Monique, jamming a finger at him.

Sam stepped around the Neanderthal woman and got himself to a place where he could see over Brunhilda's tail. The bleating, lowing swarm of dinosaurs stormed by, changing course ever so slightly to pass on either side of her, kicking up dust as they went. Diedrich patted her side, keeping her calm and still. A small raptor bounced against her hide, tried to scrabble over her, and the German kicked it away.

Noah stepped forward, setting his hands against Brunhilda's shoulder, and Sam could barely hear his words over the noise filling the air. Asking Diedrich about getting to the Castle. A quick exchange, a gesture at the Empress. Noah shaking his head.

At least a hundred dinosaurs must've stampeded by, moving fast enough Sam could only pick out random details. Big. Small. Horns. Teeth. Colorful fins. Yellow eyes. Black eyes. Armor plates.

And just like that the bulk of the stampede had passed by, leaving a few final dinosaurs desperately trying to flee the earthquakes and falling trees. Sam could see at least two dozen members of the Klaa and a few raptors that'd been crushed under the dinosaurs. Before he could stare too long, though, three crocodile-sized, yellow-brown iguanas slither-ran out of the trees, each with a massive fin like the sails of old Chinese ships. They ran low to the ground, their rough bellies battering the knee-high grass and their wide legs scattering more Neanderthals. Weaving between the fin-backed dinosaurs, a dog-sized raptor took bounding steps as it ran past them. The last finback's long, straight tail had just passed Brunhilda when a trio of the little raptors dashed out of the trees, rushing to catch up with the other dinosaurs.

Breaker smashed one of the small dinosaurs away with his axe-club. It went down and he hit it again. And again. He bellowed at the other Klaa around him and turned to march toward the group circling the fallen Empress.

Pure dedication? Angry and murder-happy? The ever-popular *why not both?*

"Hey! Breaker's coming!" Sam looked over, but nobody could hear his shouts over the echoes of the stampede and the earthquake and shit another section of cliff broke loose, like watching an iceberg cleave off a glacier. Noah was still shout-talking to Diedrich. The Neanderthal woman glanced at Sam, clearly not understanding a word he was saying. Parker was over . . .

An ultralow roar echoed across the clearing, shaking Sam's bones harder than the quakes. Not an echo, he realized. Two roars almost overlapping each other.

Two shapes moved in the shadows of the forest, tall enough to be seen over Brunhilda's high back. So many heads turned at the subsonic roars. So many creatures came to a nervous halt. For others, raw instinct kicked in and they scattered in terror.

Burn and Gnash came striding out of the trees. Sam saw the wedge-like, horned heads a dozen feet up in the air. The plate-sized, hawk-like eyes. The teeth. So many teeth.

They stomped in a dozen yards apart. Chasing the stampede? Part of it? Whatever role they'd started with, the two allosauruses gazed back and forth across the clearing like they'd found themselves at a buffet.

Gnash brought her foot down, pinning a Neanderthal under her toes. Her jaws opened and she tore off the man's head and arm with a quick yank. Sam got a quick glimpse of skin and muscle stretching out and then a wash of blood.

Burn grabbed a raptor in his massive jaws. Had there been a rider on its back or not? Now they were all thrashing too much to be sure.

Breaker paused at the roars and screams, glanced back over his shoulder. He was maybe six yards from Brunhilda and the cluster of Roanoke folks and Neanderthals. Was Sam the only person who'd noticed him?

Gnash took two big loping steps forward, crushing a Neanderthal's leg as she did. The allosaurus looked down at the shrieking man. Over at the little group of people huddled by the unmoving styracosaurus.

A few of the Klaa goaded their raptors across the shaking, shifting clearing toward Burn. The dinosaurs shrieked and hissed at each other.

Sam looked at the group. Took a few quick, nervous breaths. They were all focused on other things. Pyr unconscious. The Empress still bleeding from her head—could Gnash smell her blood? Parker. Noah. Thate.

Somebody had to do something.

Sam took a deep breath, ran around Brunhilda's tail, and screamed. Long. Hard. He could barely hear it over all the other screams and shouts and cracks and roars. He sucked in another breath and let out another long holler. Then he took a few more steps away from Brunhilda and waved his arms, jumping as high as his squat build would let him.

Breaker grinned and let out a howl of his own. Raised his axe-club and slashed it down through the air. He stomped forward, big heavy strides to keep his balance, and Sam tried to hop backward, further away from the group. Still waving his arms. Still trying to be the center of attention. Still trying to be heard over all the other noise.

Then it didn't matter anymore because Gnash let loose another subsonic roar Sam felt from his teeth to his bowels. She'd seen the bouncing and hand waving. Maybe heard it too? It'd gotten her attention as so many things scattered and she loped across the clearing toward Sam.

And toward Breaker. So focused on Sam he hadn't noticed the allosaurus coming up behind him. Normally her massive footfalls would probably give her away, but with all the chaos in the valley . . .

He felt that roar, though. Sam kept hopping back and Breaker turned to see Gnash all of ten feet behind him. But the allosaurus was still looking at Sam, coming for Sam, and for a brief moment he thought she was going to step right past the bloodthirsty Neanderthal without stopping and then Breaker slammed his axe-club dead center into her lower jaw.

Gnash stopped looking at Sam. She swung her head down and whipped it to the side. It was like watching Breaker get hit by a bus, the impact hurling him across the wide expanse of the clearing.

Sam took the moment to turn and run away after all. Away from the group. Couldn't lead her back there. He'd have to hope he could make the trees.

A dinosaur lumbered alongside him and a hand reached down. Noah. On Brunhilda. "Come on," he shouted.

Sam grabbed his hand and jumped. Noah leaned back, dragging him up onto the dinosaur's back. Brunhilda's thighs slapped against Sam twice and he was pretty sure that whole side of his body would be bruised. Then he was on her back. Riding a dinosaur.

He felt another subsonic growl behind them.

Diedrich smacked the bamboo stick against Brunhilda's shoulder and the styracosaurus galloped forward with a bubbling holler. Sam grabbed Noah's waist even as Noah grabbed Diedrich's. The rumble of the ground vanished beneath the heavy rhythm of the dinosaur's footsteps.

Sam twisted his head around. Saw Gnash diverting, heading for the group on the ground, and then a blast of white light hit her below her eye horn. She staggered, kept moving, and then she passed the cluster of his friends and focused on Brunhilda again. He caught a glimpse of Parker letting Pyr's arm drop. No idea how they'd coaxed another shot out of her blaster.

And then the trees closed around them and they were in the forest. Branches whipped at him. Leaves and splinters bounced off his face. He remembered the earlier stampede bouncing off the tree trunks and imagined his leg pulped between a dinosaur and a tree.

Brunhilda threw herself across the forest. She bounced up and down as she leaped forward again and again. Sam imagined it was a lot like riding an out-of-control carousel. He tightened his grip on Noah's waist, even as Diedrich shouted and urged her on with choice blows from the swagger stick.

A tree leaned toward them, crashed to the ground behind them. The quakes rocked the valley. How much of his shaky point of view was Brunhilda, how much the collapsing lifeboat?

The styracosaurus shuddered, and Sam felt a nervous twitch run through his back and arms. He looked back over his shoulder and saw Gnash maybe fifty yards behind them, her feet kicking up dirt and branches as she tore through the forest. The allosaurus had her head stretched out low, her butt high, like a cat ready to pounce. One of those poses that'd be impossible if you weren't moving faster than you could fall. Her mouth opened wide—so goddamned wide—and—

"She's gaining on us," he yelled.

"We can outlast her," Diedrich shouted back.

"She's gaining really fast!"

The German reached down. Gave Brunhilda a few firm slaps with his bare hand. The styracosaurus heaved and huffed and her legs hit the ground even harder.

They burst out of the forest and into another savanna. Yellow-green grass. A few wide trees with low branches. If there was a path, Brunhilda ignored it, plowing ahead in a straight line, kicking up clouds of grit and dust as she went.

Noah shook Diedrich. "Wrong way! We're going the wrong way!"

Sam tried to ignore the allosaurus smashing out of the trees behind them and saw the gleaming tower of the Ice Castle two miles away, maybe more. Brunhilda definitely wasn't headed toward it. Sam thought of the round valley, tried to do orbital math, wondered if she might be taking them *away* from the Castle.

"Give her a few moments," Diedrich called back.

"We don't have a few moments!"

"The earthquakes and the running, it unnerves her."

The landscape went sharp around them as the sky glitched again. Dark, harsh shadows appeared everywhere. Familiar shadows.

Sam looked up and almost forgot he was riding a dinosaur.

For half a moment his mind tried to tell him the sky had shut off for the night, but that wasn't exactly true. The sun still burned above them, but all the bright blue around it had vanished. Squinting against the brightness, he could see stars up there in the blackness. He recognized the harsh view from so many photos. The sun seen from space.

The sun without miles of atmosphere in the way to diffuse it.

Only the lifeboat shutting different systems down, he told himself. The comforting sky-view filter turning off. Tons of math ran through his head—gravity, gas pressure, temperature—so many reasons he knew the top of the valley couldn't actually be open to deep space right now.

It would've been more reassuring if the wind hadn't picked up then.

Sam slid on Brunhilda's back, felt momentum shift, and the dinosaur leaned into a wide turn. She pounded through the grass, under a tree branch that almost decapitated Noah, and the Ice Castle slid back into view in front of them. Diedrich cheered her on in German, rubbed her neck behind the big armored frill.

Then another subsonic roar hit them and jangled Sam's nerves.

Gnash was still gaining. And apparently could turn better. She'd cut the distance between them by half. Forty feet away. Fifty at most. Sam could see red on her teeth. See her eyes gleaming in the stark shadows under her brow-horns.

He swung his head around again. Saw the Castle. Definitely getting closer fast.

But not as fast as Gnash.

They weren't going to make it.

He pulled his knife from his belt. Stupid, but all he had. Tried to think of any knife throw he'd ever seen in movies or TV or random YouTube videos. He swung his arm, put as much force as he could behind the knife, and sent it spinning back at the allosaurus. It bounced off one of the brow-horns.

Gnash didn't blink, but Sam felt a deep certainty he'd annoyed her.

He looked for anything else on Brunhilda's simple harness he could throw, anything that might fly as a weapon—even just for a few seconds. Nothing. He thought about grabbing Diedrich's bamboo swagger stick but wasn't sure how necessary it was to guiding Brunhilda.

He felt Noah shift. The older man looked back. Seemed to do the same mental math about Gnash's speed versus theirs.

The sky glitched again. It turned bright blue for a few seconds, then went back to deep space.

Not much time left. They had to get Noah to the Castle. They needed some kind of weapon. Something to throw at her. Into her path.

He swung his head back to look at Gnash and his eyes caught something on the ground as it flew past. A straight line. The savanna ended and there were marble flagstones. Brunhilda cut across the corner of a plaza.

Maybe fifty yards away he saw the outline of an obelisk. Almost invisible against the marble. Because they were the same color.

The marble obelisk. The one that—

No time to second-guess or talk himself out of it. Sam let go of Noah's waist and swung his leg over Brunhilda's broad back. Momentum added force to his leap and he hit the flagstones hard. He went down, hit his knee, then his shoulder, somehow protected his head, and *no time no time* rolled back to his feet, trying to balance on the shaking ground. Brunhilda was already half a football field away. And Gnash . . .

Gnash couldn't've been more than thirty feet from him. Her pace slowed. Another tough choice. Keep chasing the bigger meal? Grab the easy snack?

"HEY!" Sam waved his arm even as he started moving backward. Speed-walking backward, hoping nothing back there would catch his heel and send him down to the ground again. His knee felt hot and sore where it had hit the flagstones. Was it bleeding? "HEY, OVER HERE!"

Gnash took her next step, turned her foot toward Sam, and he ran.

Short legs, but he'd always been good at running away. Grade school. High school. College. He'd been running away his whole life but holy fuck he wished he'd actually trained or something. He threw one leg in front of the other, pumped his arms, kicked off the trembling flagstones.

A subsonic roar washed over him. Shook his gut. Hot air washed across the back of his neck. He threw himself to the left as hard as he could. Fought to keep his balance as the ground shook under his feet. To ignore the pain in his knee. To ignore the massive jaws slashing a few feet from his head, like a cloud of hot knives whipping through the air.

And now he ran for the obelisk. Thirty feet away. Twenty feet. Gnash's breathing almost drowned out the rumbling of the ground. Her heavy strides overwhelmed the tremors. Ten feet. Five. The wet smell of saliva and meat washed over him.

Sam crouched low and stopped running.

His heel caught inches from the obelisk, close enough to see the thousands of tiny runes. He whipped his head around, saw Gnash's teeth and tongue, and leaped to the side again. She was ready this time, too smart a predator to get fooled the same way twice. Her head swung, her mouth caught his arm, her teeth snagged his skin, and then her momentum carried her against the marble obelisk and she collapsed onto the flagstones.

Dead asleep.

Sam hit the ground. Landed hard on his shoulder. Rolled two or three times, and halfway through the last one his head dipped down and whacked against one of the marble slabs. Right on the temple. The world went white for a moment and filled back up with a special kind of pain.

He crawled to his knees—oh fuck, his knee hurt too—and looked over at the sleeping dinosaur. Gnash's beet-red tongue sprawled out of her mouth, draped over her teeth. Her nostrils flared open. Closed. Open. He couldn't be sure, but he thought she might be snoring.

A shock wave blasted through the ground—and through his knee—knocking him down on all fours. A wave of pain shot back up through his arm. He was bleeding. A lot. Gnash must've had the lightest hold on him with her teeth when she sent him flying. Enough to leave him with a—no, with two deep slashes from above his elbow almost to his wrist. Didn't seem to be pulsing, but blood was coming out pretty fast.

If he could wrap it up with his shirt, he was pretty sure he'd survive it. With the valley's help.

Assuming the valley was still here a few minutes from now.

52

NOAH

"SAM!"

Noah's shout was lost in the sound of the charging styracosaurus, the noise of the collapsing valley. He saw Sam roll to his feet, saw Gnash change course to go after him. Saw the marble obelisk and realized what he was trying to do.

And then one of the low savanna trees tipped over and blocked his sight. He got a glimpse of Gnash lunging forward and then . . . Nothing.

He turned his head and saw the sky around the Ice Castle flicker and flash in a distinct hexagon pattern. Geometric lightning, and one of the points aimed almost directly at them. He'd bet a year's salary they lined up with the six obelisks.

A moment later the sound hit them. A deep bellow, as if all the air in the valley had groaned at once. The wind surged toward the Castle. Toward the hexagon in the sky.

The air felt thinner. Colder. Noah puffed out a breath and saw thin wisps in the air.

Diedrich leaned his head back. "This seems bad."

"It is. Can she go faster?"

He rubbed the dinosaur's neck. "This is the most running she's done in a long time. I think it is all she has to give."

They hit the edge of the swamp and Brunhilda charged ahead, spraying the shallow water in waves around herself. A few last hadrosaurs who hadn't joined the stampede stopped staring at the sky long enough to trumpet at her as she sloshed by them. The mud and water slowed her, but the styracosaurus had enough momentum to carry her across a dozen yards of soggy ground and back onto dry land.

The Ice Castle loomed in front of them, even starker under the harsh sun. It looked cold. It looked fake, like an old movie backdrop. Too sharp and in focus to be real.

Brunhilda got back on solid ground but the swamp had bled her strength away, or reminded her how much she'd already used. Or maybe the sudden chill in the air drained her. They still moved faster than Noah could run, but not by much.

Diedrich patted the big bony frill. Leaned down to talk to her. The dinosaur trotted around the tower. She let out a long sigh and her pace dropped to a tired walk. "Go," said Diedrich.

Noah had already slid down Brunhilda's side. He pushed off, gave himself space to go around her as she lumbered forward, and ran. A shock wave threw him into the side of the tower. He got back to his feet and kept going.

There. The crystal bridge. Two Klaa guards, a man and a woman with spears. They braced themselves against the front of the walkway, the man on his knees, the woman on her feet. Both of them stared up at the sky in horror and confusion.

A flash of light behind them caught Noah's eye as he ran. Something moving on the bridge. No. The bridge itself moving. Shifting. Melting.

The woman saw Noah running toward them and swung her spear around. He shouted a handful of words at her. *Friend. Help. Scared. Sun. Mother. Safe.* He wasn't sure if she heard him over the thunder of moving ground, but she didn't impale him when he ran past her. The man never moved, never took his eyes from the sky.

Noah made it four long strides up the walkway before the section under his foot vanished and sent him sprawling. The surface folded itself away, one square section at a time, in places leaving sections of the ramp hovering unsupported in the air. The squares folded and slid themselves in different directions. A few flipped themselves over. They never seemed to actually go anywhere, but after two or three moves they vanished just the same.

Fucking multidimensional technology.

Noah looked for thicker, more stable areas and hopscotched his way up the ramp. The tremors didn't seem to affect the walkway. Not as hard, anyway. He couldn't feel the valley collapsing, but he could still hear it echoing back and forth between the tall cliffs.

He slipped one more time, near the top, tricked by the stark light and the odd shadows the shifting squares made. His leg dropped down through an opening that hadn't been there seconds before. He caught himself, rolled back to pull his leg out of the hole, and realized there wasn't any walkway behind him. At least not enough to stop him from plunging ten feet to the ground if he'd shifted his weight any further. He wiggled his leg free, crawled cautiously to his feet, and mapped out three last leaps. They got him to the top, and he dove through the cave-like entrance into the Ice Castle.

Barely any light made it through the crystal walls now. The gray tunnels felt . . . deserted. It reminded him of the old cave. So still and lifeless, like no one had set foot here in years.

He'd been there yesterday.

He started to run, but a few quick steps put him in complete darkness. And as he stood there, arms wide, he felt a tremor work its way through the Castle. The walls shuddered around him.

Not much time left.

Noah closed his eyes and let childhood memories guide him through the darkness. The same ones that'd let him find the Castaway's chambers so quickly yesterday. Small steps got longer, more confident. He held his hands out at first, but they drifted down as he walked further and further without finding a wall or pillar to block his path.

Then the air shifted, the rumbling grew more resonant, and he knew he'd entered a large space.

He opened his eyes to reveal the dim expanse of the Castaway's chamber. The throne room of the Empress. Where he was supposed to be.

Hopefully.

Enough of the harsh sunlight bled through the walls to give the cathedral-like chamber a Gothic gloom. A few of the furs and pelts had fallen, shaken loose by the vibrations working through the tower. He could see his breath, too. Big clouds of it in the thin, chilly air.

The walls muffled the sounds from outside but he could still hear stone crumbling, trees falling, the faint, mournful cries of terrified dinosaurs. All still happening. He forced down a swell of despair and guilt. Everything Parker said had made sense. He was supposed to be here.

Now what?

He looked at the walls, looking for the glimmers of light and brilliance. Anything that showed the lifeboat was still working. That some part of it was still active. But they'd either gone dark or faded to the point they blended in with the gray light of the chamber.

"I'm here," he called out. "It's me. Billy Gather. The Castaway wanted me to be here."

Another faint rumble of collapsing stone echoed through the tunnels.

Think think think. Did he need to say something or do something or be in a certain . . .

A few quick steps and he leaped up onto the dais. Where the Castaway had always stood. Where the Empress had placed her skull throne. Noah held out his hands in a commanding way and . . .

Still nothing. No change. The floor still shook. Definitely cold in the room now. Lifeless.

He remembered some of the patterns and gestures he'd seen the Castaway make, but most of them involved multiple arms or hands with too few or too many fingers.

What was he supposed to do? What did the Castle expect from him? Why had it accepted the Empress but it ignored him?

The Empress.

He looked around at all the ways she'd changed this room. Her decorations. Her trophies.

Her throne room.

Her home.

Noah leaped off the dais and kicked her collection of skulls away with a few swings of his foot. He pulled the last few pelts and hides down off the wall. Went to the little alcove where he'd slept and swept down all those skulls, too. Gathered up the random stones and weapons and other things she'd used to make the chamber hers.

He went back to the dais. Back to the throne she'd made out of Fang's skull. Tried to ignore the low wailing leaking through the walls from outside. It could've been Brunhilda. Or the hadrosaurs. Or the last bits of air whistling away into space. Too muffled and distorted by echoes for him to be sure.

He threw all the furs and skins out of the lower jaw. Braced his hands against the upper half of the T-Rex skull and pushed. It weighed a lot. At least double his weight. But he had a bit of leverage, got to use his legs, and he just needed to get it off-bal—

The top of Fang's skull tilted back, off the dais, and crashed to the floor. One of the eye sockets broke. Pieces of old bone scattered across the floor.

Noah barely looked at it. He stepped out of the lower jaw, grabbed an oversized tooth in each hand, and threw his weight back. The jawbone slid a little bit.

He braced his feet against the side of the dais and pulled again, torquing his waist as he did, taking a deep breath of thin, stale air. The jaw slid, swung around, and he hopped out of the way as one side of it thudded off the dais. One more hard yank and a tooth broke off in his hand as the other side of the jawbone fell to the chamber floor.

He grabbed one of the furs—mammoth, maybe—and swept it back and forth across the dais, removing as much dust and hair and grit as he could. Then he balled up the fur and tossed it at the pile of skulls and hides.

He stood tall on the dais because he didn't know what else to do. Looked out at the chamber. It wasn't perfect, but it looked a lot more like the place he remembered from childhood. The place he'd felt safe. The place he'd always been welcome.

Noah let out a sigh and realized he couldn't see his breath anymore. He blew out a lungful of air to be sure. He couldn't feel any vibrations through the floor, either. He wasn't sure when they'd stopped. Sometime after the skull had crashed down off the dais.

A little spark of light appeared inside the wall in front of him. It pulsed twice and slid up toward the vaulted ceiling. Halfway there it split into two sparks and they went their separate ways. Another light appeared in the wall to his left. A quartet on his right drifted down from the ceiling. More and more appeared, and the walls became the sparkling constellations he remembered from so many childhood visits.

Noah felt the tension drain out of his neck as he watched the lights brighten and spread. His shoulders sagged with relief even as a weight seemed to settle across them. He stepped forward, decided to risk sitting on the edge of the dais, and somehow knew it *wasn't* a risk. The certainty of it settled in his brain like the name of an old friend.

Sitting there put his head at the height it used to be on so many visits. A twinge of nostalgia ran through him as he gazed up at the light-filled vaulted ceiling. It looked right again. It *felt* right.

It felt like somewhere he could call home.

53

PARKER

"On hang. You that of feel did any?"

Parker glanced back at Olivia. Reordered a few words. "Feel what?"

"Vibration. The in ground."

Sam crouched to set a hand on the ground like some old west tracker, an impression only emphasized by his drawstring shirt. "Yeah, something big coming this way. Let's hang out for a minute."

They retreated across the line, out of the savanna and back into the trees.

"Good catch," said Parker.

"Right damn." Olivia leaned back against a tree and smirked confidently. Over the past weeks she'd gained back all of her motor skills, along with the ability to say any word she wanted, in sentences of any length she wanted. But they still came out in reverse-alphabetical order. They'd all gotten used to it. It made her sound like Yoda sometimes, but it definitely wasn't the strangest language barrier in the valley.

Parker rolled her shoulder and let the backpack's weight readjust the strap.

"Problem?" asked Pyr. She'd stopped a quarter mile back to gather some bark Monique needed for homemade aspirin or something. The pause had let her catch up.

Sam gestured at the open savanna. "Something coming. Just being cautious."

She nodded. Hiked her own bag up on her shoulder. Leaned into the tree.

They didn't have to wait long. The faint vibrations became impacts and Burn came striding through the tall grass. Not running, not chasing anything, just trying to get somewhere.

Sam shivered a bit as the big carnivore went by. He still had scars from his encounter with Gnash, back when the valley had almost . . . collapsed? Shut off? Folded in on itself? Thate had found him half a mile from the marble plaza with a bloody arm and a flock of the little microraptors greedily following him. He'd gotten bandaged up and the lifeboat systems had taken care of the rest. Monique assured them even the scars would probably be gone in another three or four months.

Burn entered the forest a dozen yards away from them. If the allosaurus saw or smelled them, they apparently weren't as interesting as wherever it was heading. They stayed still and watched the dinosaur stride off through the trees. If Parker's sense of direction was right, he was headed more or less toward the giant mech-robot. Where they'd first seen him. Where he'd killed Kyle. Almost two months ago.

Sam and Pyr exchanged a look. "Let's go," she said.

They crossed the savanna, heading for the Ice Castle. Parker had been this close a dozen times now, but it still amazed her. An alien artifact. Part of a multidimensional alien starship. Its size and origins and the look of it amazed her every time.

Easy to see why Sam had been obsessed with this place.

The open ground let her see in a few directions. The cliff walls loomed in the deep distance, whole and intact again. They'd been in ruins that day, she'd looked away, and then they'd been whole again. Reset like a video game, with no sign anything had ever happened to them.

Well, not to the cliffs, anyway, but the valley still had plenty of damage. Fallen trees. Toppled statues. Tumbled hills. So many things trampled when the dinosaurs stampeded. The jet they'd seen when they first arrived, embedded up in the cliff walls, was now a pile of scrap metal at the edge of the valley. Even here on the savanna approaching the Ice Castle there were two or three trees that had tipped over during the quakes, and many more with broken branches.

They walked around one of the fallen trees and the big circle of dirty roots that had pulled free of the ground. It'd left a hole three feet deep, with dozens of wiry, broken roots sticking out from the loose soil. Parker idly wondered how far down the dirt went. If you dug far enough, would you hit spaceship? Or maybe just . . . space?

Lan stood patiently ahead of them. The lone Neanderthal had been at the base of the ramp-like entrance to the Ice Castle whenever anyone had come over the past months. She had a spear and one of the axe-clubs but didn't seem interested in using either of them. More like a long-performed ritual she didn't know how to break.

Parker tried to remember the word for "hello" and then Sam barked it out and waved to Lan. The Klaa woman responded with a few words and a sort of waist-high salute.

"Has anyone figured out why she keeps showing up for work?" asked Parker. "She knows the Empress isn't here anymore, right?"

Sam glanced back at her, grinning. Visiting the Castle always put him in a good mood. "I think this is her job. She doesn't care about the change in management."

"It's her duty," said Olivia.

"Nicely done."

"You thank."

Pyr shook her head. "It's just that nobody's told her to do something else."

Parker gave Lan a smile and the woman smiled back in the awkward way of people who don't really understand each other. "No one had to tell any of them to stop following the Empress."

"Fair enough."

They headed into the Ice Castle and through the strange shifting corridors. Every time Parker had walked through them they were different.

If she counted footsteps she never got the same amount. If she tried to map the turns, there'd always be one more or one less, or some going in different directions than they had last time.

But no matter what, they always led to the central chamber.

"Hey," said Noah, stepping down off the dais. "What news from the outside world?"

Parker hadn't seen the cathedral-like room before Noah took up residence, but she guessed it hadn't looked so much like . . . well, an office. Diedrich and his girls had spent a day hauling supplies out to the tower on a big sled, and now the chamber had a desk, a very sprawlable couch, and a trio of shelves.

And the chair. They'd brought him one of the high-backed wooden chairs from the main hall, but Noah'd been uncomfortable with how throne-like it looked up on the dais. So the Roanoke woodworker, John, had built him a new one. Plain. Low backed. Comfortable enough to sit in for hours on end, if need be.

"Ross says hello," Pyr told him.

"Thank you."

"We found Breaker," Sam said, shaking Noah's hand before he slipped his pack off his shoulders. Not the little thing he'd brought to the valley, but a larger, rougher one of wood and leather the size of a suitcase.

"Part of Breaker," corrected Pyr.

Noah's face twisted up as he squeezed Parker's hand. "That sounds gruesome."

"One of his arms," she explained. "Half an arm. It's pretty chewed up, but it's got three of his tooth bracelets on the wrist."

"Soooo probably him," said Olivia.

Noah stopped shaking her hand and smiled. "You beat it?"

"Yet not no. One lucky just a." She handed her pack off to Sam.

Noah sighed. "Sorry."

"Sometimes it's fuck as annoying."

"Do the Klaa know about Breaker? B'Kar?"

Sam nodded. "Warwick and Neith returned the—the remains to them. What's left of the Klaa."

The Empress had died from her injury there in the clearing, apparently minutes after Noah had taken over. The valley no longer trembled beneath her feet and the Klaa had fractured. At least four different Neanderthal tribes existed in the valley now. All of them accepting—to varying degrees—that things had changed. Most of them wanting to live in peace. Hell, a week ago a trio of visionary Neanderthals had shown up at the gates of Roanoke with all their belongings, hoping to join the tribe inside the wall.

Parker swung her own pack around. "Got a surprise for you."

"Oh?"

She pulled out a small bundle. The edges were frayed, they weren't perfectly flat, and in places the fiber of the reeds made it pretty dark. "My new daytime project."

Noah's face lit up. "You're making paper?"

"Closer to papyrus, I think. I know it's not much, but I've got the hang of it now. I'll have more ready by the time you're done with these."

"There's a waiting list," Sam called out from the shelves. He'd emptied the water bottles from his pack and started unloading the food from Olivia's. "Lots of people have things they want to write down."

Noah carried the sheets to his desk. Over the past few weeks he'd filled the two little notebooks he'd brought with him to the valley, and one they'd scavenged from Logan's pack. "Thank you. These will help a lot."

"Which brings us to . . . anything new since our last visit?"

"It's only been a couple of days."

"A couple of days of you controlling a multidimensional spaceship," Sam said.

"I'm not controlling it. Really, we're still at the stage I think it's more controlling me."

"Creepy," said Parker.

Pyr frowned. "Still can't go outside?"

He shrugged. "I think I could, but I get this sort of gut feeling it'd be bad. Maybe someday, for a little while, but not yet. The valley's still patching itself back together. For now, it's just the view from the top of the ramp." He waved a hand at the ceiling. "I've been exploring more in here, though."

Parker's interest flared. "And? Anything interesting?"

"More empty rooms."

"No command center or navigation or anything?"

He shook his head. "I'm not sure, but I think this is the only room that matters. The Castle might even be making the other rooms just because I'm looking for them."

Sam put the last of the food up on the shelves. "So it's responding to you."

"I think so."

They all stood quietly. But now they were exchanging glances and Olivia and Sam clearly wanted Parker to say something. One thing on everyone's mind. The thing they'd carefully not talked about. They'd agreed not to bring it up for a while. Didn't want to put extra pressure on Noah. "So," Parker said, "I know it hasn't been long, but we were wondering—"

"Updates on if I can get you home?"

"Yes," said Olivia.

Noah nodded. "Not yet. There's a lot of variables to this, time and space-wise. Figuring out how to control it is like . . ."

Parker waited. "Like?"

"It's like when you've owned a car for a long time. It hits that point where you register all these little things when you drive, things a casual passenger never picks up on. You might not be able to put a name to them, but you can feel that little pull to the right or left. Or hear the engine's a tiny bit off, or something's scraping a wheel."

Sam tapped his fingertips slowly against each other. "Okay, sure."

"That's what this is like. I don't quite understand the lifeboat, but I can sort of feel how it works. Like how I can sense it'd be wrong for me to go outside. It's all . . . instinctive? Intuitive? Maybe partly because I'm trying to do it all with my pathetic little three-dimensional brain."

Olivia snickered. "With to that some of more might I help be able." She reached up and tapped the side of her own head.

"I wouldn't turn it down."

"But you are figuring it out," Parker said. More statement than question.

He gestured at the desk. At the notebooks. "A little bit every day. A very little bit. But . . ." He nodded. "I'm going to be able to get you home. To get everyone home. Or to wherever they want to be."

Parker felt light. Relieved. Olivia shrieked with glee. Sam grinned and said "Yes!" four or five times. Even Pyr looked relieved.

"I'm not going to lie," Noah continued, talking over them, "it's probably going to take me a while to get the hang of this. And I'm probably going to start with rocks and trees, for practice. And then the big predators. Gnash and Burn. The dimetrodons. The Utahraptors. Make the valley a little safer overall. But eventually . . . everyone gets home."

"Everyone?" asked Pyr.

He nodded. "Yep. All the dinosaurs. Everyone at Roanoke. The Klaa. Everyone. Part of the problem, working all this out, is understanding where and when everyone came from. Some folks will be easy. You know where you're from, and that's information I can understand. Others, like Neith for example . . ."

"You don't have a frame of reference," said Parker.

"Yep. I'll need to look at it a little differently."

"Averted vision."

"Yep."

Olivia made a little sound in her throat. "We'll to things some need explain. What to Logan happened. Kyle. Josh."

"And you," Sam said, looking at Noah. "You'll have to—you're probably going to still be here after us."

"One day you'll call this place home," said Parker.

"Yep. I do and it is." Noah stepped back up onto the dais and dropped down into the chair. "But I had a crappy little apartment while I was getting my master's. I called that place home for two years. Didn't mean I was going to stay there forever."

"And when you leave . . . the lifeboat collapses? For good?"

"Yep. I'll be the last one out."

She followed his gaze up to the vaulted ceiling, where little sparks of light bounced off each other and drifted down the walls. "How?"

"I'm sure I'll think of something. It's a ways down the road."

"Question." Sam's face balanced somewhere between worried and curious. His fingers tapped against each other.

Noah gestured for him to continue.

"So the Castaway—they could've sent you home all along. You and your family."

Noah's shoulders slumped a little. A strange, vaguely familiar expression crossed his face, one it took Parker a moment to place. A guy she'd dated for a few months her senior year, explaining the holidays might be awkward because his grandmother could be "just a little bit racist."

"I don't think so," Noah finally said. "Not the way we wanted, anyway. They couldn't quite wrap their head around our view of time well enough to do what we needed. They might've sent us back 'home' to right when we wanted. Or a year after we left. Or back to the day my dad was conceived."

"Ewwww." Olivia put up a hand.

"Okay," said Parker, "counterpoint, though?"

"What?"

"They *did* send you back, didn't they? When you were a kid? I mean, how else did you get out of the valley?"

Pyr's biomechanical eyebrow went up.

Noah nodded. Pressed his mouth into a line. "I think they might've. Like I've said, the Castaway was very big-picture in the way they saw . . . well, everything. It kind of makes sense they'd send me home because they knew I needed to find my way back here and take over the lifeboat. Because . . . y'know, that's what happens."

"Paradox," said Sam.

Olivia shook her head. "Time loop."

"Same thing."

"No."

Pyr sat down on the edge of the dais with a doubtful look on her face. "They couldn't send your family home, but they could send *you* home because they'd seen you come back here in the future?"

"Either they planned it that way, or they set me up to take over here and—by absolute, sheer coincidence—I'm also the only person who ever found the way out of the valley."

"I'm not sure which one I like better."

Parker shrugged. "Either way, it's like you told us. The Castaway was always right."

AP WIRE
September 24, 2023

Four people are missing and one hospitalized after a routine astronomy field trip went awry.

A group of 42 Monrovia University students had hiked to a Mount Wesley plateau to do a series of imaging exercises with their instructor, Dr. Noah Barnes. The routine trip went as planned until one of the graduate students, Olivia Martinez, began to have trouble speaking shortly after arriving at their campsite. Two other students, fearing a stroke, rushed her to Coleman Medical Center.

Not long afterward, it was discovered that Barnes, grad students Kyle Davis and Logan Smith, and trail guide Henry Gale had disappeared from the base camp. The remaining students searched for an hour before contacting the authorities. Search teams have turned up no sign of the missing persons . . .

Gabe McAllister @THEGabeGabriel7.bsky.social · 17h

WTF Thought my ex Sam and I were ending things on good terms. 3 days ago everything was fine, today he comes back from his work/field trip thing and tells me to get the hell out of HIS apartment. Told him I live here too and he says I don't pay rent and I'm not on the lease so I can go live with—

1/

Gabe McAllister @THEGabeGabriel7.bsky.social · 17h

—my new boyfriend. Tried to tell him I couldn't and he says it stopped being his problem when I broke up with him. Anyway I've got 22 hours to find a place before he dumps my stuff on the sidewalk so if anyone's got a cheap sublet or a free couch I can crash on for a few weeks that'd be really—

2/

FOXNews.com
September 27, 2023

Plot Thickens in Mount Wesley Case

ONE OF THE MISSING REVEALED AS A DRUG DEALER WITH A STOLEN IDENTITY

A drug deal gone wrong may be the culprit in a mysterious set of disappearances during a routine Monrovia University excursion to Mount Wesley.

A professor, two graduate students, and a trail guide disappeared during a college field trip on Sept. 22. The trail guide, originally identified as Henry Gale, has since been discovered to be white-collar drug dealer Joshua Redd.

State police are now treating the missing persons case as gang related and a possible homicide, saying Monrovia professor Noah Barnes and his students may have been caught up in a drug deal gone wrong . . .

May 30

Fellow Colleagues

Please join me in welcoming Dr. Olivia Martinez, who will be a member of our full-time faculty in Monrovia University's Astronomy Department this fall. Martinez earned her BA in Astronomy at the University of Massachusetts Amherst and spent two years on staff at the Mount Wilson Observatory in California. She came to MU in 2019 to pursue her doctorate. In 2023 she suffered a stroke that left her with Broca's aphasia, but which she also credits for inspiring her pioneering work in multidimensional astrophysics. In her first semester she will be teaching Astronomy and also joining MU professor Parker Sangthong on a joint project with JPL researcher Samael Jones studying extraterrestrial communication . . .

54

BEAU

On the morning of her twentieth birthday, according to Ross's expert timekeeping, Beau wrote her suicide note.

It wasn't serious. Probably. Just an outlet. More her being dramatic than any sort of message. Not like anyone would ever read it.

And it wasn't like she was actually going to kill herself on her birthday. She'd go sit at the mouth of the cave and eat breakfast alone. Again. Go do all the random chores she needed to do for the day. Again. Come back here. Have dinner. Cry herself to sleep. Alone.

Again.

But she wasn't going to kill herself.

Probably.

She didn't eat breakfast. She stood at the mouth of the cave and stared through the pillars at the valley. She'd memorized every feature over the past two years and sixteen days since Billy had . . .

Billy was dead. He'd "disappeared" because that fucking bitch Scarnose had killed him. Probably twisted his arms and legs off and cooked him over a fire, then sliced him up and fed him to . . .

No. No, thinking about it always led to dark days, sinking deeper and deeper into a funk. Only happy memories about Billy and Dad and Mom. That was the rule. Especially today.

Didn't want to ruin her birthday.

Beau threw a rock out between the pillars, listened to it thud and bounce down the big stone steps.

This wasn't how her life was supposed to be. She knew people said stuff like that all the time. She'd heard the line on TV shows and in movies and some trashy books. She knew having to deal with tragedies, having your life go in an unexpected direction . . . they weren't exactly unique problems.

But fucking hell, this felt pretty unique.

Her twentieth birthday should've been during her junior year of college. First semester. Turning twenty in the dorms. Partying with friends. Probably some underage drinking. Maybe a random hookup later—a friend with benefits or some cute guy from a class or a total stranger because it's her birthday and she's doing something wild. Or maybe she'd be in a serious relationship. Hell, maybe she'd be doing . . .

Beau almost laughed at the unexpected thought. The long-forgotten plan. The big dream.

Maybe she'd be doing that year abroad she always wanted.

She looked out at the valley. Thought about her chores for the day. Thought about how far it was to the Pakka camp.

Definitely didn't think about killing herself.

She walked back into the cave and grabbed her pack. Her wooden club—she hadn't thought of it as "Dad's" for over a year now. Looked at her open notebook on the mostly-flat rock she called her desk. Left it sitting there. Again, not like anyone was going to wander by and read it.

Ever.

Ross watched her. She'd stopped talking to him four or five months ago. Maybe six. Every now and then he'd make a random statement. An attempt to start a conversation. Thankfully those came less and less. Maybe once a week. With only her to talk to, and with nothing new to ever talk about, Ross's conversational skills had devolved to the level of a doll with a string on its back, parroting back the same phrases again and again. The same dead eyes, too.

She left the cave without saying goodbye to him. Because he was just a machine. An appliance. And it wasn't really goodbye. She'd be back later.

Probably.

Quick check for Fang or a wandering raptor and then hop, skip, jump down the stone steps. She crossed the wide-open space to the edge of Dickwood Forest. Thought briefly about looking back at the cave one last time. Didn't.

Crossing the valley, all six miles, would take around two hours. It used to take longer, back when she had Billy with her. Or Dad. But she'd improved. Gotten faster. No one holding her back.

No one she could depend on for anything.

Beau followed the edge of Dickwood to the Cut Rock, and then headed straight into the Dead Forest. The gray, barren trees broke up the sky without blocking it, and made zigzag shadows everywhere. She moved quick and quiet across the soft, mulchy ground, her club ready.

She felt the push in the air, the all-but-noiseless sound that shook her chest, and froze. Habit moved her feet, pressed her against a nearby tree. She took a deep breath. Held it.

Branches snapped and fell. Crumbled under massive feet. The air shifted as lungs bigger than her sleeping bag sucked in the smells of the forest.

Fang pushed between two trees, scraping off dry bark and cracking stiff branches.

Beau leaned to the side, not moving her feet, putting more of the tree between her and the tyrannosaurus. How fast had she been moving? Fast enough to sweat? She didn't feel any sweat on her, but Fang could catch the faintest scent.

And then a thought bounced around in her head. She'd written the note. She could just walk out in front of him. Throw her club at that giant head and close her eyes. It'd hurt, but it'd be quick. She'd seen Fang kill raptors and duck-billed dinosaurs and Neanderthals.

And Dad. Dad had screamed, but not for long. Maybe . . . maybe ten seconds? Ten seconds of screaming, tops.

Could she deal with ten seconds of pain? Of that much pain? After all this, she wanted to say yes, but Fang's massive jaws still terrified her.

She leaned harder into the tree.

Fang strode forward, snapped off some more branches with his head and neck, and a pair of the four-winged dinobirds threw themselves into the air. Their wings flapped in his face and the big tyrannosaurus took a few lazy chomps at them. It steered him a little away from Beau. Three steps away. Four. Five. Six. And then something skittered across the mulchy forest floor and Fang launched after whatever it was, picking up speed as he went.

She waited until she couldn't hear his heavy footsteps. Couldn't feel his growls under her skin. Then she counted to a hundred again and let go of the tree.

She made it through the Dead Forest to the edge of Saurus Swamp. Billy had given everything here such stupid names. She still used all of them.

Wide circuit around the swamp. Don't want to get stuck in the soft mud on this side. One of the duck-billed hadrosaurs watched her go by. She didn't care.

She reached the wrecked riverboat. And the Ice Castle. Halfway to the Pakka camp. She tightened her grip on the club. Thought of the impact when she'd hit things with it.

Her pace quickened as she traveled around the tower of crystal and glass, and found herself in front of the Castle's drawbridge. Another Billy name. He'd only used it twice, but she remembered it. Still used it.

She looked up the shiny ramp to the entrance.

Through the trees toward the Pakka camp.

Back up the ramp.

Her grip loosened on the club.

She went in to see the Castaway.

Beau had visited the alien several times. She thought learning the secrets of the universe might distract her from her life in the valley. The Castaway had tried to oblige, but so many of the terms and things they told her were so, well, *alien* she'd barely understood any of it.

Also, they had a bad habit of drifting off into other languages she didn't recognize.

She wandered the tunnels until she found the big room. The Castaway currently had dozens of long tentacles, or maybe roots, stretched across the dais. The central mass of its body looked like a giant purple pea pod with a star-shaped flower on top. As she approached, they stretched out a set of wings, each one the size of a bedsheet, and then pulled them back into themself.

"Forgive me, Beau Gather. My attention was on other matters and I did not note your arrival. Salutations."

"Hi, Castaway."

The tentacle-roots pulled back, wove together, lifted the Castaway's body a little taller. The flower-shape curled in on itself and became more of a head. "Do you require my assistance?"

"I need . . . I need a straight answer from you."

The rippling purple body moved to the edge of the dais. "Certainly."

"You told me once, I'd get out of here someday."

"I said, 'Yes, you will get out of the valley, Beau Gather.'"

"Right. When?"

"Today. Just now." A pair of long arms grew out of the Castaway's body. Their head took on a more triangular shape.

"No, when will I get out? I can't . . . I can't do this anymore. I can't do it alone."

"Which action are you no longer able to complete?"

She thought of the note back at the cave. The note that wasn't just her being dramatic. "Living? Existing? I'm . . . I've been alone for over two years now. I know you and Ross have tried to help, but I need . . . people. My own people."

"The Neanderthals are your own people. We are merely life with different origin points."

Beau squeezed the handle of the club again. "No, I mean . . . I need to know how much longer I'm going to be here? When do I leave? When does it happen?"

"Today. Just now."

"I don't . . . Just one straight answer. Please."

"Forgive me. This is the correct response to your question. Today is the day you leave the valley."

The words rattled in her head. "I . . . what? Today?"

"This is correct."

She heard the club clatter on the floor. It echoed in the big room. "You're sending me home?"

The Castaway's bottom half rotated, twisting into a coil. Their triangular head softened, and a pair of eye shapes formed. "I am not. As I will tell you when you first ask, it is a task beyond my understanding."

Had she misunderstood them after all? "Then what . . . how . . ."

The Castaway retreated to the center of the dais. It stretched out one of the long arms and the end split into thin fingers, gesturing to the other side of the room. "Another resident of the Castle shall make these events transpire."

"What?" Again, it took her brain a minute to catch up, to make sense of the words. Was this what it was like to be drunk? Or stoned? She turned, followed the gesture.

A few yards away, an old man stood at the entrance to one of the side tunnels. She wasn't great at ages, but she guessed he was . . . sixty-five? Seventy? He had gray hair gone white at the temples—like that Neanderthal bitch—and a fair number of wrinkles around his eyes and mouth. His threadbare clothes looked like he'd had them for years. The first thought in her head, which made no sense, was her grandfather. Mom's dad. But a nervous smile spread across the man's face and it clearly wasn't Grandpa Bob.

Something stretched in the old man's arms. A tan cat. Holy fuck he had Charlie, Billy's cat that had gone missing years ago. He looked fine and healthy and sprawled in the old man's arms while he scratched its head.

"Hello, Beau." The man had an old voice. Not creaky-old, but definitely-seen-some-shit old. Probably a lot like how her own voice sounded.

"This entity is currently known as Noah," explained the Castaway. "He resides here."

Beau looked at the man. The human man. Not her imagination. Not a Neanderthal. Another human being. Who spoke English! "Have you been here all along?"

The man—Noah—smiled again. "Sort of, depending on how you look at it. The important thing . . ."

His breath caught for a moment. He stopped petting the cat, reached up, and wiped his wet eyes with his hand.

"What matters is, I've come to take you home."

AFTERWORD

I was, as some folks say, a very impressionable child.

Lots of stuff scared me, mostly because my imagination took everything and ran with it. My uncle Tim, only a few years older than me, left some horror comics sitting out once that resulted in little me staying awake late into the night for several months. There was an episode of *Fantasy Island* that gave me nightmares for a year or three. I read Stephen King's "The Boogeyman" when I was way too young and to this day I can't sleep with the closet door cracked even the slightest bit. That door needs to be latched solid in order for me to close my eyes.

But the most terrifying thing, the thing that led to so many sudden-waking shrieks and screams and sleepless nights, was a show called *Land of the Lost.* In the little-kid way of things, I was convinced it was a new show even though a glance at Wikipedia tells me it had to be at least in its first cycle of syndication. The special effects are simple—almost crude—in retrospect, but at the time they managed to give me a recurring nightmare of a tyrannosaurus outside my bedroom window that copied one of the stock shots from the show.

I kept watching, though, because one of the other appealing ideas of the series was this underlying sense of mystery. That the whole strange setting of *Land of the Lost* was some gigantic puzzle. That there was more going on here, a strange logic that my little brain could almost recognize even if I couldn't understand it.

As I got older I learned *Land of the Lost* was one in a long history of "lost world" stories about strange valleys, islands, and plateaus that were somehow disconnected from the rest of the world. Books, movies, TV shows, comics, and more. I read so many of them growing up and still love finding new ones.

And then, of course, I thought about writing one. I poked at the idea of this book for ages, adding little thoughts and notes. At one point it was going to be an elaborate D&D campaign (I hadn't played in years, but for this . . .). Then it was a movie pitch. And eventually it'd built up enough momentum in my head that it became . . . well, the book you're reading right now.

Which is normally my cue to start telling you some cute little factoids and easter eggs and trivia about this book and some of the things in it. And there's a *lot* in this one. Like some of the other people Ross spent time with over the years. Where that Egyptian riverboat came from. Why Marissa was in Queens the day she was sucked into the valley. Thate's connection to a sci-fi detective story I wrote, and the long process of deciding what color his skin should be (and then realizing months later I'd inadvertently turned him into a *Rogue Trooper* homage). Some of you may have already realized who the Castaway's people are at war with. And Monrovia University . . . well, we may be hearing a lot more about that place in the future.

All that and more. But if I told you all of it that'd be another ten or twenty pages to this book. So for now we'll just have to leave those as little mysteries to get answered later. And I'll get right to thanking the people who helped me a lot with this.

So thanks to . . .

Dr. Lisa Will, who let me ask weird questions about orbital mechanics, the night sky, looking across the solar system, and much more for about an hour. Anything astronomical here that really impresses you probably came from her. Anything that's glaringly wrong definitely came from me.

Dr. John Tansey, who helped me design Josh's study drug, Hawking's Dream. Also he, M. L. Brennan, and Kristi Charish all answered random questions about academia and grad school.

Brooke Binkowski helped me get the newspaper clippings just right.

Kristi, Brennan, Stephen Blackmoore, Autumn Christian, and Rob Brockway all read an earlier version of this and pointed out things they absolutely loved and a few things they weren't too fond of. They're all fantastic writers and good friends. Then my agent, David, pointed out a few more things and all of that led to a pretty big rewrite.

Many thanks to Josie, Rick, Megan, Candice, and everyone at Blackstone who decided to take on this big, weird book and show it to the world. Extra thanks to Toni who helped me tighten a few places I didn't even realize were loose and pare things down a bit more. Yes, this is the pared-down version of the book.

By nature of making a book, there are so many other people involved. I know I've missed someone here and if it was you, my deepest apologies and sincerest thanks.

And thanks to all of you. I'm still regularly in awe that I get to do this for a living, and that's because folks like you enjoy reading my twisting little stories. So seriously, thank you so much.

One more round of thanks for David, who continues to find homes for all my work and shows interest even when I have the wildest ideas.

And as always, so many thanks to screenwriter, novelist, sympathetic ear, my first set of eyes, and my partner in crime of twenty years as I write this, Colleen. How you put up with all of this—and me—I'll never know. But I'm so very glad you do.

P. C.
San Diego,
November 26, 2024